THE WIDOW'S CHASE

Also by Cap Daniels

The Chase Fulton Novels Series
Book One: *The Opening Chase*
Book Two: *The Broken Chase*
Book Three: *The Stronger Chase*
Book Four: *The Unending Chase*
Book Five: *The Distant Chase*
Book Six: *The Entangled Chase*
Book Seven: *The Devil's Chase*
Book Eight: *The Angel's Chase*
Book Nine: *The Forgotten Chase*
Book Ten: *The Emerald Chase*
Book Eleven: *The Polar Chase*
Book Twelve: *The Burning Chase*
Book Thirteen: *The Poison Chase*
Book Fourteen: *The Bitter Chase*
Book Fifteen: *The Blind Chase*
Book Sixteen: *The Smuggler's Chase*
Book Seventeen: *The Hollow Chase*
Book Eighteen: *The Sunken Chase*
Book Nineteen: *The Darker Chase*
Book Twenty: *The Abandoned Chase*
Book Twenty-One: *The Gambler's Chase*
Book Twenty-Two: *The Arctic Chase*
Book Twenty-Three: *The Diamond Chase*
Book Twenty-Four: *The Phantom Chase*
Book Twenty-Five: *The Crimson Chase*
Book Twenty-Six: *The Silent Chase*
Book Twenty-Seven: *The Shepherd's Chase*
Book Twenty-Eight: *The Scorpion's Chase*
Book Twenty-Nine: *The Creole Chase*
Book Thirty: *The Calling Chase*
Book Thirty-One: *The Capitol Chase*
Book Thirty-Two: *The Stolen Chase*
Book Thirty-Three: *The Widow's Chase*
Book Thirty-Four: *The Sacred Chase*

The Avenging Angel – Seven Deadly Sins Series
Book One: *The Russian's Pride*
Book Two: *The Russian's Greed*
Book Three: *The Russian's Gluttony*
Book Four: *The Russian's Lust*
Book Five: *The Russian's Sloth*
Book Six: *The Russian's Envy*
Book Seven: *The Russian's Wrath*

Stand-Alone Novels
We Were Brave
Singer – Memoir of a Christian Sniper

Novellas
The Chase is On
I Am Gypsy

THE WIDOW'S CHASE

CHASE FULTON NOVEL #33

CAP DANIELS

ANCHOR WATCH
PUBLISHING
** USA **

The Widow's Chase
Chase Fulton Novel #33
Cap Daniels

This is a work of fiction. Names, characters, places, historical events, and incidents are the product of the author's imagination or have been used fictitiously. Although many locations such as marinas, airports, hotels, restaurants, etc. used in this work actually exist, they are used fictitiously and may have been relocated, exaggerated, or otherwise modified by creative license for the purpose of this work. Although many characters are based on personalities, physical attributes, skills, or intellect of actual individuals, all the characters in this work are products of the author's imagination.

Published by:

** USA **

13-Digit ISBN: 978-1-951021-75-7
Library of Congress Control Number: 2025949017
Copyright ©2025 Cap Daniels – All Rights Reserved

Cover Design: German Creative

Printed in the United States of America

The Widow's Chase

CAP DANIELS

Chapter 1

The Misery of the Living

Summer 2017 – Oak Grove Cemetery, St. Marys, GA

I sat on the perfectly manicured, four-by-eight-foot piece of earth that had become, at least in my mind, the holiest ground in existence, and I cried. The sweat and tears blurred my vision, but I didn't need my eyes to read the chiseled inscription on the headstone.

Here lies Nicole "Penny" Fulton, beloved wife and daughter, accomplished screenwriter, and faithful believer.

November 1, 1972 – June 3, 2016

Her grave was the only thing in my life that I cared for, and the memory of her in my arms and in my heart was all I had left of the most beautiful person I ever knew. A jagged trail of empty whiskey bottles and tiny pieces of my heart littered the previous year of my life. I didn't know what day it was, let alone the month. I only knew my heart lay shattered on the ground on which I sat, and the relentless low-country sun beat down like cascading drops of Hell on my sagging shoulders—the same shoulders that once bore the burden of defending freedom and all we hold dear in this country.

But those days were gone, and these shoulders could hardly bear their own weight with bone so near flesh that I looked as if mine should be the body beneath the ground instead of Penny's.

Where was my country when a known Russian operative brought down the Citation jet in which Penny was flying with Anya Burinkova? Where were the power brokers who lent me out like a prostitute in every godforsaken corner of the world?

Where was fairness and mercy and goodness? Apparently, they'd left the empty world, along with the woman I loved.

The baritone voice of the only person on the planet I wanted to hear cut through the rancid midday air overlooking the St. Marys River in coastal Georgia.

"She's not here, brother. Tell me you know that."

Jimmy "Singer" Grossmann, a man who lived every moment of his life in endless communion with God, planted himself on the hard ground beside me and brushed away the few leaves I'd missed. I looked into the eyes of my dearest brother-in-arms, but I couldn't speak.

Singer was not only a devout man of boundless faith, but he was also one of the deadliest long-range snipers who ever lived. The dichotomy of his existence was incomprehensible to the broken man I had become. I doubted he had ever questioned God about anything, and I was too weak to have the faith Singer wore like armor. I was too empty, too hollow to believe that I would ever again know how loving and being truly loved could feel.

I wanted to scream at Vladimir Putin, and myself, and God. I wanted to unleash the beast inside me and let it devour what little of my world remained. And somehow, Singer knew and understood that.

He laid a muscled arm across my shoulders and pulled me against his side. With his free hand, he lifted the bottle from mine and poured its contents onto the ground as far away from Penny's grave as he could reach.

I watched the amber liquid fall and succumb to the ground's endless thirst. "I'm a coward."

He squeezed me tighter and gently rubbed his hand across the closely cropped blanket of grass beneath us. "If it were you under this cold, dark ground, what would you tell Penny if she were the one sitting here with a bottle in her hand?"

I placed my hand on the ground beside his and studied the contrast. His fingernails were clean and short, while mine were filthy and tattered. His hand was rock solid, while mine trembled with every beat of my worthless heart.

It would be impossible to count the number of hours Singer and I had spent just like that miserable afternoon. I cried, cursed, and questioned everything while he sat stoically and just listened.

"It should be me," I whispered through quivering lips.

He nodded, and for the first time, he joined me in the misery of the living. "It should've been both of us a thousand times, my friend."

I should've known a lesson in profound understanding was knocking at the door.

"We don't get to make those decisions, and I'm endlessly grateful for that blessed kindness from God. Choosing who lives and who dies is too much for one human soul to bear. We are left only to celebrate the living and to remember those whose souls have moved on to endless reward."

"Why are you here? Why do you do this? Why do you keep coming back? Is it some morbid fascination? Do you revel in seeing the great Chase Fulton reduced to a blithering idiot in an empty, crumbling shell? Can you tell me why you do it?"

He let me rave, but he didn't let me go. Instead, he held me as if I were his lifeboat instead of him being mine.

After an hour, or perhaps all eternity, Singer said, "Let's get you home and cleaned up. There's somebody who's been waiting fifteen years to meet you, and you can't show up looking like this."

It wasn't a conscious effort, but I shook my head in a slow, wavelike motion. "I don't want to see anybody. I don't care how long they've been waiting."

"Yeah, well, it's not about you, big boy." He hopped to his feet and cupped me beneath each arm. "So, let's go, Great Chase Fulton."

He walked, and I staggered five blocks to the barber shop where I used to get transformed from a woolly mammoth into something resembling a human. It was going to take more than a barber to make that happen again.

"Fine, I'll get a haircut, but I'm not meeting anybody today."

Singer paid the barber, and we ended our walk at the back gallery of Bonaventure, my ancestral home on the banks of the North River. Bonaventure had been a pecan, cotton, and tea plantation through the centuries, but most recently, it had been the neglected home and tactical training center for the team of covert operators I once led. The property seemed to mirror my own demise with its unkempt yard and cavernous emptiness.

Singer held open the door and encouraged me inside with a not-so-gentle hand on my back. "Get a shower. Put on some clean clothes. And please, in the name of all that's holy, brush your teeth."

"No! I told you I'm not meeting anybody. Now, get out and leave me—"

He grabbed me by the arms and shook me as if trying to dislodge my brain. "Shut up and get in the shower. You can be a horse's ass tomorrow, but today, you *will* get cleaned up, and you *will* meet this person who's waited a lifetime to see you."

"No!" I barked. "Why can't you just let me be?"

He froze me in place with what he said next. "Because I love you, and I'm finished watching you destroy yourself and everything around you. So, for once in your muleheaded life, just do what I ask . . . please."

When I wiped the fog from the mirror and dried my hair with a towel that I still believed smelled like Penny, I looked into the face of a man I didn't recognize. The emptiness in his eyes and desperation on his face spoke of unimaginable pain that nothing could soothe, but I forced myself to believe that if I went along with Singer, maybe he'd finally leave me alone and let me drown myself in the next bottle I opened.

Dressed, but moving against my will, I let Singer lead me through the kitchen and back onto the gallery. Between the house and the river-bank sat the gazebo I once loved, but I hadn't stepped foot into the structure in over a year. And I had no intention of changing that streak on that day, especially because of the woman who sat alone in an Adirondack chair with her eyes cast over the marshland beyond the river.

I turned back for the house. "No. I'm not doing this. I don't have the . . . *whatever* to deal with *her* today."

Singer caught my arm. "This isn't optional, Chase."

I jerked away and threw up a hand toward the gazebo. "You lied to me. You said the person who wanted to meet me had been waiting a lifetime. That was a lie."

He softened. "I've never lied to you, and I never will. Yes, that's Anya out there, but she's not the person you're going to meet. She's just part of the situation."

"Part of the situation? What does that even mean?"

He spun me back around and again *encouraged* me down the stairs. "Let's make a deal."

"What kind of deal?"

He smiled. "When this is over, if you still think it was a bad idea and a waste of time, I'll buy you a whole truckload of whatever you want to drink."

"I'll take Gentleman Jack, and a truckload should cost about a hundred grand. I don't have the number, but they're in Lynchburg, Tennessee. Go ahead and make the call now."

He continued his not-so-subtle encouragement. "You're getting ahead of yourself. First, you have to talk with Anya and meet someone new."

"Why are you being so cryptic about all of this? Who's this guy I'm supposed to meet?"

"Just try a little patience. You can borrow some of mine if you're on empty."

As I fought against every step towards the gazebo, I collided with the flash of an ancient memory. I had once loved the Russian sitting in what had been my spot long before I met Penny, but I choked on the thought of loving anyone, especially myself, ever again.

It took every ounce of strength I could muster to climb the two steps into the wooden structure, but I did it, and Anya stood.

"I can give to you hug, yes?"

The centerpiece of the gazebo was a seventeenth-century naval cannon that my first real training officer and dear friend, Clark Johnson, and I pulled from the mud and muck of Cumberland Sound.

I stepped around the gun and placed its heft between the Russian and me. "No, you may not. Now, what's this about?"

She returned to her chair and cocked her head. "You look like . . . I do not know English word for this."

I huffed. "The word you're looking for is *death*. I look like death, and I feel a lot worse than that. So, would you please just tell me what this is about?"

She furrowed her brow as if fighting back tears of her own. "You are not eating. You are so skinny. You must eat. You must—"

"Is that why I'm here? So you can berate me about my diet? Well, let me tell you something about me. I'm none of your business, or anyone else's, and nothing you or anyone can say will change that."

Anya bowed her head. "This is not true. You are wrong, and you will see. You will please wait here, yes? I will be back in only one minute."

I turned to Singer, who'd propped himself against a post. "So help me God, if this is some job I'm supposed to do, or that we're supposed to do, I'll shoot this guy in the face and sink him in that river."

Instead of throwing up his hands and walking away, Singer said, "Patience, please. And remember, you've got a hundred grand worth of some whiskey I've never heard of on the line."

"Don't do that," I growled. "Do not patronize me. I'd rather you bury me under this cannon than do that."

He offered a nod and turned before ambling back up the path to the empty house.

As soon as the back door closed behind him, Anya came around the corner of the house with another female walking beside her, and I couldn't look away.

I wiped my eyes and refocused on the woman beside the Russian. It was my mother . . . or at least my mother as she'd looked in pictures years before I was born. She was beautiful, with chestnut hair, bright blue eyes, and an elegance that women no longer possess.

I stood, out of some chivalrous remnant of a bygone era, and the young woman stepped into the gazebo ahead of Anya. We stared at each other for an eternity until Anya said, "Chase, this is Pogonya, and she is your daughter."

Chapter 2

I Happened to Me

As if everything in creation collided in some cosmic impossibility, the world in front of me was both too brilliant to see and blanketed in utter darkness. Pogonya seemed to be suspended in the same realm of disbelief and wonder, but hers shone on her face as a curious ensemble of questions emerging from what might have been fascination.

I ran my hands through my newly trimmed hair and begged the oracle of time to erase the misery of boundless self-neglect from my face. In a moment of indescribable emotion, I couldn't look away from the beautiful young woman with her mother's flawless features and eyes, taken as if by some miracle, from the mother who'd been ripped from me so many years before.

A thousand questions without possible answers poured from my very soul, but I couldn't muster the courage, or perhaps the strength, to speak. For the first time since Penny's murder, I saw the world through the eyes of a man who'd seen only himself doused and drowning in loathing and anguish. In that minuscule moment in time, every human emotion overtook me, and a force that could not be named or measured crashed down upon me.

I loved her without explanation or understanding, and she seemed to perceive me as nothing more than a curiosity—something foreign and abstract. Perhaps that was the truest observation of what I had become since losing Penny, and in that frozen speck of eternity, I suddenly yearned to erase the lines left behind by untold gallons of whiskey, loss, and warfare. I was ashamed and wanted to hide from her, yet I wanted nothing more than to give her everything she could ever yearn to possess. And more than all of that, I ached to hear her speak my name.

The first words from her lips sounded rehearsed and saddled by anxiety. "Hello, Father."

In those four syllables, my painful existence collapsed around me, and my world was restored around her as if she were the core of all that had ever been.

I spent the bulk of my life making decisions in fractions of seconds to save—and sometimes destroy—the lives of those around me. Warriors—brave, battle-hardened fighters of enormous valor—followed me onto battlefields, the names of which I'll never remember, in slices of the earth nestled upon precipices of crumbling stone. I'd led valiant, fearless gladiators into valleys of certain death and onto mountaintops of undeniable victory, but standing before a teenage girl on the brink of becoming a woman, I lacked the wherewithal to lead even myself into the next footprint I would create.

"How . . . ?"

Had I not been lost in the swirling torrent of endless intrigue around Pogonya, I may have shared Anya's amusement at my question, but in that moment, and in my distorted state, her laughter felt foreign and distant.

Anya smiled with everything she was and said, "Come now, Chasechka. Surely you know how a baby is made."

The comedy of the moment wasn't lost on Pogonya, and she smirked and covered her mouth with a delicate hand to perhaps hide her embarrassment. "Mama, *pozhaluysta*."

I stammered. "But . . . when?"

Anya stepped closer and rested her hands on the cannon still between us. "You risked life and lives of others to rescue me from inside Black Dolphin prison in Sol-Iletsk."

In a mission that seemed so distant in both geography and the passage of time, I had led a small team to free Anya from the Black Dolphin, the most notorious of Russia's prisons, near the border of Kazakhstan, by replacing her with her half-sister, Captain Ekaterina Norikova, of the *Sluzhba Vneshney Razvedki*, the Russian Foreign Intelligence Service.

She looked at me as if hopeful. "Please tell to me you remember this, yes?"

I swallowed the lump in my throat but couldn't yet speak, so I nodded slowly.

She reached across the cannon, and I let her take my hand in hers. "You remember also time after you gave to me money and car and freedom?"

I continued nodding as the memory replayed in my mind until it was all I could see.

She said, "After you gave to me these things I needed so badly in that moment . . ." Anya stroked Pogonya's arm. "After this, you gave to me most beautiful gift in all of world."

I grasped the cannon—the mighty iron relic—to save myself from collapsing where I stood on trembling knees. "But . . . why? Why didn't you tell me?"

At this, Anya looked away, perhaps embarrassed, or even enraged. "What would you have done, Chasechka, if you had known?"

"I don't know, but . . ."

She squeezed my hand and then placed it in Pogonya's. The girl's hand felt warm, so much like her mother's had from memories of years before that floated through my head, more like a dream than an actual envelope of time in my life.

In a transformation I hadn't expected, the girl withdrew her hand and gently whispered, "You don't look like the man in the pictures."

"What pictures?"

She pulled her phone from a pocket, brought up a folder, and passed it to me. Four pictures of me when I was young and strong appeared, and they felt like photographs of someone I never knew.

I said, "These were taken a long time ago."

She nodded and reached for the phone. After a few swipes, she surrendered the device back into my hands, the screen filled with a black-and-white photograph of Anya and me on the deck of a ship.

I caressed the screen with my fingertips until the moment settled into my mind. "This was aboard the RV *Lori Danielle*. That's a ship I used to have. This was the last mission your mother and I—" I froze, suddenly in fear that using the word *mission* may be more than Anya was ready to have Pogonya hear.

But Anya reassured me with little more than a glance, and I continued. "Your mother and I used to work together."

Pogonya giggled again. "I am proof that you did more than merely *work* together."

"Yes, well, I suppose that's true."

She reclaimed her phone. "What happened to you?"

Her voice was that of an orchestra, with only the slightest hint of a British accent and none of her mother's lingering Russian tone. "I mean, I don't mean to be offensive, but you are—"

I rescued her. "No offense taken, I assure you. *I* happened to me. What's left of the man you see in front of you is entirely my fault, but if I had known . . ."

It was her turn to rescue me for the first time of what would be thousands to come. "But you are still alive, and often, this is what is most important."

That eternal truth was one of the first lessons I learned from Clark Johnson, the man who'd mentored, taught, and protected me while I learn to become the weapon I had once been, but the wisdom from her mouth felt endlessly different than it had when Clark baptized me in the ageless truth so long ago.

I looked between the two of them and grew lost in thoughts of what might've been if I had only known.

I finally settled my gaze on Anya. "Can we talk . . . privately?"

She stepped around the cannon as if making some gesture of things to come, but I took a step back, and she said, "We can have talk together, all three of us. Pogonya is child only in years, but not in mind or spirit. You will see this soon."

Of the cacophony of emotion roiling in my mind, anger seemed to be the cream that rose to the top of the churn. As misguided and undeserved as it may have been, it still reared its horrific head.

"Anya, how could you keep this from me?"

She bit her lip before saying, "I tried so many times to tell you, but think of what it would have done to you—to your life. Your life with Penny."

"But children need a father."

Anya smiled. "Yes, they do, and now, our daughter has one."

I tasted the bitterness of shame. "But I'm not . . ."

Anya extended her hand toward Pogonya. "Give to me telephone."

The girl obeyed, and Anya held it up in front of me with the black-and-white image taken from the ship's security camera filling the screen. "You are still this man. He is still inside you because even you are not strong enough to destroy him. You have now someone else to live for. You have now daughter who wants to know man her father is —man in this picture."

My anger was quashed by one more look at the perfect child Anya and I created together, and I sank back into my chair. Pogonya sat to my right and Anya to my left.

Our daughter laid her hand on my arm. "Are the horses yours?"

I furrowed my brow. "What horses?"

Pogonya pointed across my shoulder. "Those horses."

I twisted to see the pair of quarter horses chewing on the summertime grass. "Oh, no, they're not mine. They're Penny's. She was my wife before . . ."

She smiled. "Yes, I know. Mama told me about her. She sounds like an amazing woman. I am so very sorry you lost her."

"I didn't lose her," I said. "She was stolen from me."

She nodded. "Yes, I know this as well, and I'm sorry. I really am."

The moment should've been awkward, but somehow, it wasn't.

Pogonya kept talking. "I've seen some of her movies. She was a wonderful writer."

"You think so?"

"Who takes care of the horses?"

I twisted again as if needing to see the animals to remember anything about them. "I don't know."

She frowned. "How can you not know? Someone must feed them and brush them. They appear to be quite healthy and beautiful."

I shrugged. "Yeah, I guess somebody does, but I don't know."

"Can I meet them?"

"Who?" I asked.

She giggled, and I fell in love with the sound. "The horses, silly."

"You want to meet the horses?"

"Yes, of course I do. I love to ride."

I turned to Anya, begging for help with my eyes, but she smiled back as if to say, "You're doing fine."

I wasn't doing fine, but her faith in me seemed to embolden my performance. "Sure, we can go meet the horses."

She hopped to her feet in the first authentic demonstration of her youth. So much about her spoke of maturity beyond her living years, but the little girl still twinkled in her beautiful eyes.

I followed her to the barn as if she were somehow the tour guide to my existence. Perhaps she would become exactly that.

Chapter 3
The Indefensible

Pogonya stepped through the gate as if she'd done it a thousand times and extended a hand to scratch the first nose that came to investigate the new girl. "What's her name?"

I shrugged. "I don't know."

She leaned against the animal and stroked her neck and mane. "How do you not know your own horse's name?"

I pointed toward the larger of the two animals. "That one's Pecan, and he hates me, but this one is just 'The Other Horse,' as far as I know."

"Are they broken?"

I recoiled. "Broken? Not that I know of."

The giggling returned, and she glanced at her mother. "You didn't tell me he was so funny, Mama."

"He's not being funny, malyshka. He does not like horses. Is very funny story. Maybe he will tell to you one day."

Pogonya planted her hands on her hips. "Mama, your English. Please."

Anya scowled but made no effort to correct her abuse of the language.

"Can we ride them?" Pogonya asked.

I froze. "Uh, I don't know."

"Does anyone ride them?"

"Penny used to."

"But why not you?"

"I just don't get along so well with them. They have a deep and thorough hatred for me."

She slapped me playfully. "Animals aren't capable of hate."

I reached for Pecan's nose, and he snapped at me.

She laughed. "Okay, maybe that one hates you a little. What did you do to him?"

"Nothing. I tried to ride him twice, and he threw me both times. I'll never give him another chance."

She snuggled Pecan's face, but the beast never took his eye off me. "He's a sweetheart. I can tell. Where's your tack?"

"I don't know what that is."

She huffed. "You cannot be serious. Tack. Saddles? Bridles? Reins?"

"Oh, that. I don't know."

She reached for my hand and led me into the barn. "Come, Father. We'll find it together."

Pogonya was becoming a better tour guide with every passing moment.

"Here it is," she said. "This is the tack room. May I?"

"May you what?"

She looked so much like her mother when she smiled at me. "Saddle them so we can ride."

I took a step backward. "I don't know how."

She placed a blanket in my hands. "Then, I shall teach you."

Occasionally, the European English she learned, no doubt at an early age, slipped into her voice, and it gave her an elegance and sophistication I'd never seen in teenagers.

She shouldered a saddle and motioned toward a second one. "Get yours."

"Mine? Oh, no. Nothing in this barn is mine, and I have no intention of changing that."

I glanced into the breezeway of the barn for a little help from Anya, but she was nowhere in sight. My heart shivered. I was alone with the daughter I never imagined I would have, and I had never been more uncomfortable in my life.

"I really don't think this is a good idea. As far as I know, no one has ridden the horses since . . ."

Pogonya ignored my protest. "Get your saddle. The horses probably miss Penny almost as much as you."

The thought paralyzed me, and for the first time, the crushing weight of my selfishness drove me into the earth. I wanted to lash out in an effort to defend myself—the indefensible—but instead, I hoisted a saddle and followed my tour guide.

We left the barn, and to my surprise, both horses stood just outside, peering at the two of us.

"See?" Pogonya said. "They're excited."

"They're planning to trample me. I can see it in their eyes. Where's your mother?"

She shrugged. "I don't know, but we don't need her. What does Praline mean?"

"What?"

She placed the saddle she'd been carrying on the ground. "It's stitched into the pommel, right here. I don't know that word."

I lowered my saddle to the ground beside hers and pointed toward the name Pecan stitched on the front. "Is this the pommel?"

I had already fallen in love with her laughter, and I was once again rewarded for my ignorance.

She chuckled and slid her hand across the leather. "Yes, silly man. That is the pommel. The handle is called the horn. Please tell me you knew that."

"I knew that one," I said. "I guess Praline is the other horse's name since this one says Pecan."

She took a knee between the saddles and smiled up at me. "You should've been a detective."

"I should've been a baseball player."

She stood and scratched Praline's nose. "Mama told me you were a famous baseball player before becoming an operator."

"Operator? Is that what she called me? Why do you know what an operator is?"

"Don't be naïve," she said. "I'm not a child, and Anastasia Burinkova is my mother."

I took a seat on Pecan's saddle that was still on the ground, and Pogonya scolded me. "No! Don't sit on the saddle on a flat surface. It's very bad for the tree."

I stumbled and staggered my way back to my feet. "What tree?"

"Not a real tree. The saddle tree. It's like the spine of the saddle."

"I didn't know."

"You're serious about hating these beautiful animals, aren't you?"

I sighed. "It may not qualify as hate. Maybe it's apathy, but I certainly don't love them."

She stared up at me with sincerity in her eyes. "Even though Penny loved them?"

I didn't want the tears to come, but I couldn't stop them. I turned my back and took a few deep breaths, but my play didn't work.

Pogonya stepped in front of me and laced her arms around me. "Crying is important sometimes. Never be ashamed of loving someone. Love is the fountain of more tears than all other emotions combined. You're a psychologist, right?"

It wasn't a conscious reaction. It simply happened, and my arms fell around her. We stood, holding each other as the horses looked on, and I cried.

When I finally composed myself, I said, "Come on. Show me how to put these saddles on."

She pulled away. "Let's start with the blankets and see how they react. If it's been a year since anyone has ridden them, they may be a bit skittish at first."

"Where did you learn English?"

"From my mother, first, but . . . well, you know."

I smiled, and it felt good. "Yeah, I know. You don't have a Russian accent. I assume you learned Russian first."

She said, "I speak Russian, but I think in English—proper English, not American English. Not yet, at least."

"Something tells me you speak more than just Russian and English."

She smirked. "Maybe a little. I'm pretty good with languages."

"And horses?"

She lifted the blankets and tossed one to me. "Just watch and do what I do. I'll take Pecan. Apparently, the two of you have . . . a thing."

"A thing. Yeah. That's a good way to put it."

She made no effort to sneak up on Pecan, instead, offering the blanket for him to sniff before sliding it across his back. Before she stepped away, the beast craned his neck, bit the corner of the blanket, and threw it from his body.

"See? I told you he was a devil."

"He's no devil," she said. "He's just playful."

I laughed. "Yeah. You'll think he's playful when he turns into a bucking bronco."

She rubbed his face with both hands. "Do not listen to him, Pecan. He doesn't understand you."

Instead of throwing the blanket back on him, she wrapped it around her shoulders and seemed to luxuriate in the feeling. I couldn't believe what was happening. I could've sworn the creature was suddenly envious of Pogonya beneath the blanket. The second time she laid it across his back, he turned his head again, but he didn't protest.

She said, "Go ahead. Give Praline her blanket."

I carefully approached and dropped the blanket over her spine. Unlike Pecan, she showed no reaction and continued nibbling the grass.

Slowly, we continued our work until each animal had a bit in its mouth and a saddle cinched on its back.

She said, "Would you give me a leg up, please?"

As I approached, I watched Pecan carefully. I could see it in his eyes—he wanted to bite me and throw me away just like he'd done with the blanket, but unlike the blanket, I'd fight back. "I'm not sure I know how to do that."

She positioned me beside Pecan's shoulder and demonstrated how to hold my hands. "Just boost me up a bit. I ride English, so it will take me a bit to grow accustomed to the western saddle. Don't worry if I skitter about a bit."

"Skitter about? I have no idea what that means, but I hope I get to see you do it."

"Just give me the boost, silly."

I helped her into the saddle, and Pecan didn't like anything about it. Just as he'd become a tornado the last time I got on him, he gave Pogonya the same treatment. His front legs rose high into the air, like Silver on the show *The Lone Ranger* that I remembered from childhood. Unlike me, though, she didn't come out of the saddle. Pogonya seemed to remain perfectly calm while Pecan danced like a wild mustang beneath her.

When his tantrum was over, she lay forward against his neck and stroked him lovingly. "That's it, boy. Now that we've been properly introduced, I'd fancy becoming your friend."

He let out a horse noise that probably has a name, but I don't care. Soon he was walking in gentle circles at Pogonya's behest, and everything about the scene made me believe I'd soon be lying on my back with Praline dancing on top of me.

"Go ahead, famous baseball player. Step into the saddle. If she gets spirited, simply squeeze with your legs and hold tightly to the horn. You do remember what the horn is, right?"

"I got the horn question right on the pop quiz earlier, so, yes, I know it well. Oh, and I was never a *famous* baseball player. I've never been a famous anything."

She moved in perfect coordination with Pecan as he continued in alternating circles. "I don't think they name baseball stadiums after average players."

"What are you talking about?"

She lifted gently on the reins, and Pecan froze a few feet in front of me. "Mama told me the university where you played named the stadium after you."

"Oh, she did, did she?"

Pogonya sat in the saddle nodding slowly. "I like having someone famous for my father. Now, stop stalling and get in the saddle."

I shook Praline's leather reins. "I'm not stalling. We're having a conversation. It would be rude for me to just turn around and hop on a horse."

"If that's your excuse, the conversation is over, so get in the saddle."

I said, "There's nobody here to give me a leg up, so I guess you'll have to ride without me."

She delivered that icy glare that only Russian women seem to have mastered, erasing any question of her heritage. There's nothing like the frozen fire from that Russian stare.

"Okay, I'm going. But I wasn't famous, and nobody named a stadium after me. They put my name up in the section right behind home plate. You know, because I was a catcher. That's it. The stadium will always be Foley Field."

She stared into the distance. "Baseball is a bit like cricket, only simpler, right?"

I stuck a foot into the stirrup and grabbed the one piece of the saddle I could name. Praline planted her front feet and swung her haunches away from me. I was left hanging onto the saddle for dear life, with one foot stuck in the stirrup and the other dragging behind me. Our dance continued, and my partner picked up the pace. Soon, I was bounding helplessly on my prosthetic foot while my real foot was firmly and completely stuck in the stirrup. I had to come up with a way to either improve my position or get Praline to stop her death spiral.

Before I could come up with anything resembling a plan, Pogonya nudged Pecan, and he stepped beside Praline, stopping the game of equine twister.

"Keep your body close to hers, and spring upward without pushing her away."

I released the reins and wrestled my ankle from the stirrup. When I was finally free, I said, "I think that's enough equestrian excitement for one day."

"No!" she demanded. "You must get on. You cannot let her win an argument, not even once."

"I'm not arguing with her. I'm trying to keep her from dragging my one good foot off."

She leaned over and took Praline's reins. "I'll hold her for you. Come on."

With both hands wrapped around the horn, I pushed off with my right leg, landing ungracefully in the saddle. Praline didn't seem to care or even know that I was on her back.

We walked side by side for an hour with barely a word spoken, but there was something magical about just being together. No one on Earth knew that feeling better than I did.

"So, you weren't really famous?"

"No, I wasn't famous, but I was a pretty good player once upon a time."

She tilted her head exactly like her mother. "I think you're being modest."

I pressed my boots into the stirrups to take a little stress from my backside. "Did your mom ever tell you about her experience with the chili dog at her first ball game?"

Chapter 4

Giving Chase

"Race you back to the barn!" Pogonya said.

Without waiting for me to accept her challenge, she dug her heels in, and Pecan was suddenly a thoroughbred. Praline glanced back at me as if to ask permission to give chase. I offered no such permission, but apparently, she wasn't really asking. I spent the next several minutes of my life being nothing more than dead weight holding on for dear life.

Praline and I lost the race, but I stayed in the saddle, which I considered to be an enormous accomplishment. When she finally came to a stop in a cloud of dust and a few profanities from me, I wasted no time dismounting.

"Beat'cha," Pogonya said. "But you did well, and you weren't unhorsed this time."

"Unhorsed? Is that what you call it when a fifteen-hundred-pound animal tries to kill me?"

She pulled the saddle from Pecan's back and the bridle from his head. He seemed to appreciate the kindness, but something in his black eyes still said he hated me. I hoped my expression said exactly the same to him.

We brushed the horses and released them back into their world of zero stress and responsibility, but Pecan made no effort to leave Pogonya's side. Praline, on the other hand, lay down and wallowed like a dog for several minutes before galloping away toward the tender grass near the river.

"Please tell me I didn't just see Mr. I Hate Horses riding a horse."

I turned to see Mongo, the biggest man I'd ever known, leaning on a fence post.

I dusted off my hands and moved toward the gate. "Yeah, that was me, and I didn't get . . . what did you call it?"

Pogonya giggled. "Unhorsed."

"Yeah, that's it. I didn't get unhorsed. How've you been, Mongo?"

He stepped through the gate. "I'm doing just fine, and it would appear you're either too drunk to realize you've been riding a horse or you're having a pretty good day, as well."

I instantly felt ashamed for not dwelling on Penny's absence for the previous hour of my life. "I'm glad you're here. There's somebody I want you to meet."

Pogonya stepped toward the giant and offered her hand. "Hello. I'm Pogonya, and you have to be Mr. Malloy."

His paw dwarfed her hand, but he shook it. "Nobody calls me anything besides Mongo. I don't even remember the last time I heard my real name. It's nice to meet you, Pogonya."

The questions in his eyes were impossible to hide, so I said, "She's my daughter."

He reached for the wall of the barn as if I'd knocked him from his feet. "Your daughter? What? I mean . . . what?"

Pogonya laced a hand inside my elbow. "Anya is my mother."

I'd never seen our mountain of a man at a complete loss for words until that moment, and I found it to be quite amusing. Part of me wanted to leave him hanging and listen to him try to solve the mystery with the teenager, but she beat me to the punch.

"You look almost as shocked as my father did when we met for the first time a couple of hours ago."

The big man's mouth was still agape as he stared back and forth between her and me. "But, I don't . . ."

It was time to let him off the hook. "Remember when we pulled Anya out of the Black Dolphin Prison?"

Realization overtook him. "Oh, of course. That makes . . . no, it doesn't. Are you saying—"

"My mother told me about you, Mr. Mongo."

"Just Mongo, please. What did she say about me?"

Pogonya smiled up at him. "She said you're one of the kindest people she's ever met. It's a pleasure to finally learn that you're real. She speaks of you as if you are some mythical, larger-than-life hero."

He blushed. "I don't know about any of that, but you'll have to forgive my shock. I didn't expect to find out Chase has a daughter today."

She said, "I don't think he was expecting it either. Other than Singer and Penny, I don't think Mama told anyone else."

That revelation hit me like a truck. "Penny knew?"

"Yes. I met her while she was in Switzerland with Mama."

"You met her?"

"Yes. We spent two days together while you were searching for Timothy Taylor."

Now I was the one with my mouth hanging open, and one more item made its way onto the list of things to discuss with Anya.

"Are you the one who takes care of the horses?" Pogonya asked.

Mongo rubbed a hand across Pecan's back. "Yeah. I keep them fed and make sure the vet and farrier come every few months. I think Pecan likes you."

She scratched his nose. "He's a sweetheart, like you. I think he just missed a woman's touch. He lost Penny, too."

"He sure did," Mongo said. "And you did something no one else could've pulled off. How did you get your old man on a horse?"

She gave him a wink. "Mama says he has a weakness for Eastern European girls. Maybe that's it."

"But you don't sound Eastern European."

"I spend a lot more time in Switzerland than Russia, but it's in my genes."

I said, "So, you've been taking care of the horses all this time?"

He picked a bit of lint from his shirt. "Yeah, somebody had to take care of them while you . . . recovered."

"About that," I said. "I've been a real ass, and I'm sorry. I know I pushed you and everybody else away, but I was hurting."

"I know," he said. "We all know. Singer's the only one who's been stubborn enough to force his way inside for months. The rest of us took a step back because that seemed to be what you wanted. And maybe that is what you needed."

I bowed my head. "I'm sorry. I should've . . ."

He took a step toward me and grabbed me by the shoulders. "Like Clark says, 'Don't be sorry. Be better.' And in this case, better means healthier. We miss you. We miss our brother and our team leader. The guys keep trying to stick me at the top of the org chart, but that's your spot."

I looked up at the man who towered over me, and the tears came again. He stepped between Pogonya and me and wrapped me in the closest thing to a real bear hug anybody could experience.

The tears ceased, and I wiped my face. "Thank you, Mongo. And I truly am sorry."

"You don't owe me an apology. I understand. Everybody does. Skipper's taking it pretty hard, though. Especially right now."

"Right now? What does that mean? Is she okay?"

He said, "Except for missing her big brother, she's doing great."

"I'm glad to hear it, but what do you mean by especially right now?"

He checked his watch. "Maybe you two should get cleaned up and come with me."

"Where?" I asked.

He rechecked his wrist. "Don't ask questions. Just get that horse smell off of you, and I'll meet you out front in half an hour."

He offered an abbreviated bow toward Pogonya. "It was a great pleasure to meet you, Ms. Pogonya. I think I speak for everyone when I say I'm so glad you look like your mother instead of this ugly old mug."

She squeezed my arm. "He's not so bad, but it wouldn't hurt him to put on a stone or two."

"Yes, somebody definitely needs to fatten him up," Mongo said. "How about you and me work on that together?"

"You're on."

He stepped into the barn to do whatever he did for the horses, and Pogonya and I headed for the house.

I asked, "Do you have any more clothes?"

She dusted off her jeans. "What's wrong with these?"

"Nothing, as far as I'm concerned, but Mongo's right. We do smell like horses."

She said, "Of course I have more clothes—as long as Mama didn't take my bag with her."

"Where'd she go?"

"I don't know, but I'm glad we got to spend some time together."

"It's not over," I said more quickly than I meant to.

She smiled. "I hope not."

We discovered her bag on the back gallery, and I directed her to a bathroom.

She and I emerged from the house smelling far less like the barn, and Mongo opened the door for Pogonya. We climbed aboard his Suburban and pulled down the tree-lined drive.

"Where are you taking us?" I asked.

"Just be patient," he said.

"Why does everybody keep telling me that?"

He huffed. "You said it yourself. You've been a little less than patient—maybe even less than human—for a while."

The shame returned. "Yeah, I guess you're right."

We pulled into the gravel parking area of the church where Singer taught, sang, and occasionally even preached. A dozen cars were parked neatly by the back door of the old sanctuary.

I scowled. "We're meeting Skipper here?"

Mongo threw open the door. "Come on. You'll see."

He led us through the back door, and nothing could've prepared me for what I saw inside those walls. Singer stood facing me from the altar, and Skipper, the most highly skilled intelligence analyst in the game and practically my little sister, stood in front of him, holding Gator's hands in hers.

Out of some primal reaction, I said, "They're getting married!"

That outburst halted the ceremony, and suddenly, everyone in the church turned in unison to see Mongo, Pogonya, and me standing in the doorway.

Skipper dropped Gator's hands and ran to me. "Chase! You're here! You're really here."

I wondered how many tears one man was capable of producing without completely dehydrating himself. "Yeah, I'm here. I'm so sorry for everything. I can't believe you're actually—"

She threw her arms around me, and we hugged as if neither of us ever wanted to let go.

When we'd finally squeezed each other as tightly as possible, she said, "I'm so glad you're here. This is just rehearsal, but Saturday's the big day. Singer and I were planning to come see you tomorrow and try to talk you into coming."

Skipper had been with me since Anya, Clark, and I rescued her from the hands of some low-life scum in Miami, too long ago to remember, and as the team grew, she became the glue that held what used to be my team together. Without her, I would've died, failed, or worse a thousand times over.

"I know I've been impossible for a long time, but of course I'll come if you really want me there."

My tears became hers, and we hugged again.

As she pulled away, she whispered, "Who's the girl?"

I said, "Skipper, meet Pogonya. She is a very long story."

In her typical hesitation to welcome anyone new into the circle, Skipper said, "Begonia? Like the flower?"

Pogonya smiled. "No, not like the flower. It's a P, not a B, and I'm his daughter."

Skipper had never spent a second of her life being speechless until that moment. When she finally recovered enough to open her mouth, she said, "Chase doesn't have a daughter. He can't have children, so whatever game you're playing, little girl, you can take it somewhere else."

The barrier that my team—and especially Skipper—constructed around me was nearly impenetrable, and it felt nice to know she was still in the fence-building business.

I said, "It's true. She's Anya's and my daughter."

"That's not possible. You can't have kids."

"It happened before the mission on the Khyber Pass when I got hurt."

Skipper grabbed my hand and led me through a door and into an office barely large enough to be called a closet. "Chase, she's pulling some kind of con. Don't fall for it. You're in a vulnerable place right now, and I'm not going to let Anya and whoever that girl is out there pull this on you. You may have been impossible to deal with, but that doesn't mean any of us stopped loving you. We just tried to give you the space you needed."

I wanted to protest, but instead, I reached inside my shirt pocket and pulled out an old picture of my mother as a teenager. "Take a look at this."

She snatched the print from my hand and studied it closely. "Okay, maybe the eyes are similar, but that doesn't mean anything. A lot of people have eyes like that."

I slid the picture back into my pocket. "She's my daughter, Skipper. There's no doubt."

"What does she want?"

I shrugged. "Maybe a father."

"Chase, I love you. You know I do. But you're in no shape to take care of yourself right now, let alone a teenager."

I took a long, deep breath and let it out slowly. "I don't think she's here expecting me to take care of her. I think she's here to take care of me."

Chapter 5
Definitely Not Pop

Apparently, our arrival was enough to shut the wedding rehearsal down, but the whole team was there as if they'd never dispersed.

Clark Johnson, the man I credit with teaching me to keep breathing and shooting when I wanted to crawl into a hole and cry for my mommy, sat beside me on the most uncomfortable church pew I'd ever met.

"How you doin', College Boy?"

"Better today than yesterday. And my whole world changed when this young lady showed up this morning. This is Pogonya—I assume Burinkova—and she's my daughter."

She smiled and shook her head. "I am the daughter of Chase and Ana Fulton, according to my birth certificate, so that means you and I have the same last name. But that's not all . . . Mama says you speak very good Russian, but I think you don't realize yet that my name, Pogonya, also means *chase* in Russian."

That sent a shockwave pulsing through the team, and she and I fought off questions for several minutes before things returned to a conversational tone and volume.

After an hour with the team who'd once been a family, I said, "I've got about a million things to be sorry for, and I owe all of you an apology I'll never be able to adequately express, but please know that I still loved every one of you, even when I was kicking and screaming for you to leave me alone."

Clark was the first to respond. "Don't be sorry . . ."

And the whole team joined in. "Be better!"

Pogonya giggled again. "I like these people. I thought I knew all of you because Mama talked so much about you, but meeting everyone is so much better than just stories."

The look on Skipper's face said she still wasn't convinced. "How would you feel about a DNA test?"

That silenced the crowd, and Pogonya smiled. "I am happy to have the test, and honestly, I'm surprised you're the first to ask. I understand and appreciate how unbelievable—and maybe even a bit shocking—my arrival is. It's only natural for some, or all of you, to have questions."

I leaned toward her. "I don't need a DNA test."

"Neither do I," she said. "But it's still a good idea."

Dr. Celeste Mankiller, our mad scientist in residence, said, "I can take care of that. I just need a cheek swab. I've probably got a sample kit in the car."

Pogonya walked away with Celeste, and the questions flew again.

Disco, our former chief pilot, tapped the toe of my boot with his cane. "You look good, Chase. It's great to have you back."

"Thanks, but I'm not so sure I'm technically back. How's the recuperation coming?"

In the final mission we worked as a team, Disco suffered a pair of traumatic injuries that left him paralyzed below the waist for several weeks before one of the best neurosurgeons on Earth rebuilt his spine. His flying days were over, but he took up residence aboard the RV *Lori Danielle*, the five-hundred-eighty-eight-foot vessel that had been the largest weapon in our arsenal. It wasn't the allure of life at sea that dragged Disco from the cockpit to the deck, though. It was a relationship with Ronda No-H, the CFO for everything having to do with dollars and cents in the world we used to share.

"Learning to walk again wasn't much fun, but at least I'm out of that cursed wheelchair."

"You look good," I said.

"Thanks for lying to me, boss."

"I'm not lying. I remember how you looked in the ICU. Trust me. Compared to that, you're practically Mr. America."

He laughed. "That's me."

Ronda poked him in the ribs. "You're *my* Mr. America."

I said, "See? How could you argue with that?"

Gator, the youngest and most athletic of the team, said, "Chase, I guess I should apologize for not talking to you before asking Skipper to marry me, but I did talk with her dad."

"Did he threaten to beat you to death with a baseball bat if you hurt his little girl?"

Skipper's father, Bobby Woodley, had been my college baseball coach at UGA and the closest thing to a father I had after my parents were murdered in Panama.

Gator wiped a bead of sweat from his upper lip. "No, a bat wasn't the weapon he chose, but the message was the same. He can be a little scary sometimes."

I grinned. "You should've heard him when his starting catcher called the wrong pitch and some second-rate batter from Clemson crushed it over the right field wall. I thought he was going to feed me my own mask that day."

"I get it," he said. "They're coming for the weekend, of course. I'm sure they're looking forward to seeing you."

"I'm not feeling exactly social yet, but it'll be nice to spend some time with them."

Shawn, the only former Navy SEAL on the team, was rarely without a guitar if he wasn't carrying a rifle. His prowess in, on, and beneath the water was second to none. He played softly as if his hands could do it without his conscious effort. "You look like you need a cheeseburger, boss. Do you think your daughter has ever been to a good old-fashioned American cookout?"

"I doubt it, but I, for one, would love that."

He placed his guitar back in its case. "I guess that's my cue to fire up the grills and get Cajun Kenny involved. Can we do it at Bonaventure?"

"It's a bit of a mess," I said. "But sure. Why not?"

The remaining operator, Kodiak, a retired Green Beret and Arctic survival specialist, stood with Shawn. "I'll make sure the SEAL doesn't set himself on fire. You know how those guys are around flammable material."

Pogonya nestled her way onto the pew beside me.

I asked, "Did you give a sample?"

"Yes. She's headed back to her lab with it now, and she said she doesn't need a sample from you."

I knocked my knuckles on the wooden pew. "Hey, Skipper. We screwed up your rehearsal, so we'll get out of the way so you can finish."

Pogonya and I stood, and she said, "It was nice to meet all of you. I'm sure I'll see you again soon."

"Sooner than you think," I said. "We're having a cookout at Bonaventure tonight."

Her grin brightened the sanctuary. "Can Mama come?"

My eyes naturally shot to Skipper, and she nodded with only a hint of hesitation.

Mongo hopped to his feet. "I'm your ride, so I guess I'll be going too."

"No," Skipper said. "Stay with us. Chase knows the way home. He just needed a reason to find it again."

I said, "We can walk. It's not that far."

Mongo tossed me a wad of keys. "Take the Suburban."

I tossed them back. "The walk will be good for us."

* * *

It was only a few blocks, but for the first time in months, I looked forward to the time spent with someone other than Jack Daniel.

As we crossed Osborne Street, I said, "Check out the tree in the road. They say it's around three hundred years old."

Pogonya rubbed a hand across the tattered bark. "That's a silly place for a tree."

"I agree, but it's been here a lot longer than the road, so it's safe to say it has the right of way."

"That doesn't seem to protect it," she said.

"No, it doesn't. People hit it all the time. I bet a hundred cars have run into it since I've lived here."

She stepped back and took in the massive oak. "I like it, and I think it should stay."

"That's kind of how I feel about you."

She smiled and squeezed my arm. "Thank you. Are you going to marry Mama now that . . ."

I suddenly felt like the old oak right after being hit by yet another car. "That's not something I'm ready to think about."

"But you love her, don't you? I know she loves you."

I wanted to have a better answer, but all I could come up with was, "I think she's in love with the *idea* of me. The reality is that I'm an unemployed alcoholic."

"That doesn't matter," she said. "Mama has money, and we can help you stop drinking."

"I'm . . . not sure this is the right time for this conversation."

As if someone tripped a switch, she changed the subject mid-stride. "What should I call you?"

"What do you mean?"

"You know. Should I call you Dad or Father or maybe Pop?"

"Pop? Is that *really* one of the options?"

"It made you laugh, and I bet you haven't done much of that lately."

"You'd win that bet. What do you want to call me?"

"Not Pop."

I laughed again. "No, definitely not Pop."

"What happens at a cookout?"

"You are far too European, you know that?"

"I can't help it, but I do have dual citizenship."

"Russia and Switzerland?"

She said, "No, Switzerland and the U.S."

"Why not Russia?"

"You'll have to ask Mama. That reminds me. I should call and invite her to the barbecue."

I said, "Yankees call it a barbecue. Down here in the South, we call it a cookout. Barbecue is smoked pork, and it's glorious."

"I've never had it. Can we get some? And is it true that you shot off Mama's toe?"

"I'm having a little trouble keeping up."

She slowed her pace. "I'm sorry. I do walk quickly. 'Walking with a purpose' is what Mama calls it."

"It's not the walking speed. It's the pace of the questions. Yes, to barbecue, and also yes to the toe thing. But in my defense, she did cut my tongue in half."

"Ooh, can I see?"

"No, you can't see. It's long since healed."

"I still want to see the scar."

I showed her, and she recoiled. "That's disturbing. Mama's missing toe looks better than that. I've never shot a gun. Will you teach me?"

"Teach you to shoot?"

"Yes. All Americans know how to shoot, don't they?"

"I don't know about all of them, but in the South, I'd say it's close."

"So, will you teach me?"

"We'll have to talk with your mother about that."

"What she doesn't know won't hurt her."

I stuck out my tongue again, and she said, "I guess you're right. We should ask, but you should do it. She can't tell you no."

"Does she still carry that little plastic American flag everywhere she goes?"

Pogonya pulled an identical trinket from her pocket. "We both have a flag. Oh, and a baseball game. Will you take me to one? I know every word to the national anthem."

"If I feed you barbecue, take you to a ball game, and teach you to shoot, you're not going to need that Swiss passport much longer."

She raised an eyebrow. "I have school there, but I don't want to go back. I like it here."

"I guess you're a sophomore, right?"

She blushed. "I'm a bit of an overachiever like Mama. I'll graduate secondary school in December if I go back in August, and then to university."

"At fifteen?"

"I'll be sixteen in the spring, and I've already been accepted to university."

"Which one?"

"Oxford, Princeton, and a little school not far from here. Maybe you've heard of it. I think it's called UGA."

"You applied to Georgia?"

She said, "Maybe I had a little encouragement from Mama on that one, but I'll never pronounce the mascot as *dawg*. Saying it that way hurts my mouth."

"We'll work on that right after we teach you to shoot."

Chapter 6
Not the Typical Woman

"Who's that person on your boat, Father?"

I followed Pogonya's outstretched finger across the back lawn and to the fifty-foot custom sailing catamaran tied alongside the Bonaventure dock. "Oh, that's Earl."

She lowered one eyebrow and raised the other. "Earl? It looks like a woman . . . sort of."

It had been exactly three hundred ninety-one days since I laughed hysterically, but the slump was broken in that moment, and I had to take a knee. "Earl is a woman, but not the typical woman. Come on. I'll introduce you."

"I never expected to meet so many people on my first day at Bonaventure. I love the name, by the way."

I said, "That's one of the best things about this place. There's never a shortage of interesting people around."

"Maybe I could be one of them."

I wiped the sweat from my forehead. "I think you're already becoming one. Are you really considering UGA over Oxford or Princeton? I mean, those are great schools and all, but to get a chance to go to Georgia? Now, that's a real honor."

"You're funny, Father. I don't know for sure. I've not been for a visit yet. Maybe you could take me and show me around since that's where you went."

"I'd like that."

"Yes, me too. Especially since they named the baseball stadium after my very own father."

I laughed again. "I told you that didn't really happen. Your crazy mother made that up."

"She doesn't make up stories. If she says it, she believes it."

"In that case," I said, "maybe she misunderstood."

"Why didn't you marry her before you met Penny?"

The Mack truck that loved running over me showed up again, and it took me a few seconds to get back on my feet. "Uh, I . . ."

Pogonya took my hand and led me toward the dock. "I get it. It was a long time ago, and you're a lot wiser now. You won't make the same mistake again."

"You're really pushing hard for this happy family thing."

That stopped her in her tracks, and suddenly, Earline and the boat weren't so irresistible. "How old were you when your parents . . . uh, you know."

"Were murdered?"

She glanced at her feet. "I didn't want to say that out loud."

"It wasn't just my parents, you know. It was my little sister, too. It happened in Panama when I was thirteen."

She pressed her lips into a thin horizontal line, and I said, "Your mother does that when she's about to say something I'm not going to like."

"Does what?"

"That thing you do with your lips. She presses them together just like that."

She shrugged. "I guess I picked it up from her."

"So, what were you about to ask?"

She squeezed one of my hands. "Whoever killed your parents, why didn't they kill you?"

I cupped my free hand behind her head and gently pulled her against me. "Because if they had, you would've never been born, and we would've never shared this moment."

She looked up. "That's really sweet. Mama says that about you."

"What? That I'm sweet?"

"Sometimes. But she also says when you're in a fight, there's never been anyone braver. Is that true?"

"No, of course that isn't true."

She gave me that beautiful smile that would break so many hearts in years to come. "Well, if Mama said it, she believes it, right?"

"It's not that I'm brave. I'm just not smart enough to know that I'm supposed to be scared."

"But you're a PhD. You have to be smart."

"You're confusing education with intelligence. Although they sometimes coexist, they're not interchangeable."

She tapped a finger against my chest. "See? That's intelligence talking. Come on. I want to see the boat and meet this person called Earl."

We crossed the lawn, and Earline stood upright to her full, almost five feet. "Hey, Sugar Britches. It's good to see you doing something other than moping and moaning. Who's the hot babe? A little young for you, don't you think?"

I glanced down, but Pogonya was transfixed on the filthy, sixty-something, spikey-haired woman.

I said, "You wouldn't believe me if I told you."

"Well, tell me anyway, Stud Muffin."

It was that instant when I learned my daughter had no idea how to whisper. "Father, why is she calling you those names? Is she flirting with you? Please tell me that you two aren't—"

Earl grabbed the portside rail with both hands. "Father? Did she just call you father?"

I was coming to treasure that title above any other. "She sure did. Earline, meet Pogonya. She's Anya's—and my—daughter."

Pogonya left more people speechless in my world than anyone I'd ever met. I was beginning to enjoy the reactions.

Earl pointed to her grease-stained, way-too-short shorts. "But I thought you were, you know—messed up down there."

Before I could respond, Pogonya said, "He is, but I'm pre—mess up."

"Anya?" Earl said. "The hot Russian chick? That Anya?"

"That's the one."

As Earl processed the revelation, Pogonya said, "Why are you on my father's boat?"

Earl finally released the rail and leaned against the cabin top. "The truth is, girlie, your father ain't been takin' real good care of stuff around here for a while, so them of us who love him have been taking up the slack. I just happen to know a thing or two about boats, so I check on *Aegis* every now and then just so she won't sink at the dock. That'd be a mess to clean up."

"Aegis?" she said. "Like Athena's battle shield?"

"That's one of the things it could mean," I said.

Pogonya said, "Sometimes, I think Mama is like Athena. Maybe she's even the Goddess of War reincarnated."

I said, "I've never seen your mother fight with a shield, but Goddess of War might be the best description I've ever heard for her."

"Can we get on the boat?"

I gave Pogonya a leg up—sort of like with the horse.

"I've never been on a sailboat. Maybe you could . . ."

I said, "Let me guess. Teach you? We're stacking up quite the pile of things you want to learn."

She offered a hand to help me aboard. "You had thirteen years with your parents, and I've had fifteen without you. So, you get it, right?"

"What amazes me is the fact that *you* get it."

She continued showing her perfect smile. "I'm pretty smart, like my father."

The best diesel mechanic in the world stuck out her greasy hand. "I'm sorry I was . . . whatever. I'm Earline, but call me Earl. I met your daddy before you were born, and I've been takin' care of his boats ever since."

"Boats? More than one?" Pogonya asked.

Earl had become the temporary center of the universe for my

daughter, and she said, "Yeah. He's had a bunch of 'em through the years. This is the nicest one, but it ain't the sexiest. You should see the hot rod in that boathouse over yonder."

"Hot rod?"

Earl pulled a somewhat clean rag from her pocket and wiped her hands. "Come with me. I'll give you the grand tour, startin' with the motors, and we'll work our way into the sexy shed."

Pogonya followed Earl below and left me alone in the cockpit with a billion questions without answers swirling in my head.

"Permission to come aboard, Captain?"

I glanced over the rail to see Singer waiting patiently. "You don't need permission. Get up here."

He said, "It's not about needing permission. It's about showing respect. She's your ship."

"I haven't done anything to deserve respect in a very long time, and this thing doesn't qualify as a ship."

He tapped his knuckles against the coaming as he stepped into the cockpit. "I wasn't talking about the boat. I was talking about Pogonya."

"Why would you call her a ship?"

A lesson was coming, and there was nothing I could do to stop it.

He pulled two bottles of water from the cooler, tossed one to me, and took a seat. "Tell me what ships do."

"They float."

He took a long drink. "Yep. Indeed, they do. But they also keep everybody on board from drowning in the relentless sea during a storm. At least good ships do."

"And you think that's what Pogonya's going to do for me?"

"Well, me and a bunch of people who care about you have been praying for your ship to show up, and from where I sit, that girl sure seems to fit the bill."

I stared through the companionway into *Aegis*'s interior. "What do you think about the DNA test?"

He polished off the bottle of water. "It's a waste of time, but it'll probably make Skipper back off a little. There's no question who that girl's daddy is. I noticed she walks like you. Well, not how you walk now, but how you moved before you lost your foot."

"You think so?"

"I'm a sniper, remember? And I'm a good one because I know and understand the first and most important rule of sniping—keep both eyes open and never stop looking."

"Why aren't you judging me for sleeping with Anya?"

Singer crushed the plastic bottle in his hands and pulled another from the cooler. "Have you ever heard of King David?"

"Here it comes," I said. "I've missed these conversations."

"Me, too. Anyway, King David did a lot of stuff wrong. Pretty high on that list was sending his friend Uriah—one of the best soldiers in his army—off to die so David could have his wife, who was already pregnant with his illegitimate baby. As sins go, that one's no misdemeanor."

I took a sip, but the old familiar feeling of being under the tutelage of the master washed over me, providing far more relief than the contents of the plastic bottle in my hand could ever do.

He asked, "How's it feel?"

"Having a daughter?"

"No. Drinking something other than whiskey."

"Okay, I deserved that one, but you're not finished teaching me about King David."

He waved a dismissive hand. "Ah, you know how that story ends. A man after God's own heart and all of that. We've all made mistakes, but that doesn't mean the results of those mistakes are always bad." He paused, presumably to let that tidbit soak in before continuing. "If David hadn't fallen in love and lust with Bathsheba, then King Solomon —the wisest man who ever lived—would've never been born, and the nation of Israel might've crumbled."

"So, that's why you don't judge me?"

"I don't judge because it's not my place to judge. I just love you, Chase Fulton. I always have, and I always will."

A new kind of tear formed, and I made no effort to stop it from falling. "I don't deserve a friend like you, and I'm sorry for—"

"We've already covered that business of being sorry, so you can stop apologizing. Have I ever told you the story about the most loving and just king who ever lived?"

"From the Bible?" I asked.

"No, this one's more of a fable than scripture."

"I don't think you have, but I can't wait to hear it."

Singer downed the second water and added the crushed plastic to the trash bag Earl had been using. "This is a story about a great king from someplace you've never heard of. He was heralded far and wide as the most loving and just king who ever lived, and everything he did proved that he deserved that praise more and more every day. No matter what crime had been committed, he was quick to hand down punishment that fit the crime, but he also truly loved everybody in his kingdom, and it broke his heart to have to punish any of them."

I tried to imagine where the story was going, but Singer didn't give me time to think too long.

"Anyway, this king discovered that somebody was stealing gold from the castle treasury, so he put out a proclamation that when the thief was caught, he'd be given three lashes for his crime. Now, these three lashes were serious punishment, but nobody ever died from three lashes."

He hesitated only long enough for me to picture someone receiving the lashes, and I knew that I, of all people, deserved them.

"So, time passed and the thief wasn't caught, but the theft continued. This caused the king to rethink his proclamation of three lashes. Perhaps the punishment wasn't harsh enough to make the thief stop stealing from the treasury. So, the king released a new proclamation that the thief would be given ten lashes when caught. Surely, that would put a halt to the thievery, the king thought. But he was wrong again. The theft continued until the good king declared that anyone caught stealing from the treasury would receive forty lashes."

He gave me a look over his sunglasses. "Forty lashes was a punishment nobody could survive, so, for all practical purposes, it was a death penalty. You'd sure think that would stop the thief, wouldn't you?"

I nodded, but I didn't interrupt.

"Believe it or not, even after the threat of death, the thievery continued until two of the palace guards caught the rascal in the act, and they dragged the thief before the king."

I was on the edge of my seat, hanging on every word.

He leaned forward until his face was the only thing I saw. "When the palace guards pulled back the thief's cloak, the king gasped and fell back onto his throne in disbelief and anguish. The thief was his own beloved daughter."

I should've known there would be a daughter in the story, but I still couldn't see how the story had anything to do with me. However, I had little doubt that Singer would find a way to weave my situation into the story.

"At this point, the king was lost in the horrible conundrum of loving his own child and dealing justly with the crime for which he had ordered death. After a week of sleepless nights and tear-filled days, the king finally decided that he could never again be considered a just king if the punishment wasn't delivered, so he ordered the executioner to deliver the forty lashes that would end the life of his only daughter."

I couldn't remain silent any longer. "But what about him being the most loving king in the world? How could he have his own daughter killed if he truly loved her?"

"Patience, Chase. Patience. The executioner had the king's daughter brought to the palace courtyard, where all public punishment was delivered, and he had her tied across the table on which she would die by the time the fortieth lash was administered. The king sat in tears on his elevated throne that overlooked the horrific tableau. The executioner ordered that the girl's garment be torn from her back, exposing the bare flesh where the lashes would be delivered. His order was followed without question, and the girl lay face-down with her back exposed for all the king's subjects to see."

"Where are you going with this story?" I demanded.

Singer held up one finger, but my impatience was swelling.

"As the executioner raised the whip, preparing to deliver the first blow, the king leapt to his feet and yelled, 'Stop! I can't let this happen!' The whole kingdom was in disbelief that the king had just spared his own daughter and destroyed his reputation for being the most just king in all the world."

I leaned back. "So, the moral of the story is that love is more important than justice, right?"

"I'm not finished," Singer said. "The king tossed off his crown, came down from his throne, tore off his royal robe, and threw himself across his daughter still tied to the table. 'Strike her now,' he commanded. 'But your highness, I can't strike the girl with you covering her,' the executioner argued. 'Deliver the punishment!' the king commanded again, and the executioner delivered the forty lashes, killing the king and setting his daughter free." With that, Singer leaned back, crossed his legs, and watched a pair of pelicans diving on baitfish in the shallows.

"Is that it?" I asked. "That's a terrible story."

He spoke softly as if speaking only to my soul. "No, Chase. That's the greatest love story there could ever be. Punishment was given, thereby serving justice, and out of the ultimate demonstration of love, the king sacrificed himself to save the life of his only daughter. That's exactly what Jesus did for all of us. He cast off his crown, stepped from his throne, bared himself, and suffered the punishment that all of us deserve. That's why I don't judge you or anybody else. Our sins are forgiven, and the justified debt we owed is paid in full because of the king's love."

He watched the pelicans dive a few more times before saying, "You love Penny, and she loved you, but now you've got your only daughter to love, and because you're the kind of man who'd willingly take her lashes because of that love, you have to step up and become the man you were a year ago. That man's still in there, and that little girl deserves to know that man as her father."

Chapter 7
A Common Language

By the time Pogonya's tour of *Aegis* and my counseling session with Dr. Singer was finished, someone had erected a family-size tent without sides, and the family I had once enjoyed was once again under the same proverbial roof.

I counted heads and came up one short. "Pogo, where's Athena?"

She rolled her eyes, reminding me that she was, indeed, a teenager. "Pogo? That's what you chose, Pops?"

"Oh, so it's Pops. Pogo and Pops sounds like a fantastic breakfast cereal. Don't you think?"

The eye rolling continued. "Oh, great. You've known you're a dad for less than a day, and you're already dispensing dad jokes."

"Sorry. What's the official time requirement for knowing I'm a dad before I can spew them out?"

"How about never? And Mama said she'd be here. You want to see her, don't you?"

"It's not like that," I said. "She's part of the family, and she should be here."

Cajun Kenny LePine ambled up and mussed Pogonya's hair. "Whoo wee. Ol' Kenny do declare if you ain't da cutest ting dat never been. Who dis be, her?"

She stepped back, straightened her hair, and stood in utter shock. "Uh, what language is that?"

Kenny and I laughed, and he cleared his throat. "Okays, how 'bout dis here? *Tu es vraiment belle. Comment t'appelles-tu?*"

Recognition replaced confusion, and she answered in what sounded like French. "*Merci, monsieur. Je m'appelle Pogonya Fulton et je suis sa fille.*"

Kenny's eyebrows shot up. "She say she be yo li'l girl, but dat can't be da troof, do it be, no?"

I silently wondered how long it would be before I could introduce her as my daughter without answering a dozen follow-up questions. "It's true. Anya and I—"

Kenny covered his mouth. "Oh! Dat be what be happenin'. I gots it now, me." He switched back to French. "*C'est un réel plaisir de vous rencontrer mademoiselle Pogonya.*"

She obviously realized I spoke no French, so she answered in the only common language the three of us shared. "Thank you, sir. It's a pleasure to meet you as well."

Kenny placed his arm around my daughter. "Come wiff ol' Kenny, and he show you all dey is to be knowin' 'bout what dees folk 'round here say be low-country boil."

She glanced up at me as if asking permission, but I didn't even understand the question. She strolled away with her newest French-speaking friend, and Anya pulled up the drive in her spotless Porsche 911 convertible.

After a glance across my shoulder to make sure no one was looking for me, I jogged toward the driveway. The strides felt somehow foreign, but good, and I coasted to a stop near the front of the house. "Nice wheels."

She planted a hip against the hood and admired her own car. "You will not remember, but many years ago—before Pogonya—you had one of these on Jekyll Island, and you let me drive."

"I don't remember *letting* you drive. I remember you demanding the keys and giving me no choice."

"This was a long time ago, so maybe your memory is not so good. You *are* getting old."

"I feel old."

She pushed herself from the car and stepped within an arm's length. "You are not old, Chasechka. You have just spent year inside terrible place. Doing this will feel like age, but it is not same thing."

I took part of a step back. "Listen, we really need to talk about . . ." I glanced back at the frivolity in the backyard.

She said, "This is maybe not good time for this talk. We can do this maybe later, yes?"

"No, I think we should do it now."

"Here?"

"Let's go inside," I said.

We settled into the library, which had once been one of my favorite rooms in the house. On that day, I couldn't remember how long it had been since I'd stepped inside. Part of me wanted to sit behind the desk and park Anya in a wingback so I could assume a position of power over her, but the psychological ploy would've been wasted on her. Instead, I motioned to one of the two wingbacks for her, and I settled into the other.

"You are angry with me, Chasechka. I know this, but please listen."

I held up a finger. "No, let's go at this from a different angle. Yes, I'm angry, extremely angry, but not at or about our daughter."

"Is nice hearing you call her 'our daughter.'"

"Don't do that," I said. "This isn't a stroll down memory lane. This is me demanding to know why you kept her from me."

She couldn't seem to look at me. "I am sorry for this. I truly am. But I have very good reason. You must understand."

"This should be good. Just what is this good reason that I must understand for keeping my daughter away from me? For not even telling me she existed? I can't wait to hear this."

She met my gaze, but only for an instant. "You had happy home and marriage, and telling you about Pogonya would have destroyed that. You do not understand inside of woman's mind, Chasechka. Penny wanted babies with you, and you could not give them to her.

She and I were not friends, but I had no reason to dislike her. I gave to her part of my liver so she could be alive. You remember this, yes?"

"Yes, Anya, I remember, and that was the most unselfish thing I've ever seen anybody do. I can never thank you enough for that, but this is different. That girl out there has spent fifteen years without a father —without a dad to teach her to throw a ball or tie her shoes or, I don't know . . . teach her to shoot a gun. I don't know what fathers teach daughters, but you robbed me of getting to do any of those things."

"A gun?" Anya said. "Why would you say that?"

I waggled a finger. "Oh, no. You don't get to change the subject. I want to know why it took Penny's murder, plus a year of hell for me, for you to finally mention that we have a daughter."

She took a long breath. "As I was saying, it would have infuriated Penny, and it would have hurt her badly to know I had your child and she did not."

"But you told her. You even introduced the two of them. What was that about?"

She rubbed her hands together as if washing them without water. "Perhaps you do not remember, but Penny asked for me to protect her while Timothy Taylor was trying to kill all of us last year. Think about this. Think about how much faith she had in me instead of team of security men with guns. She trusted *me*, Chasechka. She trusted me to keep her alive and safe."

I drove a fist into the arm of my chair. "This *isn't* Penny's fault, and I won't let you get away with blaming her. She'd dead, for God's sake. Find a way to have some compassion. Can you do that?" She reached for my hand, but I withdrew. "No, Anya. That's not what this is. I need to understand why you could tell her but not me."

She pressed her lips into the same thin line as Pogonya, and I looked away. "I introduced Pogonya to Penny because she trusted me with her life, and I needed to show her I trusted her. We were going to tell you about Pogonya when we came home from Switzerland last year, but the crash and your pain was too much. Telling you about our daughter at a time like that would have been cruel for both of you. You needed time to be angry and sad, but that time is no more. You can still be sad and maybe also angry sometimes, but—"

I shook her off. "You don't get to dictate when I'm ready for news like having a teenage daughter. That's not something you keep from somebody."

She sat upright. "Think about what it would've done to Pogonya."

"What are you talking about?"

Her tone was no longer flirtatious or even friendly. "What did the two of you do today while I was away?"

"We rode horses, went to Singer's church, and spent some time on the boat. She met Earl."

The thin line almost became a smile. "Could and would you have done any of those things with her one year ago?"

"I don't know."

She said, "I know. I know you could not, and not even Penny could make you ride a horse. How did a fifteen-year-old girl do that?"

"She likes horses. You know that. And she's really good with them. She told me she took riding lessons."

The smile came. "Yes, our daughter is very good cowgirl."

"I don't know about that," I said, "but she rides well, and even Pecan liked her."

"I cannot believe this. He does not like anyone."

"Well, he likes her. And she keeps asking me if you and I are getting married. Did you plant that seed?"

"No, of course I did not. She is only girl. She does not always understand things of being adult yet."

Suddenly, I was angry for not being angry anymore, and it pissed me off. "You're not keeping her from me anymore. You got that?"

She stared at the floor again. "I never wanted to keep her from you. I left for you message on tiny tape recorder inside hangar many years ago, but maybe you never found this."

I replayed the memory in my head. "Are you serious? You left me a taped message saying we had a daughter?"

"I did not give to you details on recording, but yes, I made it and left it for you."

I leaned back in my chair and tried to digest everything, but I was so overwhelmed by all of the things in my life that I couldn't process any of it. As I sat with my eyes closed tightly, specks of orange and white flashing against a field of obsidian, the screen door between the kitchen and back gallery slammed behind what sounded like bare feet.

"Father, where are you?"

My eyes flew open, and Anya smiled like a kid on Christmas. "Do you hear that, Chasechka? Our daughter is calling for you."

"I'm in the library, Pogo."

Anya frowned. "You cannot call her this name. That is terrible."

"Uh, I don't know where the library is. Keep talking so I can find you."

My suspicion was confirmed when she came dancing through the door on dirty bare feet.

"Where are your shoes?" I asked.

She held up one foot. "I was dancing with Kenny, and he said it's better without shoes. At least, I think that's what he said."

Anya reached for her, and Pogonya nestled on the edge of her chair. "Your father and I were having discussion about you. He is angry."

I cut in. "But not angry about you."

She tilted her head. "Please don't be angry with Mama. Maybe she was wrong for not telling you about me, but if you think about it from Penny's perspective, maybe you can understand why."

"That's not fair. I can't win an argument with either of you alone, but when you gang up on me, I've got no chance at all."

I was still mad, but like most anger, it was wasted on history that could never be undone. All we had was the moment without a promise of the future. I learned that when I carried my wife's dead body from a burning airplane.

"What kind of dancing were you doing with Kenny?" I asked.

"He called it Zydeco, but I don't know. He's playing the violin, and Earl has a metal thing hanging on her chest, and she's playing it with thimbles on her fingers. It's all so very odd, but I like it."

"That's a washboard—or at least that's how it started. Never mind. None of that matters as long as you're having fun."

"I am, Father. It's all brilliant, and I love it."

"Is the food ready?"

She hopped from the chair and took my hand. "Yes, that's why I came looking for you."

The three of us descended the gallery stairs where my great uncle, Judge Bernard Henry Huntsinger, married Penny and me. Pogonya would've been less than two years old at the time. Again, I cried, but only for a moment.

Earl rolled out butcher paper across the tables beneath the tent, and Kenny poured the contents of two enormous pots onto the paper. Mounds of crabs, crawfish, shrimp, corn, onions, and potatoes filled the tables, and Pogo was once again completely lost.

"What is all this, Father? Is this how you always eat?"

"It's a low-country boil," I said. "And no, this is for special occasions when families get together."

Singer offered a prayer of thanksgiving and asked God to bless the food he provided for us. Seconds after the mutual amen, Pogonya said, "I don't have any utensils."

"You don't need any for a low-country boil," I said. "It's all finger food tonight."

I taught her to peel shrimp with one hand, just as Penny taught me shortly after we met. I didn't tear up . . . much.

"Are these baby lobsters?"

Kenny jumped in before I could explain crawfish to my European daughter. "Dees here be mudbugs, girly. Watch ol' Kenny, and he'll cho' you how to do's it, him. Here goes. First, you pinch off da tail from da head and squeeze out dat good ol' sweet meat from dat tail. You tries."

She hesitantly lifted a crawfish and broke it apart. Staring at the red shell, she said, "Are you sure it's okay to eat these?"

"It's okay," I said. "But you're not going to like what comes next."

She squeezed the white meat from the tail and savored the combination of flavors that only Kenny knew how to make. "Oh, my. That is good. Why did I not know about these, Mama?"

Kenny didn't give Anya time to answer. He said, "Now come dat bestest part. Yous jus' gots to hold him head by him's eyes and suck out dem brains."

He demonstrated the age-old ritual, but Pogonya screwed up her face. "Do I have to?"

"No, you don't have to do nuffin' you don't wanna do, girly. But I'll tells you dis. If you do it one time, you won't never stop. It's 'zactly dat good, it is. I garun-told-you dat much, me."

I was surprised beyond words when she stuck the mudbug's head in her mouth and emptied the shell.

"Mama! Have you tried this? You simply must."

Anya protested, but Pogo wouldn't be denied. She walked her mother through the steps, and soon, the two of them were biting tails and sucking heads like good little Cajuns.

Out of the corner of my eye, I saw Clark stick his phone to his ear. A few seconds later, he stood and walked toward the river. I didn't like anything about the scene, but I had no choice other than to watch it unfold.

After a minute or so, Clark turned and curled a finger at Mongo. The big man stood, wiped his mouth and hands, and headed for the dock.

"What is happening?" Anya asked.

"I don't know, but it's something. I can count on one of your feet how many people's calls Clark would answer during dinner."

Pogonya giggled. "That's still a dad joke, but it's funny because Mama only has nine toes."

A moment later, Mongo motioned for Skipper to join them. She did, and they formed a huddle around Clark's phone.

When their meeting broke up, they returned from the water's edge, and Clark leaned against the table beside me. "It's time to go to work, College Boy. I think we just found the guy who shot down Anya's airplane."

Chapter 8
Who Are We?

In the previous year of my life, I spent exactly zero time thinking about work. The agony of losing Penny was all-consuming, but Clark's words rang like a Klaxon inside my head. I was immediately on my feet and headed for the house in locked step with the team.

As everyone left the table, including her mother, Pogonya asked, "What's happening, Father?"

"It's work," I said.

"May I come?"

"I'm sorry, but not this time. I'll tell you what I can when we finish the briefing."

There was no time to wait for her protest, and the pace of the team increased until everyone was jogging up the gallery stairs. We continued to the third floor, where Skipper's state-of-the-art operation center waited. She keyed in the code and scanned a thumbprint, sending the security door swinging inward. While everyone rushed inside, I took a knee at the top of the stairs to catch my breath.

The day Penny was murdered I was in peak physical condition. I could run five miles at a six-minute pace without breathing hard. I could swim almost endlessly. And I could bench press Mongo. But that was three hundred ninety-one days ago. On the day in question, I couldn't even climb three sets of stairs without my legs burning like wildfire and my lungs begging for more air.

Clark spun before stepping through the door. "Are you all right, College Boy?"

I huffed and nodded. "Yeah, I'm good. I'm just a little out of shape."

"You don't say."

I finally made it to the chair that had once been mine at the round-table of valiant knights, and Skipper tossed me a water bottle.

With the door sealed, a pair of faces I didn't recognize appeared on elevated, side-by-side monitors.

Clark took the floor. "Good morning, Generals."

"Good morning, Mr. Johnson. I see you've added one to your fold," the younger of the two men said.

"Yes, sir. I think you know Chase Fulton by reputation, if nothing else."

He said, "I do. It's a pleasure to finally meet you, Dr. Fulton, even though it has to be electronic for the moment. I'm Brigadier General Clinton McFarland, and my colleague is Major General Bradford Michaels—both retired from long and fruitful careers with USSOCOM."

"It's a pleasure to meet you both," I said.

General Michaels said, "Forgive me, Doctor, but are you operational again?"

All eyes fell on me, and I said, "No, sir, not yet. But I will be."

The generals nodded, but each still wore an incredulous look. I wondered if I wore the same expression.

"Well, then, let's get started," General McFarland said. "The first order of business is a bit of shocking information. The president and director of national intelligence have made the decision to disband and permanently stand down the Board. I assume all of you are familiar with that entity."

Clark said, "Yes, sir. We're quite familiar."

The general continued. "What you may not know are the names and pedigree of each of the former members of the Board. Elizabeth has complete dossiers on each of them, and she'll provide you with your own copies. Treat it as the classified material it is."

I had been in the meeting less than five minutes, and I was already hopelessly lost.

Elizabeth "Skipper" Woodley, in addition to being a remarkable analyst, was the second most observant member of the team, coming in only slightly behind Singer, our sniper.

She could obviously see the confusion enveloping me like a blanket, and she turned back into the little sister I could always count on. She covertly offered the diver's okay signal with her thumb and index finger forming a perfect circle. I returned the sign and was no longer worried about being out of the loop.

General McFarland lifted a file marked TOP SECRET from his desk and shook it in front of the camera. "There's no reason to beat around the bush on this one, folks. This is our guy, and his name is Scott David Delauter."

I lifted the tablet from its slot beneath the table and brought up an electronic version of what I assumed to be the same file the general was holding. Thumbing through the summary, a long line of military and civilian service stretched out in front of me.

"He's an academy grad," I said, apparently loud enough for the microphone to hear.

General Michaels said, "That's right, Chase. May I call you Chase?"

I waved a dismissive hand. "Of course, General. There's no reason for this to be any more formal than necessary."

"Thank you. Let's carry on. During the investigation that General McFarland and I led, we discovered some—let's call them abnormalities—in Mr. Scott David Delauter's life. For one, we discovered that he held a financial interest in a Russian natural gas company."

I dropped my tablet. "Are you saying a guy on the Board owned, at least, part of a Russian company?"

"That's precisely what we're saying, Chase, but it took a bit of tunneling to discover it. Technically, Delauter's ex-wife owns a holding company, which owns a second corporation that held an interest in Sibirskiy Geotekhnicheskiy Kholding. That's the parent company of the natural gas operation."

I was the only one at the table not taking notes, and that made me a little self-conscious. Thirteen months previously, my station at the table would've been well stocked with notepads, pens, highlighters, and various detritus for use by the leader of the team, but in my absence, the stockpile had been pillaged.

The general kept talking. "When we untangled the web of shell and holding companies and followed the money, we learned that the former Mrs. Delauter was also the former Mrs. Ivan Sakharova." He paused long enough for us to let the revelation sink in before continuing. "Ivan Sakharov is the eldest son of the Sakharov family, who made their fortune, such as it is, in sugar beet production."

Clark's eyes started to glaze over, so he raised his pen. "Excuse me, General, but I'm not sure how we got from a Naval Academy grad to a Russian sugar beet farmer."

General McFarland took the reins. "Don't feel lonely, Mr. Johnson. It took a while for us to wrap our heads around it, as well. The important thing to remember is that Delauter and his ex-wife aren't as ex as they'd like for us to believe. We have video. Elizabeth, do you have the Cayman Islands video?"

Skipper said, "Yes, sir, I do, and I'm bringing it up now."

"Good. Play that for your team."

The primary monitor filled with a crisp, well-focused shot of Scott Delauter and a woman in what appeared to be the lobby of a bank.

General McFarland said, "Here you can see Delauter and Dianne, his former wife, in the Cayman Capital Bank in Georgetown."

"I have an account with that bank," I said. "So, are you suggesting that Scott and Dianne are back together after she married and divorced this Russian guy, Ivan Sakharov?"

"No. We couldn't find any evidence of a divorce filing anywhere for the Sakharovs, but more importantly, we can't find Ivan Sakharov."

"Did she kill him?" I asked.

The generals shrugged in unison, and one said, "Maybe. By all indications, he is deceased, making the ex-Mrs. Delauter the current widow Sakharova."

"How much?" I asked.

The generals smiled, and McFarland gave a respectful nod before saying, "It's nice to see that you're paying attention, Chase. The answer to your question is, we don't know. It's somewhere between a quarter of a billion—with a B—and a quarter of a trillion—with a T—American dollars. But that's not the end of the story."

I let the massive number wash over me. "Let me guess. You found a tie between Sakharov and Timothy Taylor, the Russian illegal who tried to kill my whole team and succeeded in murdering my wife."

His answer was disappointing. "No. At least not a direct tie. The microscopic thread that likely ties Delauter to Taylor slipped out in something Delauter said to you during the operation that ultimately led to Mrs. Fulton's murder."

I probed my memory, but far too many gallons of Gentleman Jack separated me from the events of thirteen months before.

General Michaels said, "We have classified audio of Scott Delauter telling you that Timothy Taylor was earmarked for your team when he completed training at The Ranch."

It clicked, and something in my whiskey-soaked memory replayed those exact words in the early stages of the previous mission. "I remember that, but how does that tie Delauter to Sakharov?"

"It doesn't," he said. "In all actuality, it separates Delauter from the remaining members of the Board. When interviewed, none of the other members had any memory of any discussion about Taylor coming to your team. It was apparently an off-the-cuff comment by Delauter that was intended to plant a seed."

Mongo said, "With all due respect, generals, there isn't enough here to crucify Delauter. He made an off-hand comment about placing an operator with our team, and he met his ex-wife in a bank in the Caymans."

General Michaels said, "We've been saving the coup de grâce, and here it is. Ivan Sakharov's paternal uncle was a former officer of the KGB, and he graduated the Yuri Andropov Red Banner Institute with none other than Vladimir Putin himself."

The room was entirely silent and apparently in shock until I asked, "So, Sakharov's uncle was KGB, and the rest of his family was made up of beet farmers?"

General McFarland shook his head. "No. Sakharov left the KGB and somehow had enough money to buy the four-thousand-acre sugar beet farm that just happened to be sitting on one of the richest reserves of natural gas in the world."

Silence once again consumed the op center as we tried to take in everything we'd just learned.

Clark finally asked the best question of the day. "So, is Delauter in custody?"

General McFarland said, "He is not. In fact, we don't know where he is, but we believe you can find him."

Clark grimaced. "So, you want us to go on a worldwide manhunt for Scott Delauter so he can be returned to the U.S. to stand trial for treason?"

The general leaned close to the camera. "We don't arrest traitors, Mr. Johnson. We eliminate them."

With that still hanging in the air, Clark said, "It sounds like we're still days, or even weeks away from moving on this thing. Am I wrong?"

General Michaels said, "Not necessarily. I'd like you to bring Dr. Fulton up to speed on the new organizational structure. It's important that he understands who we are before he straps on a sidearm and starts killing alleged enemies of the state."

Skipper ended the feed, and I was left with a thousand questions. The first one out of my mouth turned out to be exactly the right one. "Who are we now?"

Clark straightened himself in his seat. "You've been here physically, but you've been mentally gone for a while. A lot has happened in that time. Where would you like to start?"

I said, "I'd like to know who the generals are, and why we now seem to work for them instead of the Board."

Clark said, "The Board was suspended by presidential action several weeks ago, and apparently, it's now been disbanded. The new leadership is called the Triad, made up of three career special ops officers. McFarland and Michaels are Green Berets, like most of us, and the third vote on the Triad belongs to Dominic Fontanna."

"Your father?" I asked.

Clark nodded. "Yep. And to say the least, he's not real thrilled about it."

"Did he not have a choice?"

Clark said, "Who knows? But according to him, he's a temporary placeholder until they can find a third retired general who's looking for something to do other than flyfish and walk his dog."

"So, are we going after Delauter?"

"I'm not sure who you're calling *we*, College Boy, but *you* barely made it up the stairs without passing out, so you're not going after anybody. But it looks like the rest of us are."

Chapter 9
Plastic Breadcrumbs

The thought of the team running a mission without me felt like molten lava in my chest, but Clark was right—I was old, crippled, and in the worst physical condition of my life. I couldn't reduce my age or grow a new foot, but I'd proven I could pound the pavement and get back to my fighting weight.

Everyone sat in silence around the table as if waiting for an invisible hand to write on the wall. When it finally occurred to me what was happening, I said, "I can't dismiss you. The team belongs to Mongo for now."

The big man twisted his face into contortions. "I'm just the substitute teacher while the real professor is convalescing."

Skipper said, "Just a minute, guys. I've been running a worldwide search for Delauter since the general said he was in the wind. So far, I've gotten just over four thousand hits."

Everyone leaned toward the analyst, and she said, "In this case, a hit is any piece of data that points to our target."

"Is four thousand hits enough to pinpoint his location?" Mongo asked.

Skipper said, "It's way too many."

I said, "What does that mean?"

"It means that most of them are contrived or erroneous. If I started a search for a normal person—Joe Nobody—I would expect to get fewer than two hundred hits. A person who isn't hiding or running doesn't take steps to actively combat surveillance they don't know is happening."

She paused as if making sure she left no one behind. "To get four thousand hits in a fifteen-minute search is way out of line. Pick the biggest celebrity in the world, and I might get a thousand hits. A Washington, D.C. powerbroker and intelligence insider isn't Beyoncé. I'd say at least ninety percent of the hits on Delauter are plastic breadcrumbs. They may look like a real trail, but you'll choke if you try to swallow them."

I asked, "Can you do anything to sort the real ones from the red herrings?"

"That's the thing. I don't have any confirmed hits, so I don't have a way to establish a baseline. I can write some code that may be able to sort out some of the obviously false leads, but take a look at this." She pointed toward a line of text on her monitor. "In the last minute or so, the hit count is almost five thousand. Something is generating intentionally misleading bits of data at a crazy rate."

"Something or some*one*?" Kodiak said.

Skipper shook him off. "No way. It can't be a person. It's happening way too fast and randomly. Even if it were a team of a hundred people constantly feeding garbage into databases, there would be some overlap."

Kodiak said, "What does that mean?"

"Tell him, Chase."

I said, "Lay your pen down, and name your one hundred favorite foods. Go."

He dropped the pen, leaned back, and rattled off a couple dozen of his favorites. Somewhere around thirty foods, he said, "Pork chops."

I knocked on the table. "Stop."

He did, and Gator tossed a pencil toward the former Green Beret. "You said pork chops twice, Klondike."

Skipper turned into a judge desperately trying to regain order in her court. "Guys, that's enough. That's exactly my point. Any human making a long list of anything will sooner or later repeat something he's already named. That doesn't happen in this list. There's not even a record of Delauter visiting the same coffee shop twice. It's malicious, and it's electronic."

"How hard would it be to create that code?" I asked.

"It's advanced stuff, but it doesn't have to be written."

I said, "Why not?"

"Because someone else already wrote it, and it's available on the black market. If you want a copy, I can find it in less than an hour."

That sent my brain into a gear it hadn't known for a long time. I said, "Do it. No . . . wait!" I had to sound like an idiot stammering and stuttering, so I backed up. "First, how much does it cost?"

Skipper grimaced. "How much does what cost?"

"The code. The program to create your five thousand erroneous hits."

"Oh, I don't know. Probably a hundred grand, maybe more. Why?"

My questions were on the verge of sounding like a man who'd been so far outside the loop that he'd forgotten what a loop looked like. "Do we have any money?"

That got a few nervous laughs from the table, but Skipper didn't flinch. "Yes, Chase. The money is fine."

"Sorry," I said. "I didn't want to write checks that would bounce all the way to the bank."

"I get it. We'll have that conversation later, but for now, you can consider our financial situation to be the same or better than it was be-fore the . . ."

I didn't want her dangling uncomfortably, so I didn't hesitate. "Good. If you had a copy of the code, could you use it to reverse-engi-neer the hits you're getting?"

She pulled off her glasses. "I'm not following. What do you mean by reverse-engineer?"

"I don't know. I'm not the computer whiz. That's you. I don't know the right term for it, but can you teach your computer to learn from the ever-expanding list of hits and work backward to find out which of the hits are authentic?"

"Wow. That's a pretty good idea. I don't have time to teach you the terms, but I catch your drift, and I'll give it a shot." Skipper spun to her computer but froze before her fingers hit the keys. She slowly turned back to the table. "Uh, are we okay with spending the money?"

Mongo said, "As far as I'm concerned, Chase is back. If he says write the check, write it."

She glanced at Clark, and he nodded his agreement.

Uncertain if the meeting was over, I slid toward Clark. "This Triad thing. Is it black?"

He said, "It is."

"So, that means we don't exist, and by extension, if we get our foot caught in a Russian snare on this one, nobody's coming to save our butts."

"That's right. It'll be a coyote ugly, and you'll have to chew your own leg off. And to be honest, that's how we've worked all along."

I said, "Not when we were sanctioned by the president."

"Well, yeah, but that's a horse of the other foot."

I laughed, and it felt good. "I can't tell you how much I've missed hearing you screw up phrases everybody else knows by heart."

"You know what I mean. It's rare."

"I get it," I said. "But if this is a national security mission, like it sounds to me, why wouldn't the president sanction it?"

Clark said, "You're the one with his personal cell number. Call and ask him."

"Not quite yet," I said. "We've got some shady stuff to do before we bring in the White House."

We broke the meeting and left Skipper working her fingers to the bone in the land of ones and zeros.

Clark hit the call button for the elevator when we left the op center. "There you go, College Boy. Why don't you take the bus?"

Anya stepped between me and the opening door. "No! You will

take stairs. You cannot get back into shape inside elevator."

I met her gaze. "I guess that means I'm taking the stairs."

Since the day I met Mongo, he'd been the bodyguard I didn't know I needed. For some reason, the big man took on that role and wasn't interested in resigning. He walked one step in front of me and matched my pace exactly as we descended the stairs. I wasn't going to fall, but if I did, I knew beyond any doubt that Mongo would catch me.

When we stepped from the house, life beneath the family tent was nonexistent. Everyone had moved inside the gazebo.

Anya cut me from the herd and took my arm. "What are you going to tell Pogonya?"

"About what?"

"The mission, of course."

"I don't know yet. This is my first day being a dad."

She surveyed the lawn, and apparently satisfied no one was listening, she said, "Chasechka, I am sorry for so many things, and I do not expect you to forgive me for any of them. Is important for you to know how much I love seeing you with Pogonya. She already loves you."

I turned to see our daughter laughing with Kenny and Earl beneath the lights of the gazebo. "She's amazing and so much like you."

She joined me in watching her. "She is so smart and beautiful on outside and also inside heart. This makes her like you."

"I don't know about that, but she's the best thing that's happened to me in a very long time."

Anya blushed. "Thank you for . . ."

She paused as if stuck, and I asked, "For what?"

She took my hands, "For being her father."

I possessed more licenses than I could count, had letters before and after my name, and was qualified to do things most people only dream of, but in that moment, I would've traded all of those just to keep the title of Pogonya's father.

"How much does she know?"

Anya sighed. "I said already that she is very smart, and this is true. For most of her life, she has known that I would go away for days, or maybe weeks, and come home with wounds and injuries. I cannot lie to her, so I told to her truth. Sometimes, when she was small, I would not tell all of truth, but now, she is almost woman. She knows."

"She asked me to teach her to shoot."

Anya perked up. "And you said to this yes, of course."

"Actually, I said we'd have to ask you."

"What are you guys talking about?"

Without either of us noticing, our daughter had snuck up on us, and I was impressed.

I said, "I was just telling your mom that I'm going to teach you to shoot, no matter what she says."

Anya bowed in feigned humility. "This is true. I am only silly woman. Man always knows what is best."

Pogo and I laughed as if we'd never laughed before, and Anya said, "What? You do not like new and submissive Anya?"

"It's just weird, Mama. You're freaking us out. But does this mean it's okay?"

I threw my arm around her. "It means your mother has become senile, and yes, I'll teach you to shoot. We can start tomorrow morning, right after our run."

We joined the party, and Pogo sat on the arm of my Adirondack with her bare feet propped on the cannon carriage. It was the first time since Penny's murder that I felt like I was part of something . . . maybe even a family.

* * *

Sleep had been elusive for much of my life, especially over that past year, but that night, it came like a warm and gentle tide. I was up before the sun, but I wasn't the only one. When I stepped onto the back gallery to stretch, Pogonya looked up from a stretch of her own.

"Good morning, Father."

"Good morning, daughter."

She laughed. "That sounds silly."

I planted a foot against one of the gallery posts and stretched my calf. "Not to me."

She hopped to her feet. "You're going back to work, aren't you?"

"That depends on how good you are as a personal trainer."

We ran at a pace that was dreadfully boring for her but agonizing for me. When I felt as if we'd run a thousand miles, I collapsed on the riverbank, panting like a dog.

Pogo jogged in place. "You are okay, yes, Chasechka?"

I lifted a few pebbles from beside my foot and playfully threw them at her. "You're not funny."

"I'm a little funny."

"Maybe a little," I admitted. "I'm not pushing you too hard, am I?"

She grabbed her chest. "Oh, yes. My heart may explode if we run another step at the blistering twenty-minute pace of yours."

With my breathing back in a survivable range, I stumbled to my feet. "Don't make me throw you in the river."

"You'd have to catch me first."

We jogged back toward the house, and Pecan noticed his new best friend. The horse galloped to the fence and ran beside us for half a mile.

Through wheezing and gasping, I said, "I think he likes you."

"And I love him," she said. "Keep going. I'll catch up."

She stopped to rub Pecan's face. I didn't look back as I pounded my feet into the ground like someone who'd never run a step in his life.

True to her promise, she caught up and wasted no time in dictating our schedule for the day. "I'm hungry, so let's have breakfast before shooting."

"As you wish, Princess Buttercup."

She frowned. "Uh, what's that supposed to mean?"

I sucked enough air into my lungs to say, "Don't tell me you've never seen *The Princess Bride*."

"I don't even know what that is."

I stopped, planted my hands on my knees, and gave myself a minute to recover. "Add that to our list. It's the best movie ever made."

She looked sincere. "Did Penny write it?"

I took a knee as my body succumbed to the exhaustion of the first exercise I'd done in far too long. "No, she didn't write it, but she loved it, too."

"I really liked her," she said softly.

"Yeah, me too."

Chapter 10
Biscuits, Gravy, and Ballistics

Rather than climbing the gallery stairs, I sat on them. It wasn't a choice. My diminished body made the pause a necessity.

"It will get easier," Pogonya said. "You'll soon remember how it feels to be strong."

I rubbed a hand across the remnant of the original stairs where the Judge married Penny and me. The old familiar knot returned to my throat, but tears didn't come, and that surprised me. "Give me a few minutes to catch my breath and grab a shower, then we'll go to breakfast."

She said, "Or I can cook while you shower."

"Well, that would be great if there were anything in the kitchen other than empty whiskey bottles and Vienna sausages."

"Then a shopping trip has to be included in today's schedule."

"Whatever you want," I said.

"Am I no longer Princess Buttercup?"

"You'll always be my Buttercup."

She smiled from her soul. "Come on, Father. You can't sit here all day."

I thought Hunter had been a tough coach, but Pogo was already putting him to shame.

"Okay, I'm coming. Give an old guy a break."

The terrifying Russian stare made its return. "Do not say such things about my father. You are not old. You are still young, and soon, you will be better than new."

The shower felt like a gift from Heaven, and twenty minutes later, we were headed for the VW Microbus.

I tossed her the keys. "You drive."

She stared down at the ancient metal keys and then back at me. "I don't know how to drive."

"You've gotta learn some time, and there's no time like the present."

"But what if I have an accident? I don't have a driving license."

I climbed onto the passenger seat. "Look at this thing. Nobody would notice if it were in an accident."

She slid behind the wheel and laced the seat belt around herself.

I motioned toward the dash. "The big key goes in there. Have you ever driven a straight shift?"

She fumbled but finally slid the key into the ignition. "I've never driven anything."

"Nothing?"

She shook her head, and I said, "Good. You won't have any bad habits. Which side of the road do they drive on in Switzerland?"

"The right side, but not in England."

"We also drive on the right here in America."

"Yes, Father, I know this. It's gas, brake, clutch, right?"

"That's correct. Your left foot is only for the clutch. Don't use it to brake. Your right foot is for the gas and brake. Start by pressing the clutch all the way to the floor and turning the key."

The bus buzzed to life like always, and Pogo said, "I can't believe I'm doing this."

I had her pull the shifter through each gear before driving away. "Now you know where the gears are. Start in first, and let the clutch out slowly while gently pressing the gas. Everything here is flat, so you don't have to worry about hills yet."

We lunged forward two feet, and the bus died.

"Not bad for your first try. Start it again, but this time, let the clutch out much more slowly."

She didn't kill it on the next attempt, and we rolled down the drive in first gear at ten miles per hour.

Her face beamed with joy. "This is amazing. What about the other gears?"

Press the clutch with your left foot, and take your right foot off the gas. When the clutch is all the way against the floor, pull the shifter to second gear and repeat the exercise of letting the clutch out slowly."

"I'm doing it. I can't believe I'm actually doing it. But how do I stop?"

I threw up my hands. "I have no idea."

"Father, quit. Tell me how to stop."

"Right foot off the gas and onto the brake. Ease the clutch in, and gently press the brake until we stop."

It was a little jerky, but her first stop wasn't bad.

"Good. Now, let's go again. Turn right onto the road, but stop and look first."

She killed the engine almost immediately and growled in frustration. "What did I do wrong that time?"

"We're still in second gear. You always have to start in first."

"Ugh. This is complicated."

"It'll get easier. After breakfast, we can go to the airport and practice on the taxiways. You won't have to worry about other cars there."

She looked up as if in shock. "What? It can't be okay to drive around at an airport."

"It is when you own the airport."

"You're pretty cool. You know that?"

I said, "I used to be."

After a series of fits and starts, we pulled into the lot at the diner, and I said, "Take us all the way to the back where it's empty. We'll learn parking beside other cars later."

She managed to get most of the bus between the white painted lines, and she shoved the keys in her pocket when we stepped out. Maybe I got both a daughter and a chauffeur on the same day.

I've read and heard that fathers love experiencing firsts with their children, and I was on the verge of testing that theory. "You should try the biscuits and gravy. It's amazing."

"A biscuit with gravy? That sounds disgusting."

"Not a British biscuit," I said. "That's a cookie here in the States. American biscuits are little fluffy clouds of love—especially here in the South."

When the plates arrived, she stared down at the mound of white sawmill gravy covering an open-faced biscuit. "What am I supposed to do with this?"

"You're supposed to eat it like this." I cut into mine and shoveled the first bite into my mouth. It tasted wonderful, and I couldn't wait to see her face when it hit her tongue.

She cut off a minuscule piece and slowly moved it toward her mouth. The hesitation was fun to watch, but as soon as she closed her lips around her first taste of biscuits and gravy, all hesitation was gone.

"This is incredible. Why do we not have this in Switzerland?"

I tapped the edge of her plate with my fork. "One more reason to go to Georgia instead of that little community college. What did you call it? Princeton?"

We ate mostly in silence, and my stomach was full long before I finished half of my first biscuit.

"You must eat, Father. We can't train if you don't eat. How much did you weigh before?"

"Around two thirty most of the time."

"And now?"

"I don't know. Probably one ninety or less."

"You're very thin, but breakfast like this will take care of that."

The waitress slid the check onto the table. "Do y'all need a to-go cup or two?"

I said, "No, thanks. We're good."

Pogo slid from the booth, and I said, "Give me a couple of minutes. I'm going to use the restroom before we go. Don't leave without me."

When I came out, I thanked the waitress and glanced through the front window of the diner to see two teenage boys standing in front of my little girl in the parking lot.

Boys are the same all over the world, I thought. *The new girl gets all the attention.*

When I stepped through the door, the scene changed. Pogonya turned to walk away from the boys, but one of them grabbed her arm.

I leaned forward and quickened my pace. "Get your hands off of her!"

The boy looked up and laughed. "What are you gonna do, Grandpa? This ain't none of your business."

The next two sounds his body emitted were the bones in the back of his hand snapping like twigs and his skull striking the concrete. With animal number one on his side and lost in the spirit world, Pogonya lunged toward the second boy. He was smarter than his friend and surrendered instantly. "Hey, look. I'm sorry. We didn't . . ."

"You didn't what?" she said. "You didn't think a girl could beat up your friend, or you didn't know it's not okay to grab me? Which is it?" She poked the boy still lying on the ground. "Your friend probably needs a doctor. You should take care of that. Oh, and try the biscuits and gravy. They are wonderful."

We climbed back into the bus as if nothing happened, and I asked, "Are you okay?"

"Of course. I'm Anya Burinkova's daughter. She may not have taught me to shoot, but she showed me a few tricks."

"It looks like the tricks worked."

She said, "Those were just silly boys. They weren't taught how to be respectful—or how to fight—so I offered a little free tutoring."

She got us back home with only one stall that she quickly remedied. I suspected driving wasn't the only thing she would master quickly.

I pressed the code and thumbprint, and the door to the armory swung open.

Pogonya's eyes turned to saucers. "This place is unbelievable. Are all of these yours?"

"I guess they are," I said, "but we're starting with pistols this morning. We'll progress to rifles tomorrow."

"Or maybe this afternoon."

"This is a Glock forty-three. It's chambered in nine-millimeter. It should fit your hand nicely."

She reached for the pistol, but I stopped her and asked, "Is it loaded?"

She said, "I don't know."

"Always assume every weapon is loaded until you've checked for yourself. Never take anyone's word for it, not even mine."

"How do I check?"

I took her through the functions of each piece of the pistol, and she memorized every detail almost before it fell out of my mouth.

We moved to the range and spent an hour on proper grip, sight picture and alignment, trigger control, breathing, and stances. She was a natural, and I loved seeing her quickly grow so comfortable with a pistol in her hand.

After a few hundred rounds, we stepped up to a rifle, and she adapted quickly and smoothly. Fighting was obviously in my daughter's blood, but I didn't know if it came from me or her deadly mother.

I taught her to clean and oil the weapons before locking them back into the vault, and then we washed up and found Anya in the library.

"Mama, you won't believe it, but I learned to drive, shoot, and eat biscuits and gravy already today."

It was easy to forget she was only fifteen, and every time the little girl inside her appeared, it made me smile. I wondered how it would've felt to see her take her first steps and say Mama for the first time.

Anya said, "You are teaching her to drive? This is dangerous, no?"

"Mama, please. I have to learn sometime."

"Yes, I know, but is difficult seeing you growing up so quickly."

I settled into the chair behind the desk, and Pogonya said, "Will you take us sailing?"

I stood. "Nothing would please me more."

A sail across Cumberland Sound turned out to be just what the doctor ordered. The wind blew twelve knots out of the south, and *Aegis* danced across the calm waters of the sound under Pogonya's gentle hand on the wheel.

Anya stood by the starboard rail, her long blonde hair blowing in the wind just as it had years before when I believed she was everything I could ever want. I wasn't ready for *anything* with her, and I probably never would be, but everything inside me cried out to spend every second of the rest of my life with our perfect daughter.

Chapter 11

Leave a Message

I found Skipper and Singer in the gazebo, and neither looked happy. Since misery loves company—or whatever—I joined them. "You two look gloomy. What's up?"

Singer patted the chair next to his. "Join us. We're working through a problem."

I took the seat. "What's the problem?"

He said, "The church flooded overnight from a burst pipe. The plumbers are coming, but there was a lot of damage."

"That's no good, but you can use one of the hangars, or even this back yard for services until it's fixed."

"That's not the problem," Skipper said. "The problem is that I'm supposed to get married in two days in *that* church."

"That doesn't change my offer. I'll be more than happy to pay for a venue wherever you'd like."

"You don't get it," she said. "We had Tony's funeral in that church, and that means something to me. That day, my world was shattered, and I want to start my new life over in the same place. It means a lot to me."

"How bad is it?"

Singer shook his head. "It's bad. One of the guys in the church is a contractor. I met him there this morning, and he said it'll take at least a month before it'll be ready to use again."

"Have you thought about getting a second opinion?"

"Yeah, and the second opinion is worse than the first."

Skipper slapped the arms of her chair. "I want to get married in that church and nowhere else. Let's postpone the wedding until it's ready. I'll talk to Gator."

I leaned forward. "Let me give you a little insight into the male brain. That boy doesn't care how long he has to wait. He wants the day to be perfect for you, so whatever you want is what he'll make sure you have."

She said, "I've been living in a boys' club for a long time. I'm pretty good at predicting what's going on inside the male brain, but thank you."

I stood. "I'm sorry. I wish I could fix it, but your solution sounds like the best plan. I have to run, literally. My personal trainer and daughter —one and the same, by the way—is trying to kill me, but I'll make it."

"Enjoy your run," they said in unison.

* * *

The running, stretching, swimming, and lifting routine continued every day until Pogonya and I began to push each other instead of the pushing being unidirectional. The more time I spent with her, the more I loved her, but there comes a time when a man has to step away from who and what he loves and put himself in harm's way to defend and protect the ones left behind.

* * *

Time passed as it does, and Skipper continued working feverishly to track down Scott Delauter and Dianne Sakharova. The harder she looked, the more elusive they became. We considered issuing a world-wide BOLO, but doing so would only warn them we were coming. I was impatient, but with every passing day, I grew stronger, faster, and more fit to fight.

The church was finally restored to its pre-flood condition, and the contractor did an amazing job making it look like nothing had gone wrong.

Skipper was radiant, but the cast of knuckle-draggers looked like fish out of water in our tuxedos, trimmed hair and beards, and polished shoes.

Skipper and Gator stood holding hands at the altar in front of me.

Singer said, "As we walk through the door toward a life as one for Clint Barrow and Elizabeth Woodly, let us go to the Lord in prayer." He bowed his head, and everyone in the church followed suit. In the moment of silence before Singer began to pray, my phone chirped, and in embarrassment, I drove a thumb against the button to silence it.

Just as Singer began his prayer, Mongo's phone chirped, and he performed the same graceless dance to silence it. Seconds into the prayer, Clark's phone joined the party. I took a peek to see Clark's reaction. The chances of three of our phones ringing in rapid succession could mean only one thing, and Skipper wasn't going to be happy.

Clark silently stepped from the altar and through a side door. Singer's prayer ended coincidentally with Clark's return, and every eye that should've been focused on the couple and Singer was instead trained on Clark.

He stepped beside me and whispered, "That was the police chief. We've gotta go. There's a school shooting in progress, and the SWAT team is tied up on another active-shooter call."

I stepped around Gator and shared the news with Skipper. Instead of throwing a fit like I expected, she laid her flowers on the communion table and said, "I'll be in the op center in five minutes. Go get 'em, boys."

* * *

Kodiak said, "Sealed door right. Going right. Plug left. Breacher up."

His size and agility earned him the temporary moniker of Spider Monkey on more than one deployment, and his precision and nearly instant decision-making ability made him one of the best point men in the game. That skill set put him number one in the stack. Singer was second. Shawn the SEAL was unstoppable in any position, but on that day, he was the number three man. I was fourth, Gator was fifth, and Mongo brought up the rear.

During my year of absence from the team, Gator devoted his life to learning, practicing, and perfecting the art of breaching. Closed doors are little more than a low temporary hurdle when a team like mine moves in to clear a building. Barricaded, hardened doors were only slightly more challenging.

Singer broke from the stack and planted himself in the opening to the left so the rest of the team could go about our deadly work without fear of being flanked. Gator moved on Kodiak's order and pressed a shaped charge to the surface of the locked door. With the explosive in place, Gator took a knee and waited for my command.

Our state-of-the-art comms meant there was no need to yell unless we were in the heat of a gunfight. Every member of the team could hear every other member without fiddling with push-to-talk buttons.

I issued the order. "Shawn, take cover. Breacher, send it."

Shawn ducked away from the blast zone, and Gator called, "Fire in the hole."

With the push of a compact plunger, Gator proved he'd mastered forced explosive entry. Exactly the right amount of energy sent the heavy door falling from its hinges, and any thought we had of surprising our target vanished in smoke and debris.

In some cases, covert entry was a better, albeit slower and much quieter, method of clearing a structure, but on that day, there was no time to waste. Human lives were at stake, and my team answered the call.

We pressed into the room like a high-speed Caterpillar and broke into singles to cover our assigned sector in the room. With the echo of Gator's breaching charge still echoing, our storming of the room sent the ten students and one teacher into hysteria. Mongo and I stepped between the gunman and the children with our rifles raised.

"Put it down! Do it now!"

The gunman's eyes were glazed over as if his body had been possessed by some force too dark to name. I continued yelling commands, and our groom and all-American free safety from K-State turned into a freight train as he lowered a shoulder and collided with the shooter. Both men hit the tiled floor and slid several feet before coming to a stop with Gator's elbow pressed into the man's Adam's apple.

Kodiak pointed to the American flag sewn to the sleeve of his shirt and then pressed a finger to his lips. The screams fell away as his message of "we're the good guys" came in loud and clear.

By my count, there were eleven innocents, including the teacher, and we herded them toward Anya, who was waiting just outside the door with two uniformed patrol officers. She counted heads and led the fortunate victims of the school invasion to safety outside the building and into the arms of half of the St. Marys Police Department.

Classroom number one was clear and safe, but we were a long way from ending the potentially deadly situation. According to the information Skipper could piece together, there were one hundred eighteen students and twelve faculty inside the school. The intel on the shooters was a little shakier. There were at least three and as many as six, based on the 911 calls.

"Coming out," I called, unsure if Anya and the patrol officers were back inside.

The Russian's voice cut through the screams echoing through the halls. "Clear out."

We stepped from the classroom and reformed into our stack in preparation to blow through door number two, but before we could position ourselves outside the door, a flurry of semi-auto fire pierced the air, and it was time for a change of tactics.

I said, "Two-man assault teams. Move!"

Mongo and I separated ourselves from the rest of the team, and my heart pounded like a bass drum. I wasn't back to full strength, but in that moment, I felt more alive than I'd been since Penny was torn from my life. It was an old, familiar feeling that I would welcome on the battlefield facing any foe who dared stand toe-to-toe with us, but the screaming, crying children inside the school added an element I wasn't ready to face.

Every scream was Pogonya's. Every child in danger was my child, and I burned with a fire I'd never known. I was driven by an instinct I didn't know I possessed, and nothing was more important than delivering every child safely home to their parents when the ordeal was over.

The first minutes of any penetration are fraught with confusion and chaos, but my team, even when split into twos, moved as if we shared one collective will. And that will, coupled with the violence we were prepared to unleash, would carry us through the mission. No force would stop us. If the gunmen mowed us down one by one, our last man standing would continue to bring the fight to their door and deliver the wrath that only warriors of right could pour out.

Mongo and I slid to a stop outside classroom number two, and I gripped the doorknob. No matter how much torque I applied, it wouldn't budge, and the barricading hardware the school installed made entry almost impossible without another of Gator's breaching charges or a bulldozer. Mongo and I had neither, but we had his three hundred pounds of muscle and stone resolve.

"Kick it!" I ordered, and the giant delivered a crushing mule kick that would've demolished most doors on the planet. That particular door, with its barricading system in place, made the classroom a fortress.

"Gator, we need a breach at two."

Small arms fire roared from around the corner, and his calm reply came with only a slight delay. "I'm in the middle of a gunfight at the moment. Leave a message, and I'll call you back if I live."

It wasn't an attempt at humor. It was an automatic response while focused on staying on the living side of eternity.

"Do you need us?" I asked.

His pitch rose a notch, but he still wasn't panicking. "We're good for now, but we're gonna need every ambulance they can find."

That sickened me and almost sent me to my knees. The thought of wounded children and teachers fueled my drive to end the situation immediately.

Mongo said, "I can shoot the door down."

"Too much chance of a stray round hitting a kid. Get me into the ceiling."

The big man looked up to see a suspended acoustic tile ceiling nine feet above the floor. In one fluid and powerful motion, he launched me through the grid. I came to rest a little disoriented and with a mouthful of whatever the ceiling tiles were made of. I dragged myself across the wall and rolled onto my butt before driving both boots through the grid on the other side.

My fall wasn't intentional, but it worked out. I had planned to de-molish the tiles and get a bird's-eye view of the classroom, but in-stead, my body followed my boots, and I hit the floor with my rifle shouldered.

A hooded figure stood inches away, and I swung my rifle to deliver a butt-stroke that would end with the bad guy face-down and bleed-ing, but he was quick. Dodging my strike, he took a long step back-ward and raised his rifle to meet mine. We had one living bad guy, so dispatching this one wouldn't hurt the investigation to come.

Before he could break his weapon to bear, I pressed my trigger and tagged him high on the chest. He staggered backward but stayed on his feet, and I was in the throes of a deadly situation. Half of the two rounds that should've left my muzzle didn't show, and it didn't matter why. I had ten pounds of useless metal in my hands and a bad guy still very much in the fight.

He instinctively checked his wound and raised his rifle back to the uninjured shoulder. I released my rifle, letting it fall against my body, and then drew my sidearm as I dived for the deck. If he got off a round or two, I wanted them well above and directed at the concrete block wall behind me.

Long before my pistol sight was aligned with my eye and the gunman's chest, I crushed the trigger four times. The wall of 9mm lead hit him like a truck and put out his lights. I yanked the dead man's rifle away from him in case he wasn't as dead as I believed.

Covering the man as a pool of blood formed around him, I motioned for the teacher. "You're safe now. Get that door open, and we'll get you out of here."

She was frozen, and her distant stare said she would be of no help.

"Does anybody know how to work this door?"

A quivering hand went up. "I do."

"Get over here and do it now!"

The boy scampered across the floor, never taking his eyes from the body bleeding out in front of me.

I said, "Room secure. Door coming open. Coming out with maybe twelve or fifteen. One gunman down."

Anya's voice played in my ear. "We're waiting by the door."

The nervous and terrified child fumbled with the mechanism until it finally collapsed, leaving the door free to swing inward. The children filed out with Anya and the officers, but the teacher stood pale and motionless by the back wall.

I double-checked the dead guy, and my diagnosis was accurate. "Ma'am, you're safe now. Come with me, and we'll get you out of here."

The woman didn't flinch, bat an eye, or let out a sound. She was a statue, and I didn't have time to thaw her out. I hefted her across my shoulder and headed for the door.

Mongo stood by the opening with his rifle at the ready, and I passed him in a loaded sprint. Once I caught Anya and the rest of the children a few yards down the hall, I handed off my cargo to the larger of the two officers.

Back at the classroom, Mongo tossed me a magazine. "Drop something?"

"That explains the malfunction," I said.

We pressed deeper into the building with the sound of sporadic gunfire still ricocheting through the air.

I said, "Sitrep."

Kodiak answered first. "Me and Gator are good. One dead, one wounded. All hostages safe."

Shawn was next. "We've got a problem at the end of the right-hand hallway."

"What kind of problem?"

"I think we found their zealot."

A chill ran down my spine, and Mongo and I sprinted for Shawn's position.

An explosion rocked the walls, and I yelled, "Somebody tell me that was ours."

My answer came in the form of crisp 5.56 mm rifle fire—and then silence.

Mongo and I continued movement on Shawn's position, and I said, "Sitrep."

Gator's voice arrived, but it wasn't the calm tone from before. This time, it was anger tempered with adrenaline. "I took one in the arm, but we're good. Two more shooters down, and we're coming out."

The patter of young, frightened feet reverberated through the hallway as the students Gator had just saved exited the building.

As I worked to paint a mental picture of our situation inside the school, Mongo and I took a knee beside Shawn.

I asked, "What have you got?"

The SEAL pointed to the half-inch space beneath the bottom of the door. "Take a look."

I lay on my side and pressed my face against the cool tile of the floor. With one eye closed, I squinted with the other and tried to focus through the slit. It took several seconds for my eye to adjust to the situation, and my heart sank. A man in a suicide vest stood near the back of the room with at least a dozen children within the blast radius of his device. In his left hand was a dead man's switch, and he was holding down the trigger.

I rolled over and looked up at my teammates. "Shawn, stay with me. Everybody else, clear the rest of the building. Get Gator outside and bring Anya in."

Everyone except Shawn vanished, and I said, "Hey, Skipper. We've got a live one with hostages and a dead man's switch. We'll need a negotiator."

She said, "The PD doesn't have a negotiator. I can call the FBI and get one of their guys rolling."

"Check with the Navy at the sub base. If they don't have one, find one. I don't care who he works for, just get him here."

"Roger."

I whispered to Shawn, "Got any hostage-negotiating experience?"

"Nope. Instead of negotiating, I usually just kill 'em."

"Me, too."

I pressed my face back to the floor and counted feet. "I've got sixteen. Did you count?"

Shawn said, "Same."

"Okay, Skipper. Start the clock. Sixteen hostages and one jackass who's trying to ruin everyone's day."

"The clock's running," she said. "No luck with the Navy. GBI is on their way with a negotiator from Savannah, and HRT is en route from Jacksonville."

I eyed Shawn. "That means we're on our own for at least an hour."

He said, "If the hostage rescue team takes over, this thing will go downhill quick."

"That's the last thing we need. Get out of here. Help the rest of the team clear the building, and get everybody as far away as you can."

"What are you going to do?" he asked.

"I'm a psychologist. That makes me the closest thing to a hostage negotiator we've got for now."

Chapter 12
Breakaway Running Backs

I said a silent prayer and pressed my face back to the floor. The thin horizontal slit beneath the door gave me a distorted and extremely limited view inside the classroom. Turning away from the door, I said, "Somebody bring me a fiberoptic camera."

Instead of *somebody* showing up, *everybody* arrived. The whole team stood in a semicircle around me, and Kodiak lay down beside me. "I'll run the camera."

"No. Leave it and get out of here. If I screw this up, there's no reason for you to pay the price for my mistake."

He didn't let go of the camera. "Yeah, that's not really how this works. If our boy in there gives us a window of opportunity, we'll do a lot more than negotiate with him."

I didn't like it, but he was right. "Fine, but at least stay back. There's no way to know how much punch that vest has, and I don't want any of us eating an oak door."

He worked the long, flexible lens beneath the door and positioned it so the bomber stood in the center of the frame. We moved a few feet away and pressed ourselves against the wall.

I studied the high-definition video on the small monitor and elbowed Singer. "Any chance you can put a bullet in his hand?"

"No chance. The angle's bad, and it's too risky for a couple of reasons—I couldn't live with myself if I hit one of the kids, and the other reason is that I may not destroy the trigger, even if I hit it. If it's holding a circuit open or closed, it's possible it would stop doing that and blow all of us to Orlando."

I held out a hand. "Give me a phone."

"Where's yours?" he asked.

I pulled it from my pocket. "Right here, but I need mine."

Singer handed over his iPhone, and I used it to dial my number. Then, I pressed the speaker button on his and shoved it beneath the door. It slid about fifteen feet into the room, and I said, "My name is Daniel, and I'm here to help you. What's your name?"

My voice boomed from Singer's phone, and the bomber took a step toward it. "What do you want?"

I thought, *He's not American, but definitely not Russian.*

"I want to help you get out of this alive. I'm not with the police, and I don't want to hurt you. Can you tell me your name?"

"My name is Amir, and if anyone comes through the door, I will kill everyone."

Middle Eastern, maybe. Perhaps Turkish.

"That's a good start, Amir. Nobody's coming in, but the FBI is on its way. What they do when they get here is outside my control. Right now, I'm calling the shots, but—"

"You are not calling any shots! I am!"

"Okay, I'm sorry, Amir. Of course you're in control. I just want you to know what's going on out here. The FBI is coming, and I can't stop them. What I can do, though, is give you what you want. First, I need to know what that is. What do you want, Amir?"

"I want my brothers released."

"Which brothers, Amir? I need their names."

"Their names are not important! They must be released."

I said, "I'm afraid that's not possible as long as you're holding the children hostage. I need a show of good faith, Amir. Send out the hostages, and I'll go to work getting your brothers released."

"No! No one is released until I know my brothers are free."

I took a long breath. "Amir, I cannot release your brothers without a show of faith from you. If you won't give me all of the hostages, give us the girls."

"I have a bomb!"

"Yes, I know, but there's no reason to die today. One of your brothers shot one of mine, so we have to take that into consideration in anything you and I work out. I can keep you alive, Amir, but the clock is ticking."

"I don't care about your clock or your brothers. Release them, and let them call me. When they are free, I will give you one hostage of my choosing."

That wasn't the path I wanted us to walk, so I took a gamble. "Listen, Amir. I'm the only friend you've got right now. I don't want you to die, and killing innocent children is the surest way for you to end up on a slab at the end of this. Innocent children are sacred to Allah. We both know this. You don't want their souls on your slate."

"Shut up! Stop talking! I must think."

I muted the phone and leaned against the wall. "I'm not cut out for this."

Singer said, "You're doing fine. That was a nice Allah reference. I think it hit home."

"I have no idea what I'm doing."

He said, "You're saving the lives of a bunch of innocent kids."

Skipper said, "The GBI negotiator will be there in twenty minutes. He wants you to keep Amir talking. I'm feeding him the audio."

I unmuted the phone and took another gamble. "Amir? Are you still there?"

"Are my brothers free yet?"

"I can do a lot of things, but until you give me something, I can't give you anything. That's how this works."

A powerful hand grabbed my shoulder, and I turned to see Mongo pointing at the screen. "He changed hands with the dead man's switch."

I touched the mute button again. "Can you play it back?"

Kodiak said, "I think so. Give me a minute."

I turned the volume back on. "Have you decided yet, Amir?"

"Decided what?"

"Which of the hostages you're going to give me. You're in charge, Amir. It's up to you. The more you give me, the more you get in return. It's quid pro quo, Amir."

"Why do you keep calling his name?" Singer asked.

"Using his name as often as possible humanizes him and plants that concept in his mind. If he thinks of himself as a sentient individual instead of just a soldier for Allah, it's less likely he'll be willing to kill himself."

"Got it!" Kodiak said. "Here's the replay."

All eyes turned to the small screen, and he played the video in slow motion. Amir wiped sweat from his forehead with one arm and then slid the trigger from his left hand to his right.

"Did it open?" I asked.

Kodiak said, "I think so. Let me see if I can zoom in."

"Are my brothers free yet?"

"Keep at it," I whispered. "I'm going to deal with him." I cleared my throat. "Amir, you and I are reasonable men. I can't manufacture results until you prove that you're serious about keeping those innocent children alive."

"No!" he roared. "I am in charge, not you. You will release my brothers, and then we will talk about my hostages."

For his benefit, I let out an audible sigh. "Look, Amir. I need you to see this from our perspective. If we believe you're going to kill the innocent children, no matter what we do, then there's no chance of your brothers going free."

"You called it an act of good faith, so now you can show good faith and release my brothers."

"You sound like a smart man, Amir. I hope you'll agree that I'm no dummy, either. We both know how these things work. Give me the girls, and I'll give you one of your brothers."

Singer said, "Chase. It opened."

I spun. "The switch?"

He nodded and pointed at the screen. "Yeah. When he switched hands, his finger was off the trigger for maybe a second."

I leaned toward the screen. "Play it again. I want to see his face."

The video played in full speed, and I watched the exchange unfold. He wiped his brow, slipped the switch from one hand to the other, and didn't react nervously when the trigger opened.

"It's on a delay," I said. "Is there any way to know how long the delay is before detonation?"

All eyes fell to Kodiak, our resident explosives expert. He said, "There's no way to know, but the fact that Amir didn't panic when he let the switch open means he knew he wasn't in any danger."

"Guess," I said.

Kodiak laughed. "Seriously? You want me to guess how long a delay is in a switch built by a psychopath and carried by a radical zealot?"

"Think about it," I said. "Now, somebody estimate the distance from this door to where Amir is standing."

Mongo said, "We don't have to estimate. There's an identical classroom next door. We can just measure it and take the guesswork out of the equation."

"Do it," I ordered. "I've got an idea."

"Are you still with me, Amir?"

He shook the switch but never looked directly at the camera, showing no real indication that he knew we were watching.

Mongo was back in seconds. "It's seventeen feet from the threshold to where he's standing."

I muted the phone. "Here's what I'm thinking. If there's more than a one-second delay built into that switch, I can get back up in the ceiling, crawl seventeen feet, and burst my way through. If I can get my hand on that trigger the instant I hit him, we can keep everybody alive."

The big man shook his head. "No good. That's just a suspended ceiling grid held up by wires. When I put you up there before, you had a wall to support you. You could never make it seventeen feet away from the wall without bringing the whole ceiling down."

I closed my eyes and leaned my head back against the concrete wall. My brain churned and burned, and I drummed my fingers against my thigh until a thought hit me. "What's Gator's forty-yard speed?"

"Gator's down," Mongo said. "He took a round in the upper arm."

"Which arm?"

"Left, but why does that matter?"

I asked, "Is he still on-site?"

Gator's voice showed up in my ear. "Yeah, Chase, I'm here. It was just a graze. I'm good. What do you need?"

"What's your forty-yard time?"

"Four-three. Why?"

I said, "In boots?"

He chuckled. "No, that's my running-shoe time, but I can probably do sub-five in boots."

"Are you sure your arm is okay?"

"It's just a scratch. I'm still in the fight."

"Get in here," I said. "And bring running shoes if you've got 'em."

Mongo asked, "What are you doing, Chase?"

I held up a finger and focused on the screen. "How you doing in there, Amir? Are you ready to give us the hostages?"

"I will give them to you when I know my brothers are safe."

"I'm working on that," I said. "I get it. You have no reason to trust me, and I understand. I'm trying to convince the police to release your brothers—at least some of them. If I can get that done, how many hostages will you give me?"

Gator showed up with a pressure bandage around his left bicep.

I pressed mute. "Just a scratch, huh?"

He waved a hand. "It's nothing. That's all we had for a dressing. I'm good."

"Okay. How much room do you need to be at full speed in a sprint?"

"Maybe five strides. What are you thinking?"

I said, "I've got a plan, but you're the only one who can make it work. I want to rig a breaching charge and blow that door to hell the same instant you sprint through it at full speed. If you can hit Amir like he's a running back and grab that switch, we can end this thing without losing anybody."

He looked down, obviously playing out my plan in his head. A few seconds later, he looked up. "Kodiak blows the door."

"This isn't foolproof," I said. "A lot could go wrong, so if you're uncomfortable with it, tell me now."

"No, I'm good as long as Kodiak rigs the charge. Skipper, are you okay with this?"

Our analyst, likely still wearing her wedding dress, said, "We have to save those kids. God only knows how badly the FBI and GBI could screw this up."

Gator stared back at me with absolute resolve in his eyes. "Rig the charge."

Kodiak pulled a shaped breaching charge from his pack and pressed it to the door. "I'm going to blow the hinge side. The barricading hardware fixes the latch side in place, and we need the door to collapse inward." He pressed two more smaller charges a foot below the top of the door and a foot above the floor. "These two will blow a tenth of a second before the main and destroy both hinges. The main charge will split the door in half horizontally and blow it into the room."

Gator grabbed Kodiak's shoulder. "Don't blow me up, please. I've got a wedding to finish."

Kodiak smiled at our free safety. "I don't kill good guys."

Gator paced off the five strides he needed to achieve full speed in a sprint, and Kodiak said, "I'll blow the charge when you start running."

I put up a hand. "Hang on. Let me try one more time . . . Hey, Amir. We just talked to the FBI Hostage Rescue Team coordinator, and they'll be here in less than fifteen minutes. I don't know how much you know about HRT, but those guys aren't as patient as I am.

If you'll give me the girls, I'll hold them off. That's the best I can do right now."

Amir growled. "No! I will kill everyone, and . . ."

I locked eyes with Gator and nodded sharply.

He took a full breath, rocked backward, and burst into a sprint directly toward the barricaded door. Kodiak watched with singular focus, and when Gator's lead foot hit the ground, he pressed the plunger.

A roaring explosion consumed the hallway just outside the door, but Gator didn't miss a stride, accelerating as smoke and debris filled the air in front of him. None of us could see the completely shrouded door when Gator disappeared through the cloud.

When the smoke cleared, we saw Gator lying on top of Amir and holding the dead man's switch firmly in his grasp.

Gator said, "Could I get a little help in here? I've got my hands full."

Mongo lifted him from the ground while I drove a knee into Amir's chest. "You should've given me the hostages, Amir. Oh, and those brothers you wanted released? They're dead."

Chapter 13

Friends in Low Places

Under the spotlight is the last place my team and I ever wanted to be, so the evening news report pleased us beyond words.

The anchor said, "An armed invasion and assault on a local Camden County school today resulted in four fatalities and one arrest. Thanks to the FBI Hostage Rescue Team and a hostage negotiator with the Georgia Bureau of Investigation, no students or faculty were injured, but four of the five attackers were killed by federal officers. The only surviving member of the alleged gang is being treated at a local hospital for wounds he received while being apprehended by one of those officers. Authorities say thirty-four-year-old Amir Ben Al-Shadi, a Yemeni man in the United States on an expired student visa, suffered no life-threatening injuries during the arrest, and will remain in federal custody following his release from the hospital. The motive for the attack is, as of yet, unknown. On a related note, a local man, who prefers to remain anonymous, has generously committed to providing the necessary funding to install security systems and hire full-time security personnel for all Camden County schools."

Glasses were raised, and Mongo gave the toast. "Here's to the feds. I'll never know *how* they could be so brave."

My glass joined the others in the air, and although the contents of my chalice looked like the golden amber bourbon in theirs, it was sweet tea.

When the revelry died down, Skipper said, "Nice job, guys. But next time, maybe send someone without a gaping laceration in his arm to do the tackling."

"He said it was just a scratch," I argued.

She pointed to the massive bandage on Gator's bicep. "Does that look like a scratch to you? I've been trying to marry this man for two months. Can't you give him a break long enough for me to say 'I do' and spend two weeks making him forget any other woman ever existed?"

"I'll see what I can do. But he did say it was just a scratch."

She rolled her eyes. "Well, now you know he's a miserable liar who deserves to be placed on administrative leave and banned from all team activities for at least fifteen days."

"I think we can make that happen, but it's unpaid leave."

She grinned. "I think we'll find a way to scrape by on my meager salary for half a month."

Before the laughter faded, Skipper grabbed her phone and leapt from her seat. Every eye followed her to the stairs, and apparently, the same thought hit the rest of us simultaneously—we couldn't catch her, but we could follow her. And that's exactly what we did.

Inside the op center, a line of text flashed at the top of a monitor, and Skipper let out a celebratory whoop for the ages.

I said, "Should we assume that's a good thing?"

She danced around her chair and high-fived each of us until she came to the guy with the boo-boo on his arm. He got a kiss.

Kodiak said, "Hey, that's not fair! Next time, I'm getting shot."

"So, what are we celebrating?" I asked.

She did a pirouette and landed on her chair. "I found Scott David Delauter."

Before any of us could react, she spun to face us with a finger pointing directly at me. "You are not leaving again before I marry that man, even if we have to do the ceremony right here."

"I know a pretty good spot," I said.

She spun back to face her monitor and dived in. After several seconds of doing something that I'll never understand, she said, "He's in Bern, and he's not alone."

"Where's that?" Gator asked.

Anya answered before Skipper could. "Is capital city of Switzerland, and I have house there."

I tucked Anya's little tidbit away for later and said, "I'm not doubting you, but how do you know he's there?"

Skipper said, "It would take the rest of my life to explain it to you, but it was actually your idea that got me heading in the right direction."

"That's me," I said. "The idea man."

"Yeah, whatever. Anyway, I bought the code on the dark web and rewrote it to fit our need. It's a really clever piece of software, and I was impressed. But none of that really matters. I started a trace on both Delauter and his ex-wife, Dianne Sakharova. She was missing, too, by the way. She finally screwed up and made a call to Sevastopol on the Black Sea."

"How is that a screwup?" I asked.

"It's a screwup because the call she made was to a burner phone that belongs to her dead husband, Ivan Sakharov."

I pulled out my chair, nestled in, and rolled beside her. "I'm still not following."

"I told you it was too complicated to explain in this lifetime, but I'll break it down for you. Check out these four numbers."

I leaned in and studied the highlighted international phone numbers on the screen.

She pointed to each of them in turn. "This one belongs to the supposedly dead husband millionaire. This one is Delauter's. This one is a humble little bank on Grand Cayman that I believe you've heard of. And here's the kicker . . . This one belongs to Colonel Oleg Volkov of the Russian Federal Security Service."

"Why would she call the FSB?"

Skipper said, "I don't care yet. What I care about is starting clean tracks on both her and Delauter. Your idea about reverse-engineering the software made all of this possible. That makes you a steely-eyed missile-man."

"And it makes you the best analyst on the planet."

She pouted. "Just this planet?"

I gave her a playful shove. "Yep, you've still got a lot to learn before you go interstellar, baby."

She typed furiously for a couple of minutes while the rest of the team and I studied a map of Bern, Switzerland.

When she finished, she said, "If I've done my job correctly, the hard part is finished. Now, all you guys have to do is go catch him."

I looked up from the map. "Is there any way he could know that you've found him?"

"There's always a way, but I can't imagine Delauter having the skills to pull it off."

"He figured out how to hide," I said. "He may have a team of techies. He was a big-time D.C. power broker, so he's probably got a lot of friends."

Skipper said, "After what he pulled, he's got a lot of enemies who *used* to be friends. My bet is that he's running from them, not us."

"I hope you're right. Can you get us a pallet of gear to Bern?"

"Probably. Give me a little time, and I'll see what I can do."

She went back to work, and I went back to the map, but it didn't take long for the front door chime to ring. I looked up at the bank of security monitors and saw Police Chief Bobby Roberts waiting somewhat impatiently on the stoop.

I pressed the intercom. "Come on in, Chief. It's open. Take the elevator to the third floor. I'll meet you there."

I stepped from the op center and waited for the elevator car to arrive.

When he stepped out, I stuck out a hand. "You look tired, Chief."

He shook my hand and huffed. "Yeah . . . it's been a tough day."

"Let's go in here where it's a little more comfortable."

He followed me through the high-security door and onto the floor of the op center. His exhausted look turned to fascination as he took in the surroundings. "Impressive. I had no idea this was up here."

"We're low-profile guys," I said. "Have a seat. Would you care for anything to drink or snack on?"

He checked his watch. "I could use a little something. I have to keep my sugar right."

Skipper slid him a pack of peanut butter crackers and a bottle of water.

I settled back onto my chair. "To what do we owe the pleasure, Chief?"

He held up a pair of fingers. "Two things. First, thank you for responding to the school. I don't even want to think about how that might've ended if you guys hadn't been there."

"It's what we do," I said. "There are very few things worse than intentionally hurting children. I'm glad we could help."

"Help? What you guys did was a lot more than just help. You saved a bunch of lives that would've otherwise been lost."

Mongo asked, "Do you have any idea what the purpose of the invasion was?"

He swallowed a cracker and washed it down with half his water. "We think so. The other active shooter was at the country club. The feds tell me they were related."

I said, "I was afraid that would be the case. Two such events, simultaneously in a town this small, can't be coincidental."

He polished off the water, and Skipper handed him another. "Thanks. So, the common thread seems to be a guy named Patrick Cassidy. He's a Navy commander from Kings Bay who skippered a sub in the Arabian Sea and the Gulf of Aden. I don't know all the details because they're classified—need-to-know and all that."

He twisted the cap from the bottle and drank more slowly. "Apparently, Commander Cassidy dropped off some SEALs to do something nasty over there. You probably know more about it than I do, but the feds say Cassidy's wife was at the club having lunch when the gun*men* stormed the place. We weren't as fortunate as you guys. The gunmen shot up the place pretty bad. Three dead and nine wounded. Two of them are critical. The apparent target was Mrs. Cassidy. She survived, but she's one of the critical."

"Were any of your officers injured?" I asked.

"We lost T.J. Knowles. Did you know him?"

"I don't think I've ever met him."

Bobby said, "Good kid. He was twenty-seven with a baby on the way."

"I'm sorry to hear that. If there's anything we can do, don't hesitate to ask."

He nodded. "So, anyway, the tie to the school was Commander Cassidy's two children. They're nine and seven, and both of them were in the school. In fact, the younger of the two was in the room with Amir Ben Al-Shadi."

"Are both of them okay?"

"They're fine physically, but they'll be shaken up for a while. The feds took custody of the Al-Shadi guy, but the SWAT team put two rounds in the shooter's head at the club. That means Al-Shadi is all we've got, and we don't really have him. Who knows if we'll ever get to interview him."

I let everything he told me tumble around in my skull for a few seconds. "So, the feds think all of this was to get back at a submarine commander for dropping off some SEALs to do what SEALs do?"

The chief's exhaustion grew more evident with every breath. "That's what I'm telling you, and I guess I'm really here asking you to see what you can get out of the feds."

I scanned the room, but no one looked like they wanted to explain our situation, so I said, "To be honest, Bobby, we don't have the best working relationship with federal law enforcement right now. You knew about Penny's murder, and that had me messed up for a long time. I've been out of the game for well over a year. The entity we worked for has been dissolved, and we're sort of in the middle of a reorganization. That's probably the best—and most polite—name for it. We'll put out some feelers, but I can't promise we'll ever know more than you already do."

He sighed. "Still, a call from you has to hold more weight than one from a small-town police chief. I heard you had an injury as well."

I pointed at Gator. "Not me. It was that young hero over there. He took one in the arm and stayed in the fight. He actually took down Al-Shadi, one-on-one."

The chief looked at Gator for a long moment. "There aren't going to be any parades for you down Osborne Street, but let me tell you—the town, especially Commander Cassidy and I, sincerely thank you. You saved a lot of lives, young man."

Gator offered a sharp nod. "Like Chase said, it's what we do, Chief. We're not looking for parades or headlines. We were happy to help."

The chief wadded his cracker wrapper and shoved it into a pocket. "Oh, yeah. There's one more thing. Can I give your phone number to Commander Cassidy? He'd really like to thank you personally."

I scratched my chin. "Please tell the commander we're glad we could help, but like you said earlier . . . need-to-know. And I don't think he *needs* to know our names."

He stood. "I get it, and that's what he thought you'd say. He does send his most sincere gratitude, and he's just been promoted to captain. An admiral's star isn't far away. He's likely going to be president some-day, so it wouldn't hurt to have his name and number in your rolodex."

I stood and shook his hand again. "We've learned that friends in high places aren't as valuable as the ones in low places nobody talks about. I'll take a couple of salty old Navy chiefs who've been busted down a few times over a one-star admiral any day."

Bobby left, and I hoped he was heading home for a night of well-de-served rest, but I suspected he was headed to the hospital to try to sleep in the torture device that nurses like to call a chair.

"I found you a ride," Skipper said.

"That was quick."

She said, "It's our old pals—Gordo, Tubbs, and Slider."

Chapter 14
My Favorite Angel

After our Gulfstream was destroyed in an attack on our airport fifteen months earlier, some shadow agency lent us a C-130 and a top-notch flight crew. We became fast friends, and I even tried to recruit them to come work for us. They declined, but I was happy to hear they were coming back.

"When will they be here?" I asked.

Skipper scanned a few lines of text on her screen. "They're wrapping up a thing in Puerto Rico, and they should be here either tonight or by midday tomorrow."

I laid my head back against the chair and closed my eyes. Over four hundred days had passed without Penny's murderers paying for their crime, and I was only days, or maybe hours, away from exacting righteous vengeance on the men who committed a sin I would never be able to forgive.

The scene played inside my mind as if on a massive screen. I'll never forget the feeling of seeing Penny's plane—only seconds away from touching down at St. Marys—getting struck by a rocket fired from Cumberland Sound. I could still feel the sting of the cabin door release burning the flesh from my fingers as I struggled to wrench it free after the burning airframe slid to a stop. Every detail of the episode scalded my soul and left me to bear the press of the red-hot brand smoking and searing into my back. I'd wear that scar for all eternity, but before I crossed the Rubicon, I'd deliver the agony that brand unleashed on me to the mortal bodies of those who deserve a wrath greater than I—or any man—could pour out.

Without a word, I stood and left the op center for a destination I couldn't name. I had to be somewhere . . . anywhere else but in that room, where everything and every word reminded me of boundless loss and my mind crashing down upon itself.

While I don't remember descending the stairs or walking the path, I remember well the nudge against my hip. I turned, expecting to see someone, perhaps Singer, waiting to walk with me through the hell that had become mine, but nothing could've prepared me for what I saw or how I would react.

Pecan, the oversized demon of a quarter horse, pressed his face against my side, nuzzling gently. I hadn't cried in days, but that record was crushed in that moment. I reached out and rubbed the creature's neck, and he appeared as surprised by my gesture as I'd been by his. I stared into his black eyes and saw a pain that somehow mirrored my own.

"You miss her, too, don't you, boy?"

He let out a sound that couldn't have been a rational reply. There was no way he understood my question, but the sadness woven throughout the noise he made resonated with that of my own tortured soul.

"She's never coming back."

Pecan lifted his head from my hand and laid it across my shoulder in an expression that said the two of us had become the unlikeliest of allies and brothers-in-despair.

"I'm going to find them, boy, I swear it. And I'm going to drive them so deep into the ground that they'll have to look up to see the underside of Hell."

Pecan didn't respond. He simply held his ground with his face pressed against mine.

It had been a pretty good week. I hadn't exploded or collapsed beneath the nearly unbearable weight of having half of me—the far better half—torn away, but that would end in the coming moments.

I shoved Pecan's head away and drove a fist into the interior wall of the barn. The oak plank absorbed my assault without surrender, and my knuckles burst into torn, bloody flesh. There was no pain, no reaction to the self-inflicted wound. The sight of my blood on the wall only served to fuel my rage until my body was too small to contain the sadness that had become fury.

I grabbed the upper half of the split stall door and ripped it from its iron hinges as if it were mere paper, then I swung the door with the maniacal rage of a madman, tearing fixtures from the walls and sending splintered oak and broken glass in every direction. When the door half finally withered and surrendered to my hate-fueled tirade, I turned to my boots to continue the assault and demolished everything within my reach.

As my energy waned, I looked up to see Pecan annihilating the stalls outside the range of my trembling legs. He bounded into the air and delivered unrelenting kick after kick against timbers, bales of hay, and the air itself. Whether he was experiencing the same sorrow-driven emotional break I was, or if he was only reacting in kind to my insanity, I'll never know, but it wasn't fear in his dark eyes. It was bottomless sadness escaping as mindless destruction, and in so many ways, I was doing exactly the same.

I collapsed, exhausted and gasping through tear-filled inhalations, my back against the only remaining stall door in the barn. Pain washed over me in wave after crushing wave until I could no longer see or hear the world around me, and I surrendered—alone and broken and empty.

"Father?"

It was impossible to focus through the haze of sweat, tears, and rage, but that voice could've only been that of my perfect daughter. Ashamed and terrified that she had witnessed me at my worst, I expected her to flee and cling to her mother after seeing her father behave like an untamed animal, but instead, she sat beside me and held my bloody fists in her delicate hands.

Pogonya didn't speak, and she didn't have to. Words in moments like those are wasted things, strings of gibberish serving only as life-giving fuel for the flames of madness.

I had allowed myself to become a carcass of a man in the hands of an angel, a child who should never have to see her father in such weakness and hysteria, but when I opened my eyes, I didn't see a heartbroken child. I saw the beautiful gift I'd been given and the singular reason I would survive. I saw love I hadn't earned, tears I had caused, and hope where I'd felt none before she came into my life.

I squeezed her close to me. "I'm sorry you had to see that. I'm not usually—"

"Father, don't do that. Don't apologize for loving the woman you wanted to watch every sunset with. Asking you not to cry would be asking a wounded man not to bleed. You're not alone, Father. Look."

I wiped my eyes and tried to focus through the dust that clung to the liquid air of the summertime South. My team, my family, was standing backlit by the sunlight, armed with hammers, saws, and nails. They were ready to rebuild what Pecan and I had destroyed, and maybe even the tormented, broken man I had become.

It was Singer, not Mongo, who took my hand and pulled me to my feet. "You knew this was coming, Doctor. Your body and mind are crying out for things that made you feel normal. First, it was Penny and that hole inside you'll never heal. Its razor-like edges will soften over time, but until you see her again, when we've passed from this world, the place she held inside your heart will always yearn for her. No one knows that yearning better than me. The second one is the whiskey. It won't be easy, but it won't take you long to beat that one."

I wrapped him in a hug that I didn't want to end. "Without you, I wouldn't have survived this."

He pulled an arm from around my shoulder and enveloped Pogonya in our embrace. "Yeah, well, now I've got a little help in that department, and I for one sure am thankful for that help. You're a handful, Chase Fulton."

Pogonya squeezed in closer. "I love you, Father."

If I had thought the tears were finished, I'd never been more wrong.

* * *

When evil rattled the gate, no better team that ever lived could beat back that evil, but nothing about my crew of hardened warriors would ever qualify as carpenters. When the hammers fell silent, the barn was usable again, but it looked more like a jigsaw puzzle forced together by a hurricane.

Pogonya pulled on a pair of farrier's chaps and called Pecan. He approached timidly, which was completely out of character. Perhaps he, like me, was ashamed of the part he played in demolishing the stalls.

Loving on him, Pogonya stroked his neck until he relaxed and gave her his hoof. She cleaned the dirt and mud from his hoof and ran a hand across the iron shoe that was well overdue for a change. Apparently satisfied with what she saw, she moved to the other side of the massive animal who'd shown me the heart I didn't know he had. She lifted his hoof, and the big quarter horse flinched.

"I was afraid of that," she said. "Do you have a farrier and a veterinarian?"

I turned immediately to Mongo, and he already had his phone pressed to his ear.

He said, "Hello, Doc. This is Mongo from Bonaventure. Do you have time to come check on one of Pecan's hooves?" He listened and then said, "I don't know, but I'll put someone on the phone who does."

He handed the phone to Pogonya, and she described in great detail the injury Pecan sustained while helping me demolish the barn.

She tossed the phone back to the big man and said to me, "He's on his way, but you'll need to get some fresh shoes for both of the horses very soon, especially since we're going to continue riding them."

"I didn't realize I signed up for that, but the demons are starting to grow on me."

"I'm not one of those demons, am I?"

"Most certainly not," I said. "You're my favorite angel."

The moment was interrupted by the sound of what Gordo, the C-130 captain, called the Four Fans of Freedom.

The turbines roared overhead, and I stepped from the cover of the barn. "There's our ride. I guess that means it's almost time to gear up, load up, and go wheels up. We've got a score to settle."

Chapter 15

Just in Case

Ronda No-H, our CFO and the baddest door-gunner under the sun, led me by the arm to the library.

She said, "We need to talk."

Those are the four most-feared words in the English language to every man I know, but thankfully, it was business, not personal.

She settled in behind the desk.

I said, "That's my chair."

"Not today, it isn't. Sit down, big boy. We've got a lot to cover."

"Yes, ma'am."

She pulled four massive ledgers from her bag and stacked them neatly on the desk. "Let's start with the Bonaventure Foundation." She opened the first book and slid it across the desk.

I said, "I'll look, but I won't understand it."

"That's okay. I understand it. You just need to know how we stand. We circled the wagons a bit while you were fighting through all that stuff."

The shame returned, and I said, "I owe you and everyone else a huge apology for how I behaved."

She smacked the back of my hand with her pen. "You don't have to apologize for being human. The rest of the world thinks you're a superhero, but those of us who love you know better."

"Tell me how bad it is."

She said, "We'll get to your personal finances later, but as far as the foundation goes, things are good. We've got a full-time grant writer now. I'll introduce you to her when we have time, but for now, just know that she's amazing." She pointed toward a figure at the bottom of a page. "This is where we are right now. Just over one point three billion."

"Billion? Are you serious?"

"I told you she was amazing. The *Lori Danielle* is still ours, and she's almost paying for herself. Captain Sprayberry is ready to drown you, though. You know how badly he hates research work. He'd much rather sink somebody's battleship."

"I know, and with any luck, he'll get to fire a few torpedoes sooner than later."

She said, "If you want to go through the figures, we can do that, but everything is in order."

"I trust you completely. If you say it's good, it's good."

She swapped books and slipped the foundation records back into her bag. "Here's the team operational budget. The figure doesn't start with a B, but we're fine. We've got thirty-one million, plus a little. It would be a little higher, but we bought a Citation for Anya after the . . ."

"Yes, of course. Go on."

She pointed at several entries that didn't make any sense to me, but I paid attention. "The insurance company paid for the hangar, the Gulf-stream, and the helicopter that was inside the hangar. I don't know if you've been to the airport lately, but the hangar is rebuilt, and it's better than new."

"I saw it last night when we picked up the flight crew."

She said, "Ah, that's right. We're holding the insurance settlement in a separate account. It's more than enough to replace the Gulfstream and the chopper. They were generous with their tools and equipment settle-ment as well. We didn't want to make any big purchases until you were back on your feet—or I should say your *foot*."

"You're funny, Money Girl. Keep it up."

She grinned. "I have my moments. Do you want to see the settle-ment account?"

118 · CAP DANIELS

"No. Again, I trust you."

She swapped books again and sighed. "Okay, this one is your personal accounts. I did a little consolidation with the overseas accounts to make it cleaner on paper. I hope you're okay with that."

I said, "We're back to that trusting-you part again."

She pointed to a number that surprised me. "This is your bottom line. It includes the life insurance payment of four million and the homeowner's policy settlement for the L.A. house. That's another two point one."

I stared at the number. "I'd give every dollar I'll ever have for just one more day with Penny."

Ronda bit her lip. "I know. We all feel the same way. Human life is priceless, but writing checks is the only way the insurance company has to compensate you for your loss."

I was proud that I didn't melt down, and Ronda continued.

"You didn't spend any money except on whiskey and the occasional Quarter Pounder with cheese, so you can walk away and live the rest of your life any way you'd like. I did my best to take very good care of your money while you learned to take care of you." She closed the book. "Is there anything you want to ask or tell me?"

I said, "Can you set up something for Pogonya?"

Ronda smiled. "Somehow, I knew that would be your first question, and the answer is a resounding yes. I would've already done it, but that would've been overstepping my bounds a bit."

"Give it all to her," I said.

"What's a fifteen-year-old girl going to do with that kind of money?"

That brought an unexpected chuckle. "I guess that's a good point. Just make sure she never wants for anything. Can you do that?"

"Consider it done. Should I write the check to UGA?"

I choked back tears. "Did she pick Georgia?"

Ronda repacked her bag. "No, Chase. She picked you."

* * *

When the finance committee meeting was over, I made my way to the op center, where the whole team was huddled around our analyst.

"This looks like a party," I said. "Mind if I join?"

"It's your party," Skipper said. "We're just waiting to pop out and yell surprise."

"In that case, I'll pretend to be surprised. Do we still have a solid track on Delauter and Sakharova?"

"We do, but it's two separate tracks now. They've parted ways, it would seem."

"Oh? Where are they headed?"

She said, "Dianne—that's easier than pronouncing her last name—appears to be on her way to Sevastopol, but Delauter is still in Bern. I've got him on four surveillance cameras across the city, so I'm a hundred percent on him, but the ex-wife is a little shaky."

"She's not the important one," I said. "I want Delauter. If he set this whole thing up, he's got a lot of questions to answer."

"That's what I thought, and that's why I focused on him instead of her. Technically, she hasn't done anything illegal that we know of."

Anya spoke up. "Conspiracy to commit treason against United States is terrible crime."

"Good point," Skipper said. "But we can't tie her to that yet. I'm still on it, but I think the bulk of our attention should be on Delauter."

Mongo asked, "Is there any way he could know we're coming after him?"

Skipper said, "We have to assume so. He probably still has a lot of contacts in the intelligence world, so we can expect him to exploit those. He's also actively trying to hide by using some pretty extreme and expensive measures. He's probably not sleeping well."

I clicked my tongue against my teeth. "I just talked with Ronda about our accounts, and that was a relief, but are we funding this one ourselves?"

Clark said, "Not a chance, College Boy. The Triad signed a blank check and slid it under our door. Whatever you need, you shall have. It's good to have you back, by the way."

"I'm not sure how much of me is left to give, but I've never wanted anybody more than I want Delauter."

Clark raised an eyebrow. "Remember what they say about digging two graves when you try to kill a mockingbird with one stone . . . or whatever."

I snapped my fingers. "For the first time ever, I know exactly what you're talking about."

He gave me a wink. "I knew you would. Have you thought about your loadout? You can't exactly hit the streets of the capital of Switzerland in full battle rattle. You'll have to play grown-up spy on this one."

I turned and patted Mongo on his landmass of a chest. "I want you beside me for every second of this one. You're the only one of us who has a chance at pulling me off the guy the first time I see him."

"I wouldn't have it any other way," the big man said.

"Okay. Let's load out for every possible contingency. We'll start this as tourists, but if Delauter turns it into a fight, I want us ready to drill his ass into the dirt with everything we've got."

I've never been a coach, but I've heard some of the best pregame pep talks from some world-class baseball coaches, and I thought I'd just delivered a pretty good one. The grunts and growls of my team confirmed my belief.

I wonder if anyone has ever taught Pogonya how to catch and throw a baseball. Focus, Chase. Focus!

I pulled myself from my distraction. "How long will it take to load out?"

Mongo said, "I don't want you to get the impression that any of us could do this without you, but the plane is loaded with nearly everything we own. All you need to do is pack some socks and underdrawers, and we can cross the big pond."

"Give me thirty minutes," I said. "I have to talk with Pogonya before we go."

Anya's smile was the brightest I'd ever seen it, and for the first time, I saw our daughter in her face. The curve of her lips when she was pleased was indistinguishable from Pogo's, and there was something about it that made me feel almost human again.

The meeting broke, and Gordo took my arm. "Can I have thirty seconds, Chase?"

"Absolutely. What's on your mind?"

He said, "Listen, we're in. All three of us are here for whatever you need. We're not door-kickers like you guys, but if there's ever been a fearless crew, you're looking at 'em."

I almost laughed. "You guys flew a Herk fifty feet off the water over Lake Huron, with Slider shooting a fifty-cal out the back at a Russian illegal, while the Coast Guard was swarming all around. Trust me, Gordo. I know what you guys are made of, and I'd gladly kick doors with you three any day."

"We'll meet you at the airport. Oh, and we brought the fifty-cal, just in case."

* * *

I found Pogonya in the barn with Pecan and Praline. The horse that I hated slightly less than I had the day before snorted at me just to re-mind me that he could kick my butt if he needed to. Maybe he and I could come to some sort of truce.

"What's up, Pogo?"

"Just bathing the horses, Dado."

"Dado? Is that what we're doing now?"

She giggled. "I tried it out, but it didn't feel good, so I'll keep work-ing on it. You're leaving, aren't you?"

"You're too smart for your own good, you know that?"

The smile came, and it was definitely Anya's. "I know. Mama said you'd try to talk to me, and it would be awkward because you wouldn't know what to say. So, I'll make it easy for you. I don't like it, but I un-derstand. You have to go."

"You're mom's pretty smart, too."

"She gets it from me," Pogo said.

"I'm sure you're right. Oh, and about yesterday . . . I'm really—"

"Stop it, Pops. Sometimes it feels good to let it all out. How's your hand?"

I studied my scabbed knuckles. "Don't tell the guys, but it hurts bad."

She held up a finger. "Wait a sec. I've got just the thing."

She disappeared into the tack room. When she came back, she had an aerosol can in one hand and a rag in the other. "Give me your hand."

I held out the wounded appendage, and she sprayed a stream of purple gunk all over my hand.

I yanked it away. "Hey! That hurts worse than the busted knuckles."

She giggled again, and I fell in love again. "It's called 'purple stuff,' and Pecan didn't act like a baby when I sprayed his hoof."

"That's because he's a demon, and he thrives on pain—especially when he gets to inflict it on me."

She wrapped my hand with the rag and tugged on my shirt. I bent down, unsure what was about to happen, and she kissed me on the cheek. "Please come home after you catch the people who killed your wife. We've got fifteen years to make up for."

I returned the kiss on her cheek. "Okay, but repeat after me. Go Dawgs!"

Chapter 16
How Immediately?

On my way back to the house, a congregation had formed on the back gallery, and they appeared to be waiting for me.

"What's all this about?" I asked.

Skipper stuck her hands on her hips. "Lest you forget, I told you that you weren't leaving until I marry"—she pointed at Gator—"that man. Now, stand still and be quiet."

"Yes, ma'am."

Pogo slipped silently beside me and squeezed my hand. She whispered, "That could be you and Mama."

I squeezed back, a little harder than necessary.

Singer gave a ninety-second sermon on the biblical blessing of marriage and moved quickly into the abbreviated ceremony. "Friends and family, we're here to witness the joining of lives and hearts until death severs one from the other. If anyone can show just cause why these two should not be joined before the sight of God, it would be best if you kept your mouth shut or risk having me shoot you from a very long way away."

That unexpected moment lightened the mood and garnered a hearty round of laughter.

The "Do yous" and "I dos" were exchanged, as were simple wedding bands, before Singer said, "By the power vested in me by the Almighty and the great state of Georgia, I pronounce you husband and wife. You may now kiss your bride."

The kiss was brief, and the two stood, silently staring into each other's eyes for one of the most sincere moments of honest, pure love I'd ever seen.

There was no doubt the entire team was thinking the same thing I was—that we needed to be on an airplane—but none of us would do anything to steal that moment from Gator and Skipper.

To my surprise, Skipper was the one to break up the party. She kissed Gator again and said, "Go. You've got work to do. And so help me, if you come home dead, I'll kill you."

I'd never been to a wedding that began and ended in laughter, but I liked it.

Skipper stepped in front of me, but I stopped her before she could tell me to take care of her husband. "I won't let anything happen to him, and—"

"Don't make promises like that. You know better. All I ask is that you don't leave him behind. I can't bury another one. It would destroy me."

I rode to the airport with Gordo, the C-130 commander. "It's going to be a long day, Colonel."

He played the song "Wipe Out" on the steering wheel. "Yep, we've done a lot of those. We'll stop in Newfoundland for fuel and one last walk-around before crossing open water. The jet stream is kicking, so we'll have an extra hundred knots after we gas up."

I said, "That'll be on our nose coming home."

His drum solo was getting out of control, but he said, "If you can talk the Russians into selling us some jet fuel, we can come home the wrong way."

"That's probably not the best choice. The eastern route doesn't interest me."

"Good," Gordo said. "I've never had the desire to overfly Siberia in anything slower than an SR-seventy-one."

"I've done it, and I've even jumped out a couple of times, but I never particularly enjoyed my time in the former USSR."

He shot me a look over his glasses. "Based on the fact that you've got a fifteen-year-old daughter, who was conceived in Sol-Iletsk, says you probably enjoyed at least one night over there."

"Touché."

We drove in silence until reaching the airport gate, and I checked my watch. "Do you mind if I borrow your truck for a few minutes before we blast off?"

"Of course not," Gordo said. "Is everything all right?"

"I don't know. Something about the police chief's story isn't sitting right in my gut. I need to talk to the sub commander. Do you remember his name?"

"Cassidy. But I don't remember his first name."

We parked, and I curled a finger at Shawn. "Come with me."

He trotted over and climbed into the truck. "What's up?"

"I'm going to talk to the sub commander who dropped off some of your shipmates in the Middle East. I'd like you to be there to pick up on anything I miss. Nobody understands SEALs better than other SEALs."

He buckled in. "SEALs don't even understand themselves, but I'll do my best. What are you thinking?"

"I don't know. It just seems odd that some Yemeni warlord could find out who was skippering the boat that dropped off a team of SEALs. Something's not right about the story, and I don't like it when cogs don't line up."

Chief Bobby Roberts answered on the first ring. "Hey, Chase. What's going on?"

"I changed my mind. I would like to talk with Commander Cassidy. Would you mind giving me his number?"

"Sure. Give me a minute to dig it up." He came back a few seconds later and read off the number. "What made you change your mind, if you don't mind me asking?"

"I can't put my finger on it, but there's too much wrong with the story. I need to pick it apart a little and see where it leads."

"That's why you're the double-naught spy and I'm just a lowly police chief. If you get anything you can share, I'd like to hear it."

"If I can share, I will. I suspect it's been bugging you, too."

"*Bugging* isn't the right word. It makes me spittin' mad is what it does. Whatever led up to two simultaneous active shooter incidents in my town is something I want to understand and prevent, if that's possible."

"Thanks, Chief. We'll talk again soon."

I dialed the number and waited.

After several rings, a pleasant voice answered. "Captain Cassidy's office."

"Good morning, ma'am. My name is Chase Fulton, and I need to speak with the captain if he's available."

"Is he expecting your call?"

"Probably not, but trust me, he'll be happy to hear from me."

"Wait one, sir."

A minute or so later, a man said, "Mr. Fulton?"

"Yes, sir. This is Chase Fulton."

"I'm Pat Cassidy, and I've been hoping you'd call. I can't thank you enough for what you did. It was nothing short of remarkable."

"It's what we do. I know this is a lot to ask, but is there any way you could spare ten minutes to have a face-to-face?"

"Absolutely. What time?"

"How about now?" I asked.

"Come to my office. Do you know where I am?"

"No, sir, I don't, but I have access to the base."

He gave me the address and directions, and I said, "Would you mind if one of my men who was on the op with me joins us?"

"As far as I'm concerned, bring the whole team. I'd love to thank them personally."

"It'll be just me plus one for now. We'll see you in fifteen minutes."

We showed our credentials to the guard at the main gate, and he waved us through. It took longer than I expected, but we finally found the building and made our way inside.

"I'm Chase Fulton, and we're here to see Captain Cassidy."

The uniformed sailor behind the desk motioned toward a door. "The captain is expecting you. Please go right in."

I tapped a knuckle on the door before opening it, and a man who appeared to be in his early forties stood up from behind a governmental-looking desk.

He rounded the desk and stuck out a hand. "I'm Pat Cassidy."

Shawn and I shook his hand and introduced ourselves. "If you wouldn't mind, we'd like to ask a couple of questions about the mission that may have led to the shootings in St. Marys."

"I'll tell you what I can, but I'm sure you understand that—"

I said, "We have the necessary clearances, signed NDAs, and if you want us to catch the people responsible, we have the need to know."

He settled back into his chair. "In that case, would you like some coffee while we talk?"

"No, sir. Thank you, though. We're about to get on a plane and fly halfway around the world to take down the people responsible for my wife's murder, and it would appear those same people may be, at least tangentially, connected to the attack on your family."

He took a sip from his mug. "The shoulder-fired missile from the sound, right?"

"That's right," I said, choking back the emotion that wanted to rise. "They took out a Citation carrying my wife and one member of our team. My wife Penny didn't survive, but the pilot is fine."

"My condolences."

"If I have my way, it'll be an eye for an eye kind of trip. Can you tell us about your mission that may have led to the shootings?"

He fidgeted in his chair, and I said, "It's okay, Captain. Nothing you tell us will leave this room except to direct members of my team who need the information to plan and execute what we're about to do."

He tugged at his khaki uniform shirt. "It was quite an unconventional insertion. Only a handful of men on the boat knew what we were doing, or even where we were going. Me, my XO, and the boat chief were the only three on board who knew the details. We picked up a team of Naval Special Warfare operators from a carrier in the Indian Ocean and carried them a thousand miles to an island called Mayyun off the coast of Djibouti."

"I'm familiar," I said. "We've done some work in and around the area. Moses led some friends across the Red Sea, not far from there, a few thousand years ago."

"That's the place. I don't know how much you know about SEAL tactics, and even with your clearances, I don't feel comfortable discussing those."

Shawn said, "I haven't polished my trident in a few years, but I wore it with pride."

Captain Cassidy smiled. "Indeed. In that case, I don't have to try to explain what was happening. We let the SEALs out about a mile south of the island. According to the chief, they would take their SEAL Delivery Vehicle ashore to do their dirty work."

"I've done that more times than I can count," Shawn said. "It's not rare."

Cassidy shook his head. "No, of course not. But that's not the rare part. What I didn't understand was surfacing."

"Surfacing?" Shawn asked. "You surfaced your boat?"

"We did," Cassidy said. "I've dropped off and picked up SEALs all over the world, but never like this. Our orders were to launch the team covertly from periscope depth, wait eight hours, and surface the boat."

"Why?" Shawn asked.

"When the president wants a Navy commander to surface his boat, we surface our boat. Asking why isn't exactly how the chain of command works."

"The president?" I asked. "Is it common to get orders directly from the White House?"

"They filter down. I've never spoken directly with the president, but it's not extremely rare for a set of orders to come from the top.

However, this was the first time I'd ever been ordered to do anything stupid."

"Stupid?"

"Yeah. Breaking the surface in the Gulf of Aden is stupid. The whole point of the submarine service is to be silent and undetected. Surfacing a nuclear sub in the Middle East makes no sense at all unless it's a show of force."

I said, "It doesn't sound like that qualified as a show of force."

"It most certainly did not, but the story gets weirder. Once we floated the sub, two SEALs who'd been left behind deployed an inflatable dinghy and motored away in the dark."

"Did they come back?" Shawn asked.

"It took them an hour, but yes, they came back. And when they did, they had two civilians with them. Our orders didn't specifically tell us to remain on the surface while they were away, so I dived the boat and loitered."

"What about the rest of the SEALs?" Shawn asked.

"We picked them up at another set of coordinates we received at the last minute. They brought the SDV back on deck and locked through. They secured the two civilians away in a compartment no one had access to—not even me."

"Who were the civilians?" I asked.

The captain sighed. "I don't know. It was a woman and a young boy. He was maybe five or six, and I only saw him twice. I never really saw the woman. She was wearing a niqab when they brought her on board and when we rendezvoused with the carrier back in the Indian Ocean."

I glanced at Shawn. "That seems like a lot of trouble and expense to pick up a woman and a boy."

Shawn said, "It depends on who the woman is and who the boy's father is. It sounds to me like an asset evacuation. It's likely that the woman and her son, presumably, were assets of the American intelligence community. They were probably promised safe passage in return for information."

I let the story run inside my head for a while before asking, "What was the date?"

Captain Cassidy finished off his mug of coffee. "You're not really asking the date, are you? You're asking what happened in Yemen immediately after the date."

"You're good at this game."

"I've been playing it for more than two decades," Cassidy said. "And the answer to your question is that a team of Delta operators took down a guy named Shakim Ben Al-Shadi."

Shawn and I locked eyes, and I asked, "How immediately?"

Cassidy said, "Exactly forty-two hours after I picked up the SEALs and the two civilians."

I said, "Shawn, why wouldn't the SEALs make the hit while they were there instead of having Delta come behind them?"

"Those frogmen had one mission, and that was to get that woman and boy off that island safely. It's basic compartmental security. The SEALs didn't know Delta was coming, and Delta had no need to know that the SEALs had been there. It's not as rare as you'd think."

Cassidy said, "He's right. The same is true for us in the silent service. We rarely know all the details around our operations."

"So, there's a leak," I said. "Somebody talked. Somebody named you as the commander of the sub that delivered the SEALs and took away the two civilians."

"Wait a minute," Cassidy said. "We were on the surface for thirteen minutes when we launched the Zodiac, and eighteen minutes when we recovered them. That's thirty-one minutes when we could've been seen. A sharp-eyed observer could've identified my boat and passed that information along to his superiors. Let's not jump to conclusions about it being an inside leak. There's room for other options."

I stood. "Thank you for your time, Captain Cassidy. It was a pleasure."

Shawn did the same, and Cassidy said, "Listen, Chase. Sincerely, I don't know how to thank you for what you did at that school. You probably saved my children's lives, and there's no way to put a price on that."

"You don't have to thank us. Just like you, it's what we do."

He shook his head. "It's not the same. I used to command fast-attack submarines, and now I fly LGMDs."

"LGMDs?"

He smiled. "Large Grey Metal Desks. You and your men . . . be careful out there. We need to keep the good guys alive as long as possible."

We climbed back into our borrowed truck, and Shawn said, "Is it just me, or did things get more confusing?"

"It's not just you, my friend. There's a lot wrong with that story, and I intend to get to the bottom of it."

Skipper answered quickly. "Op center."

"I need some background on Shakim Ben Al-Shadi."

She said, "I'm on it. How deep?"

"Right now, I just want to know who and what he was, but I eventually want everything you can find on him, his family, and his associates."

"Well, we can start with the fact that he's dead. It looks like Delta got him."

"We already know that much," I said. "It's a pretty big coincidence that he and the shooter your husband body-slammed have the same last name. That's what this is all about."

Chapter 17

What I'm Made Of

Life in the back of a C-130 was quite a different experience than it was in the Gulfstream *Grey Ghost*. Everything rattled, a lot of things leaked unknown fluids, and the noise level was a lot like a sawmill. Normal conversation was impossible without yelling or wearing a headset. Thankfully, Slider, the loadmaster, passed out David Clark headsets to the team. That made the ride a little better, but it didn't do anything to stop the leaks.

I grabbed Slider's arm as he walked by. "What's the red stuff leaking from that hose?"

He looked up, examining the leak closely. "I'm not sure, but if it stops leaking, let me know. It makes me nervous when it stops."

I missed the *Grey Ghost*, but I loved the cargo capacity of the Herk. There's a reason the venerable C-130 has been around since the fifties. We've got bigger, faster, and sexier airplanes today, but so far, nothing can replace the Hercules.

Just as Gordo planned, we touched down in Newfoundland for fuel, food, and a real bathroom. The trusty old honey bucket wasn't how any of us wanted to offload our last cup of coffee, so the combination of porcelain and running water was hands-down the winner of the day.

The remainder of the Atlantic crossing was relatively uneventful until, just as Slider feared, the old girl stopped leaking. The dry hoses, though, were the least of the Herk's—and our—problems. The airborne, noise-making beast suddenly became nearly silent, and nothing about that felt right.

I yanked off my headset and searched for the loadmaster, but he was nowhere to be found. The rest of the team followed my lead, and their useless headsets hit the deck.

Gator was the first to open his mouth. "Uh, does anybody know what's happening?"

"I wish we did," I said, "but *what's* happening isn't as important as *where* it's happening."

Mine wasn't the only brain on board concerned with our position. Mongo said what I wasn't willing to put into words. "Does anybody know where we are? Last time I looked outside, there was nothing but cold, grey water in every direction."

I shoved my sat-phone against one of the few windows. It seemed to take an eternity, but one by one, satellite symbols appeared on the tiny screen. The connection took longer than I wanted, but the words I longed to hear came through loud and clear.

"Op center."

"Skipper, it's Chase. Please tell me you're tracking us."

"Of course I am. Don't I always?"

"I need to know where we are."

"Are you okay?" she asked.

"We're everything *except* okay. It appears that we've lost all four engines somewhere over the North Atlantic."

"That's impossible! Four turbines don't just stop at the same time, unless you're out of fuel."

"Just tell me where we are."

"Uh, one sec . . . Okay, got it! You're halfway between Cork, Ireland, and Land's End, England."

"That's not much help," I said. "I failed European geography twice. Give me a distance to England."

"Eighty miles."

"What's our altitude?"

She said, "You were cruising at thirty thousand, but you're descending through twenty-eight-five."

My brain launched itself into a whirlwind of calculations. "Find the glide ratio for the J-model C-one-thirty."

"I'm working on it." She finally said, "Based on what I could find quickly, the glide ratio is between twelve and sixteen to one, depending on the weight and configuration."

Thirty thousand feet is roughly five miles, so sixteen to one would give us the eighty miles we need to find British soil, but twelve to one would leave us with a twenty-mile swim in frigid water and horrendous seas.

Skipper apparently did the same math and said, "Based on your descent rate, you're not going to make land."

"That's encouraging," I mumbled.

Slider made his return in dramatic fashion, leaping from the elevated platform from the cockpit. "Everybody move forward, now!"

Following orders wasn't one of my team's strong suits, but no one hesitated, and we were at the forward bulkhead in seconds. Slider pulled on an oxygen mask and wrangled a lever from its stowed position, then pumped it with everything he had. The ramp slowly opened at the back of the cargo bay, and the loadmaster kept hefting, huffing, and sweating with every cycle.

The air inside the formerly pressurized compartment turned cold and thin, but at our descent rate, we'd be well below twelve thousand feet and breathing with ease in no time.

Mongo watched Slider struggling with the manual ramp control and shoved me aside. He hip-checked Slider and took the handle in his massive grip, becoming part of the machine. After catching his breath, Slider deployed the drag chutes, sending both pallets of our gear overboard and descending toward the depths of the Celtic Sea. The desert patrol vehicles followed our gear, and finally, the Toyota Hilux with the mounted fifty-cal vanished into the sky.

Lightening the load would increase our gliding distance, but I had no idea how much.

Slider said, "Flip the switch and keep working."

Mongo obeyed, and the ramp crept its way back into the closed position, but Slider didn't wait for the ramp to seal. In an instant, he disappeared back up the stairs and into the cockpit.

With the ramp closed and our gear headed for Davy Jones's locker, Mongo took a seat and panted like a dog.

Gator asked, "You okay, big man?"

Mongo held up a finger and blew out a long breath. "I will be. Just give me a minute. That's quite a workout, and the air's a little thin up there."

I surveyed the cavernous belly of our gliding beast and wondered if it was empty enough. Singer caught my eye, and the fear bouncing inside my skull subsided. Our Southern Baptist sniper was kneeling with his eyes closed and whispering to what was likely the only force in existence that could save us.

We strapped ourselves back into our seats and joined Singer in talking to God. I had faith in the flight crew up front, but even if we lived through contact with the planet somewhere below, we'd have a lot of surviving left to do, and the hands of the Almighty were the ones in which I wanted to land.

When I closed my eyes, Pogonya's beautiful face flashed before me, and I swallowed the bile rising in my throat.

What if I never see her again? Will she know how much I already love her?

I opened my eyes and saw Anya wrapped in what must've been the same emotions I was experiencing. She stared back at me and tried to smile, but it wouldn't come. I wanted to give her some semblance of hope, but nothing about our situation pointed to a positive outcome. So, I was left looking into the eyes of my daughter's mother and sharing mutual fear and dread.

Anya released her restraints and crossed the cargo bay. Without a word, she settled into the netting beside me and strapped in. Before I knew it, her hand was wrapped around mine.

She said, "She knows, Chasechka. She knows how much you love her."

How Anya could've known what was swirling inside my head, I'll never know, but somehow, her words were enough to ease the anguish I felt until Slider bounded back into the cargo bay.

He yelled, "Get out!"

No one moved, and I said, "What?"

He yelled even louder. "Get out! Some small islands are coming up, and you can land there. We're not gonna make the coast."

I shook my head. "Our chutes were on the pallets. We're in this thing 'til every piece stops flying."

He threw his head back and cursed before heading back to the flight deck.

Anya leaned close. "How do we get out if we land in water?"

"We'll go out the hatch," I said. "If we have to ditch, I'll make sure the hatch is open before we hit the water. It's going to be cold and rough, but hopefully a ship will see us hit the water and pick us up."

"What if there is no ship?"

My heart sank. "Then it's going to be a very long night."

Slider rejoined us and said, "All right, listen up. We're planning to ditch off the coast. We've got life jackets and two life rafts. The ditching procedure varies based on conditions, so I'll brief you on those when we get closer."

"What can we do to help?" Kodiak asked.

Slider shrugged. "Just stay out of the way. We've got this. Gordo and Tubbs have done this once before, but it was in warm water and flat seas."

"You got any Ziploc bags?" I asked.

"No,"—he almost smiled—"but we've got honey bucket bags."

"We'll take 'em," I said. "We need to keep our sat-phones dry if possible."

Slider pulled a fistful of bags from the locker and threw them at me. "We've got two water-resistant radios in each raft, but those sat-coms of yours will sure come in handy if we survive this." He opened a bin and tossed water bottles to each of us until he'd exhausted the supply. "Stick these in every pocket you've got. There's emergency water in the rafts, but there's no such thing as too much fresh water."

We tucked the bottles away, but Slider stared intently at the remaining one in his hand. He twisted off the cap and chugged the contents, then he held the bottle upside down and swung it through the air in an effort to shake out the last drops still clinging to the plastic.

Anya said, "What is he doing with empty bottle?"

"I don't know," I admitted, "but he's definitely up to something."

Apparently convinced that his bottle was truly empty, Slider turned to our giant. "Come here, big guy. I need a boost."

Mongo stood and followed the loadmaster. The rest of us watched in amazement as Mongo hefted Slider onto his shoulders and stood erect beneath a collection of hoses, valves, and various other unidentifiable parts. After several minutes of twisting, banging, and dropping tools, Slider stuck his empty bottle beneath a valve and collected sixteen ounces of whatever had been inside that line.

Mongo let him down, and he capped the bottle that went immediately into the cargo pocket of his flight suit. I wanted to ask him what that was all about, but I was halted by the sound of a jet engine whirring to life.

Singer smiled, "Is that the engines restarting?"

Slider burst the sniper's bubble of hope. "No, that's the auxiliary power unit. We need it to jettison the fuel to get our weight down as low as possible. Plus, we don't want a bunch of jet fuel in the water with us if we ditch hard."

After one more visit to the cockpit, Slider returned and checked the latch on the side parachute door. He then planted himself in the same netting as the rest of us and pulled the strap tight across his waist.

Every eye was on Singer, and he did a relatively good job of appearing calm. "Listen up! Here's the ditching procedure. Gordo says to leave the door closed until we hit the water. So, as soon as we stop, I'll open it and deploy the rafts. They're on a tether, so we'll be able to keep them close. Don't inflate your life vest until you're outside the airplane. If anybody's unconscious, I'll carry you out the door." His eyes fell on Mongo, and he said, "I may need a little help if you go down."

The big man said, "Just roll me toward the door. What I'm made of floats."

The Herk banked to the right, and Slider yelled, "We're turning into the wind. Brace for impact!"

I had no idea how to brace for impact, or for anything else for that matter. We were sitting in net seats with a single strap across our laps. There was nothing to hold onto except our faith and Gordo's experienced hands on the controls.

I pressed myself into the netting as hard as my legs would push and ducked my chin to my chest, just like I'd done a thousand times at home plate when a runner from third was about to bulldoze me into the dirt.

The banking ceased, and Gordo pulled the nose of the dying airplane above the horizon, slowing our forward motion as much as possible without stalling.

I tried to imagine how many water landings I'd made in my life. It had been hundreds, at least, and most likely thousands, but I'd never done one in the open ocean, in a C-130, without floats, with four dead turbines, and from the cargo bay. I wondered if it would be legal to write that one in my logbook if I survived.

The hiss of the belly kissing the waves lasted only an instant before it felt like we hit a brick wall. Grunts and groans escaped our bodies in a mighty chorus of grateful pain, but by all indications, everyone was still alive and conscious.

Slider was on his feet before the rest of us moved. He forced open the door, kicked both rafts into the water, and yelled, "Go! Go! Go!"

Kodiak grabbed Anya by the arm and threw her toward the open door. The rest of us remained still until her blonde ponytail disappeared through the opening. I guess chivalry wasn't dead after all.

We filed out quickly but smoothly, and I watched every boot of my team step through the door before I considered abandoning the behemoth that had delivered us safely to the surface of the deep. I scanned the cargo bay, determined to be the last man to step into the raft, but to my disbelief, Slider was gone. It was as if he'd never been there.

I yelled, "Slider! Where are you?" Hanging my head out the door, I counted my entire team huddled in the first life raft. "Anyone seen Slider?"

Heads shook, and I feared he might have fallen through the door.

Relief overtook me when I heard Gordo yelling as he descended the stairs to my rear. "Get out! We're right behind you."

Slider was hefting Tubbs, the copilot, across his shoulder just like I had carried Penny's body from the burning Citation back in St. Marys. My heart sank, but I followed Gordo's command and stepped into the raft with the rest of my team.

The wind howled, and the waves lapped at the side of the floating Herk and across the inflated tubes of our raft. Mongo reached up to take Tubbs from Slider's arms and then carefully lowered him onto the deck of the raft. A massive wound lay open across Tubbs's forehead, but his chest rose and fell in a continuous rhythm.

Singer moved into position and examined Tubbs from head to toe, and I pulled my med kit from my belt and tossed it onto the copilot's chest. Singer ripped it open and dressed the laceration.

Slider landed beside me, and I looked up to see Gordo rubbing a hand across the fuselage as if comforting a weeping child. He mouthed something I couldn't make out before stepping from his wounded bird that he loved so much.

Chapter 18

In the Arms of the Angels

With obvious concern, Gordo leaned toward his wounded copilot and spoke softly to the loadmaster. "Seal the hatch, Slider."

His quiet confidence spoke of decades of doing things lesser men could not. The fight had not ended. Surviving the ditching was but one of the battles of the war in which we found ourselves still entangled. Having a man with Gordo's confidence to manage the elements that were his gave me the freedom to fight the battle that was mine and to face the beast still gnarling in the distance.

"How are we on wounded?" I asked.

Singer gave a brief shake of his head as a report on Tubbs, but the rest of the team reported no injuries. A check on rations gave us the assurance that we had sufficient water and food for six days if we carefully rationed what we had on board. We weren't yet certain of our position, but that was only a matter of electronics. Our situation wasn't great, but everyone aboard our boat had been in far more dire circumstances and survived. We were likely hours, or at worst, days from rescue. In my opinion, keeping Tubbs alive and getting him into the hands of competent doctors was our highest priority.

With that in mind, I, as team commander, slid beside Gordo, the flight crew commander. "You doing okay, Flyboy?"

The seasoned aviator shrugged. "I've had better days. How about you, Shooter?"

"I'd say it's a pretty typical Tuesday."

He glanced at his watch. "It's Thursday."

"Oh. In that case, we're screwed."

He said, "I've been screwed before and came out the other side. I'm worried about Tubbs, but from the looks of things, your man qualifies as a pretty good doc."

I studied the peaceful expression on Singer's face and the unhurried pace of his care. I didn't have the heart to tell Gordo that Singer was our sniper, so I said, "Those are exactly the hands I'd want to be in, but I think it's time to make a call and get him an airlift out of here."

Gordo nodded. "I agree, but I need to bring you up to speed on a few things first. Are you keeping a log?"

I pulled a thin hardback binder from my cargo pocket. "Always."

He began. "I'm going to give you times in Zulu, which I can only assume is plus one from here. We came to rest at seventeen forty-seven. Time now is eighteen twenty-two. Do you agree?"

I jotted down his times and checked my watch. "I do."

He continued. "The last fix I took was at forty-eight point eight-seven degrees north by seven point four degrees west, just southwest of Bishop Rock Light. That's a piece of granite in the ocean with a light-house stuck on it that nobody cares about."

He seemed to ponder the likely useless nature of the information before continuing. "The auxiliary power unit failed just before touchdown, I assume because of the same malady as the four primary turbines. I haven't wasted time concocting a theory yet, but it doesn't matter at this point. *Why* the turbines stopped spinning is less important than the fact that they did stop, but I'm sure Slider has a few hundred theories of his own. I recommend focusing on staying alive and making it ashore. We'll study the mechanicals later."

"Agreed."

Singer glanced up, and Gordo took in the sight of his motionless copilot.

Singer said, "It's not as bad as it looks. The laceration is superficial, even though it's ugly. Head wounds always bleed a lot, but I've got it under control. He's unconscious, and that's merciful in this case. He'd otherwise be in a lot of pain, and I wouldn't want to administer morphine to a patient with a head injury unless it was absolutely necessary. His vitals are strong, and he's showing no other signs of injury. He's stable, and by all indications, comfortable. I'm going to wrap him up, hold him, and keep him warm. I don't want him waking up in pain. I don't see any reason to make decisions that would surrender our tactical advantages—if we have any—for the benefit of moving him. Do you understand what I'm saying?"

Gordo slapped our chaplain/sniper/medic on the shoulder. "Thank you, Singer. Keep him alive, and keep me posted."

"You know I will, sir."

Gordo winked. "Nobody is a *sir* in a lifeboat, Singer."

The pilot and I nestled back against the tube of the raft, and he continued the briefing that he somehow made feel far less formal than it was. "It'll be dark in less than an hour, and it's going to get cold. These rafts are built to stack. We'll flip the empty one on top of this one and lash it down. That'll keep us out of the wind, and it'll keep us dry. We've got flashers and EPIRBs, but that's something we need to talk about. Your medic is right about our tactical advantage."

I took a long breath. "I've been thinking the same thing. Having the whole world believe you botched the water landing gives us a huge advantage in the remainder of our mission."

He chuckled. "That's what I like about you SOCOM guys. You fall out of the sky and crash in the middle of the ocean, but to you, it's just a hiccup in the overall mission."

I said, "We're not Special Operations Command, Gordo. We're No Operations Command. We don't exist."

He nodded slowly. "Even better."

"So, back to not existing," I said. "Is the emergency locator transmitter running?"

"It is for now, but I can have Slider shut it down in a matter of minutes. Same for the EPIRBs on the rafts."

I laid my head back against the tube. "Give me thirty seconds to think about it."

I let my hand fall against the plastic trash bag that contained a collection of satellite phones that could put me in almost instant contact with Skipper or a thousand other people who could pluck us out of the water in no time. The problem with such a plucking was the fact that whoever sabotaged our airplane—and sabotage was the only explanation—would know immediately that we'd survived. The only thing I liked better than the thought of shoving the muzzle of my pistol down Scott David Delauter's throat was having him falsely believe I was rotting on the bottom of the cold grey ocean.

"Kill the ELT and EPIRBs. Let's have ourselves some fun with this thing."

Gordo's maniacal grin was almost as big as mine as I dumped my bag of radios over the side of the raft.

He gave the order, and Slider disappeared inside the belly of the C-130 still floating dutifully beside our rafts.

The loadmaster had been gone less than thirty seconds when Gordo sank against the wall of the raft and pointed into the darkening sky. "We waited one minute too long, my friend."

The sound arrived before the sight, and it was unmistakable. It could've been nothing other than a heavy-lift chopper of some design. I suspected it would bear the markings of the British Royal Navy, and I didn't think I'd have to wait long for my suspicions to be confirmed.

The noise grew until the shape of a truly massive helicopter materialized against the sky. Every eye in our raft was cast upward, and Slider returned to the hatch to join the skyward gawking. His face wore the same look of disappointment as the rest of us. Any hope we had of remaining anonymous and pretending to be dead was gone, but we were minutes away from rescue, and Tubbs would soon have a forehead full of stitches and a bellyful of painkillers.

The helo slowed as it descended until coming to a hover thirty feet above the sea. The wind was still strong enough to blow even the massive aircraft around in oscillations I wouldn't want to experience. I shaded my eyes against the wind and water, expecting to see a rescue swimmer descending on a cable alongside a metal basket to haul each of us back aboard the airship, but I was wrong.

Instead of a stainless-steel cable lowering a brave swimmer into the waves, two swimmers with fins, masks, and snorkels pushed themselves from the door of the hovering helo and fell into the raging water below. They disappeared beneath the waves and reappeared moments later, each hanging by one arm over the tube of our life raft. They gave the thumbs-up signal to the chopper, and the pilots backed away, quieting the environment and reducing the pelting wind and water in the air.

The first of the swimmers pulled his mask from his eyes and let it hang downward around his chin. "Oi! Fancy runnin' into you blokes out ere where we're goin' for a swim, eh. Ain't that somefin'?"

I don't remember exactly what my expectation had been, but that certainly wasn't it, and I was left hoping that somebody in my boat understood what was happening.

The second swimmer mirrored his buddy's motions with his mask and wiped the salt water from his face. "Ever heard of the Special Air Service, mate?"

Before I could tell him that I had enormous respect for the elite British special forces unit, he said, "No, 'course you ain't. Neiver have I. Mind if me and my mate come aboard and have a look at that bloke there wiff the bad head on 'im?"

Mongo hoisted the SAS troopers over the tubes in a breath, and one of them inspected Singer's handiwork.

After looking in each of our eyes, checking pulses, and giving Anya a little extra attention, one of the men leaned back, crossed his ankles, and said, "You wouldn't have a spot of tea about, would you? Or maybe a biscuit?"

Gator tossed him a bottle of water. "How 'bough a bah-ul o' wah-uh?"

The man caught it. "Not bad for a Yank. We're jammin' your ELT and EPIRB, by the way, so don't nobody know you're out 'ere. Which one o' ya be Chase?"

I raised a finger, and he said, "Your little daughter, Begonia, sends 'er love. Told 'er meself I'd make sure her ol' man was safe 'n' sound."

"Her name's Pogonya," I said.

He took a long swallow of Gator's water and shrugged. "I reckon you Yanks gave us a pretty solid whippin' say, a couple hundred year ago. Got anythin' you'd like to maybe say to us now that we're way out 'ere and we're the ones with the aero and all?"

I should've known it would be Kodiak who spoke up for all red-blooded Americans, and he did not disappoint. "Now that you mention it, there is a little something we should say. We really appreciate you guys showing up. As you can see, we're in a bit of a fix and a long way from home. It's awfully nice of you to lend a hand. And it's even nicer of you not to wear your red coats so we didn't have to shoot you in the face."

The roar of an engine cut through the howl of wind and waves as the bow of a vessel appeared from the south. The ship appeared to be in the sub-hundred-foot range and came at an impressive clip. The skipper of the craft laid her alongside the C-130 and ordered the deck crew to lash the plane to the portside beam. The order was instantly obeyed and followed by a maneuver that brought the whole massive assembly across the wind, using the heft of the airplane to block the howling wind and waves from our temporary home in the life raft. For the first time in hours, we were physically comfortable, dry, and relatively warm.

I caught the attention of one of the SAS troopers and mouthed, "Who are they?"

He said, "Oh, those blokes? They're the Special Boat Service swimmers. They're the little girls who couldn't hack it in the Air Service."

The SAS chopper reappeared and came to a hover above our boat in the lee of the Herk. Finally, the basket I expected appeared and descended. The two SAS troopers loaded Tubbs aboard and rigged him to be hoisted away.

Before they rode the cable skyward, one said, "Good luck to you Yanks, whatever you're doing out here. Your man is wiff us now, in the arms of the angels you might say, but the rest of you are stuck wiff them Boat Service blokes, so godspeed to you. And how about having a little tea for us next time, eh?"

Chapter 19
To Cornwall She'll Go

My grasp on American rank insignia was weak, at best, having never served in uniform, but the garbage the Brits pasted on their shoulders could've been from *Star Trek* as far as I was concerned.

A booted, mustached gentleman offered Gordo a hand and said, "Why are you the only one without a beard, mate?"

The pilot accepted the hand and climbed to his feet with a well-rehearsed look of sincerity on his slick face. "Has it fallen off?"

The British—whatever he was—said, "Get aboard. I haven't the time for American foolery."

We followed Gordo and filed aboard the Special Boat Service vessel still in the lee of the crippled C-130 Hercules. Crewmen placed us on well-padded seats and passed out mugs of steaming tea. The SAS troopers may not have cared for the boys in the boats, but so far, they had my vote.

Gordo wrapped his hands around the offered mug and spoke in his typical soft, confident tone. "I'd like to speak with the skipper if I may. I'm the aircrew commander."

"Give us a bit to get all sorted and counted, if you please, and you'll have your audience with the cap'n."

"Fair enough."

Mongo leaned his tree trunk of a frame against me. "You doin' all right, boss?"

"I'm good. You?"

"I've never been a fan of being the one getting rescued, but as rescues go, this one isn't bad."

I touched the rim of my cup to his. "The Brits do it in style, don't they?"

He took a sip. "Next thing you know, we'll be playing cricket and eating crumpets . . . whatever those are."

I said, "They're little bugs, kind of like grasshoppers, that rub their legs together and make noise."

He rolled his eyes. "I should've drowned you when I had the chance."

A rugged-looking man with a beret tucked beneath an epaulet stepped from somewhere forward in the vessel and landed without a sound on the deck in front of us. "Gentlemen. Welcome aboard Her Majesty's Vessel *You Don't Need to Know*."

His accent was English, but just barely. He could've pulled off New England just as easily as Old England. The man said, "This is my ship, and as long as that big ugly aeroplane of yours is lashed to her, it's mine as well. If I so much as get the itch in my belly that she's about to take us down, I'll cut her loose and motor away. That thing is not my priority. Queen and Country, this ship and crew, followed by you. Those are my charges. Do you have any questions? Good."

I both liked him and wanted to fight him at the same time, and I didn't really know why.

He spoke seemingly without breathing. "My orders are vague, and I wouldn't have it any other way. And those orders are thus . . . Feed, harbor, house, heal, and protect the bloody Americans against all boogers, real and imagined, until such time as I can toss the lot of you ashore at some other poor bloke's boots, be it the will of the Crown."

Gator caught my eye and mouthed, "Did he say boogers?"

I learned in that moment exactly how uncomfortable it felt to have lukewarm tea erupt from my nostrils, and Captain Booger was clearly less than amused.

Intimidating operators like those drinking tea from tiny cups aboard the HMS *Who Cares* isn't possible, and I was happy to learn the same was true of beardless Herk drivers.

Gordo cleared his throat and said, "Look, Skippy. You can prance around and play fancy-pants *Pirates of Penzance,* or whatever this is, all you want, but you're going to tell *me* what you plan to do with *my* airplane. And if I don't like it, I just might cut *your* little boat loose and take my chances on whatever rocks I wash up on. Then you can tell your friend the Queen, and her little dogs too, how you screwed up a simple mission to fix us bloody Americans some decent tea."

The British officer took a step toward our pilot, and the man who'd been my self-appointed bodyguard for a decade stood to his full height of two English meters and—if my math was right—just over twenty-one stone, and placed himself between Gordo and the Brit. "Whatever you're thinking ain't what you should be thinking. Take a step back, and let's start over."

The officer looked up at Mongo, and part of me wanted to let it play out, but we were a long way from home and in the middle of a mission I badly wanted and needed to finish.

I patted the big man on the leg. "Let's everybody take a breath. Tensions are high, and there's no reason for them to be. The airplane isn't going to sink. We appreciate you picking us up, and at the end of the day, we're all on the same team. There's just a bunch of questions we all want answers to, and I'll be glad to go first."

I didn't know if my psychologist's couch approach would help cooler heads prevail, but I didn't want to watch Mongo pound half a dozen British Special Boat Service commandos into the deck of their bathtub toy. The thought that the big guy and the rest of us might lose the skirmish didn't enter my mind until later. Much later.

Mongo took his seat, and the Brit with the tucked beret stepped back.

I breathed a little easier and said, "Okay, boys. Here's the truth. You know the game. You play it, too. We're off the reservation and looking to settle a score."

The shoulders of the SBS team softened, and a few of the battle-hardened fighters even leaned in a little.

"There's a guy in Switzerland who's responsible for killing my wife. He didn't put the gun to her head, but he ordered it done, and I carried her body from the wreckage."

I'd never been prone to moments of emotional weakness, and story time in front of some of the most serious badasses on the planet wasn't the place for tears on my cheeks. The feeling in my gut didn't seem to care about my audience, but somebody in the belly of that British boat did, and she took the helm.

Anya said, "It should have been me. I was flying airplane when missile struck tail. We were on fire, and I crashed on first part of runway. I should have been dead. It should not have been Chase's wife. She was perfect woman in all ways, and I am exactly opposite of this."

If her intention had truly been to dam my tears, she was failing. In one respect, though, she crushed a mighty stone I was uncertain could be reduced to rubble.

The commander took a knee between my boots. "Who is this bastard, mate? What's his name?"

Shawn, our stalwart SEAL who hadn't said a word since we'd climbed aboard the life raft, hooked a powerful hand inside the Brit's knee and pulled him across the deck. "His name is Delauter—Scott David Delauter—and he's a piece of treasonous turncoat trash. You plucked us out of that water because we've got some powerful friends back in the States, who made some phone calls to some of *your* powerful friends, who sent you out here to get us."

Shawn didn't say much, but when he spoke, it was time to shut up and listen. His English counterpart seemed to sense exactly that, and the look on his face said that he let our SEAL's sermon sink in.

"We're going to Switzerland if I have to swim these guys there one at a time, and we're going to find Delauter. When we do, we're going to stand in a circle around him while our buddy, Chase, tears him into bite-sized pieces and feeds him to the devil himself."

Even the ocean seemed to hold its tongue in respect—or perhaps fear—as Shawn continued. "Now, I know who and what you boys are because I'm a SEAL. I've got a lot of respect for you. You're the real deal, but so are we. So, tell us what you're out here to do, because I know it ain't to sit here tied to an airplane in the dark. That's not what Special Boat Service boys do."

The man who'd made no secret of being in charge stuck out his hand. "Captain James Millgood, and these are me swimmers, a fine bunch all."

Instead of shaking Captain Millgood's hand, Shawn motioned toward me. "He's Dr. Chase Fulton, and you might say we're his merry band of misfits all."

I shook, and everything about the air inside the boat changed. Maybe it was the brotherhood of SEAL and SBS, or maybe old Jimmy Millgood was afraid of Mongo. I'll probably never know, but I was thankful for the change and the progress.

Millgood said, "Here's what lies ahead for the night. I meant what I said about your aeroplane. I can't let her sink us, but if she gets a bit wobbly, we'll do what we can to get her into shallow water. We're under orders to keep her here and dark until a pair of Royal Naval seagoing tugs arrive to tow her ashore at Pendennis Castle."

That was apparently Gordo's cue to dance with the captain. "Pendennis Castle?"

Millgood said, "Yeah, sure. Know where that is?"

Gordo said, "Never heard of it."

"It's 'round Lizard Light into Falmouth at the National Maritime Museum Cornwall."

"Nope. Still nothing. Why would you take my Herk to a maritime museum?"

"Think about it, mate. Where else can you haul out something that weighty from the sea, dismantle her, and load her on a barge without nobody asking a basket o' questions? Me swimmers here, they're crack hands at demolition. We can send her to the rock bottom if you don't want to fly her again, but if she were mine, to Cornwall she'd go."

Gordo chuckled for the first time in days. "To Cornwall she'll go."

As the minutes became hours, tensions continued breaking and warriors became brothers, regardless of how they pronounced a mostly common language. War stories are war stories over coffee or tea, and all three flowed until the tugs made their appearance.

I stood in absolute awe as they approached. "I had no idea tugboats came in Mongo size."

Shawn tapped his knuckles against the rail. "I didn't join the Navy to spend my life on a boat, but those are big'uns. I've never seen any American tugs that size."

"They shouldn't have any trouble with the Herk."

He said, "They wouldn't have any trouble with a continent."

The tugs worked in practiced precision, connecting lines and moving in a well-choreographed ballet that would've made the Bolshoi proud.

When the command came for Captain Millgood to cut away, Gordo stepped to my side. "Uh, Chase. I need to talk with you about something."

Part of me wanted to have a little fun with the man who'd saved all of our lives and performed a task fewer than a handful of others had ever done in the history of the storied C-130 Hercules, but I couldn't do it. I laid a hand on the shoulder of the man, who, in my mind, had become a legendary pilot and a friend I'd treasure as long as I drew a breath under Heaven. "Go, Gordo. I understand. You and Slider belong with your girl. Delauter is ours. When all of this is over, we'll smoke a Cuban, drink something old, and watch a sunset somewhere beautiful together."

Instead of a word, he threw an arm around me, and we stood, two men, somehow understanding the other when neither could explain how or why.

When he backed away, I said, "Before you go, I've got a question."

"Sure. What is it?"

"Right before we left the Herk, Slider put a sample of some liquid in a plastic water bottle and stuck it in his pocket. What was that?"

Gordo looked back at his loadmaster. "He did?"

I nodded, and he said, "I don't know, but when I find out, I'll be sure to let you know."

"I look forward to it. Oh, and Gordo . . . thanks for not getting us dead."

Chapter 20
My Two Quid

Captain Fancy-Pants—and that's who he'd forever be to me—motored away to the southeast without a single light shining anywhere on the exterior of what he called his ship. I skirted my share of maritime laws, but running completely dark at the speed we were making, beneath a moonless sky, wasn't on my lengthy list of nautical sins.

"They've probably got pretty good radar," Shawn said.

"No doubt. Where do you suppose the good captain is taking us?"

The SEAL glanced into the cloud cover as if he possessed some sort of GPS the Navy issued him in Coronado during Hell Week that the rest of mere mortals lacked. "Some place out of the wind and waves, I'd guess."

"We can hope," I said.

He unrolled his previously pushed-up sleeves. "Where would you take us if you were at the helm?"

I took my own glance into the looming clouds. "I guess Switzerland is a little short on seaports, huh?"

"A little."

"I sure would like to chat with Skipper," I said.

"Wouldn't recommend it. I'd say Delauter's either listening or he's got folks doing the listening. If we want him to keep believing we didn't make it through our little dance with the Celtic Sea . . . That was the Celtic Sea, right?" I nodded, and he continued. "If we expect him to keep believing that pretty sloppy lie we're trying to feed him, we'll have to stay off the phone."

"Yep, you're right about that. It's been a long time since I've run an op without an op center."

He slapped me on the back. "Well, old buddy, you've got me now, and I'm the kinda guy you can drop off on a rock with a Q-tip and screwdriver and I'll build you a Walmart."

I laughed. "Good to know, but I'm plumb out of Q-tips."

He glanced over his shoulder. "I'll bet one of them pretty-boy Brits has one."

"Seriously, what do you think of those guys?"

"They're the real deal," he said. "Not exactly SEALs, but I'll take 'em three to two with frogmen any day."

"That's high praise."

He packed a dip of snuff behind his lip and offered me the tin.

I shook him off. "No, thanks. Penny doesn't like . . ."

Like the brother he was, he just tucked the few grains of finely chopped tobacco back into his pocket and said, "You know, in this part of the world, nights like this qualify as fine evenings."

I took a long breath. "Then I'm thankful to God that we don't live in this part of the world."

"I hear that, my brother. I hear that."

We stood in silence as the crisp air cut through our damp clothes and memories of the woman who'd loved me deeper and stronger than I could've ever deserved. Her wild head of hair danced on every breath of wind, and I swear I could hear her beautiful voice singing every time the hull cut through the spray of salty wash. Maybe she was out there —out there on the wind and in the spray. Maybe she could see me chasing her killer like the madman I'd become, the man she always knew I was. She hated that man in me, and she loved him more than she'd ever say out loud. Scott Delauter was a coward—a lying, slithering snake—but maybe he'd send my soul to join Penny's. Maybe that was the ending written in the stars I couldn't see a billion miles above my head. Maybe that had been my destiny from the day God stuck the sword in the angel's hand in the ruined Garden of Eden. Or maybe I'd borrow that angel's sword just long enough to carve the obsidian soul from the chest of the man who'd feel neither mercy nor grace from my vengeful hand.

"Why do you reckon they call it *The* Hague?"

Shawn's question pulled me from my godless rage.

"What?"

He turned his head and spat overboard. "The Hague. I can't think of another city they call *The* anything. The Atlanta. The San Antonio. The Nashville. It just sounds stupid. Why *The* Hague?"

"I don't know. What makes you ask a question like that?"

He pointed to what I believed to be the northeast. "I saw it in a spy movie once. It's somewhere over there by Denmark, I think. You're supposed to be the smart one. I'm just the guy who can build you a Walmart out of a Q-tip and something else. I forgot what."

"It was a screwdriver," I said.

"Yeah, that was it."

"I don't know why they call it The Hague, but I'll bet your buddy, the two-thirds of a SEAL, knows."

Shawn raised his eyebrows. "Don't you call him that to his face. He'll probably kick both our butts, at least two-thirds of the way."

I laughed again. "Not as long as we've got Mongo."

"There is that."

I said, "You know, The Hague isn't a bad idea. We've got a lot of assets in the community there, and we don't need a telephone or an op center to have a cup of coffee with them."

He clawed the expired lump of black debris from his lip and sent it over the rail. "Do you think they need a Walmart built?"

"They just might."

I made my way back inside the vessel and found Mongo holding court with a handful of SBS swimmers gathered around. It was the perfect audience to relay Shawn's question to. "This looks like a bright group. Why do they call it The Hague?"

I don't think I'd ever seen Mongo stumped before, but I was

amused by the look and promised myself I'd never forget it.

One of the SBS swimmers scoffed as if I'd asked for the recipe for ice. "It's from Middle Dutch, mate. Doesn't everybody know that?"

"I'm afraid I slept through Middle Dutch and instead favored baseball fundamentals. Why don't you enlighten me?"

He said, "The original was the old 's-Gravenhage. It meant the Count's Hedge, or more formally, really, the Count's private enclosure or hunting grounds. They say it was surrounded by quite a row or two of hedges of a couple meters, or more like your big mate 'ere. Don't seem much for sportin' if you ask me, but them Dutch counts. What can you say, eh? I reckon it boils down to modern English as just 'the hedge,' or The Hague, as it were. Does that suit you?"

"I reckon it does," I said. "Thanks."

"Is that where we're takin' ya? It'd be a fine choice for my two quid, it would."

I shrugged. "Got no idea what that means, but it sounds like you like it."

Mongo returned to his grand tales of the Green Beret, and I found Captain Fancy-Pants at the helm with one hand on the wheel and a hip on a cushion.

"Permission to come aboard the bridge, sir."

"Yeah, yeah, come. And thanks for askin'. Some don't, you know."

I stepped into the pilothouse that was clearly built for men who'd never grown to my height.

The captain motioned toward a second cushion. "Plant yourself over there. You'll keep that noggin' o' yours off the o'erhead."

The accent he'd buried while chest-thumping an hour before was back, and I liked the authenticity.

A glance at the dimly lit instrument panel gave me pause. "I can't take that cushion. Nobody puts himself between the captain and the wind."

The stone facade broke. "A man of the sea, are we?"

By way of an answer, I offered nothing more than a slight nod, and he stepped back. "In that case, take the helm, and I'll take the cushion. I'm overdue for a tea by any measure."

"I have no idea where we are."

"It's the English Channel, old boy. Nothing's ever gone awry in these waters. Well, maybe the Vikings, but even they didn't cause much trouble, now, did they?"

"Not for us Yanks," I said.

He actually laughed. "No, I suppose not."

I took the helm of his "ship" and searched in vain for the nonexistent autopilot control. The pirate of Penzance was the real deal. "So, where are you taking us, Captain?"

"Plymouth. It's a couple hundred kilometers with a nice breakwater to hide behind. From there, you and your men can hop a train, ferry, or plane anywhere in Europe wiffout issue."

Perhaps it was my silence or my failure to immediately thank him, but he caught on quickly.

"Don't like it, do you, mate?"

I checked the radar and tried to concoct a plan to dodge the bevy of echoes filling the waterway ahead. "It's not that I don't appreciate what you're doing for us. It's just that I was thinking about 's-Gravenhage."

"The Hague? Good god, man. That's eight hundred kilometers. I ain't got the petrol for that. What do you think I am, some sort of long-range ferry service for American mercenaries?"

I pulled the throttles to their stops and turned to face the captain. "How much? How far? And how long?"

He braced himself as we drifted to a stop against the current. "What are you asking me?"

I locked eyes with the rock-hard British commando. "I'm asking you how much fuel you want me to buy because I don't care if it costs a million dollars a gallon. I'll write the check. I'm asking you how far you'd want me to take *you* to find your wife's murderer if the roles were reversed and you were on *my* boat. And I'm asking you, Captain, if our roles were indeed reversed, how long would you stand here and negotiate with me before putting a bullet in my head, taking my boat, and driving yourself to The Hague?"

The echoes on the radar drew nearer by the second, but I didn't move. Neither did our darkened vessel. The captain stared back at me, no doubt wondering if his first punch could subdue the American bent on revenge.

I was finished talking, and I was willing to face piracy charges before a British military tribunal or whatever they have over there. The Hague was my best opportunity to sit at a tiny metal table at a streetside café, across from a real spy with real connections, who could do some of the cloak-and-dagger stuff nobody thinks is real, and put me in front of Scott Delauter. The one thing standing between me and that meeting was the closest thing to a Navy SEAL the Brits had, and I wasn't certain I'd win the fight.

He stood, just as I expected, but he didn't lunge, and his hand didn't become a fist. Instead, it became a pointed finger between the two of us, and it landed on my chest.

"Let me make one thing crystal clear, American. The day will come when I will ring your bell, and I will not be asking for the return of a favor. I will be calling in this marker that you're signing tonight. When this happens, you will not hesitate. You will not falter. You will step to my side, or if necessary, you will step between me and whatever threat I am facing, and you will destroy that threat without question. Look into my eyes and make me know that you understand this better than anything you have ever known in your life, American."

As if I were going to rip his shirt from his body, I grabbed it with both hands and shook him so violently the muddy body of the English Channel felt it. "You listen to me, Captain. You put me and my men on dry ground in The Hague, there isn't an army on Earth or a demon in Hell I won't slay for you, so help me, God."

The lunge I expected came, but it wasn't at me. It was toward the throttles, and the captain's hands shoved them to their stops, sending the wheel hard over just in time to avoid the bow of a freighter that would've sent us to the bottom like a child's bath toy.

The lights came on, and the captain said, "Get some sleep, American. You've got a long road ahead, and you're going to need the rest."

Chapter 21
Mongo's New Clothes

I left the pilothouse, still uncertain that the captain wasn't going to slit my throat. I'd been out of line, but my points were valid, especially with a war fighter of Millgood's caliber. His quid-pro-quo demand spoke volumes and even suggested he might occasionally step outside the stringent world of the Queen's rigid rulebook to take on some off-the-books vigilante work of his own. At the very least, I'd met and solidified a bond with a true brother-in-arms. In my world, I'd take a single friend in a low place over a dozen high-placed ones any day.

As I passed through the main cabin of the vessel, the revelry of earlier was clearly winding down, and I took a seat among the mix of American operators and British fighters. "We're going to The Hague."

No one reacted. Not a single expression changed, and not a sound left a tongue, with one exception—Anastasia Robertovna Burinkova flinched, and Chase Daniel Fulton noticed and wanted to know why. I did not, however, want to take her by her beautiful hand and search for a secluded compartment on the boat Fancy-Pants called a ship. Those weren't the rumors, or truths, I needed swirling about the crew . . . his or mine.

"The captain says it's eight hundred kilometers. That's five hundred miles for us colonist traitors, and it'll require at least one fuel stop."

"It ain't eight hundred kilometers from 'ere," one of the swimmers said, pointing through a porthole. "See, yonder? That thar's Lizard

Light. Ain't but seven hundred from 'ere. I've done it in me twelve-meter and won twice single-handed, I have."

"Much better," I said. "Is there a place on this fine vessel where a shipwrecked crew and a fellow sailor might lay down their weary heads for a couple of hours?"

"Sure, there is," he said. "Take them stairs there, and you can have our bunks for the night. They ain't much, and I wouldn't put girlie there in Dingo's bunk if I was you."

Anya said, "And which one of us would be girlie?"

The swimmers froze for a moment and pointed at Mongo.

Our Russian giggled. "That is what I thought. Now, which one is Dingo?"

"Oh, we don't let him inside 'ere. Up topside, he is, likely howlin' at the moon."

"There is no moon," Anya said.

"Don't tell him that."

They were right. The racks weren't much, but they were better than sleeping on the steel deck. Cold War submariners probably had more luxurious digs, but the canvas laced into aluminum frames kept us from rolling out, even when we passed close abeam something big enough to nearly swamp us in the channel. Sleep was scarce, but the rest was a welcome relief from the day we'd spent trying to crash the Herk and ride the rapids of the open ocean in Slider's life raft.

Morning came both far too slowly and way too fast. The sun that broke through the slit-like portlights was more gray than orange, and I wondered if the sun ever really shone east of Greenland.

My boots hit the deck at the instant Anya's hand landed in mine. "We need to have conversation privately."

"Good morning to you, too."

"Yes, of course, good morning. Where can we talk?"

"Can't the rest of the team hear whatever you have to tell me?"

"This is your choice, but it might make you sound like not so good leader. You make decision."

"Fine, but I need coffee first."

She said, "You will not find coffee. Only tea. I will make for you and meet you on back of boat. It will be warmer with less noise there."

"As you wish, Princess Buttercup."

She cocked her head. "Gwynn said to me same thing, and I did not understand. Maybe you will explain to me."

"Maybe. Just don't start calling me Farm Boy."

She shrugged. "I saw you with horses and Pogonya. Maybe this is not such bad name for you."

A Special Boat Service swimmer came through the bay with a laundry bag in one hand and an eye on each of us as he passed. He held up a pair of pants and said, "These will have to do, but they'll be a bit short. Do you care for boxers or briefs?"

"Are they Dingo's?" I asked.

He laughed. "Oh, heavens, no. He doesn't wear underpants."

"Then, boxers sound great."

"Good choice, mate. Here you go. Shower, such as it is, is frough there, and I'll take your dirties."

Interesting. Laundry service from the British special forces. I can't wait to see what they give Mongo.

I crammed myself into the smallest shower I'd used since I lived aboard *Aegis*, my first sailboat, but the fresh water felt nice, and my prosthetic appreciated the maintenance. The pants were short, just as promised, but they were much better than the saltwater-dampened pair that fit.

I met Anya at the stern rail, and she handed over the somewhat warm cup of tea. "You have kept me waiting, and you went shopping."

"Something like that. There's a shower and some clean clothes in there if you'd like to freshen up."

"I would, thank you, but I will wait until after we talk. Drink your tea. It will be cold."

I emptied the cup. "Oh, that's good. Thank you."

"Of course it is. I made it for you. Everything I have ever made for you is better. Think of our daughter."

"She rarely leaves my mind."

"Mine also," she said. "She adores you, Chasechka."

"Is that what you called me back here to talk about?"

She looked away. "No, but is truth."

"Yeah, I know. And I adore her. I only wish I had known her from the moment she was born."

"It was not possible. You know this, and you know why."

I wasn't so sure I knew either of those things, but that chilly morning in the English Channel wasn't the time or place for that discussion or that fight.

"So, what's this thing that's going to make me look like a terrible leader?"

She turned back abruptly. "I did *not* say this. You could never look like terrible leader. You are best of leaders. All of us would follow you into any fight, no matter the odds. You know this. I hope I did not make you think I was questioning your—"

I took her arms in my hands. "No, no, you didn't. Just tell me what's on your mind."

"You do not have real plan for The Hague, do you?"

I sighed. "No, not really."

"You cannot walk inside city looking for man in trench coat and hat and ask if he is spy."

"I suppose you've got a better plan."

Anya said, "You should maybe hope I have better plan."

"Okay, please tell me you have a plan."

"Do not worry, my Chasechka. I do, and I will find for you perfect spy, but you may not call him, or her, this name."

"What should I call them?"

"Whatever I tell to you."

"As you wish."

She drank the last of her tea. "Where is shower and clothes? I will look ridiculous in British uniform."

"You've never looked ridiculous in anything."

She smiled for the first time in my recent memory, and I saw our perfect daughter in her face. Then I heard Penny's voice singing in the spray again.

* * *

Anya was right. She looked a little bit ridiculous in British pants, but for the first time in history, nobody was looking at her. All eyes were on Mongo. The captain had just lost the title of Fancy-Pants, and rightfully so.

"Go ahead," Mongo said. "Somebody, please laugh at me. If I don't kill you, Dingo will. He stayed up all night making these for me while the rest of you jokers cuddled up and slept in your nice warm beds."

"In our defense," Kodiak said, "nobody cuddled, and there's nothing nice or warm about any of those racks."

I think Gator was joking when he eyed Anya and asked, "Are we sure nobody cuddled?"

It seemed Anya wasn't so sure he was joking. In an instant, a pair of fighting knives appeared from somewhere near the waistline of her new pants and came to rest a fraction of an inch from Gator's nose. "We are very sure no one cuddled, unless it was you and maybe Englishman."

Silence ruled the moment until the swimmers who'd sewn Mongo's new clothes giggled. "Oh, me likes her."

The moment came to a halt when the captain approached. "Mr. Fulton, you will come with me, if you please."

As it turned out, I did please . . . whatever that meant. We made our way through a pair of companionways barely wide enough for my shoulders and into a compartment I assumed was his quarters. He had a real mattress, but it clearly wasn't from Buckingham Palace.

"Is everything all right, Captain?"

He sat at one end of the rack and motioned toward the other. "For now, but I can't speak for the remainder of your day. I'll have you in

The Hague inside three hours. I see our quartermaster, such as he is, managed something to wear while he's tidying up your kits."

I tugged at the britches. "He did, and we appreciate that. You and your crew have been more than accommodating."

"We covered that last night, you and me. Things are straight between us. We're men of action, not words, are we not?"

"We are," I said.

"Speaking of that action," he said, "I have the impression you and your men might be more the knockin'-heads types than the sneakin'-about-in-shadows blokes. Would I be on the mark there?"

"You would be."

"Thought so. That's why I sent a wire to an old schoolmate of mine overnight—an old chum you might say. We took the different path, we did. His was a bit moss-covered while mine had a bit more blood and smoking shell casing about, if you get my meaning."

We may have spoken the same language on paper, but in practice, I was lagging. He saw it on my face and drew a knife from his boot. I hadn't expected that, but there was nothing threatening about the move.

The captain picked at something beneath a fingernail with the gleaming point of the blade. "You're dangling out a bit on this one, ain't you, brover? Working wiffout a net, as they say."

"You might say that. I'm accustomed to a high-tech network, nearly bottomless pocketbooks, state-of-the-art equipment, and an operation center MI-Six would drool over."

"Exactly what I thought," he said. "The girl, is she Russian, Ukrainian, or Belarusian?"

"Russian by birth. KGB and SVR by education and training. American by heart and by choice."

It wasn't threatening, but he tapped the worn tip of his knife against my chest. "How much of *you* is in that heart and choice of hers?"

"A good bit, I suppose."

"How solid is she?"

I'd been asked a billion questions in my life, and I'd given almost as many answers, but I'd never answered one with as much confidence as I did that morning somewhere between England and France and a universe away from home. "A hundred percent, Captain."

"I'm going to put you ashore and introduce you to a man named Nigel Anderson. He's my schoolmate I told you about. Maybe that's the name his dear old mother gave him, or maybe it ain't, and you ain't gonna ask 'im. As I said, he laces his leather shoes and treads on mossy stones and sidewalks with butts of cigarettes in their gutters. I've worn the boots of the Queen's soldier since I could be called a man. Gettin' the picture, are you?"

"I think so," I said.

"So, this gent, Nigel, he's not your man, but he knows your man . . . or at least the man of that Russian of yours. You better hope she is what you believe, 'cause if she ain't, she'll get the whole lot of you killed, and probably me to go with you before this is finished. I'll tell you by all that's holy, I wish I'd never been dragged into none of it."

"Me too, Captain."

He studied the well-worn blade in his hand. "Ever killed a man with a knife?"

I nodded.

"Filthy business, eh?"

"Sure is," I said.

"Got yours with you?"

My response clearly wasn't what he was expecting. I laughed, and he recoiled.

When I drew my Leatherman, he seemed to understand. "I've never slit any throats with this one. Anya's our slicer and dicer." I drew my highly customized Glock, spun the muzzle away from the captain, and offered him the butt. "This is my guillotine of choice."

He accepted the offered weapon, racked the slide, locked it to the rear, caught the ejected 9mm round in the air, dropped the magazine, and examined the polymer and steel tool of our shared trade. As he seemed to stare through my favorite piece of weaponry with what might've been a bit of disdain, he slipped the handle of his blade into my palm and said, "I've never fired the American Glock."

"It's not American," I said. "It's Austrian. Well, that one's a little bit American, but the frame was built in Austria. I've done some tweaking."

He thumbed the release, dropping the slide, and raised the weapon into perfect firing position. "And how many times have you heard the awful, dreaded click when you pressed the plastic, American trigger?"

"I've only put maybe a million rounds through that one, but just like every one of my men out there, and especially the Russian, it's never failed to fire."

He locked the slide to the rear, reloaded the ejected round, and slammed the magazine home before slipping my pistol into his belt. With a flourish, he motioned to his scarred and tattered knife. "And neither has that one."

Just as he'd done with my Glock, I slipped his blade into my belt. I didn't understand the tradition, if it was in fact a tradition. Maybe Dingo could explain it to me.

Believing our exchange had reached its end, I stood, but the captain placed a gentle hand on my shoulder. "Tell me, Fulton. Do you know who Prince Yusupov was?"

"He killed Rasputin."

At that moment, the captain did something I wasn't certain he was capable of doing. He smiled. "The way I hear it, the prince cut off a few of the mad monk's favorite parts with a knife that was a lot like the one you just tucked away. Would it be outta bounds for a man in command of the best team he's ever known to ask somefin' of another such man?"

"Ask anything you'd like, my friend."

He locked eyes with me. "Should you be given the honor, may you make the man who killed your wife know my blade just as Rasputin knew Prince Yusupov's."

Chapter 22
The Only Real Spy

The Hague was not what I expected, but the captain's British boat drew no more attention in the small harbor than an errant rowboat. One of his men tossed a line to a boy ashore, who made it fast around a cleat that was probably older than the country I called home.

"How much cash do you have?" Captain Millgood asked.

"Maybe a couple thousand American and a thousand euros."

He curled his hand, and I followed him back to his cabin, where he spun the dial on a shoebox-size safe. "Give me your dollars. They'll only get you killed."

I handed over the bills, and he stuck a respectable stack of well-used euros in my palm.

"Pocket half and dole out the rest to your men, save the big one. I'm takin' him with me. I gave Anya five thousand of her own. She knows what to do with it."

"Did you say you're taking Mongo?"

"'Course I am."

"That won't work for me."

"O'er here, he'll do nothin' but get you killed, or worse, shunned."

"What are you talking about?" I asked.

"Look around out there. You're bigger than all of 'em yourself, man. What are you, one ninety?"

"One ninety what, pounds?"

"No, centimeters," he said as if that's how my brain was supposed to work.

"I have no idea. I'm six feet four inches, whatever that is in British English."

He locked the safe and laughed. "Close enough to one ninety, and your ship's mast of a mate out there is over two solid meters. Ashore in Holland, no one, not even my mate, Nigel, would be seen with him. You're a stretch yourself. I'll take care of him and deliver him back to ya, fit and fair. Don't you fret none."

I stuck out a hand, and he accepted. "You be well, mate. And don't be gettin' yourself killed, ya hear?"

"I'll do my best. Thanks for everything, Captain, but are you sure you've got enough provisions on board to feed my giant?"

"Let's make it James, shall we? And I'll make him fish for his supper if I must."

"James, it is, then. So, about that petrol bill?"

He said, "It weren't no million per liter, but I think the Queen can manage."

"Fair enough."

With the boat tied loosely, we stepped from the gunwale onto the centuries-old seawall.

The swimmer holding the line leaned close. "Split apart and walk in twos. You stay with the Russian cutie. That makes you the lucky one, I reckon. The others can mill about like tourists eatin' and drinkin'. Try not to look like you look. There ain't nobody dangerous about, so don't be startin' no fights. The cap'n gave you some spendin' money, yeah?"

I nodded and slipped my hand into the Russian cutie's, just like a tourist would do.

Leaving Mongo behind tied my stomach in a knot I wouldn't soon be able to untwist, but for reasons I couldn't explain, I trusted Captain Fancy-Pants.

Anya squeezed my fingers between hers and whispered, "You are pretending, yes?"

"What do you mean?"

She squeezed again. "That I am her."

I pulled my hand from hers. "No, that's not what I'm doing."

She wasted no time in reclaiming my hand. "Is okay, Chasechka. I will be for you whatever you need."

"Right now, what I need is that rock-hard Russian who almost killed me on St. Thomas. I need that girl with those instincts, those wits, and that gut. I need you to disappear like a chameleon when necessary, and I need you to cut a man in half when that's what needs to be done."

Those frozen Siberian eyes that could drive stars from the sky made their return. "And I am also to be 'hold hand and be girlfriend tourist in European city.'"

"How are we going to find this Nigel guy?"

"*We* are not going to find him," she said. "I am going to find him, but I have first question."

"So, what's your question?"

"When you said you need gut of Russian girl on St. Thomas"—she pulled my hand toward her and placed it on her stomach—"did you mean gut as in instinct, or firm and flat like this?"

I didn't want to smile, but resisting was impossible, and Siberian ice turned into warm turquoise water of the Caribbean.

We walked for half an hour, just as tourists would.

"Do these people have some moral opposition to cars over here?"

She said, "City is large, maybe one-half million people, but most walk or ride bicycle. There are many cable cars and buses. Some have cars, but is not like America."

"How about the hedges? Where are they?"

She frowned. "What hedges?"

"Hague means hedges, right?"

"It used to. That is hundreds of years ago, silly boy. Come, I will show to you Plein."

"Plane as in airplane, or plane as in simple?"

"Do not be so American all of time."

I stopped in my tracks, stepped in front of her, and slipped two fingers into her left front pocket.

She raised her eyebrows. "I think this is not appropriate, sir."

When I finally found what I was looking for, I pulled the plastic, two-inch Stars and Stripes from her pocket and twirled it between my fingers. "I think perhaps Betsy Rossonova may be calling me 'too American.'"

She grabbed the trinket she'd carried for years and shoved it back into her pocket. "Do not do that."

"Why not? We're tourists, remember?"

She rolled her eyes. "You should have been baseball player."

"No, you're wrong about that."

"What? I have never heard you say this. Why do you now believe you should have not been American professional baseball player for Braves of Atlanta?"

I took both of her hands instead of just the one. "Because if I had become a pro ballplayer, we never would've had Pogonya."

Before that instant, I could've counted the tears I'd seen fall from Anya Burinkova's eyes on one hand. Even if I still had all ten of my natural toes and my fingers, I couldn't have come close in those few seconds. She buried her face against my chest and became a mere mortal with real emotions, if only for that fleeting moment. Part of me loved it, but something about it also made me worried that the focus I needed from the deadliest woman I'd ever known wasn't on point.

Before she pulled away, she whispered something in Russian that I pretended not to hear and chose not to acknowledge.

When her face appeared, her eyes were dry and focused, and she was expressionless. That's exactly what I expected from the honor graduate from the Yuri Andropov Red Banner Institute—if the CIA's file on my make-believe European girlfriend-for-the-day was accurate.

"Was all of that an act for our friend Nigel?"

"Not all of it," she said. "I have never heard you say anything so nice as what you said about Pogonya. Did you really mean she is more important to you than baseball?"

I squeezed her hand. "Anya, our daughter is more important to me than anything else."

"Even more important than finding Scott Delauter?"

Before I had to force an answer from somewhere between my gut and my soul, an undeniably British voice spoke from inches behind me. "Release her hand, Dr. Fulton, and continue walking at a slightly increased pace, if you please. I assure you, neither of you is in any danger."

Everything in me wanted to throat-punch the man who'd somehow stepped close enough to whisper in my ear without me hearing or sensing him being there, but Anya put me at ease by gently tapping my hand with two fingers and pressing me forward.

I didn't look back, but I scoured the area for absolutely anything reflective. I needed to see his face, his height, shape, dress, anything. There were no storefronts, no windshields, and not even a person wearing eyeglasses. Nigel, and I had to assume the man was Nigel, was very good.

Precisely eight strides ahead, I reached my limit and turned. Four dozen people milled about as if they had absolutely no agenda of any kind. Six carried umbrellas as if they were walking canes. Four were talking on cell phones. Eleven wore earbuds or headphones. And nine rode bicycles. The remainder could've been anyone from anywhere, except Nigel Anderson or Anya Burinkova.

Kodiak's voice appeared as if it were coming from the two-hundred-year-old wall beside me. "Five feet ten inches tall, a hundred eighty pounds, light brown jacket just past his hips over dark pants tailored well and cut to break just above good shoes. The shoes were dark brown with relatively new soles, heels, and laces. They'd been polished within the last day or two. His shirt was olive with blue pinstripes. Montblanc pen that looked out of place. Hat was wool and not new. He wore it tilted maybe half an inch to the back. Plain watch, leather band. No other jewelry."

I smiled and followed Kodiak's voice into a coffee shop. He ordered two cups of something—I didn't care what—and we sat in the front corner by the window.

"Good eyes. How long have you been shadowing us?"

Kodiak took a sip. "Hmm. This is pretty good. I've been on you for three or four minutes. We've been leapfrogging."

"That probably wasn't him," I said.

He took another sip. "Yeah, probably not, but it was somebody, and Anya didn't seem concerned."

"Who's on them now?"

"Shawn," he said.

"I sure wish Clark was here."

Kodiak laughed. "Clark Johnson in Denmark . . . Now, that's a picture."

I took my first sip and agreed with Kodiak's assessment. "I've been all around the world with him, and he's as good as they come. He could be wearing a clown suit and squeaky shoes and sneak up on a polar bear on an iceberg."

"Yeah, I know. It's just that he would've choked the guy out and stolen his Montblanc."

"You're probably right. Speaking of the pen, why did you say it didn't fit?"

He shrugged. "I don't know. Everything else was so common and tidy. No Rolex. No Italian loafers. No rings. And the pen was crooked in his pocket."

"Maybe the guy's got a thing for nice pens."

"Maybe, but for my money, it's a mic or a tracker."

I took another sip. "You're right about the coffee, but it's stout. What bothers you about the pen being either of those things?"

He said, "Nothing, as long as the dude is Nigel or one of his guys. If he's not, we just lost the only real spy we've got."

A single knock came at the window of the coffee shop, and Kodiak stood. I followed, and we headed for the door. When we hit the sidewalk, Shawn rounded the corner half a block away.

Kodiak said, "You take him and tell him I'll meet him at Falke."

The Arctic survival specialist turned espionage guru vanished, and I suddenly felt like I was wearing a flashing light on my head and dragging a banner declaring myself to be the world's worst covert operative.

I rounded the same corner I'd watched Shawn make, but he wasn't there. A street performer with a guitar caught my eye, though, and my search was over. I don't know the Dutch word for ice cream, but I learned it had about four hundred letters in it, and it was plastered on the glass windows of the shop directly across from the guitarist.

"They don't have those flat little wooden spoons over here. Who knew?"

It was impossible to predict what Shawn was going to say, but it was always going to make me feel better. He stuck a paper bowl of ice cream and a real spoon in my hand.

"Thanks. Who's on Anya now?"

He filled his mouth with a glob of cream in a color for which there is no English word. When most of it slid down his throat, he said, "Gator, but don't worry. He's doing fine. Singer's backing him up."

I took a bite. "This is good. Have you had the coffee?"

"Coffee ice cream? No, I'm not into that."

"No, I meant real coffee."

He said, "Oh, yeah. I had some. It's pretty good. So, anyway, the original dude, hat guy, handed Anya off to another guy."

I put down my ice cream. "You could've led with that."

He said, "I tried, but you wanted to talk about coffee. He's a little guy. Maybe five three or four and a buck forty. Late fifties, maybe sixty. Round, wire-framed glasses. Grey hair, balding, one of those Andy Capp hats. Tweed jacket, light blue shirt, brown corduroy pants, worn-out leather lace-up shoes."

"That sounds like our guy."

He shoveled in another mouthful of ice cream. "That's what I thought. Oh, and the first guy passed off the ink pen to the second guy."

"What did he do with it?"

"He stuck it in the left pocket of his jacket."

"The breast pocket or the waist pocket?" I asked.

Shawn patted his left hip.

I nodded. "Got it. Kodiak told me to tell you he'd meet you at Falke, whatever that is."

Shawn pointed at my paper bowl. "You gonna finish that?"

I pushed it toward him, and he polished it off. "I know this isn't really our kind of gig, but don't worry. You heard what those swimmers said. This whole place is an old hunting ground. When was the last time you knew any of us to go hunting and not come home with a trophy to hang on the wall and a freezer full of meat?"

Feeling better is what Shawn made me do, and he wasn't finished.

He asked, "Have you heard of a place called Plein around here?"

I nodded, and he said, "There's a big statue of an orange guy out there. He must be a Tennessee graduate. I don't know. Anyway, there's a café on the south side of the square with a bunch of tables and umbrellas. Buy something that'll take you a long time to eat, and we'll find you."

"I'm pretty sure that guy is William of Orange."

"Did he go to Tennessee?" he asked.

"Probably not."

Chapter 23

Semper Fi Welcome

I'm ashamed to admit that I wasn't sure exactly what William of Orange did or who he was, but he didn't look like a Tennessee Volunteer at all. His statue was impressive, though, and the Dutch pigeons seemed to especially like it. I tried to look less like a tourist, but that's more challenging than most people realize. There's a lot to see the first time in a new city.

I had no fear of anyone taking a shot at me. Just as Captain Millgood said, I was bigger than most everyone else in the hedge, so the thought of anyone running up to pick a fight hadn't entered my mind either. I strolled across the square of a port town that was nearly a thousand years old, and I thought it should've had cobblestones, but it didn't. It was paved mostly of brick laid in a herringbone pattern, but I couldn't understand why. I suppose I'd tuck that curiosity away in my little black bag of European mysteries, like my Russian, who was somewhere in the city. She was no doubt doing one of three things: learning from Nigel Anderson how and where to find Delauter, being handed off between British spies on her way to finally meeting Anderson, or gutting somebody like pig because they wouldn't take her directly to Anderson. My money was on options one or three.

Doing what I was told had never been my preferred way of whiling away the hours, but when in Rome . . . or The Hague. So, I ordered a couple of things I couldn't pronounce—Gugen-flufen and Haagendorkinboog, or something. They cost eighteen euros, and when I tried to get the Dutch teenager behind the register to keep the change, she seemed to believe that I was from another planet. I was on the verge of agreeing with her.

When the Hoogin-doogin-flippin-floopin showed up at my table, they were a gorgeous sandwich and a bundt cake the size of a softball. I hoped one of the things I ordered was something to drink, so I made the universal signal of pretending to lift a cup to my mouth, and the waitress returned an even more common signal by showing me her palms.

I also hadn't a clue what the Dutch word for water was, but the good old American word did the trick and cost me three more euros. Still, though, the concept of a tip sent the girl into a tailspin. I was going to run out of room in my little black bag of things I didn't understand, and I suddenly wished Clark were sitting across the table from me to help with my Dutch pronunciation skills. I tried to laugh only on the inside, but it was impossible. He would somehow have the pigtailed waitresses eating from the palm of his hand, even though he'd butcher even the simplest of their lexicon.

I missed having him on operations with me. I missed his lessons. But most of all, I missed knowing that he was always exactly where I needed him to be, every time, without exception. If a would-be assassin's blade were inches from my throat, Clark's supersonic pistol round would be millimeters from the man's temple. If the rotten timber of the bridge from which I was hanging were an instant from giving way, Clark would be drifting beneath in a Zodiac, a cocktail in one hand and a pair of bikini-clad beauties in the bow waiting for me to land amidships. It was uncanny, but I suppose guardian angels come in all shapes and sizes. Mine just happened to have a crooked smile and a penchant for good whiskey and young brunettes. I missed Clark without question, but that wild-haired woman who loved me no matter how many times I got hurt halfway around the world, and whose smile could always erase every pain I felt, no matter how deep, was the one person I'd never stop longing to hold again—the one voice I'd hear every time I closed my eyes, and the hand I'd forever reach out for each time I closed my eyes to fall asleep.

The past forty-eight hours of my life had been spent without a cell phone, satellite phone, or radio. In many ways, it had been beyond terrifying, but something about sitting alone and silent at a cast-iron table, beneath an umbrella, eating a plorken-klofpfor and maggen-fiendor in a place named for some hedges a thousand years ago, was peace that my mind, body, and soul needed more than I could've known. And peace was something I'd forgotten could exist.

Something else occurred to me as I sat there with my sandwich, cake, and water in a city between the hedges where men hunted, likely with their dogs, for hundreds of years. Dooley Field at Sanford Stadium, where my beloved Georgia Bulldogs tore up the gridiron on warm autumn Saturday afternoons at my alma mater, boasted two rows of hedges known as Chinese privet bushes. Just like every other UGA graduate, I once knew the botanical name for the sacred bushes. It was something like *Ligustrum sinense*, but that's probably not exactly right. Although I played a real sport that required hitting a two-point-nine-inch piece of leather, cork, and twine racing through the air at a hundred miles per hour with a two-point-six-inch bat, those hedges on that football field named for the legendary Vince Dooley were a staple and glorious Georgia tradition since before the Great Depression. And there I was, nearly a hundred years later, still between the hedges and still a Dawg on the hunt.

The waitress who'd delivered my water reappeared and took a knee beside my chair. She leaned close. "*Spreek je Russisch.*"

I screwed up my face. "Do you have any English?"

She made the same face and asked, "*Ty govorish' po-Russki?*"

It wasn't English, but it was close enough. "*Da! YA govoryu po-Russki.*"

We'd found a common language. Her Russian may not have been great, but communication had suddenly become possible.

I wondered, *What about me led her to think Russian was the best place to start? Why not German or Spanish? Either would've worked, but why Russian? All right. Let's give it a go in old Russki.*

She spoke slowly, and her grammar wasn't solid, but the pronunciation wasn't bad.

She said, "Do you know where the embassy is?"

"The Russian embassy?"

She nodded. "Da."

"No."

She huffed, and I imagined trying to translate Dutch street names into Russian for an American.

I smiled and said, "Draw me a map with Dutch street names, and I will find it."

I wasn't certain about the Russian verb for the word *draw*, but she seemed relieved and darted away smiling.

She returned in a flash with a colorful map obviously designed for tourists and then pulled a pen from her apron. "*Wij zijn hier.*"

The Dutch came out of her mouth naturally, but I had to direct her back into a language I understood. "*Russki, pozhaluysta.*"

She apologized in some language and continued mostly in Russian. "We are here, and embassy is here, but it is not labeled on map. I do not know why."

"I do," I said.

She laughed. "Da."

I studied the map and turned my attention back to the waitress. "Why do I need to know where the Russian embassy is?"

She bit her bottom lip and closed her eyes for a moment longer than seemed comfortable. "Because that is where the woman said you should go."

"The woman? What woman?"

"The tall, blonde woman."

"Was she Russian?"

"I do not know. She spoke Dutch."

"Dutch? Are you sure?"

She nodded aggressively. "Yes, I know Dutch very well."

I still didn't understand the rules of or the objections to tipping in Holland. Still, in my mind, the young lady and I had departed the land between the hedges. We danced between the frozen world of the tsars and my world of capitalism long enough to justify my insistence on rewarding her for her patience with my ignorance and Americanism. I took her hand in mine and pressed a one-hundred-euro note into her palm. She made a noble effort to reject it, but I folded her fingers around the bill and pointed toward my empty plate.

"That was the best floggen-doogen-horten I've ever had."

She cocked her head in obvious bewilderment, and I laughed and returned to Russian. "Seriously. What is the Dutch word for water?"

She pocketed the tip, grinned, and said, "Water."

* * *

I took one more stroll by the only statue I knew in The Hague, gave old Billy a high-five, and said, "Go Vols!"

It hurt my Georgia Bulldog heart to do it, but I needed a moment of silliness. I was on my way to the Russian embassy on foot, by myself, in a country in which I didn't speak the language. I had no idea where my teammates were, I had no comms, no clothes other than the ones I had on, no weapon other than a British special forces officer's knife I was supposed to mutilate an American traitor's genitals with, and no plan for exfiltration. And the whole world was supposed to believe my team and I perished in a horrific airplane crash off the Irish coast. What could possibly go wrong?

The walk was just under two miles, or whatever unit of measurement the flying Dutchmen used. It took me forty-eight minutes for three reasons:

I doubled back six times, searching for anyone tailing me, and honestly, I hoped I'd find someone. My choice would've been the tall Russian blonde I brought with me, but in that moment, Shawn would've done nicely. What I didn't want to find tagging along was an operative I couldn't identify. To my dismay, though, either I was terrible at street tradecraft, or there was no one in my wake.

The second reason my trek was slow was because I was endlessly amused by how many letters the Dutch could cram onto a street sign that spelled absolutely nothing any sane human could pronounce.

Finally, I was stalling. I didn't want to go to the Russian embassy.

I finally found the ridiculous address of Andries Bickerweg 2, 2517 JP Den, The Hague, and I walked past it as if I were on a midday stroll in search of a dike to stick my thumb into. Folks in the espionage business call that a reconnaissance pass, but I called it a cowardly avoidance of the inevitable. I kick down doors and shoot people in the face. I don't pass secret envelopes in shadowy alleyways while wearing a trench coat.

I'd seen a lot of embassies in my time, regardless of my job description. I'd even run toward a great many of them, firing a pistol over my shoulder while blood was spurting from my body and I was screaming, "I'm an American! Open the gate and shoot the guys behind me!"

Hollywood never gets it right, but Marines love it when you do that. I've learned that if there's anybody in the area above the rank of kindergartener, they'll usually throw open the gate and put a few hundred holes in the bad guys. That's one of the things I love about Marines. They have a mindset of taking care of right-now problems right now and worrying about tomorrow-problems tomorrow. I dig that.

I'd never tried that trick at a Russian embassy, but something tells me I wouldn't get the same Semper Fi welcome.

The embassy was a gorgeous three-story mansion, painted brilliant white, with a medallion of the Russian Federation mounted boldly— as Russians tend to do—on the second floor. There was a somewhat modest-looking two- or maybe three-car garage out back and cameras everywhere. The former Soviets do love their lenses. The thing I didn't see was humans. A few SUVs and a spattering of sedans, all with blacked-out glass, were parked in positions that would make them quite easy to mount and drive away without using reverse. It made me proud to see that the FSB, SVR, GRB—or whatever collection of meaningless letters they threw together to name the intelligence service behind the well-locked doors of the mansion—were still smart enough to avoid nosing into a parking space. I wouldn't want them to make things too easy for us Americans.

Why am I here? What is behind those walls that I need to see, hear, taste, or smell? I don't want their vodka, and I don't even like caviar. Their girls aren't bad, but the only one I'm interested in is fifteen years old, has half my DNA, and a weird affection for demon horses.

With no idea what I was going to say when I rang the bell, I took my first intentional stride toward the gate. The list of reasons the Russians would like to tie my ankles together and drag me to Red Square was longer than the Dutch street signs. I couldn't come up with any reason they would want me behind that fence and inside those walls that could possibly benefit me.

A few steps before the dreaded black button I didn't want to press, a voice filled the air behind me. "Jolly good. Good of you to come, old boy."

I turned to see the man Shawn had described to a T.

Instead of sticking out his hand like any normal human would do, he threw an arm across my shoulder. "Nigel Anderson's the name. I understand you know my mate, Jimmy Millgood."

"We've met," I said. "He had a lot to say about your shoes, if I remember correctly."

He cast his head back and roared with laughter, exposing a mouthful of mismatched teeth. "Indeed. He is a bit of a man's man, isn't he? A believer that a man should be a wearer of boots and a bearer of arms, if I'm not wrong, he is."

"That'd be a fair description."

He patted my waistline. "Old Jimmy wouldn't have bestowed upon you a weapon, now, would he?"

I glanced up, identifying as many of the Russian cameras as I could find, and turned my back to them. "Just a knife."

"That'll never do. Those damned Soviets'll make great sport of keeping that for a trophy, for sure. Give it up, old boy. I'll manage the thing."

I slid the blade from concealment and slipped it into his palm. Keeping himself well in my shadow between my heft and the Russian's camera array, he vanished into a row of thick shrubbery and returned as if having relieved himself. "Sorry about that, but sometimes, a man can't wait. You understand, I'm sure. Let's go see these chaps, shall we? I think you'll like what they have to say."

I pressed a firm palm into his chest. "Where's Anya?" I'd never seen a horse with worse teeth.

"Fancy that one, do you? I can certainly see why. She's quite the prize. Rest assured, my good man. She's quite fine in every way and managing precisely the bit of business you would no doubt have her do. Come, come now. No time to waste. You know how these Russians are . . . a fastidious lot when it comes to tardiness."

Chapter 24

A Tank in the Dining Room

"Tardiness?" I asked. "Did somebody make us an appointment?"

Nigel pushed up his sleeve and raised his chin just as my favorite psych professor and mentor, Dr. Robert Richter, used to do when he peered through his bifocals. "Not exactly, but nonetheless, we shan't be discourteous."

"Shan't? This whole thing is starting to feel and smell like a giant crock of shan't if you ask me. What's going to happen in there, Nigel?"

He adjusted his hat. "Oh, you Americans and your bloody irreverent tongues. Just come along and have a bit of faith, won't you?"

I was running short on faith in British spies, or whatever Nigel was, if, in fact, the cat I was following was Nigel at all. For all I knew, he could've been Ivan Petrov with an Oxford education and accent.

I was walking into a trap. Everything in my gut knew it. I'd been disarmed, separated from my team, and I was steps away from being taken into custody by the Kremlin. It was a fancy, well-manicured finger of the Kremlin, but the Kremlin, nonetheless.

Nigel pressed no button, lifted no phone, inserted no key. He merely pushed open the black iron gate with the crest of the Russian Federation embossed at eye level—well, eye level for him. For me, it was spitting level, and I took full advantage of the golden opportunity. I wondered how many cameras caught it, and even more, I wondered if they'd give me a copy of the tape if I survived.

I followed my tour guide down the southern wall of the embassy. "What? We're not going in the front door?"

He'd obviously either grown tired of my sarcasm or realized I'd grown wise to the game he and his fur-hat-wearing comrades inside were playing on the American who was supposed to be too smart to fall into such an elementary snare.

I was furious, but more than rage, I was determined. Determined to find a weapon, kill everybody inside the wrought iron fence, and get home to Pogonya. I should've wanted to take her flying. I should've wanted to sail around the world with her. I should've wanted to watch her grow into the most beautiful and brilliant woman the world had ever seen. But to my utter disbelief, I wanted to go horseback riding with her along the North River. The only thing standing between me and that ride with my daughter were three dozen extremely well-armed and incredibly well-trained foreign service officers with more cameras and microphones than Warner Bros. Studios. But a psychotic horse named Pecan and I destroyed a hundred-year-old barn together, so surely I could take care of a few leftover KGB wannabe commies and get home to my little girl.

Nigel turned at the rear of the embassy and climbed the four steps onto what the Russians call a *porog*. At Bonaventure, I called it the back gallery. I didn't follow him for two reasons: First, I wanted to have a peek inside the garage. I'd never seen a Russian T-90 main battle tank in person, and I was sort of hoping there'd be one in there that I could take for a joyride through the formal dining room of the embassy. The second reason was to test the foreign service officers' response time when I didn't remain in locked step with comrade Nigel.

I was disappointed on both fronts. There was no tank in the garage, and there was no response time at all. No one came to fetch me. When I turned to look for the AK-47-wielding Reds, I only saw Nigel with his arms crossed and tapping a foot like a disgusted schoolmaster.

I took one final hopeful glance into the garage—still no tank—and climbed the stairs to the porog.

Nigel didn't have the same access to the back door as he had to the front gate, and that interested me. He lifted an iron cap and pressed a recessed button with his thumb for several seconds. I'd never rung the doorbell at any embassy, especially not a Russian version, but the amount of time he spent with the button depressed surprised me.

Several bolts released inside the doorframe, and it opened outward. Suddenly, I had a reason to like these guys. It's tough to kick in a door that opens outward, and for an old door-kicker like me, that earned at least part of a point for respect.

A rutty-faced man in his thirties exposed just enough of his head and shoulder around the heavy door to demonstrate his understanding of entryway security, and that earned one more fraction of a point for the bad guys.

Seemingly convinced that Nigel and I were no threat, or at least one he could manage, the man pressed the door further and said, "*Pozhaluysta, voydite.*"

Nigel led the way, and I said, "*Spasibo.*"

The man showed no surprise that I understood his invitation to come inside, nor that I thanked him in Russian. His suit was cheap, but it fit nicely, and by all indications, he was unarmed except for what appeared to be a folding knife in his left front pocket.

We rounded a corner, and I let the toe of my boot catch beneath the edge of a carpet. When I stumbled, the Russian turned and extended an arm to keep me from falling. He simultaneously smiled and helped me reestablish my footing. After taking a step backward, he opened his jacket and pointed behind his right hip. His English was terrible, but I appreciated the effort. "Is very small and good hiding back here. You are for this looking, yes?"

He was right. The pistol was quite small and very good hiding. I said, "*Da, prodolzhat'.*"

He led the two of us up a flight of stairs, through a pair of poorly hidden metal detectors, and into a small room with a desk, three chairs, and a painting of Premier Putin.

Nigel sat down, and I nestled into the interesting chair I'd seen and sat in before in the woods of Virginia twenty years earlier.

Nigel crossed his legs and picked at imaginary flecks of nothing on his very British breeches.

I said, "This is going to be fun, isn't it?"

"I should say so."

"You're not staying for the chat, are you?"

He found an actually existent fleck. "I should say not, but you should make a show of tossing me."

"You said I was going to like what they had to say. So far, I'm finding that unlikely."

"Patience, my dear boy. Patience."

The door to the office opened, and Nigel rose. I did not. In walked a fastidious little man I would not have picked to be a Russian intelligence operative of any flavor. Perhaps he could've been an accountant or a patient of some incurable illness, but I doubted that he had a pair of pliers in his pocket with which he planned to remove my fingernails at any point in the coming interview.

The man carried a leather attaché case and a long canvas satchel that rattled with every step. He placed the case on its side and aligned its edges perfectly with the table's limits. He then pulled a glass bottle of water from the canvas bag and placed it on the floor. With a handkerchief he produced from inside his jacket, he created a perfectly square coaster and positioned the water bottle on it. Two glasses came next and landed equidistant from his seat and mine.

My seven years of psychological education found his behavior to be a well-practiced three-ring circus, so I'd play along.

Once he was finally situated in his chair that didn't resemble mine, he said, "*Privet, Naydzhel.*"

My English companion nodded without a word, and the Russian turned to me. "*Angliyski ili Russki?*"

I said, "I choose English. Thank you for asking. That way, when you analyze the biofeedback monitors built into the seat and armrests of this chair, it will be much easier for your analysts to synchronize the data with my answers in my native language. If I have to think in English and then answer in Russian, there will be a delay in the data, and it may skew your results."

A bead of sweat formed on his forehead between his heavy eyebrows. "You are mistaken, Mr. Filtson. We have no reasons to do this."

I shrugged and let out a breath. "I'm sorry. I meant no offense. I'm just a little nervous. This is my first time inside a Russian embassy, and you know, I've read too many spy novels, I guess."

When he reached for his handkerchief, I pointed toward the bottle of water.

His eyes darted wildly. "Oh, yes," he said, and then wiped his brow with the back of his hand.

I wondered if the nervousness was an act or the result of a cocktail of drugs designed to produce the effect. Either way, it was time to have a little fun, so I reached for the bottle, uncorked it, and poured the man a glass. "You look like you could use a drink. Are you okay?"

The Russian lifted the glass, raised it in front of himself, and said, "*Spasibo.*"

Two seconds later, it was empty, and that was rude, even for a Russian. I poured him a drink, but he didn't pour me one. So, as part two of my experiment, I poured myself a glass and placed the bottle half on and half off the folded handkerchief.

The man hadn't hesitated to drink it, so I didn't. It was water, or at least it tasted like water, and it was cold and refreshing. Ice cubes weren't common in Russia, so I was surprised by the temperature of the drink. Perhaps the comrades were growing accustomed to the comforts of the western world of the Dutch.

My interrogator, or whatever he was, seemed to realize he missed the opportunity to pounce on another of his OCD moments and jerked to relocate the bottle to the center of the handkerchief. While he was fiddling with that, I slid my glass a few inches out of place and said, "You haven't introduced yourself yet. You obviously know my name, but I don't know yours. Would you mind?"

"I am sorry. I am Sergei Kozlov, political affairs officer."

"Yes, of course. Nice to meet you, Sergei."

His English wasn't bad, but his acting was terrible.

"So, Sergei, what do you want from me?"

He shuddered. "No. This is wrong. What do you want from us is question."

I squinted. "You think I want something from you?"

"*Da*. Yes. You are here. What is do you want?"

I turned to the Brit. "Okay, Nigel, get out."

"I'm sorry?"

"Get out," I said. "I've had enough. You don't need to be involved in what this is about to become. Just walk away so I don't screw up the arrangement you've got with these guys. I don't want to muck up the works, or whatever it is you call it over here when Americans start breaking stuff."

Nigel leaned toward me. "Listen to me . . ."

"Yeah, I did that already, and you brought me to this clown who wants to play games. I don't have time for it. Get out, and don't you dare touch my knife. That was a gift from a friend, and you don't want him or me unhappy with you. Just walk away. I've got this."

Brits don't have the same facial expressions as us Yanks, but a good ol' American wink is as good as a thousand words, and the spy got the picture. He stood, ignored Sergei, and tapped on the door.

Someone opened it, and Nigel disappeared.

After centering my chair in front of Sergei, I uncorked the bottle and drank it dry without using either glass. I made a show of rolling the bottle across the floor. "The gig's up, dude. Your name's not Sergei. You don't have OCD. And you're the worst liar in the history of Russian liars. By the way, that's a really long list."

I dug three fingers beneath the armrests of my chair and pried the vinyl trim from the metal frame. A collection of brightly colored wires dangled from the trim, and I waved them in front of the man's face. Suddenly, his sweating was real.

"I was trained on these biofeedback chairs two decades ago, liar. You called me Mr. Filtson instead of Dr. Fulton to establish a baseline reaction for the biofeedback monitor, liar. Someone with OCD would never place a bottle of drinking water on the floor, liar. Someone pretending to speak terrible English would never use the Russian word for English before the Russian word for Russian in a sentence, liar."

He swallowed hard and unbuttoned his jacket, so I reached across the table and grabbed his attaché case by the impressive handle that had two extra stainless-steel cables running from beneath the stitching and through the upper flap. With a swing harder than I'd ever swung a baseball bat, I sent the case colliding with the leg of the table between us, releasing the handle and exposing the garrot designed to wrap around a man's neck and end his life in seconds if it were in the hands of a well-trained assassin.

I was across the table and behind him with the wire encircling his neck in an instant. In calm, flawless Russian, I said, "I'm bigger, faster, and stronger. I won't make it out of the building, but you won't make it out of that chair. The game is over. The next man I talk with will be the Russian ambassador, or you get to find out if Russian Orthodoxy was the right choice of religion."

The door opened just as I expected, but it wasn't the muzzle of a Kalashnikov that came through first. It was a ruby-red cuff link against a brilliant white shirt and a deep Russian voice that should've been the first one I heard upon entering the embassy.

"Doctor Fulton. My apologies. I am Ambassador Alexander Shulgin. If you would like to speak with President Putin to verify my identity, that can be arranged."

Chapter 25
Three-Thousand-Euro Clucker

I released the garrot from my right hand, allowing it to fall slack around Sergei's chest, and the nervous little man fell limp in his seat, obviously grateful to be alive.

I turned to the new man in the room. "Hello, Mr. Ambassador. Let's not call Vlad just yet, but maybe there's someplace we can talk where the chairs aren't wired and the interrogators are a little more competent."

His English was solid, but there was no question that his mother tongue had been the same as Anya's and Mr. Putin's. "Certainly. We should continue conversation inside office. We have only one thing to discuss, unless you have questions."

His absence of a jacket made a surprising statement, though it was likely intentional. Russians in the intel game rarely do anything that isn't. He wanted me to believe the situation was casual. Formality tends to breed tension, while more casual settings lead one to feel at ease. I wasn't as uncomfortable as the water boy behind me who was still pawing at his neck, but I was a long way from being at ease.

"Come with me someplace more comfortable, Dr. Fulton."

I glanced back at the guy who wanted me to believe his name was Sergei and tossed him the folded handkerchief. "Take it easy, Mr. Spy Man. You'll be okay."

The ambassador led me to the third floor of the Dutch mansion, where the accommodations were far more Vladimir Lenin and less Albertus Van Raalte. No one followed, and no elegant, former Bolshoi blonde graced an outer office before reaching Shulgin's lair. It was merely stairs, a landing, and a heavy, ornate door.

We stepped through, and he said in Russian, "Close the door."

His office was neat but not overdone. After motioning to a comfortable chair, he settled into its twin a few feet away, nothing but a nicely woven rug between us. "We can use any language you prefer," he said in formal Russian. "I am equally comfortable in yours or mine."

"In that case, Mr. Ambassador, let's make it mine. I don't get to use yours enough to remain what you call 'comfortable.'"

He nodded and motioned toward a small side table. "I have tea, coffee, water, bourbon, and of course, vodka."

"What are you having?" I asked.

Russians don't smile very often, at least not on the outside, but I thought I detected one of those internal versions they try to hide when he said, "Coffee. How do you take it?"

"Black, please."

He poured two cups, and we drank.

"Not bad," I said.

"Is Cuban."

"They have nice soil, those Cubans. So, Mr. Ambassador, thank you for the coffee, but please tell me what that fiasco downstairs was all about with the guy calling himself Sergei."

He took a sip and placed the cup on the table. "You met real Sergei, Doctor, but he was FSB officer who escorted you inside rear entrance to embassy. The man you tried to garrot—"

"Pardon the interruption," I said, "but I don't *try* to garrot people. I proved I could have garroted him. There is an enormous difference in any language, sir."

"So there is. This man is a, what you would call, clerk, and now he is a frightened clerk who will likely request to be sent back to his mother in Minsk, or wherever she lives, so she may feed to him porridge and coddle him like baby boy."

I laughed. "I'll give him a hug and apologize on my way out if you'd like."

"Would you?"

The unlikeliest of men in the unlikeliest of places in the unlikeliest of circumstances shared the briefest moment of laughter before saying, "We have common enemy, Doctor."

He wanted to get down to business, but I wanted to set some ground rules and control the conversation. "First, call me Chase. I'm not a real doctor. I can't write you a prescription, but I can explain your clerk's mommy issues and probably hypnotize the real Sergei into clucking like a chicken every time somebody says *dobroye utro*. Second, why did you pull that stunt downstairs? None of that was necessary."

He took another sip. "I pulled what you call 'stunt' because I needed to know beyond all doubt that I had right man inside my embassy. If you were not Chase Fulton, I was not willing to waste my time with impostor. I see you are real doctor of psychology because of diagnosis of fake condition of fake interrogator. I saw that you were real intelligence operator because of chair. And I saw that you were real warrior because of noticing and using garrot inside handle of case. I do have for you one question, though. Why did you roll bottle across floor instead of breaking to use as weapon?"

I made no effort to hide my American smile. "You watched me drink from the bottle. I didn't want the water. I wanted to taste the bottle. It was spun sugar and lacquer—a movie prop, not real glass."

Shulgin nodded once. "My point is made, and I say yes."

"Yes to what?" I asked.

"Please hypnotize real Sergei. I must see him cluck like chicken when I say to him good morning."

"Consider it done. Now, about this common enemy of ours. Who is he?"

The ambassador resituated himself in his seat. "The enemy is not man. The enemy is woman."

I didn't know how much force it would take to rip the arm from my chair before beating a Russian ambassador to death with it, but I was seconds from finding out. "If this is about Anya . . ."

"Relax, Dr . . . excuse me. I mean, Chase. Russian Federation does not care about Anya Fulton. She is now yours. There was time when we wanted her dead, but she is no longer threat to us. Please allow me to express my sincere condolences for loss of your wife as well. Please believe me when I tell to you we had nothing to do with that."

"You'll understand when I tell you that I don't believe you, but let's move on," I said. "Who's this common female enemy of ours?"

"Her name is Dianne Belford Delauter Sakharova. She is the surviving widow of Ivan Sakharov, formerly of Sibirskiy Geotekhnicheskiy Kholding."

"Oh, I know exactly who she is, and as of four days ago, I know exactly *where* she was. In fact, the whole reason I'm in this part of the world is to find her American ex-husband, Scott Delauter, and turn him inside out."

"I know all of this already," he said. "And we will come back to subject of Mr. Delauter." He lowered his gaze for a moment before continuing. "This woman murdered very important man who is friend of Russian Federation and friend of President Putin."

"So, why is she still alive?"

He looked at the floor, and I immediately knew the answer to my own question.

"You don't know where the money went, do you?"

He poured each of us another cup of coffee. "You are a dead man, Chase Fulton, and there is no greater gift in all of world. You are not Jesus Christ, and Vladimir Putin is not God, even though he may sometimes think himself to be. But in this case, we can resurrect you. We will feed you, clothe you, arm you, equip you, and support you. Best of all, no one will know."

I stalled and took a drink. "And in return?"

"Find for us woman and money she stole from Ivan Sakharov."

"What are you going to do with the woman?" I asked.

"Why do you care?"

I placed my cup back on the table and leaned toward Shulgin. "I don't care about the money. You can have it. I want the woman."

He narrowed his eyebrows into one continuous line. "Why?"

"Because I plan to hang her upside down in front of Scott Delauter, set her on fire, and make him watch her burn."

The ambassador stood, stuck out his hand, and said, "You would have made very good Russian, Dr. Fulton."

"I'd make a terrible Russian. Because just like a friend of mine once said, 'I do not drink vodka. I detest cold, and I cannot eat caviar. Is terrible. I drink tea. Vodka makes my mind soft. I eat chocolate because it tastes better than fish egg. I would rather chase you through Caribbean than build *snegovik* in Mother Russia.'"

He laughed. "Anya told you that, did she? She was right. She is terrible Russian, but it appears she is pretty good American. Will you do for me one more thing?"

"Sure, why not."

He produced a leatherbound book and opened it on his desk. It contained a list of handwritten names in several languages—some I recognized, and some I couldn't read. He handed me a beautiful Montblanc pen and asked, "Would you sign my personal guestbook? It is not official embassy document, only personal memento I cherish. Look. George Bush. Both of them."

I signed his book, recapped the pen, and handed it back.

He raised a hand. "Please keep pen. It is gift from me. I think you will find it very useful."

The Montblanc went into my pocket, and the book went back into his desk. He had my fingerprints, my DNA, a handwriting sample, and at least an hour of recorded audio of my voice. I wondered if he'd like to have a blood and urine sample while I was on the property.

"So, where can I find my team? Who gets my shopping list? And where should I wire the money when I find it?"

Shulgin laid a hand on my back. "You will find friend Nigel downstairs. He will take care of everything. Well, almost everything. I will have visas delivered to your home."

"Visas?"

He said, "Yes, of course. Lifetime visas for you, Anya, and of course, Pogonya, to travel at will in and out of Russian Federation. That is, of course, once you have found Dianne Sakharova and our money."

"Of course."

"There is one more small thing," he said.

"There always is."

He rounded his desk, pulled a locked case from a drawer, and extended it toward me.

"What's this?" I asked.

"The . . . forgive me. I do not know English word. *Kombinatsiya zamka* is President Putin's birthday."

I took the case and shook his hand again. "I still don't trust you, Ambassador."

"Is good. I do not trust you, either, Chase, but you will still make Sergei cluck like chicken, yes?"

* * *

I spent twenty minutes with the real Sergei Kozlov, but making a man that uptight relax enough to be hypnotized is outside even Svengali's wheelhouse. So, instead of mind control, I turned to bribery. For three thousand euros, he swore he'd cluck like a chicken every time the ambassador told him good morning for the next week. I doubted he'd keep his word, but on the off chance that he did, it was three thousand buck-bucks well spent. Besides, it wasn't my money. It was the Queen's.

* * *

I found Nigel smoking a cigarette on the back gallery.

I said, "Those things will rot your teeth, you know."

"Perhaps, but they calm my ulcers."

"I recommend habanero peppers and raw garlic. The ambassador says you've got a blank check for me."

By way of an answer, he waved a hand across the parking area. "Pick a car, any car."

"Are any of them hardened?"

His shoulders sagged in obvious disappointment. "We're at the Russian embassy, old boy. Must you insist on asking ridiculous questions?"

"What's in the garage?"

"The ambassador's official Range Rover. A pair of 'em, I'd say."

"Either of those will do. Let's roll."

He grumbled. "You can't have the Russian ambassador's official . . ."

I assumed he kept talking, but I didn't listen as I strolled toward the gate. It was probably locked, but the small walk-through portion might've still been unsecured, just as it had been upon our arrival. If I was right, though, it wouldn't matter.

Half a dozen strides from the gate, a black Range Rover pulled to a stop beside me, and the darkened window came down a few inches. "For God's sake, man, get in."

Instead of following Nigel's instructions, I ambled around the vehicle before settling into the back seat on the passenger's side. "Diplomatic plates. Nice. Let's pick up the team, do a little shopping, and find ourselves some passports."

"We can't keep this motorcar, of course."

"Why not?" I asked. "The ambassador said we could have whatever we needed."

"Yes, of course, but we can't drive a Russian Federation diplomatic vehicle all the way to bloody Switzerland."

"Oh, of course not," I said. "Then we'll fly, and we're not going directly to Switzerland, James Bond. We're going by way of Sevastopol, Russia."

Chapter 26

The Warrior Poet

"Russher, you say?"

"You know, Nigel, to be the guys who invented English, you folks aren't very good at it. I said Russia. Sevastopol, to be precise. But we're going to need the rest of my mates and a bit of kit first. How'd I do?"

"Dreadful," he said. "But the part about your mates wasn't so bad."

He pulled to a stop just as the rain began . . . again. "Here we are at Falke. Geofrey will get you fitted for what you need in the way of clothing, and I believe you'll find your, uh . . . buddies inside. How'd I do?"

"Not bad, but this place doesn't look like my kind of shop. Do you think we could find an REI or maybe a Bass Pro?"

"I should think not, but you'll be pleased to know that Captain Millgood does his shopping with Geofrey."

"Is that so?"

Nigel squirmed in his seat. "Oh, and this'll be the last time you'll have me for a chauffeur. You've sailed beyond your letter of marque, I'm afraid."

He handed over a card with a handwritten number on one side. "After you've seen Geofrey, call this number and ask for Michel. He will arrange transportation for you and your team to his shop in Amsterdam, where you will be kitted out with all of the communications equipment you will need. It isn't up to the standard of MI-Six, I'm afraid, but it's the best the Russians can afford."

I pulled the Montblanc from my pocket. "What's the story on this thing? I noticed there seems to be a lot of them floating around."

Nigel motioned for me to hand it over. He unscrewed the snow-capped end, plucked the metal pocket clip from the cap, and stuck it into the hole. Then he pulled the barrel into two halves, revealing a tiny number pad with a sliver of plastic wedged into a slot. After handing me the white tip that identified the famous pen as its namesake, he said, "Stuff this bit into your ear. Dial with the pick, and speak into the cap. It's a secure satellite uplink charged by the warmth of your body and the light of the sun, such as it is here. There are believed to be fewer than a thousand of these in existence. How did you come by yours, might I ask?"

"My new buddy, the Russian ambassador."

"Sign his book, did ya?"

"I did."

He chuckled. "Got your handwriting sample now, they do."

"He's got my left-handed sample."

Nigel laughed once again, exposing those teeth that would've made Pecan the demon horse quiver. "There may be a bit of tradecraft in you yet, my boy. If only you were twenty centimeters shorter and shed of that horrid beard. Now, get out before we get marked."

"What are you talking about?" I asked. "You've got diplomatic plates. You could park here all week and dance naked on the bonnet, and nobody would say a word. Where's my knife?"

He rolled his eyes. "It's in your belt, just in front o' your hip pocket. You may be not bad wiff your tradecraft, but you're shite by close-up handwork. I put it on you whilst you were preachin' 'bout me smokin'."

"Hey, Nigel. One last thing."

"Yeah, yeah. What is it?"

"Thanks. We couldn't have done it without you."

He huffed. "You ain't done nothin' yet, Yank. And you know that Russian girl's in love with you, don't ya?"

"That's the rumor."

He pulled the car into gear. "It ain't no rumor. How 'bout makin' sure you just need one of them graves you dug before you set off on this quest of revenge, huh? The way I see it, mate, the world's a bloody better place if you stay in it. Take care of yourself, and give Geofrey a good tip. He's a good lad and got himself shot up in the war."

"Which war?"

"Ain't but one, Chase, and it ain't never ended, has it now?"

I watched him drive away with his wisdom trailing behind like the wake of a ship that had no need for an anchor. Since the day Cain's rock met Abel's forehead, the battle had raged. And until the moment the heavens split open and the mightiest of all swords sever the evil from the good, nothing will change. Until then, men like me will continue to fight the battles that must be fought to prolong civility one more day and thwart ruin one more moment, for such is our destiny, our calling, our commandment.

A brush of my hand against Captain Millgood's knife pulled me from my trance of the warrior poet, and I stepped inside Falke, a clothing store that looked older than The Hague itself. Without looking up from her bolt of cloth, a lady said, "Geofrey *staat achterin.*"

Although I understood only one word of what she said, the fact that she pointed her scissors toward the rear of the shop implied that Jeff—which probably started with a G—was likely in the back.

I parted the curtains, and it felt as if a legion of angels had descended upon me. Singer was first to his feet, but the rest of the team was only an instant behind. "Where have you been, man?"

"You wouldn't believe me if I told you."

Kodiak said, "We've got a few tales of our own that fall into that hard-to-swallow category."

Underhand shakes and man hugs all around made the moment exactly what I needed, and from the looks on the faces of my brothers, they felt exactly the same. When the revelry fell away and the team parted, the mother of my perfect daughter stood ten feet away wearing the look that could've meant she loved me and wanted to have a dozen more beautiful daughters or that she was about to gut me like pig. I doubted I would ever be able to tell the difference.

The look finally melted into what could've almost been a smile. "I am pleased they did not kill you, Chasechka."

I chuckled and pulled the Montblanc from my pocket. "Me, too. We had a nice chat, and they even gave me a pen. Oh, and I almost forgot. I paid an FSB officer three thousand euros to cluck like a chicken for the Russian ambassador."

Every member of my team produced an identical pen, and Anya produced something I never expected—genuine, American-girl laughter. "I must hear this story of clucking like chicken."

"We'll get to that. Did anybody explain the pens to you?" Heads shook, and I said, "You're going to like them, but we'll get to that, too. Tell me about Geofrey."

Shawn said, "Oh, you're going to like him a lot more than we like ink pens. Come on."

I followed them through a second set of curtains into a central issue facility that would make any military unit in the world drool. In minutes, we were kitted out from boots to hats and everything in between.

Geofrey didn't appear to speak a word of English, but Anya's Dutch from her days in the tourism business on Bonaire served us well.

With rucksacks full of everything we could need, I asked her, "Did you pay him?"

"No, your chicken-clucking comrade did. Make phone call. You have number, yes?"

I pointed toward my pen, and she shook her head while pointing to a telephone on the wall.

I dialed, and a man said, "*Ya?*"

"Michel?"

"*Ya?*"

"English?" I asked.

He said, "Come behind Falke," and the line went dead.

With every passing minute, I was more thankful I'd fallen into the door-kicking arm of the covert-ops world instead of the cloak-and-dagger pit.

"He wants us to meet him out back."

I approached the man who'd made sure we had everything we needed, slipped a very nice tip into his hand just as Nigel had ordered, and spoke the only Dutch I knew. "*Bedankt*, Geofrey."

He smiled and sounded as if he were from Dump Truck County, Mississippi. "You're welcome, Chase."

I really need a door to kick and a bad guy to shoot in the face.

When we stepped through the back doors of the shop, I was surprised and overjoyed to see the sun, but I didn't like the bright-white tour bus covered in painted tulips and windmills, parked only inches in front of us.

"Why did somebody have to park this thing right here right now?"

Anya grinned, and I said, "Stop doing that. It's freaking me out."

She said, "Stop doing what?"

"Smiling. There's a giant bus in our way, and you're smiling. Have you been smoking the local dope? You never smile. What's going on with you?"

She said, "No, of course not. I do not do this. But this is bus for us. Put gear in bins on bottom and get inside. Is perfect camouflage. We are tourists in Holland. Hold hand of girlfriend, and pretend to be happy."

I threw my two bags into the cargo bay in the belly of the rig and slammed the door. I grabbed Gator's hand, gripped it hard enough to keep him from pulling away, and skipped toward the door of our camouflaged bus to Amsterdam. Anya giggled, and at that point, I was thoroughly convinced she was thoroughly stoned.

Gator sat beside me. "Since we're apparently dating now, could you at least give me some clue about what's going on and where we're going?"

I turned to Anya. "Is it safe to talk on this bus?"

"I do not know, but driver knows where we are going, so you can say this much at least."

I motioned for the team to huddle up. "We're headed to Amsterdam to meet a guy named Michel. He's hooking us up with some comms."

Shawn frowned. "Who's financing this little shopping trip?"

I mouthed, "The Russians."

That did not imbue confidence on the faces of the team, but Anya leaned in. "It will make sense. I promise to you this. We do not have to trust them to spend their money."

Shawn said, "Okay, I don't have to like it, but we did get some pretty cool stuff from ol' Jeff back there. How far is it to Amsterdam, anyway? Have I got time for a nap?"

Gator gave him a shove. "It's an hour, so you've got time for a nap. I'll wake you up if we see a windmill."

He said, "Don't do that. I've seen windmills. But if you see somebody jousting with one, take a picture. I'd kinda like to see that."

"I don't have a phone, remember? They're somewhere at the bottom of the ocean."

"Oh, yeah. Well, in that case, I guess you can wake me up."

Gator's estimation was spot-on, and nobody gave our tour bus a second look. Michel's two-hundred-year-old, three-story building had a roll-up door barely big enough for the bus, but the driver squeezed us in. If Geofrey's store had been an equipment haven, Michel's place was a technology paradise. The best part was that two of his technicians spoke English, and one of them even spoke American.

It took fifteen minutes to explain the bone conduction devices attached to our mandibles that worked in conjunction with our satellite communications, and ten minutes after that, my team and I were talking with each other handsfree, without earpieces or microphones, using satellites the Americans had never heard of. Yuri Gagarin would've been proud.

We loaded up on batteries, chargers, solar panels, spare parts, tool kits, short-wave radios, and even a few jammers, just in case we needed to cause a little havoc somewhere along the way. And havoc was one of our favorite games.

In addition to what we packed up to carry with us, at least twice as much base station gear went into Pelican cases to be shipped to St Marys, Georgia, by the fastest means possible.

I pulled our American-speaking friend aside and slipped him a little cash he didn't inspect. He simply tucked it away, and I appreciated his style.

"Thank you for not asking who we are or what we're doing."

He said, "I don't know what you're talking about, Tex. I've never seen you, never heard of you, never met you, none of that."

I put on one of Clark's crooked grins. "Tex . . . ha! How'd you guess?"

He didn't say a word, so I made a pistol with my index finger and thumb.

He sighed. "I wish I could help, man, but you're in the wrong part of the world for that. I can hook you up with some Tasers that'll knock you into football season, but that's it."

"Can you manage a dozen and plenty of batteries?"

"I'll talk to Michel. And, hey, man. Whoever you're going after . . ."

I stood and checked across my shoulder. "He killed my wife."

"For real?"

I nodded, and he said, "You sure a dozen is enough?"

* * *

Back beside the tulip-covered tour bus, Michel muddled through enough English to let me know he'd been well compensated and that a Russian cargo jet was waiting for us at Schiphol Airport. I thanked him the best I could and called Anya over.

"Tell him I need a landline phone. A simple, non-satellite, non-cell-phone. Can you do that?"

She blurted out something that could've been a recipe for one of the things I ate at Plein, for all I knew. When their conversation was over, she led me from his building and across the street to a telephone booth. It was a beautiful, ancient, wooden telephone booth with a two-hundred-pound hunk of metal and ceramic and a handheld receiver like nothing I'd ever seen. "Who is person you want to call?"

I said, "The only person left on Earth I know with a real telephone —Earl at the End. But I don't know how to use this thing, and even if I did, it would take two hundred dollars in quarters to make the connection."

Anya pushed me aside. "I told to you already. I make for you everything better. Tell to me telephone number."

I gave her Earl's number, and she lifted the receiver. After three minutes and at least as many languages, she handed me the phone. I parked myself on the triangular seat inside the booth and listened to the irregular ring. It continued until I believed there was no chance of making the connection. I shook my head in frustration and pulled the receiver away from my face just as Earl said, "Yeah? Hello?"

I slammed the receiver back against my ear. "Hey, Momma! It's your baby boy, but don't you dare say my name. Just listen."

She gasped, and I thought I heard her fall to the floor. "It can't be."

I had to think of something to say, so I blurted out the first thing that came to mind. "If anyone touched those engines besides you, I hope Kenny buried them a hundred feet deep."

"Oh, Baby Boy, where are you?"

"Just listen. I need you to do something for me, and I need you to do exactly what I say. Write it down if you have to."

"All right. I've got a pencil. Go ahead."

I said, "Get a couple hundred bucks in cash. It has to be cash. And buy a prepaid phone from a gas station in Alabama. Go to Alabama. Don't buy it from Florida or Georgia. You got all of that so far?"

"Give me a little credit here. Rob a bank, get a phone, Roll Tide, then what?"

I secretly wished Earl could see where I was and meet the people I'd encountered over the previous few days, but I vowed to sit in the gazebo and tell her all about it when I got home.

"I'm sorry. I didn't mean to imply that you weren't keeping up. I've got a lot going on. So, when you get the phone, take it to Celeste. She's still there, right?"

"She's that smart doctor lady, the Indian chief, right?"

"Earl . . ."

She giggled. "You had it coming, Baby Boy. Yeah, she's still here. I'll take her the phone. Then what?"

"Have her program the phone number I'm about to give you into it."

I gave her the number, and she read it back.

I said, "Then, give the phone to Skipper. I don't know what time it is there, but I'll call exactly twelve hours from right now, and it'll be from a crazy number that won't make any sense. Can you do all of that?"

"I'm gettin' in the truck right now. I'll have that phone to Celeste in six hours if none of them state troopers don't haul me off to jail for runnin' ninety on the interstate."

"Hey, Earl," I said. "Your brother's got an airplane."

Chapter 27

I'm Batman

Back on the bus, it was Singer's turn to be my seatmate, but we didn't hold hands.

He said, "They're going to listen to every word we say and track every step we take."

"The Russian?" I asked. He nodded, and I said, "Of course they are, but who cares? As Clark would say, the goose that's good for the gander fell right into our lap."

The sniper chuckled. "That sounds like something he'd say, but I don't have a clue what it means."

"It means the enemy of our enemy doesn't necessarily have to be our friend, but we can still accept their golden eggs."

"I'm starting to think you're turning into Clark, and it's freaking me out a little."

"Think about it," I said. "We want Delauter, and we're going to get him. He's in Bern, Switzerland, or at least he was. The Russians believe his ex-wife, Dianne Sakharova, killed one of their golden boys, Ivan Sakharov, and took all his money. Whether she killed him or not doesn't matter. She took his money. That happened, and following the money is always rule number one when it comes to catching the bad guys."

Singer's eyes lit up. "And Scott Delauter is bad guy number one."

"We think Delauter and Sakharova are probably back in some sort of romantic relationship, and their original divorce may have even been a ruse to get her in with the Russian billionaire to set all this up."

He said, "That's a big mess, but yes, it appears they're back together, even if it's a business arrangement."

"Exactly. So, we know Delauter has some kind of network to track us based on his former contacts through the Board, right? Now, Delauter thinks we're dead, and just like the Russian ambassador told me, there's no greater gift in this game than to have your enemy believe you're dead. He—Delauter—probably isn't trying very hard to find us now. He knew we were coming after him, and he knew us well enough to know that quitting wasn't in our repertoire. Now that he believes we're out of the picture, he probably feels pretty comfortable, and comfortable people make mistakes."

Singer lowered his chin. "You're starting to sound pretty comfortable yourself."

"That's why I've got you, shooter. Don't let me get comfortable. Here's what I'm thinking. I'm okay with the Russians listening and tracking because they don't have any love for Delauter. Maybe they don't hate him, but they don't care if he lives or dies. What they care about is getting back Ivan Sakharov's cash from the widow Sakharova."

He said, "But they can find her just as easily as we can. They don't need us. Why are they using us?"

"You're not wrong very often, my friend, but this time you're missing something. If the Russians find her, kidnap her, torture her, and she gives up the money, she's smart enough to have a skyscraper full of thousand-dollar-an-hour attorneys already locked and loaded to unleash legal hell on Putin, and everybody within three thousand miles of him, to tell the world what he's done. The Kremlin's in enough trouble right now without stacking that geopolitical, billion-dollar scandal on top of it."

Singer leaned back in his seat. "Ah, the golden goose is coming home to roost."

"It sure is. If the Russians can get us to do their dirty work for them, they keep their hands clean, get their money back from Sibirskiy Geotekhnicheskiy Kholding, which the Kremlin probably owned anyway, and we get Dianne Belford Delauter Sakharova to take us by the hand and lead us right to her ex-husband, Scott Delauter, in exchange for her life."

He said, "And now that we've got all this Russian comms gear, we can talk to Skipper without Delauter and the former Board knowing anything about it."

"That's exactly right, and I don't care if Putin himself listens in. As far as I'm concerned, he can strap on a Makarov and ride along with us if he wants."

"That's pushing it a little, don't you think?"

"Yeah, probably. So, tell me the truth. How are you doing? You took a pretty nasty blow at the airport last year, and I've been a mess since then."

"I'm good," he said. "Disco, not so much. You should talk to him when we get back. You're not the only one who's a mess."

I bowed my head. "I've got a lot to be ashamed of."

He threw an arm around me. "No, you don't, brother. You lost your wife. Everybody understands. I'm proud of you for climbing out of the bottle, though."

"I didn't climb out," I said. "You yanked me out of the bottle and beat me over the head with it. Then, Pogonya showed up and made me never want to look at another glass of whiskey."

He looked up at Anya and pointed a finger at her a few seats away. "You know, the day's gonna come when we're going to have to talk about *that*."

I looked at the long golden hair cascading down her back, just as it had the first time I'd ever seen her on top of that water tower at Belmont Park in Elmont, New York, a lifetime ago. "She and I were two entirely different people back then, and that's not something that's going to be on my mind anytime soon . . . maybe ever."

He sighed. "Well, those two entirely different people made another person, who's a fifteen-year-old young woman now, and you can bet your shot-up, crippled old butt that thing that's not on your mind—

maybe ever—is on hers, so we're going to have to talk about it when we get home."

* * *

Just as Michel said, there was indeed a Russian jet waiting on the ramp at the Amsterdam Airport, but it wasn't what anybody would consider a luxurious means of transportation. The Antonov An-72 was a hunk of aluminum with a pair of giant engines stuck on top of a pair of hideous wings, but sometimes, even the ugliest of girls can dance, and the An-72 Coaler could certainly dance. She could leap off the ground in fewer than two thousand feet and stop herself in fourteen hundred. She was essentially a less attractive copy of Boeing's 1970s YC-14 design that was simply too hideous looking for America to build.

We climbed from the bus and stood in awe of the Coaler. Kodiak spun in a circle, apparently scanning the airfield, and finally pointed at the Russian beast. "That? Really?"

I said, "Hey, she may be ugly, but at least she's slow."

The bus driver somehow got permission to take us and the bus all the way to our luxury airline charter, where we loaded our own gear and tied it to the deck with pieces of nylon rope we found tucked in various places throughout the airplane.

We searched, but there was no crew to be found. Gator had never flown anything in Europe, and I couldn't read Cyrillic well enough to know the difference between air speed and hydraulic pressure. On top of all that, I hadn't been inside the cockpit of an airplane since Penny's murder. I was far from legal, and even further from competent to fly a kite, let alone a 1970s Russian freightliner.

In frustration, I parked my butt on a mostly inflated, worn-out tire on the port side of what barely qualified as an airplane.

Gator made a better decision and squatted on the tarmac in front of me. "Any ideas?"

"Yeah, I've got one. The Russians screwed us . . . again."

"There's a big surprise," Shawn said. "Can you fly this thing?"

"Probably."

The SEAL studied the underside of the wing that appeared to be a mile above his head. "I think I've got a better question. Can you land this thing?"

"Probably not."

Shawn grabbed a landing gear strut and gave it a shake. "Want me to blow it up?"

"Yep, but not yet. I believe I'll wake up the ambassador first."

Our SEAL grinned. "Can you do it in English and on speaker-phone so we can all enjoy it?"

I pulled one of the phones Michel provided for us and dialed the number I'd memorized from the Russian ambassador's card on his desk. He didn't present me with a card, and that was a reasonable decision. He didn't need the bloody remains of an American covert operative on the ground in Sevastopol with his business card in my pocket.

A woman answered in sleepy Russian, and I imagined her to be the former dancer I expected to see sitting outside his office on the third floor of the embassy.

I spoke in Russian because her English language proficiency probably wasn't why she was answering the ambassador's phone in the middle of the night. "Wake up the ambassador."

She mumbled an excuse, and I pressed the speaker button. Still in Russian, I said, "Tell him that he has five seconds to wake up and talk to Dr. Chase Fulton, or I'm calling Vlad Putin."

It didn't take the full five seconds.

"*Da*, Chase. *Chto eto takoye*?"

I switched to English for the enjoyment of my crew. "Hey, buddy. Listen. I'm sitting here in the cockpit of this An-Seventy-Two in Amsterdam. Thanks for the gear, by the way. Your boys hooked us up. Anyway, I can't find the keys to get this airplane started, and I'm not real good at reading Cyrillic. Would you mind telling me which one is the fuel gauge?"

"What are you talking about?"

"I'm talking about the airplane you gave me, Alex. It's cool and all, but I don't really know how to fly it, and the only other pilot I've got with me is a little green."

"Are you telling to me there are no pilots?"

"Yeah, Alex, that's exactly what I'm saying. So, do you want me to watch a YouTube video or two and give this thing a whirl, or would you like to rattle some cages and get me a couple of pilots out here so I can find your girl and wire you a couple billion dollars?"

I thumbed the red button, dropped the phone back into my pocket, and Shawn shoved me backward off the tire that had been my throne. "You're Batman."

I scrambled to my feet and checked my watch. "That's right. I *am* Batman. What's the over/under? Ten minutes?"

Kodiak said, "If there's not a pair of pilots in that cockpit in five minutes, I'd bet a grand there'll be a pair of Russian bullets in their heads, and you can take that to the bank, Batman."

* * *

Kodiak was wrong. Three minutes later, four men came running across the tarmac, pulling flight suits across their shoulders and apologizing in rapid-fire Russian.

Soviets understood three things: fighting, hitting on women who were way out of their league, and establishing dominance. All three of those things carried over well after the wall fell and the Soviet Union became the Russian Federation. My team understood Russians almost as well as the Smirnov company understood them, and we put that intimate operational knowledge to good use.

When the four men got their flight suits zipped and got close enough, Shawn punched the largest of them in the center of his chest, sending him onto his back gasping for breath and his boots slapping on the tarmac as his body convulsed like a slammed running back.

Anya stepped within inches of the youngest, and clearly most self-confident of the crew, smiled seductively, and then hissed, "If you look at me one more time for any reason, I will cut out your eyeballs with plastic spoon and force them inside part of your body where they were never meant to be. Then I will shove also rest of head inside same part of body so maybe eyeballs can find again their home."

With the fighting and flirting covered, it was my turn to take care of the dominance. I chose the man who appeared to be the most senior of the crew, stepped beside him, and drew my phone. In gentle but confident Russian, I said, "Take this, and dial the last number I called."

He did, and Ambassador Shulgin answered on the first ring. "Pilots arrived, yes?"

The flight commander and ambassador had a rather unpleasant discussion in Russian without a word from me, and the phone returned to its place in my pocket.

I made sure the preflight inspection was done thoroughly without haste while Shawn helped the heavyweight champion of the Russian Air Force Academy boxing team catch his breath. There was little doubt about who was in charge, and we were airborne in half an hour with Sevastopol fourteen hundred miles ahead and Holland seemingly a million miles astern.

The airplane was dreadfully slow. Gordo's Herk would've run circles around the lumbering Russian lump of coal, but we were equipped, operational, moving, and mostly reunited. We just needed Skipper and one more missing piece. Part of me was thankful we didn't have that one additional piece on the plane, though. Mongo's extra three hundred pounds would've likely slowed us down another fifty knots.

Chapter 28
Defense Wins Ball Games

Gator kicked a heel against the floor of the Antonov An-72. "Wooden decks? Are you kidding me?"

"They worked onboard the USS Corregidor," I said.

"That thing burned to the waterline."

"Yeah, but they rebuilt it."

"Not with wooden decks."

"Beggars can't be choosers."

He rolled his eyes. "Since when did we become beggars?"

"Since we wrecked our airplane in the North Atlantic, got rescued by a bunch of British special ops maniacs, and fell into the loving arms of a fruitcake who thinks he's some combination of James Bond and Sherlock Holmes."

Gator chuckled. "That's tough to argue with. I gotta tell you, man. When I was playing ball, I never thought I'd end up on a Russian cargo plane chasing the billionaire ex-wife of a dead Russian sugar beet farmer."

"Join the club, my friend. I was supposed to be a retired catcher and hall-of-famer for the Braves by now."

He said, "Funny how stuff works out, huh?"

"Look around. Maybe it's funny, and maybe it's how things are meant to be, but don't get hung up on Dianne. She's not who we're really chasing. Have you ever done much fishing?"

"Not really."

I said, "Sometimes, you have to stand on the end of the dock and cast a net to catch the little ones so you can use them as bait to catch the ones you really want later in the day. That's what Dianne is. We're going to catch her and force her to take us to Delauter, the traitor who soured the Board and ultimately killed Penny."

"Fishing isn't my thing, but there's not much I don't know about the secondary in football. Between safeties like me and the corner-backs, we're the edges of that net you were talking about. We can't let anybody get past us when the D-line falls apart. Didn't anyone ever tell you that defense wins football games, boss?"

"I've heard that a time or two," I said. "But don't forget that I was a defensive player, too."

"Yeah, but they let you step up to the plate and take a few pitches every game, didn't they?"

"They did, and I made 'em pay for a few hanging curveballs I crushed into the bleachers."

Gator grinned. "I picked off more than my share of passes and ran them back for six on our side of the scoreboard."

"We may have changed uniforms and sides of the ball, but we're still on the good guys' team," I said. "What we do now is never going to be repetitious. We're not building Toyotas, young man. We're saving the world, one bad guy at a time."

"Maybe so," he said, "but I've never worked a mission *this* crazy be-fore. We're doing a bunch of stuff I've never done. Oh, and speaking of stuff we've never done, I'm calling dibs on crushing the next Rus-sian sternum that needs crushed. Shawn made that look like way too much fun, and you know how I hate to miss out on hitting a dude that doesn't know he's about to get hit. That's some of that free safety stuff right there."

"You can take that up with Shawn. He'd call it SEAL stuff, but I'm not getting in the middle of that one."

* * *

We finally landed as if we'd crashed into a construction site, but nobody complained. Being back on the ground was enough of an accomplishment for us. The pilots—if they truly qualified as such—had us off their airplane minutes after most of the moving parts came to a stop, and I pulled the apparent senior member of the crew aside. We spoke in what I assumed to be the only language he knew well enough to understand my sarcasm.

I said, "When you get back to the embassy, thank the boss for the luxurious ride, would you?"

He wore the look of a man who understood no language of any kind, but the words that came out of his mouth were undeniably Russian. "Embassy? We are not going to embassy. We are staying with you. Think of us as private crew only for you, comrade. Talk only to me, and I will deliver you to wherever you must be. We have, of course, limitations of speed and distance, but she is good airplane, no?"

The answer I wanted to give was not the one he wanted to hear, so I gave him a slug on the shoulder and said, "*Da, spasibo.*"

We found a shower, food, and most importantly, a clock. Twelve hours passed as if it had taken months, and I prayed Earl had talked her brother Cotton into flying her to Alabama to buy a throwaway phone that Dr. Celeste Mankiller could turn into Frankenstein's monster.

Why did people assume the monster's name was Frankenstein? That was the doctor's name. Mary Shelley never named the monster.

I pulled the Montblanc from my pocket and admired its craftsmanship as I considered making my first call on its internal phone. The hours of time and devoted precision that went into its creation rivaled that of Mary Shelley's doctor himself, but I tucked the piece of Maxwell Smart spy gear back into my pocket and opted for a more conventional, yet equally monitored, chunk of Dutch Michel's work.

I dialed what had been my childhood home phone number and the very first complex number I learned in kindergarten. I owned the number I'd instructed Celeste to program, so fearing someone I'd never met answering never entered my mind.

The exact voice in the perfect tone came bounding across the four thousand miles separating us. I expected three minutes of tongue-lashing, but instead, the woman I'd always see as my baby sister said, "Imagine that. The great Chase Fulton being right on time. Say something so I can hear your voice."

"I've missed you, old girl."

Skipper said, "Yeah, there's been a little of that going on around here, too. So, I hear you're in bed with the Russians. I guess I can't stop you from that anymore."

"Don't worry. The bed is only figurative and financial. The other one isn't happening. I've got too many other things screwing me to add another—"

She cut me off. "That's funny, but maybe you should stop before you take it too far. How and where?"

"Physically, we're good. Nobody's hurt except Tubbs. The Brits have him, and his wounds are relatively minor. He hit his head during the water landing. Psychologically, we're a little beaten down. We've been through a lot, and we're out of our element. We're shooters, not spies, and this thing is turning into an Ian Fleming novel."

"Don't stop now," she said. "Where?"

"Sevastopol. I cut a deal with the Russian ambassador in Holland to get what he calls 'his money' back."

Skipper said, "A deal implies give and take. What's he giving?"

"He says we can have Dianne Sakharova if we get her to give up the money that she stole from him and Putin when she supposedly killed Sakharov."

"How nice of him," she said. "Did he tell you where she is?"

"He did not. In fact, he implied that he didn't know. I told him I knew."

"Why would you tell him that?"

"Because you told me she was in Sevastopol, and I needed a bargaining chip."

"She *was* in Sevastopol," Skipper said. "But not anymore."

"So, you've still been tracking her?"

"Not exactly," she said. "I do have friends, though."

"Do you know Putin's birthday by any chance?"

"What?"

"Vladimir Putin, the president of Russia."

"Yeah, I know who Putin is, but why do you need to know his birthday?

"It's a long story. Do you know it or not?"

She said, "I'm going with *or not*, but you can Google it."

"Thanks, so where is Dianne?"

"Before we get to that," she said, "what's the deal with these two-dollar phones?"

"Phones? Plural?"

She said, "Yeah, Earl showed up with three of them in case Celeste screwed up the first two. She says you owe her two hundred and forty bucks, by the way."

"I think we can handle that. The phones are a long story, so here goes . . ."

I spent twenty minutes bringing our analyst up to speed on every detail. I couldn't tell if she was taking notes, but I had no doubt she would never forget a single word of any of it.

When I finished, she said, "Okay, here's the brief from our end. Ginger is doing the op center work from her underground base, and no, you've never been there, and before this instant, you didn't even know it existed. Honestly, neither did I, but she's on it. The best part is the Board didn't know about it, either, so it's as close to one-hundred-percent secure as possible."

"That's great news," I said. "So, have you found it?"

"You're expecting me to say 'found what?' but I'm way ahead of you. Yeah, we found the money Dianne inherited from her dead Russian husband. It's roughly three point four billion dollars, depending on today's exchange rates. It's in various currencies. She has it spread out all over the world in Switzerland, Aruba, the Caymans, South Africa, and Oceana."

I said, "You're expecting me to ask what Oceana is, aren't you?"

"Yep."

"You know how much I hate to disappoint you, so I'll do it. What the heck is Oceana?"

"It's a little love nest off Anguilla in the British Virgin Islands, off a private island that sits in two hundred eighty feet of water."

I could almost see James Bond strutting out of the surf and onto the beach in his Speedo while holding a speargun, with a bikini-clad beauty on each arm and a bag of Russian rubles dangling from each shoulder.

I said, "Two hundred eighty feet, huh? That's a long way down. Recreational divers aren't making that one."

"I suspect they have themselves a sexy little submarine or an elevator."

"What's the fun in that?"

She said, "Just in case you're wondering, the *Lori Danielle* is steaming for Oceana as we speak, and they'll be there in less than seventy-two hours."

"Is there any chance they could pick up Mongo and a boatload of British Special Boat Service swimmers along the way?"

I expected her to have a dozen questions and an argument or two, but she said, "I'll talk with the generals and see what I can do. Oh, by the way, your girl is in Thessaloniki."

"Dianne?"

She said, "Yes, Dianne. She's in Thessaloniki in a hospital called Ippokrateio General."

"Why?"

"I don't know," Skipper said, "but something tells me that Dr. Chase Fulton can find out."

"What name is she using?"

"Donna Belford."

I said, "I'll give it a try, but we'll have to play it by ear and see what happens. Now, I have the most important question of the conversation."

"I thought you'd never ask. Hang on. She's sitting right here beside me and squirming like a worm."

The next voice on the phone made me tear up with three simple letters and one beautiful syllable. "Dad?"

I was practically speechless. "You called me dad."

"I am sorry. I meant to say father, but I am excited. How are you?"

"Never be sorry. I'm fine, except I miss you."

"I thought you were dead. Everyone thought you were dead."

"I know, but it was necessary."

She said, "I know. I spoke with a man from the Special Air Service, and he promised me he would save your life."

"He told me, and he did. He saved all of us."

"I know. We've all known, but we had to pretend you were dead, and that was hard."

"I'm sorry I put you through that."

She said, "It's okay. I understand, sort of. Is Mama with you?"

"She's here. Do you want to talk to her?"

"Yes, but first you. As she would say in her terrible English, I have for you geeft."

I laughed. "I can't wait."

"When will you be home?"

"I don't know, sweetheart. We still have a lot of work to do, but we'll be there as soon as possible."

She said, "Father?"

"Yes?"

"I love you."

The tears came again, and I said, "Daughter?"

"Yes?"

"I love you, too. Here's your mother."

They spoke for a few minutes, and the phone ended up in Gator's hand. No doubt, Skipper needed to hear his voice as badly as I needed to hear Pogonya's.

I gathered the team and briefed the conversation I had with Skipper, including the part about Dianne being in the hospital in Thessaloniki. When the Q&A was over, I said, "I've got a thousand bucks for anyone who knows Vladimir Putin's birthday."

Anya said, "*Sed'mogo Oktyabrya tysyacha devyat'sot pyat'desyat vtorogo goda.*"

Gator threw up his hands. "That's not fair. She's Russian. Of course she'd know."

Anya leaned toward him. "I will give to you ten thousand dollars, plus one thousand dollars Chase is giving to me for knowing Putin's birthday, if you can tell to me birthday of your President Donald Trump."

Gator stammered and finally gave up. Anya eyed the remainder of the team, but no one offered a guess. She pulled the tiny American flag from her pocket, gave it a twirl, and said, "June fourteen, nineteen forty-six."

I pulled out the impressive-looking case Ambassador Shulgin gave me in his office and dialed 10-07-52, hoping Anya was right about the day Putin drew his first breath on the planet, but when I thumbed the releases, nothing happened. I double-checked the dials, but again, nothing.

"I thought you said October seventh, nineteen fifty-two."

She said, "Yes, this is correct."

"According to the ambassador, that's supposed to be the combination to the case."

She took the device from my lap and spun it to examine the lock before shaking her head. "You are being again too American. Put day first, not month. You are in Europe, you silly colonist."

I dialed 07-10-52, and the pair of latches sprang open. Inside the velvet-lined container rested three vials of fluid with no markings in any language. I spun the case back to face Anya. "Any ideas?"

She closed the box and relocked the latches. "Yes, I know exactly what this is, and we must go now to hospital in Greece."

Chapter 29
Out-Greeked

A long time ago, Clark Johnson told me that although we didn't descend from monkeys like good old Charlie Darwin may have believed, warriors behaved a lot like animals and responded to most of the same stimuli in very similar ways. His way of putting it may have been a little harsher, but his lesson was spot-on. Feed your men first, especially when you're the hungriest of all of them, and they'll respect you for it and fight harder for you than you'll ever be able to fight for yourself. That's why I made sure the flight crew ate before any of us when we climbed off the airplane in Sevastopol, even though their landing was more like a wrestling leap off the top rope than a thing of aeronautical excellence.

And that's one of the reasons they didn't hesitate when I said, "Get us to Thessaloniki, now." It is possible that their fear of the ambassador played a role in their haste, but I'm sticking with the food thing.

The flight was far shorter than our previous trek across the galaxy, and we touched down like a delicate-toed dragonfly just over an hour after our departure from the scene of our previous crash.

I turned to my team. "Please tell me somebody speaks Greek."

Singer waggled his hand. "I can read a little Koine Greek. That was the common language of the Mediterranean during Jesus' time on Earth."

"Yep, that ought to come in real handy if we run into any Scribes or Pharisees," I said.

"Actually, those guys would've spoken Hebrew," Singer said. "But I get your point. Koine isn't all that different from modern Greek, but reading it and speaking it are two very different things. I'll be able to muddle through a little, but I'm worthless with anything technical, especially medical stuff."

I turned to our Dutchess Tzarina. "How about you? Got any Greek?"

She held her index finger and thumb an inch apart. "A little."

I patted Singer on the back. "I'm sorry, my friend, but you've been out-Greeked. Congratulations, Anya. You've been promoted to head nurse and translator. Let's go find our patient."

We fed the crew again, sort of. In truth, we gave them enough money to feed themselves but not enough to escape. "Meet us back at the airport in ninety minutes. With any luck, we'll have an extra passenger with us."

Anya hailed a cab, and the six of us crammed inside a car that would've been cramped with only four. She said, "*Na mas páei sto Ippokráteio Genikó Nosokomeío.*"

The driver nodded, started the meter, and yanked the car into traffic without checking the mirror.

I said, "It sounds like you know a lot more Greek than just a little bit."

"I have maybe done little bit of travel."

I twisted in a wasted effort to get comfortable and found myself, once again, thankful we'd left Mongo with the SBS team. "Ask him how far it is to the hospital."

"*Póso makriá eínai to nosokomeío?*"

Instead of an answer, he asked a question, but in Russian. "You are Russian, no?"

"*Da,*" Anya said.

Their conversation continued in the language I could understand, but I played the part of the dumb American that comes so easily for me.

"Then why are you with Americans? Is it about sick woman?"

"Which sick woman?" Anya asked.

"Very sick woman. American woman, but she is also Russian somehow. Very strange, I think."

Anya put her arm around me. "I am nurse, and this man is American doctor. We are here to help her. Your Russian is very good. Where did you learn?"

"Is not so good," he said. "I was married to Russian woman. She was once beautiful like you, but no more. She is now old and very mean."

"And she is still your wife?"

The cabbie shook his head. "No, she is back in Russia, and I hope she is freezing to death. Her wicked heart should feel at home in world of ice."

Anya said, "Tell us what you know about woman inside hospital."

"I know only what I hear. People say things inside taxi, and I pretend I do not understand. She has maybe poison. If this is true, you have come very long way to see her die. There is nothing you can do."

Anya squeezed my arm. "My husband is wonderful doctor. He can do many things other doctors cannot."

The driver looked into Anya's eyes in the mirror. "You are Russian. You know that even best doctor in all of world cannot save woman if Kremlin wants her dead."

He pulled beneath the portico of the hospital, and we climbed from the car like a troop of clowns.

Anya whispered, "Give to him only very small tip, maybe only three euros."

I was a guppy in a goldfish bowl, way out of my world, so I did as I was told, and we stepped through the pneumatic doors into the hospital.

I said, "I need to look like a doctor. How about a little help?"

"We're on it," came somebody's reply, but it didn't matter whose.

A few seconds later, I was wearing a lab coat that almost fit, a stethoscope, and I had a pager and six ink pens of various colors in my pocket. A clipboard and stethoscope almost completed the look, but I needed an ID badge. Everyone except me seemed to have one, and Shawn appeared determined to change that.

He returned a few minutes later with a look of great satisfaction, but not the same look he wore when he'd just punched somebody in the mouth who truly deserved it. When he pinned the badge on my "borrowed" lab coat, he turned it so both the picture and name faced inward. I was grouchy enough to get away with the mistake, and I just hoped Anya's Greek was as strong as it sounded in the cab.

I took her by the sleeve of the scrubs she somehow acquired and donned. "You do know what we're trying to do, right?"

"Yes, of course, but we are not trying. We are doing. We are going to get both of us inside room of Donna Belford, read her chart in Greek, and convince her to take us to ex-husband, who we hope she is still in love with. I am, of course, correct, yes?"

"And you're going to sound like a nurse during the whole thing, yes?"

"Perhaps not all of thing, but maybe most. Ready?"

"Sure. What could possibly go wrong?"

Anya's expression turned from kindness to one-hundred-percent business as she nabbed a stack of charts from a basket and opened one in front of me. She motioned with one finger and spoke in angry Russian about a baby bear she once saw at a zoo when she was a child. In any other language, the story would've been heartwarming and cute, but it sounded as if she were describing how the patient's intestines were on the verge of exploding if I didn't perform the emergency surgery in the coming seconds.

"Argue with me," she demanded.

"About what?"

"No! In Russian, and it does not matter about what. You, Dianne, and I are only three people in all of building who probably speak Russian. Just sound angry and maybe throw something."

I raised my voice and demanded that she hadn't seen a baby bear at all. She was making up the whole story. I said that there weren't even bears in Russia.

That did it, and the fight was on. She closed the file and waved it in my face until I yanked it from her hand and shook it so violently the paperwork inside took flight. It was precisely at that moment she did something I'd never seen her do. She retreated as if afraid of me. Something about it made me uncomfortable, but I had to admit, my daughter's mother would've made a fine actress.

She turned to a pair of nurses behind a tall console, wiped her eyes, and with the same fearful tone in her voice, spoke in what must've been Greek. The only words I recognized were Dr. C.D. Fulton and Dianne Belford.

Perhaps it was sisterly compassion for their fellow abused nurse, or maybe shared hatred for the overbearing American doctor, but whatever it was, it worked. One of the nurses produced a red file and slid it across the counter as she motioned toward the mess of paperwork on the floor.

From all appearances, Anya apologized profusely, but the seated nurses apparently reassured her that they would manage the fallout. When the exchange was over, the three women hugged, and I earned a single-finger salute from at least two of them.

Inside the elevator, my nurse got the giggles. "That was fun, no?"

"Maybe for you, but not so much for me. I was starting to think they might burn me at the stake."

"Perhaps they might if we go back that way, so we should find other direction. They think you are terrible doctor."

"They're right," I said.

She took my arm. "This is not true. You are wonderful."

"I'm wonderful at killing people and breaking things, but I'm not that kind of doctor."

"This does not matter here. Probably here they would have you to make surgery for heart or maybe even brain transplant, if this is what you wanted to do."

"I'd rather just grab her and get out of here."

"This will not be easy, but we are very good at doing not easy things."

The bell rang, and the doors opened onto a dimly lit corridor. Thankfully, Dianne's room was only three doors down on the right.

Beside the door sat a well-dressed young man who spent enough time in the gym to require tailored jackets, and above his shoulder hung a sign with a message written in Greek.

I turned to my nurse.

She said, "No persons except medical staff."

I opened the door, as if we qualified, and the bouncer didn't protest. We stepped inside to find a woman who looked very little like the photographs I'd seen of Dianne Belford Delauter Sakharova. Her dossier said she was fifty-one, but she looked at least two decades older. The oxygen mask over her nose and mouth hissed and distorted her face with a wispy cloud of white gas. Her hands were drawn and bruised from IV needles, and her legs were bent unnaturally at the knees.

Beneath her fluttering eyelids, her pupils seemed to focus on me. "You are not my doctor."

"I am today," I said. "My name is Dr. C.D. Fulton, and this is Nurse Ana."

"What do you want?" she breathed.

I turned with my back to our patient. "Take pictures of every page of that file and get them to Skipper, stat."

Anya bit her lip to avoid laughing. "Did you say stat?"

I whispered, "I've always wanted to say it, but psychologists and gunfighters don't ever get to."

Anya pulled the rolling table near the window of the small room and began the task of photographing everything while I turned back to Dianne.

She said, "I demand to know what you want."

"I'm not sure you're in any position to make demands, Mrs. Delauter Sakharova."

Dianne reached for a wristband strapped to her left arm and pressed a pair of buttons before I could stop her.

I said, "Anya, she just pressed two call buttons on her wrist."

Anya dropped the files and ran to the edge of the bed. "Tell to me what you have done, or you will die before you can see result of effort."

"So that's it," Dianne said. "You're just another Russian here to kill me."

Anya said, "Quite opposite. We are here to keep you alive. What do buttons do? Tell to me now, or I will no longer be able to help you."

Dianne smiled through the fog of oxygen and spoke in flawless Russian. "It is you who cannot be saved now, whoever you are."

The door burst inward, and I lunged for the opening. Our little rich girl was more resourceful than I expected. Her one-man, rather lax security detail outside wasn't impressive, but I didn't expect the panic button.

Anya ripped the handle from the rolling table and leapt through the air, prepared to impale muscle-boy when he came through the door and created a human barricade for the subsequent security personnel to follow, but she yanked away her makeshift weapon at the last possible instant.

First through the opening was Gator's forearm and elbow with a bulky Scandinavian man in a perfect chokehold. The Viking's knees were already soft, and a second later, he was little more than a doormat.

Shawn had the doorman and his tailored suitcoat in an even more precarious situation. One of the man's arms was laced between his own legs while the other was folded across his shoulders, and our SEAL was carrying him like a purse. When he dropped him, the concussion of the man's face colliding with the floor eliminated any threat he may have once represented.

Kodiak had a third man by the elbow and was making him prance like a prized stallion at a horseshow. "Look, he can do tricks." He frog-marched his show pony around the room and gave him a little tactical baptism in the room's small shower. "Do you want to die?" Kodiak asked as the man spewed water from every orifice north of his belly button.

"No! No! What do you want?"

Kodiak dried his face with a handful of paper towels. "I want to know where Scott Delauter is."

The man said, "I don't—"

Before he could finish his lie or truth, it didn't matter which, his head was back beneath the shower, and a thin towel was wrapped around his face.

It takes between four and five minutes for a calm, adult human in relatively good shape to drown. That number is inversely proportional to the level of stress the individual is under when panic is factored into the equation. Okay, none of that is true. People drown for all sorts of reasons at all kinds of times. Needless to say, our new friend's stress level was off the charts. He was in good shape, but he was in the hands of some fairly dangerous guys, so he wouldn't make it four minutes if he chose not to play nice. Kodiak showed some mercy and shut off the water at ninety seconds.

"How about now? Did we jog your memory about Mr. Delauter's whereabouts?"

The man spewed, sputtered, gagged, and coughed, but he didn't have an answer, so Kodiak changed tactics. He raised the lid, sat on the toilet, and said, "Hey, Shawn. I could use a little help with this guy's feet. Wanna come play?"

Shawn was in the bathroom almost before the question left the air. Waterboarding isn't enjoyable for anyone, and any interrogator who says he enjoys nearly drowning a detainee is a sick individual who needs intense psychological intervention. The key is making the detainee believe we enjoy doing it, regardless of how much it tortures us. No one on the team was as good an actor as Anya, but Shawn and Kodiak were close.

Seventy-five seconds and two flushes later, our boy was ready to draw a map and give us GPS coordinates to Scott Delauter's last known position.

"Why are you doing this?" Dianne asked through agonizing wheezing.

"Because we have to find your ex-husband," I said. "It's a matter of life and death."

"Whose?"

That question made me smile. "That's up to you, ma'am."

"I'm already going to die, so it isn't me."

Anya stepped close beside the woman. "This is not true. Dr. Fulton knows exactly what is wrong with you, and we have the cure. It is not too late yet, but it soon will be. Do you want to live?"

The woman nodded.

"This is very good answer," Anya said. "Is this man who is very wet and afraid correct about where your ex-husband is?"

"No, but he believes he is correct, so please do not kill him. As far as he knows, he is telling the truth."

"Do you know where he is?"

She nodded.

Anya glanced up at me and then back down at the dying woman. "If we give to you antidote for poison Russians gave to you, will you take us to your husband, Scott Delauter?"

"He is not my husband anymore."

Anya smiled. "Yes, but you want him to again be husband, yes?"

Dianne nodded. "Yes, very much, and yes, I will take you to him if you will save my life."

Chapter 30
A Doctor Without Borders

I stepped beside Anya. "Do you really think they'd let me do heart surgery?"

"I was saying only joke."

"I know, but how much do you really think I can get away with? Is it possible we could score some sedatives for these guys to keep them asleep for a few hours while we get her out of here?"

She handed me a pad of paper from the pocket of her scrubs. "Write for me what you want, and I will get, but I have only one rule."

"What rule?"

"I am nurse, so I must give injection."

Being nothing more than a psychologist, I couldn't legally prescribe so much as an aspirin anywhere in the world, but I knew the names of a few drugs that would bring Dianne's security team some sweet dreams without sending them to meet their maker, so I made a few notes, and Nurse Anya went shopping.

My team of the most loyal hitters any leader could ask for stood security, just as they'd been trained and practiced for years.

"Thanks for following us up here, guys."

The team laughed, and Kodiak said, "You write us a great big beautiful check every month, boss. You don't have to thank us for doing our jobs."

Singer piped up. "Truth is, we'd do it even without the checks."

"Don't worry, guys. The checks aren't drying up. Nice move with the toilet, by the way."

Kodiak said, "I call it swirly-boarding."

I chuckled. "Clark would be proud."

Anya returned with a pocketful of syringes and dispensed the love.

Gator pulled back the blinds. "Have you got a plan for getting her out of here yet?"

I pulled the phone from my pocket and called the Alabama throwaway back at Bonaventure. "Hey, Skipper. We found our girl."

"Great news. How is she?"

"Not great, but she's alive and agreeable for now. You said the ship was steaming for a particular destination I won't name. Where is she now?"

"In the Med, coming off a research gig. Why?"

"How soon can she be in Thessaloniki?"

She said, "I'm en route to Thessalo–Virginia. You'll have to give me a couple of minutes, and I'll call you back."

"That may be a problem," I said. "You should receive a big package from Amsterdam that'll make the two-dollar crack-deal phone obsolete. I was hoping you'd be there to receive it."

"Yeah, I know. I've got that handled. It'll be where I'm going a few hours after it lands in Georgia."

"I should've known," I said. "Call me back soon. We're running out of time over here."

The line went dead, and the room was full of eyes staring at me for answers.

"She's checking with Captain Sprayberry and calling back."

In typical Skipper fashion, it didn't take long. "How soon can you be in Algiers?"

I palmed the phone. "Does anybody know how far it is to Algiers?"

The boys looked like I'd asked how far it was to the moon, but Anya closed one eye and started thinking. "Maybe two thousand kilometers."

Dianne pulled the oxygen mask from her face and waved away the white mist. "Eleven hundred miles by air and seventeen hundred by sea, but if you're taking me by sea, just kill me now. I'll never survive it."

I pressed the phone back to my ear. "Six hours if the airplane will start."

Skipper said, "What are you talking about?"

"Nothing. It was a bad joke. We'll be there in less than six hours."

The phone went back into my pocket, and my attention turned back to my team. Gator was first.

I said, "Hey, free safety, have you ever done any blocking?"

"More than my share of tackling. Does that count?"

The SEAL was next.

"Can you drive an ambulance?"

He said, "If it's got wheels and an engine, I can."

"Good. Go steal one. We'll meet you downstairs. Singer, get every bag of fluid you can throw onto that bed, and round up as many oxygen bottles as you can find. If she's been poisoned, can she survive sedation?"

The closest thing we had to a real doctor shook his head. "Probably not."

I took Dianne's hand. "We're getting you out of here, and it's going to suck bad. It'll hurt, it'll be loud, and you're going to see us break a few Greek laws, but if you stay here, they're going to let you die. If you come with us, I won't let that happen. Are you ready to roll?"

She squeezed my hand. "You're not a real doctor, are you?"

"Oh, I'm a real doctor. I'm just not the kind who believes in borders."

Singer emptied several drawers of medical supplies onto Dianne's bed, piled bags of fluid on top of them, and shoved bottles of oxygen everywhere he could. Blankets and pillows became airbags, and the carnival ride began.

We only started three fights, unless we count the skinny security guard. He surrendered too quickly to qualify as a real fight in my book, but I had some respect for the pair of young doctors who did okay against Kodiak and Gator until Anya got involved. She didn't cut anybody, but I didn't envy the headaches they had coming.

Shawn was right. He could drive, but what he couldn't do was find the airport. Thessaloniki isn't laid out like any other city on the planet. The streets looked like a pile of spaghetti in the spin cycle. Perhaps the Apostle Paul should've written Third Thessalonians and given them a little direction on how to build a decent system of roads. Google on a phone built in China and programmed in Amsterdam wasn't much help, so I yelled into the back of the ambulance. "Hey, Dianne. You got any idea how to get to the airport?"

She was weak but witty. "I would look up and follow the airplanes."

Since the minute I left the Russian embassy, my plan had been to stand Dianne in front of Scott Delauter and shoot her in the face with the highest caliber weapon I could find while somebody forced his eyelids open and made him watch, but with every word out of her mouth, I liked her more. My willingness to kill the woman Delauter loved was fading a little more with every passing minute, but my hatred for Penny's killer was still festering and growing more malignant with every breath.

Shawn leaned forward and peered skyward. "Why didn't you think of the airplane thing, College Boy?"

"Don't start calling me that. Clark gets away with it because he earned it, but I'll dock your pay and do terrible things to you while you sleep, you no-navigating frogman."

He grabbed his chest. "That's hurtful."

"Good."

Dianne's plan worked, and even the Greek police couldn't navigate the streets of Thessaloniki well enough to stop us before we made the airport in the stolen EMS vehicle. Our Russian aeronauts hadn't dismantled the Antonov, sold the parts, and made a run for freedom in the West, so we had that to be thankful for.

"*Opustit' rampu,*" Anya ordered, but none of the crewmen moved.

I pulled the phone from my pocket, and suddenly, the crew understood their native language when spoken from the lips of a woman. The phone went away, and down came the ramp. Shawn drove up the steep incline, and we strapped the requisitioned ambulance to the wooden deck of the An-72 with everything we could find, including seat belts we sliced from the cockpit. The medical equipment inside the ambulance was far too valuable to leave on the ground, and the nonexistent heater inside the Antonov worked almost as well as the sunshine in Siberia.

"What are we going to do about the exhaust from the ambulance's engine?" Gator asked.

"Maybe we could pipe it into the cockpit," Shawn said. "It might improve their landings."

Singer said, "All we can do is run it a few minutes at a time and hope to keep Dianne warm enough to stay alive without killing the rest of us with carbon monoxide."

While the team readied the cabin for the trip across the Med, I climbed into the cockpit. "Do we have the fuel to make Algiers?"

The crew looked up in utter confusion, so I shook off my native tongue and tried again, this time in Russian. That seemed to work a little better.

"If wind is good, maybe."

The captain listened to a weather briefing on the radio and said, "Probably, but if not, we can make fuel stop in Tunisia."

"Let's go. When we land in Algiers, your work with us is finished."

All action in the cockpit froze, and the captain said, "It does not have to be. We can do more. You are good man to work for."

I pointed westward. "Algiers, comrades."

* * *

I checked on Dianne only enough to keep up the charade of being a real doctor, but Singer kept her alive. His training as a medic in the Ranger battalion was powerful. I could talk her through the trauma of losing her husband, or maybe even help her stop smoking, but he could dig a bullet out of her gut and plug a sucking chest wound at the same time.

We leveled off, and it got cold in the belly of the Russian cargo liner. Wrapped up in blankets, we stayed as close together as possible until one of the crewmen came back and manhandled a series of valves and levers until warm air flowed into the space.

Our SEAL, who'd been conditioned by the Navy to endure cold beyond the limits of most polar bears, shook his head. "Really, dude? Now you do that?"

The crewman, whose breath Shawn had knocked from his lungs the day we met, took a knee and opened his flight suit, revealing a massive bruise still covering his chest and the imprint of our SEAL's knuckles embedded in his flesh. He pointed toward the ambulance that we'd been running for only minutes at a time in a futile effort to keep Dianne warm.

The man's attempt at English was terrible. "Is for you, no. Is for her, yes."

Shawn bumped me with his shoulder. "How do I say 'I'm sorry, take your shot' in Russian?"

I thought about it and worked out the pronunciation for him.

The SEAL stood, opened his arms, and said, "*Izvinite. Sdelayte snimok.*"

Shawn braced for the coming blow, obviously concerned it was coming about two feet lower than he'd delivered his strike in the center of the man's chest. The Russian stood, wrapped his arms around our SEAL, and patted him on the back. With that, the moment was over, and the cargo bay of the worst airplane I'd ever seen grew warmer in far more ways than any of us could've imagined possible.

* * *

The landing was flawless. In fact, I wasn't certain we had actually touched down until we slowed to a stop.

Singer said, "It must've been the missing seat belts."

I stuck my head inside the ambulance. "How's she doing?"

"Not great," Singer said. "BP's a hundred over fifty-five. Pulse is thirty-one. Respirations are eighteen to twenty-two on fifty percent oh-two."

"Conscious?"

"Sometimes."

By the time the ramp of the Antonov An-72 touched the ground, our Boeing Vertol landed only feet behind the Russian monstrosity, and two flight nurses, along with Dr. Shadrack, descended the ramp with a high-tech gurney between them.

"You brought the whole ambulance?" our doctor said.

I threw up my hands. "It's Shawn's fault. He punched a giant Russian and stole the ambulance. I'm completely innocent."

Dr. Shadrack said, "Those are the exact words I think of every time you enter my mind, Chase—completely innocent. Where's my patient?"

I pointed into Shawn's ambulance.

Minutes later, Dianne Belford Delauter Sakharova was aboard the Vertol and airborne, making a hundred fifty knots toward the Research Vessel *Lori Danielle* and our ship's world-class medical facility.

The Antonov commander approached and tried his English. "Is has for been very . . "

I shook him off. "Let's stick with Russian, my friend."

He nodded. "Your helicopter came and left. This means you are still with us?"

"Only temporarily. They will be back for us. They took our medical patient first, but they are coming back to get the rest of us."

"This is sad for us. We like flying for you. Is always interesting, and food is very good."

"You have to get yourself a better airplane," I said.

He appeared offended. "What is wrong with this one? Is strong and good to land anywhere."

"Perhaps an Antonov Two-Twenty-Five," I said.

He recoiled. "No! Too big. Needs too much runway and always

concrete. I can land this one on football field. Two-Two-Five is like weight-lifting girl. She is strong and powerful but takes too much room and eats too much. This one is like dancer. She is also strong but can leap and twirl. She is my ballerina."

Our Vertol returned, and Ronda No-H, our CFO and door-gunner, ran from the chopper with a Halliburton case tucked beneath her arm. She stuck the case into my hand and ran back to the helo. I took a peek inside at the neatly stacked and banded bills. I loved how Ronda always knew exactly how to pick the perfect gift. The Russian flight crew was going to love it, and the ambassador never needed to know.

I stuck the case in the commander's left hand and shook the other one. "*Spasibo*, comrade Colonel."

Without opening the gift, he took a step back, gave a sharp salute, and turned for the cockpit of his beloved ballerina.

Chapter 31

So Cruel?

I stepped from the Vertol onto the helipad of the RV *Lori Danielle*, the five hundred eighty-eight-foot warship cleverly hidden beneath the veil of one of the world's finest scientific research platforms, and took in the sights, sounds, and smells of a place I hadn't experienced in nearly sixteen months. "Home again, home again, jiggety jog."

Gator froze beside me. "What does that mean?"

"I have no idea," I said. "It's just something my father used to say every time we came home from a trip."

"You're a weird dude, Chase Fulton."

I gave him a nudge toward the ladder. "Hello, pot. I'm the kettle."

He hooked the handrail and slid down. "I get that one."

"Thought you might," I said. "Get the rest of the guys settled in, and I'll meet you in the mess hall in an hour. I'm going to check on our patient."

The medical facility aboard the L.D. made most big-city trauma centers look like neighborhood walk-in clinics. Doctor Shadrack—whose first name I'd never known for some reason—insisted upon merely calling it his sick bay, but it boasted two surgical suites, some of the finest diagnostic imaging equipment available, a laboratory second to none, and a staff whose name tags could've read Mayo Clinic, Johns Hopkins, Mass General, or any hospital they chose, but they all opted for Bonaventure Historic Trust instead. At least that was the name on their paychecks. Who they worked for and exactly what they did had far more to do with *making* history than discovering it.

"How's she doing, Doc?"

Dr. Shadrack pulled off his glasses and rubbed his forehead. "She's dying, Chase, and the only person who seems to have any idea why is your pretty little girlfriend. Care to tell me what that's all about?"

The doctor and I had an interesting relationship. He saved my life on a regular basis, and I gave him a few more stomach ulcers and grey hairs every time I showed up in his "sick bay."

"Let's have a sit-down," I said.

The doctor huffed. "That's what mafia guys do when they're deciding who to whack."

"Exactly."

Shadrack, Anya, and I huddled around his desk, and I said, "Show him the vials."

Anya slid the box across the desk, and the doctor said, "She already showed me. The problem is that we have no idea what's inside."

"This is not truth. Inside is antidote for poison she was given."

Dr. Shadrack furrowed his brow. "Maybe, or maybe it's more poison or an accelerator to make the original poison kill her even quicker. The first thing I need to know is what she was given, and if it was, in fact, poison."

Anya said, "Believe me, Doctor. It was definitely poison. I am certain of this."

"Did you give it to her?"

"No, of course not."

The doctor's glasses came back out of the pocket, but instead of returning to his eyes, he stuck a stem into the corner of his mouth. "Then how do you know it was poison? In fact, how do you know she was given anything, poison or otherwise?"

"This is what Russians do. She was given a slow-acting toxin with antidote. Is common tactic of Cold War. We give poison. Person gets very sick. We say to person, 'Give to us what we want, and we will give to you antidote.' They give to us what we want, and sometimes we give to them antidote. It sometimes works, and they live. Sometimes not, but most of time, we get what we want."

The doctor shook his head. "You Russians have always been on the cutting edge of humanitarianism. God bless you, everyone."

I asked, "So, let's assume Anya is right. What kind of poison do you think she was given?"

He said, "The folks in the lab are tearing it apart as we speak. We'll know in half an hour. Whatever it is, it's making her body incapable of absorbing oxygen at a survivable rate. Do you remember the day you and I met?"

I waggled a hand. "I was a little woozy that day."

He said, "Yeah, well, you remember the circumstances. You'd been blown a couple hundred feet out of the water from beneath the Bridge of the Americas at the south end of the Panama Canal on some crazy mission involving a Chinese spy ship sunk in the Miraflores Locks . . . or some insanity."

"It's all coming back to me now."

"I'll bet it is," he said. "You had the worst case of the bends anybody should've ever survived. I was working on Captain Stinnett's boat back then. We had two recompression chambers, and one of them worked most of the time. I threw you in there and forced enough pure oxygen under pressure into your stupid little twenty-five-year-old body to bring you back from the dead, mostly."

"And I appreciate that, by the way."

He laughed. "I'll bet you do. Anyway, as soon as I'm sure I won't kill your victim in there by squeezing her with compressed air, I'll do the same thing to her. If I can't get her body to absorb oxygen naturally, I'll force it into her under high pressure. You bought me a nice set of upgraded chambers, so we've come a long way since I stuck you in that old phone booth with an air compressor."

I said, "That's just a temporary fix, though, right? You still have to figure out what's actually wrong with her and fix it."

"I assume you've read at least part of the Hippocratic Oath, haven't you? The whole, 'first, do no harm' crap?"

"Sure."

"That's not really all that relevant here," he said. "If I understand it correctly, my sole purpose here is to keep this woman alive long enough for her to tell you her ex-husband's location, right?"

I took a long breath and heard one of Singer's even longer sermons echoing in my head. "That's the primary purpose, but not the sole one. If you can save her, do it. She's not the one who killed Penny."

He leaned back in his chair and spun his glasses by the stem while staring at Anya. "All right, Red Sonja, let's hear it. Tell me about the antidote. Is there a specific order, timeline, storage requirement, shelf life? What do you know?"

"I am sorry. I do not know any of these things."

He blew out his cheeks. "How about quantity? Does it require absolutely every drop of every vial, or can I draw off a minute sample and test it?"

Anya beamed. "This one I know. It does not require all of antidote. Sometimes, only small amount is enough. You can test it."

Dr. Shadrack stood. "Come with me, both of you."

We followed, and he drew four vials of blood from each of us.

"What's that for?" I asked.

He said, "You're a terrible spy, kid. Look at that woman in there. I need to know if the two of you have been exposed to whatever they stuck her with, and if you have, I need to know if I can replicate whatever's in those vials in Anya's magic box. Oh, the box is mine now, by the way."

He taped a piece of gauze over each of our arms where he'd drawn the blood, and I said, "Bring an injection of anything that won't hurt her, and come with me. We're going to tell a lie, and you're going to back me up."

Shadrack reached into his pocket, withdrew a syringe, and said, "This is my favorite part."

We strolled into Dianne's small room, and I took the syringe from the doctor's hand. Without a word, I inserted it into her IV and slowly pressed the plunger.

She looked up through weak eyes, and I said, "Dr. Shadrack and I know exactly what's wrong with you, and we know exactly how to treat it. You're going to be perfectly fine. It'll just take a little time and a few rounds of medication. We're also going to place you in a hyperbaric chamber to help your body absorb the oxygen you need. It won't hurt, but you will be isolated for a while. I've done it many times, and it's actually quite peaceful."

She tried to smile. "Thank you, Doctor."

Shadrack giggled, and when I stomped on his foot, the giggling ceased.

"Now, it's time for you to keep up your end of the bargain. I promised I'd get you out of Greece and save your life. I kept my word. Now, where is Scott Delauter?"

She closed her eyes, and I squeezed her hand. "Where is he, Dianne? The medicine I just gave you is only the first dose. I'm not interested in playing games with your life. Dr. Shadrack and I took an oath."

I raised the heel of my boot, and the threat was enough to ward off a second round of Shadrack's giggling.

Dianne said, "He's in the British Virgin Islands."

Once clear of the room, Shadrack grabbed me to keep from falling to his knees in uncontrollable laughter. "She thinks you're a doctor?"

I pushed him away and let him fall. "I am a doctor."

He composed himself. "Oh, thank God. That means you don't need me anymore, and I can finally retire and go fly-fishing in Montana."

"Okay, cut it out. We had to put on a little masquerade to get her out of the hospital in Greece. It worked, didn't it?"

From inside the lab, a technician in a full-body protective suit stuck her head out the door. "We've got it, Dac."

I stared down at the real doctor. "Did she just call you Dac or Doc? Please tell me your full name is Dac Shadrack, because if it is, this is the best day of my life."

He pretended to ignore me, but I was terrified he was already tying flies for Montana in his mind, so I followed him into the lab.

"What have you got?"

The tech said, "It's complex but also quite simple. I know that's weird, but take a look."

The doctor pressed his face to a microscope and then studied a computer screen above the scope. He whispered, "Cyanide? It can't be cyanide. It's not behaving like cyanide."

The technician said, "Look at the glucose levels."

Dr. Shadrack rubbed his temples. "Something's wrong. You've got to run it all again. Something has to be contaminated."

The tech said, "I ran it six times, and Bruce ran it four. We took the samples three times. There are zero variances. The data is flawless. Forgive me if I'm overstepping, but what did the patient do for a living?"

Dr. Shadrack turned to me, and I said, "She killed her husband, a Russian sugar beet farmer."

The tech yanked off her mask. "Oh, you've got to be lying."

"I'm not a hundred percent certain she killed him, but he was definitely in the sugar beet business."

She said, "This is going to get weird, but stay with me, okay?"

Dr. Shadrack's impatience started to show. "Speak!"

She said, "Sugar beets are these horrible, ugly, sweet potato–looking things. They just look nasty. Anyway, to turn them into sugar, they have to be refined by first turning them into a form of molasses. You know what that is, right?"

Shadrack said, "Yes, we know molasses. It's rum before it becomes rum. Get to the cyanide part, would you?"

She said, "Right. So, the water that comes off the molasses—and there's a lot of it—is full of byproducts, and a small percentage of those byproducts is Prussic acid, better known as . . ."

In stereo with the tech, Dr. Shadrack said, "Hydrogen cyanide."

I grabbed the door frame to the lab. "My God! They poisoned the woman with sugar beets, the very thing her husband made his fortune producing."

Anya said, "Russians can be sometimes terrible people, but not

246 · CAP DANIELS

only Russians. Hydrogen cyanide is same poison used to make product called Zyklon B by Germans. It was used in gas chambers inside Nazi death camps. Why must people inside world be so terrible?"

Anya's question was a good one, but I had a better one in the moment. "Can you save her?"

Dr. Shadrack said, "Yes, probably. We'll load her up with hydroxocobalamin, sodium nitrite, sodium thiosulfate, and all the fluids we can push. And she's going into the chamber immediately."

Chapter 32
Unicorn Octopus

It was time for a little housekeeping, but an unexpected reunion caught me by surprise on my way through Ronda No-H's door.

I said, "I just came by to go over some . . ."

Disco, retired Air Force A-10 driver and our former chief pilot, hoisted himself from the chair across from Ronda's desk and stepped into my arms.

When we parted, he said, "It's good to see you with your boots back on, boss."

The best pilot I'd ever flown with endured back-to-back unimaginable injuries that would've killed a lesser man. That lesser man I was dived into a whiskey bottle and lay on my wife's grave while my friend suffered alone, without the man who was supposed to be his friend and copilot in and out of the cockpit.

In wordless shame, I stood three feet away from Disco, who needed me when I was too cowardly and selfish to be there for him, but he seemed to bear no disdain for the man he should've despised.

"Don't, Chase. There's only so many people any one man can save at a time, and you had more stew than you could stir, as my mother used to say."

"That's no excuse. I was supposed to be—"

He hugged me again. "Don't. We'll talk later. We've both got a lot to talk about. I've missed my friend and flying buddy. Now, go ahead and have your talk with my girlfriend. Just don't flirt with her. I hear she's pretty handy on a gun."

"I've seen her shoot."

He made a sound from the lungs that used to churn like turbines but now sounded more like the little engine that couldn't quite. "That makes you one of the lucky ones. From what I hear, most people who've seen her shoot never get up again."

He wandered off with one hand on the rail, but without the confident stride of the fighter pilot I'd once known.

I took a seat. "How's he doing?"

She shook her head and tossed me a box of tissues. "Not great. He could use somebody who understands, and somebody with a license to listen. Know anyone like that?"

Suddenly, the box of tissues made sense.

She didn't seem upset with me exactly, but I obviously hadn't picked the best time for the interruption. "So, what do you want to talk about?"

I cleared my throat and sat upright. "Everybody's getting paid, right?"

She cocked her head. "We talked about this back at Bonaventure, Chase. All the finances are in order. I'm taking care of everything."

I nodded and studied the scuffs on the toes of my left boot that didn't match my right. When I composed myself to avoid the necessity of pulling another tissue from Ronda's box, I motioned out the door with my chin. "How about him?"

It was her turn to clear her throat. "You carried the same long-term disability policy on Disco that you carry on everybody else. He's still getting paid through the policy, and thanks to you, there's no debt."

"Is his clearance still active?"

"His security clearance?" she asked. "You'd have to talk to Skipper about that, but he's on this ship with access belowdecks, so I'd have to say yes."

I pointed toward her computer. "Write up a job description, and make the title something like Senior Aviation Operations Officer or Master of All Things Aeronautical Under God's Heaven."

She giggled. "That's sweet, Chase, but don't do stuff out of guilt. That man's a war fighter, not a charity case. You can't put him out to pasture in a fancy hat and pay him a stipend to sit on his cute little butt."

"Let me finish," I said. "That's just his title. Make the job description 'your errand boy' or whatever you need. We'll cut a hole in that bulkhead and rip out whatever's back there to make him an office."

She said, "Behind that bulkhead is the primary electronic control module for the ship's independent defensive weapons systems. It's encased in lead, hardened steel, and the linings of unicorn octopus ovaries or something mystical. Are you sure that's the bulkhead you want to cut out?"

"Okay, so maybe I pointed in the wrong direction, but you get my point. Find him something to do. Teach him accounting or something."

She laid down her pen. "Where'd he go to college?"

"I don't know."

"What was his major?"

"I don't know."

"You're lying," she said. "You may be the psychologist on this boat, but just because you've got the license doesn't mean I can't look at your face and know when you're fibbing, big boy. You know he went to the Air Force Academy and graduated second in his class with double majors in aeronautical engineering and economics. After that, he earned a master's degree in accounting while on active duty. Overachiever much?"

"Okay," I said. "I knew he went to the Academy, but I didn't know the rest."

"I'll write his job description, but he's the Deputy Financial Operations Officer. Do you want to talk about a salary?"

I asked, "How much do you make?"

She dropped her chin and glared at me over her glasses.

I shrank in my seat. "Is it more than me?"

She said, "It should be."

I needed a chuckle, and I got one. "Make his salary whatever it was when he was flying full-time, plus whatever the disability insurance payment is, and cancel that garbage. He's not disabled. He just can't fly anymore."

She made a note, and I asked, "Are you going to marry him?"

"If he'll get his mind right."

"How's your cabin?" I asked.

She laid down her pen again. "It's great now that we did the refit, and it's just fine for newlyweds, if that's what you're asking. Disco's quarters are right next door, and they're nice, too."

"It sounds like the welders can open up a wall and—"

She stuck up a finger. "Oh, no. The wall stays. I like the idea of having some place to send him if he acts up. Is there anything else we need to talk about?"

"There is one more thing. I'm going to bring on a few foreigners. Don't worry. They're friendlies. And if all goes well when the mission is over, we're going to take a little R and R in the BVIs. Do you think you can handle that?"

She said, "I'll try to suffer through it, and I'll tell the quartermaster to get ready for your foreign guests. How many, and they don't eat fish heads or anything crazy, do they?"

"Even worse," I said. "Bangers and mash."

* * *

It took me a minute to remember the layout of the ship well enough to efficiently make my way to the mess hall, where the team was gathered with some old friends.

"Well, it looks like you guys are having a little reunion," I said.

The team looked up from the hundreds of firearm parts spread out on mat-covered tables in front of them.

"There's only so long a man can go without his best girl," Singer said as he stroked the well-used and fully disassembled .338 Lapua Magnum in front of him.

Shawn pointed toward an empty seat at the end of the table. "Yours are down there. We figured you wouldn't want to miss the party."

An M4 and a pair of Glock 19s waited for my attention. The armorer had obviously taken very good care of them, but it was nice to run rods down the barrels and cycle the actions. Fresh batteries in the optics and a few adjustments completed the tune-ups.

I said, "Once we're in the Atlantic, we'll do some live-fire drills to freshen up."

Kodiak leaned back and propped his boots on the table. "Is this thing going to turn into that kind of fight?"

I pulled Captain Millgood's knife from my belt and slid it onto the table. "I hope not, but what wins games, Gator?"

The boy-wonder chanted, "Defense, baby. Defense!"

"I don't plan to do much of that on this op," I said, "but if you feel the need to tackle somebody, don't resist the urge."

Singer, as I should've expected, asked, "How's Dianne?"

"You'll never believe it. The Russians poisoned her with a type of cyanide derived from sugar beets."

"Sugar beets?" the sniper said. "The same kind of sugar beets her former husband grew for a living?"

Gator jumped in. "The ex-husband she killed for three point four billion dollars' worth of sugar beets?"

"Exactly," I said.

Kodiak snapped his fingers. "This would be the perfect time for Clark to explain his definition of the word *irony* to us."

With our weapons clean and back in our holsters and slings where they belonged, we filled our bellies with some of the best shipboard food ever served at sea. The luxury liners of the golden age of sea travel may have come close, but I doubt it.

My next stop was the combat information center. The CIC was the waterborne equivalent of Skipper's op center back at Bonaventure and Ginger's lair, wherever it happened to be, but mine was growing cobwebs. I assigned a crew to get it cleaned up and operational while I headed for the navigational bridge.

"Permission to come aboard the bridge, sir?"

"Get your butt in here, and cut that 'sir' garbage."

Captain Barry Sprayberry didn't put down his cup of coffee for many reasons, but I was honored to be one of them. He threw his arms around me, and we made up for the man hugs we missed for too long.

"It's good to see you, Chase. I wondered how long it'd take you to get up here."

"I had a few things to take care of. It's good to see you, too, Barry. How've you been?"

He reclaimed his cup. "Care for some?"

"Absolutely."

I should've known he wasn't offering to serve it to me. "You know where it is. Good luck finding a clean cup."

"Clean cups make coffee taste funny," I said. "How long will it take us to get to Anguilla?"

"Not long after we hit the Atlantic. We have to be careful in the Med. I'm still nervous about running on the foils in heavy-traffic areas."

The *Lori Danielle* could rise out of the water and onto foils resembling wings beneath the waterline, giving her the ability to make speeds in excess of sixty knots in relatively smooth water, and even fifty in seas up to fifteen feet. We made great effort to keep that—and many of her other remarkable capabilities—under wraps, though. The research vessel, which, from all external appearances, she was, shouldn't have such abilities. When angered, her fangs could come out and dispense a venom more deadly than that of most of the world's navies, but even more so than her speed, we tried to keep her fangs well hidden.

"We'll easily make the BVIs inside of four days as long as that tropical storm doesn't overdevelop."

"I haven't seen any weather reports in a while," I said.

He pointed to the electronic chart plotter. "We'll outrun her as long as she doesn't turn north and start gobbling up energy from the warm water."

"Global warming, huh?"

He took a sip of coffee. "Yep, it's a strange phenomenon. Happens every year. We call it summertime. Anyway, are you on some kind of a tight schedule?"

"That depends on a couple of factors. We've got a sick woman downstairs with Dr. Shadrack. Did you know his name is Dac, by the way?"

"Sure, didn't you?"

I said, "No, but we'll come back to that. I need her to live long enough to get to the British Virgin Islands. I also need to pick up Mongo and some British Special Boat Service swimmers along the way. Can we make that happen?"

"SBS guys, huh? Can you keep your SEAL on a chain so they don't kill each other?"

"Believe it or not, they actually get along pretty well."

He laughed. "No, they don't. They just haven't found themselves in a football stadium big enough to start a fight yet. But sure, we can pick 'em up. Where are they?"

"I don't know. Last time I saw them, they were dropping us off in The Hague."

"The Hague. That means 'the hedge.' Did you know that?"

"Of course I knew that. Doesn't everybody?"

He huffed. "Just when I thought I knew something you didn't. Oh well. Figure out where they are, and I'll have Mr. Sulu lay in a course. Wasn't he the guy from *Star Trek*?"

I finished my coffee. "I don't know. I'm not that old. It's good to see you again, Captain."

"You too, Chase. Oh, and it's still your boat. You don't have to ask permission to come on the bridge."

I grinned. "Yeah, I know, but you like it when I do."

I found the CIC again, and even though I didn't know how to use everything, I did remember how to make a secure phone call. The cleaning crew was impressive and already had the place spick-and-span.

Surprisingly, it wasn't Skipper's voice that came on the line. "Good evening. Long Leg's Pizza and Subs. Will this be delivery or carryout?"

Maybe I only thought I knew how to make a secure call from the CIC.

As I tried to decide what to say next, Ginger, Skipper's less-than-five-feet-tall mentor, broke into raucous laughter. "Gotcha, didn't I, hero?"

"I'll have a large meat lovers with a side of kiss my butt."

She ignored my quip. "I see you found your pretty little boat."

"She's neither of those things. She's gorgeous and huge."

"Just like you, right?"

I said, "I'm not letting you off the hook that easily. I need to know where Mongo and his British babysitters are. We'd like to have them join us for a little tropical vacation."

Ginger said, "Skipper's coming on with us. Is that cool?"

"Of course."

Skipper said, "Hey, Chase. How's Dianne?"

"She's going to live. Dr. Shadrack has her in the recompression chamber, and he's treating her for cyanide poisoning."

"I didn't know recompression therapy was part of the treatment for poisoning."

"It's not, but apparently, cyanide kills a person by destroying their cells' ability to absorb oxygen. Dr. Shadrack's theory is that he can force oxygen into the cells under extreme pressure while also using the conventional treatment protocols."

She said, "There's a reason he's the medical officer and you're the . . . whatever you are."

"Exactly. So, the Brits and Mongo?"

She said, "They're near Dover."

"Delaware?"

"No, dummy. The original one. Where do you want them, and how soon?"

I said, "Oh, that one. How about Gibraltar tomorrow or Anguilla in four days? Oh, and tell them to plan on taking a little holiday down island on our dime afterwards."

"They're Royal Military, Chase. It's not like they can just go galivanting off whenever they want."

"Oh, they can't? In that case, get me the number to Buckingham Palace. I'll talk to the Queen about a permission slip."

Skipper huffed. "I'll take care of it. Let's make it Gibraltar. The airfare is cheaper."

I said, "Ronda will appreciate that. We just hired her a new assistant."

Chapter 33
Not His Secretary

"They've got themselves a bloody road runnin' right 'cross the runway o' the aerodrome, don't you know?"

Captain James Millgood seemed entirely unimpressed that I'd arrived to pick him up with an American Boeing Vertol helicopter with a supermodel for a pilot and a pair of M134 General Electric Miniguns hanging from mounts on either side of the remarkable airframe.

I said, "They ran out of room. It's a spit of land that sticks out into an inlet of water they call the Strait of Gibraltar, with an enormous rock at one end if you hadn't noticed."

He said, "It is, isn't it? At least they had the decency to name the bloody road after one of the greatest men ever to smoke a cigar."

"They named it Chase Fulton Boulevard?"

He rolled his British eyes and motioned toward the street sign. "Prime Minister Winston Churchill, you pompous Yank. How've you been, old boy? I see Nigel didn't run you through."

"He let me live," I said, "but he seemed disgusted that I was ever born."

"He's disgusted that his own mum ever bore him, he is. Just his way. Don't think nothing of it."

I asked, "Where's my giant, you imperialist bully?"

"The bloody crew's prying his oversized arse from the cargo compartment. He wouldn't fit up top with us human folk. Big 'un, ain't he?"

"Bigger than most," I said. "But he's got the brain to match."

"Noticed that. How goes that hunt? Did you give the trumpets a blast and send the hounds a runnin'?"

I reached for his bag. "Come on. We'll talk about it on my ship. She's not as nice as yours, but I'm afraid she's all we've got."

The rest of his Special Boat Service swimmers deplaned with Mongo bringing up the rear, as usual, and I wanted nothing more than to wrap the giant sequoia in my arms.

"I was getting worried about you, boss. I told the rest of the guys they'd have to answer to me if anything happened to you."

"They took good care of me," I said. "It sure is good to have you back."

"It's good to be back. I'm looking forward to some groceries I can identify that taste like . . . well, that just taste. Those Brits aren't exactly the gourmets of this side of the Atlantic."

"Get on the chopper. There's plenty of good chow waiting for you on the ship."

We climbed aboard the Vertol and settled in. The SBS swimmers had the reputation of rarely being impressed, so they hid it well, but their commander's eyes betrayed him.

"Not bad, old boy. Must be nice to have the keys to the black-ops coffers."

"If 'by keys to the coffers,' you mean killing a team of hired guns in the Brazilian rainforest who were slaughtering innocent babies and doing their best to murder one of our former teammates turned missionary, then, yeah, I guess we got this thing by having that coffer key in our hand."

"You blokes are the real deal, aren't you, mate?"

"We're just shooters like you, Captain. I'm glad to see you got rid of those fancy pants of yours."

We touched down on the helipad aboard the RV *Lori Danielle*, and the Special Boat Service swimmers' legendary ability to avoid being impressed melted like butter.

Captain Millgood said, "Don't tell me you found this tub in the rainforest, too."

I gave him a wink. "There may have been a coffer involved in this one, but we're debt-free these days. Except to you, of course."

He slapped me on the back as we neared the top of the ladder. "We worked out a payment schedule for that one. I'll ring your bell some late night."

"Looking forward to it," I said.

After a tour of the ship, we settled into the CIC for a briefing, and I brought the Brits up to speed on what we knew.

"Dianne Sakharova is down in sick bay being treated for cyanide poisoning, and according to our ship's doctor, she's improving with every breath."

"The Russians?" one of the swimmers asked. I nodded, and he asked, "If they stuck her with the poison, how'd they lose her?"

"She was worth almost four billion American dollars. It's easy to disappear with that kind of money, even from the Russians."

He let out a whistle. "So, how did *you* find her?"

I said, "A combination of your skipper's friend, Nigel, and my Skipper."

"Your skipper?"

I said, "Yes, my Skipper with a capital S. Here she is now." I brought up the CIC's main monitor. "Skipper, meet the British Special Boat Service team who delivered us from tentacles of watery death and into the slippery grasp of MI-Six in Holland."

More whistles ensued, and Gator rattled a chair. "Take it easy, boys. I may not be able to whip all of you at once, but the ring you see on her left hand belongs to me."

Dingo, my favorite of the swimmers, asked, "Can I have it if I chew it off?"

Gator lowered his chin and balled a fist, but Mongo grabbed his arm. "Take it easy. There's no way to know if he's talking about the ring, the hand, or Skipper. He could even be talking about the computer monitor. Just toss him something edible and let it go. Trust me."

Gator took his advice, tossed the animal a protein bar, and reclaimed his seat.

Skipper said, "Nice to meet you guys. Thanks for taking care of my boys. They get themselves in a mess from time to time."

Anya said, "I am not boy, but she sometimes forgets this."

"I consider you one of the boys, and you know it."

The Russian said, "This is for me compliment. *Spasibo*."

Skipper continued. "Everybody's got a clearance, right?"

Dingo ate the protein bar, wrapper and all, while everyone else nodded, so she continued. "I've got the money."

"All of it?" I asked.

"Every penny except for what they've got at Oceana in cash and whatever other medium they chose. I suspect there's some gold, maybe some bearer bonds, probably some diamonds, and stock certificates or other securities. We won't know until we, or you, get your eyes on it."

"Do you have coordinates yet?" I asked.

"I do, and they should be on the secure server in the CIC. The weapons officer can run the systems, and Ronda No-H can do a lot. I wish I was there."

"You can be. Just catch a flight. We'll be in Anguilla in three or four days."

"That's up to you," she said. "I'm running double duty here. I've got a security team on Pogonya as she checks back into her final quarter in Bern before early graduation, and I'm running this op with Ginger from here. So, it's your call."

I spun to Anya. "What do you think?"

She said, "You and I will make decision together privately."

Millgood's eyes betrayed him again, and I liked it. He loved knowing every detail of every situation, and he had no idea why a Russian would make a security decision about my daughter's return to boarding school.

I said, "We'll table that one and get back with you within ten minutes of wrapping up this briefing."

Skipper nodded. "Okay, back to the money. Like I said, I've got it, but nobody knows. From all outside appearances, it looks like it's never moved. It can still be moved, watched, played with, fondled, whatever, but I can nab it anytime I want. You say the word, and I'll stick it in any account anywhere in the world."

"What's the current value?"

She typed and clicked. "Three point six two five. Do you want me to keep going?"

"No, that's fine. They're making money."

"Duh. You should make money with that much money. I even did a little investing for them behind the scenes."

"Is that legal?"

She huffed. "If you're going to start asking that question, so am I."

"Forget I said it. Have you heard from Gordo, Tubbs, and Slider?"

"Thought you'd never ask."

Another monitor came to life, and our hotshot flight crew came into focus, huddled around a moderate-quality webcam.

They waved in unison. "Hey, guys!"

"Look at Tubbs," I said. "Nice stitches. Chicks dig scars."

Gordo's copilot touched his forehead. "I prefer to sleep through water landings."

I said, "It's good to see you with your eyes open again. Are you doing all right?"

"I am. It was just a little concussion and a few stitches. The docs say I'll be as good as new in no time."

Gordo laughed. "Yeah, but we're hoping for a little better than that. He wasn't all that great when he was new."

"How's the Herk?" I asked.

Gordo said, "She's got a little more than a concussion, and it's going to take more than a few stitches to put her back together."

"Is there a diagnosis yet?"

Gordo pointed toward his loadmaster. "Go ahead, Slider. Give it to him."

He said, "I'm sure this'll come as no surprise, but it was definitely sabotage. The J-Model Herk burns fuel outboard in. That means we use the fuel in the outboard tanks first before switching to the inboard tanks. You may have noticed Mongo boosting me onto his shoulders to take a fuel sample before we left the plane after we ditched in the water."

"So, that's what you were doing," I said.

"That's what I was doing. I'm not just the loadmaster. I'm the closest thing we've got to a flight engineer in that monster, so I wanted to know what those big, beautiful turbines were drinking. I knew something had to be wrong."

I said, "Four fans stopping at once is a pretty good indicator."

"You're telling me. Just like I always do, I drew samples after we took on fuel in Newfoundland, and it looked right, smelled right, and it weighed what it should've. I was primarily checking for water in the fuel. I had no reason to believe it was anything other than JP-eight, our turbines' favorite cocktail."

Slider paused and took a sip of water. "We'll come back to the weight in just a minute, but let's talk about the sample I took when I was on Mongo's shoulders. When I tried to drain what should've been the same JP-eight I saw in Newfoundland, it was soup. Naturally, I thought the plane would sink and take every drop of evidence to the bottom with her, so I kept what little bit I could collect to prove to anybody who'd listen that somebody messed with our fuel."

Mongo put on his enormous, geeky smile. "Please let me tell them the next part."

Slider said, "There's no way you know what's coming next."

My whole team laughed out loud, and Mongo said, "I'll bet you a hundred grand to whatever you make in a week that I've already figured it out based on what you've told us so far."

"You're on, big man, but let's make it two hundred grand to two weeks of my pay."

Mongo said, "Done. Food-grade gelatin in powder form weighs between six point two-five and six point four pounds per gallon. JP-eight weighs six point seven to six point eight pounds per gallon. Your Herk's inboard tanks hold just under seventy-eight hundred pounds each for a total of about fifteen thousand five hundred pounds of fuel. Twenty pounds of powdered gelatin would be more than enough to contaminate that much fuel and kill all four engines, plus the APU. The difference in weight between fifteen thousand five hundred pounds of jet fuel and that much jet fuel minus enough fuel to be replaced by gelatin is eight point five pounds. Nobody, not even NASA, would've noticed an eight-and-a-half-pound fuel difference in a fully loaded cargo plane. How'd I do?"

Slider sat with his mouth agape. "How did you figure that out based on the fact that I said it looked like soup?"

"You said a lot more than that. I just listen differently than most people. So, how and where is the airplane?"

Gordo reclaimed the floor. "The airframe is in pieces and headed for Lockheed Martin for a refit. Her new engines and APU from Rolls-Royce will meet her there."

"Speaking of meeting," I said, "where are you guys?"

"We're hanging out in London waiting for a call from you. We thought you might need a lift somewhere if you could find an empty cockpit for us."

Kodiak asked, "Are you type-rated in the Antonov Seventy-Two?"

"The what?"

"And we thought you guys were real pilots," Kodiak said.

I tried to take control of the peanut gallery. "Grab a flight to the BVIs or Anguilla. Skipper, can you make some arrangements for them?"

"Sure, no problem."

I stood. "That's all we've got time for right now. We've got a lot of work to do, but we'll catch up on the island. Oh, wait! One more thing."

Gordo leaned toward the camera, and I asked, "Do you have a rotor ticket, and are you a CFII?"

"Yes to both."

"Good. Since you wrecked your previous employer's airplane, you're probably looking for work, so doctor up your résumé, iron your best flight suit, and call my secretary to schedule an interview."

Skipper almost yelled, "I'm *not* his secretary!"

Chapter 34

Man Overboard

I said, "Calm down, Skipper. I wasn't talking about you."

She huffed. "When in the history of calming down has telling a woman to calm down actually worked, *Doctor* Fulton?"

"We've got a lot of work-up to do in prep for Oceana. Do you have anything else for us?"

She said, "Are you hiring Gordo and his guys?"

"I don't know. We don't even own an airplane right now."

"We can get another airplane, Chase. I just need to know if I should start the prep work for them."

"Ronda will handle most of that, but yes, if they want the job, we need a flight crew. Disco is out. Gator isn't ready. And I'm . . . well, I'm no good for a while, so get the ball rolling just in case they say yes."

"They're going to be expensive," she said.

"All the good ones are. We'll find a way to pay for them. Get me some satellite coverage over the BVIs and especially Oceana. I need to know what we're walking into."

"We're already on it," she said. "It's a fortress."

"I knew it would be. That's why I wanted the Brits. They seem to have a fetish for knocking heads, and I plan to parade them right into the middle of a dandy."

Dingo growled like one of the hounds of Hell, and I took that as a very good sign.

Skipper said, "Can you have everyone give us the room? Everyone except you and Anya."

I turned. "Shawn and Gator, get the SBS swimmers down to the armory and geared to the teeth for a shooting house op. I want to see them shoot. A few days from now, we're hitting a seriously hardened facility with high security on the surface. We'll have headcounts and physical security inventory in a few hours, but that's the easy part. Once we ring that doorbell and they invite us in, we've got a second facility underwater that we believe to be two hundred eight feet or eighty-five meters—if my math is correct. We've got exactly zero intel on the wet one, and that may not change until we put eyes on it. Gear up for the shoot house today, but go ahead and draw what you need for the actual assault as well."

Captain Millgood asked, "Why are we hitting this facility?"

I locked eyes with the commando. "It's where my target is."

"The man who killed your wife?"

I nodded once.

He said, "Then I reckon it don't matter how many of 'em there are nor how hard the target is. As long as that armory of yours is stacked deep enough, we can manage."

"Full disclosure," I said. "There may be a pretty good-sized stash of cash and other valuables when we hit this place. I made a deal with a Russian ambassador to get the money that's owed to the Kremlin back to Red Square in return for them giving me the woman who can lead us to Scott Delauter, the man who's responsible for Penny's murder."

Millgood said, "And I take it that's the woman you've got down in sick bay, eh?"

"That's right."

"Then this ain't 'bout the money, then?"

I shook my head.

"All right, then. Let's see this armory of yours whilst you have a chat wiff the girls."

The CIC emptied, and Anya and I slid closer to the screen and camera.

Skipper said, "I want to make sure our security doesn't overlap in

Bern. I don't need my guys shooting at your guys and vice-versa."

Anya said, "And I want to make sure it does overlap. I have team of twelve Norwegian and Swiss Special Forces watching her. They are very good. I will send to you dossier on each of them."

Skipper said, "I've got five former Rangers, four Green Berets, and one former Delta operator. Their dossiers are on the secure server in the CIC. WEPs or Ronda can retrieve it for you."

"I can do this," Anya said. "I am not just pretty face."

Skipper laughed and waved a hand. "You've never really been all that cute, but you've got a decent personality, so that makes up for it. So, you're taking the Brits in with you?"

Anya sighed. "I think this means you should be very glad you are pretty."

Skipper gasped. "Ouch. Nicely done. Now, about the Brits."

I said, "I'm not sure what's going on with you two, but you're scaring me. We're too light without them, and it's the BVIs. I figured a Union Jack flying with our Stars and Stripes on our stern wouldn't hurt."

"You're a thinker, Chase Fulton. I'll give you that much."

"Speaking of thinking," I said, "I need some ideas from both of you. What do I tell Dianne?"

Anya didn't hesitate. "You tell her you are going to feed ex-husband to sharks in tiny bits and take all of her money."

"She'll figure that out," I said. "Do you really think I need to tell her?"

Skipper piped up. "Didn't you tell her you were going to save her life?"

"I did tell her that, and that's exactly what I'm doing. I didn't tell her how long I'd let her keep that life I'd save, though."

The analyst tapped her chin with a pen. "I can't believe I'm saying this, but I sort of agree with Anya. I say you tell her the truth, mostly. Tell her what Delauter did, and give her the option to choose sides."

Anya said, "This is terrible idea. She loves him. She does not care what he did. Chase could kill president of United States and destroy also moon in sky, and I would still love him."

That silenced the room until Anya said, "I mean, I was only making example. Of course no one can destroy moon. Maybe Chase, if anyone, but probably not."

Skipper closed her eyes and shook her head. "Please tell me you two haven't moved in together already."

"This is ridiculous thing to say. Of course not. I have now much better idea of what to tell to Dianne."

"Thank God," Skipper said. "Let's hear it, and please tell me it doesn't involve the moon."

"I think we should tell to her nothing. If she knows nothing, she can make plan to do nothing to screw up plan we have. She is very smart. Chase saved her life. Even if she does not like him, she has sense of, maybe word is *favor* for him. Perhaps we can use this to advantage for us. If we cannot, she is only woman, and she is easy to control physically."

Skipper widened her eyes. "I like it. As long as she's an asset, we use her to the full extent of her value. If she becomes a liability, we lock her up."

Anya said, "But cutting throat is much quieter."

I leaned back in my chair, relieved the craziness hadn't gotten completely out of hand. "My father had an interesting saying about assets and liabilities. He used to say, 'If a man's got too many liabilities, his assets in jail.' I think *ass sets* may have been two words when he said it, but I'm pretty sure you get the point."

Anya frowned. "I do not understand this."

Skipper frowned. "Go to work. I'll call you when the satellites get into position."

* * *

The North Atlantic Ocean is a misunderstood body of water. Most people tend to think of it as the iceberg-ridden bit of frigid water where the *Titanic* met her fate. That's only a tiny portion of it. The North Atlantic is the whole of the Atlantic Ocean, lying north of the equator. Much of it is temperate water teeming with unimaginable life, and some of that life was aboard the unimaginable RV *Lori Danielle* that afternoon as we put the Mediterranean well astern and steamed westward. My team was busy installing the shooting house on the stern weather deck while the Brits were gearing up in the armory.

I helped slide the final panel into place. "What are we going to see when they get inside?"

Kodiak said, "They're hardcore operators. We don't need to see them press a trigger. We need to learn to adapt and operate *with* them. If we don't move as one, we die as many."

"That's deep, man. You've been reading bathroom walls again, haven't you?"

"I heard some old guy say it one time, and now I'm an old guy, so I figure I've earned my stripes."

"I'd say you've earned yours and a few others, my friend. Have you ever worked with the SBS before?"

"No, but I know a bunch of guys who have, and they say they're good. They're just faster than us, and I don't love that. We either have to find a way to slow them down, or we have to speed up."

"Not necessarily," I said. "We can just let them go first."

"There is that."

"I don't want to get any of the good guys hurt, though, and with the money Dianne has, she can afford to buy some of the best security there is."

Kodiak said, "Look at the jokers she bought in the hospital in Greece, and she didn't buy us."

I sighed. "No, the Russians bought us."

He said, "No, the Russians rented us, and that's worse. But don't you worry. I'll wear that scarlet letter for you or anybody else on this boat because we're brothers, and that's what brothers do. Now, let's push these limey goats through the gate and watch them shoot."

Gator and Shawn, my two favorite sheepdogs, herded their flock of

Englishmen to the weather deck while kitted out in gear befitting the commandos they were, and I wasted no time taking command.

"Gentlemen, and Dingo, the course of fire is this. You will clear this structure of an unknown number of hostiles and hostages. These individuals will be simulated by lifelike mannequins in various positions, and they will have the ability to return fire. Their fire will be hard plastic munitions that will sting but will not cause permanent damage. Dingo, do not eat the hard plastic pellets. This is a live-fire exercise. The rifles you've been issued are chambered in nine-millimeter, as are the sidearms. The rifles you'll be issued for the actual mission will be chambered in five-five-six but will otherwise be identical to these. Do not kill each other. Do not kill any hostages. Kill only hostage takers and direct aggressors. If you can subdue a potential bad guy without killing him, do so, but do not put yourself or your team at risk by doing so. Any questions?"

Captain Millgood asked, "Are there directional restrictions for fire?"

"No, these walls were specifically designed for this type of training aboard this vessel. Shoot in any direction you wish. The deck is steel, so rounds will ricochet. The walls and overhead will absorb the rounds."

"How will you observe?" one of the swimmers asked.

"We have cameras everywhere, including on your gear. Ignore them, and operate as you've been trained. We want to know exactly what to expect of you when we hit our target. And gentlemen, make no mistake. We will hit a target—a very hard target—and that target will hit back. Do it right, and do it hard. After we've seen you work it a few times, we'll start blending teams, and we'll learn to do it together."

I studied the swimmers' eyes, and they looked identical to those of my men before we'd stepped through a thousand doors together. "Men, there are no limits on ammunition. We have thirty tons of it. Train hard, and train as if the lives of the men behind and in front of you depend upon it. It's your op, Captain Millgood. Make a good show of it . . . or whatever you guys say."

My team and I backed away and fired up the monitors.

Millgood's men broke into two squads of four and discovered our first obstacle. The lead man tapped a fist to his helmet, signaling breacher up. An instant later, the obstacle was obliterated beneath the head of a twelve-pound sledgehammer without the use of a single ounce of explosives. The teams moved like lightning, clearing left and right without hesitation at any opening. Pistol-caliber rifle fire raged until planned malfunctions arose, and the fighters responded in textbook fashion by switching to pistols and continuing the fight. At precisely the right times, they resolved the malfunctions with their rifles, returned their sidearms to their holsters, and brought their primary weapons back into use. I loved everything about their tactical precision.

Bad guys with hostages fell like sawn timber. Threatening fighters with weapons ate bullets and met the same fate, but careful and well-covered abduction and securing of prisoners was yet one more of the team's flawless skill sets. The second team evacuated the hostages to safety, covered for security, and triaged for injuries.

Not a single muzzle swept the back of another swimmer. Not a single word was uttered above a tone that would draw adverse attention to the rapidly moving squad. Not a step was missed. No corner was uncleared. No overhead space was ignored. No hostage was even brushed by a supersonic round. The Special Boat Service swimmers were some of the finest close-quarters operators I'd ever seen.

As they neared the end of the exercise, I called Shawn and Mongo close. "Pick one of them—I don't care which one, as long as it's not Millgood—and put him overboard the instant he comes through the door."

My men answered in perfect unison. "Yes, sir."

When the swimmers reached the limits of the shooting house, they performed a maneuver my team had considered but rarely done. They back-cleared the structure, moving back through the building and double-checking that every inch had been vacant and secured. No more hostages or wounded were in need of rescue, and no more bad guys were in need of additional pain.

I slapped Mongo and Shawn on the shoulders. "Go!"

The instant the door to the shoot house opened, Mongo grabbed the first man's shoulders, and Shawn wrangled a boot. The Brit was overboard before he drew another breath. My men backed away, and the swimmers identified the drill immediately.

One of them yanked a life ring from the stern rail and threw it with all of his might toward his teammate. He froze in position, never taking his eyes from the man in the water. A second man ran forward and up every ladder he approached, yelling, "Man overboard!"

A third man glared upward at the sun for an instant, then down at his watch, took a compass bearing, and ran for one of the life rafts in a white barrel mounted on each stern quarter. He and another man hefted the barrel overboard and followed it over the rail without hesitation.

The line came tight, and the barrel parted, activating the compressed-air cartridges inside to inflate the raft. Within seconds, the two swimmers were inside the raft with the paddles deployed and rowing toward their brother, who was well astern of the ship.

Millgood stood against the stern rail, keeping careful mental notes of everything his men did and the precise timing of their every move.

I stepped beside Shawn. "Take Millgood into the water, and go with him."

"Aye, sir."

Shawn hit the SBS commander like a linebacker, and over the rail they went.

This time, it was Dingo who responded. He took the second life raft over the rail by himself, but an entirely different reaction came from the remainder of the SBS crew.

They dropped the magazines from their rifles and pistols, cleared the chambers so there was no question the weapons were safe, and pinned my team to the bulkhead of our own ship.

"On your knees with your hands over your heads, now!"

The ship slowed and initiated a turn. "Attention, all hands. This is the captain. This is a training drill. This is a training drill. Multiple men and equipment overboard. We are coming about to starboard and initiating recovery procedures. All recovery personnel report to recovery stations immediately. Medical personnel, stand by to recover wounded. All other training exercises shall cease immediately. That is all."

Chapter 35

A Madman, Absolutely

As the recovery crew plucked men and equipment from the water, Anya sidled up beside me. "What did you learn?"

"I learned that I want every single one of them on our team. I've never seen anything like it. They love each other more than they love anything else in the world. Did you see the way they sacrificed themselves first?"

"I did," she said. "That cannot be taught. It must be already inside man's heart when he is born, and we have it already in ours."

"I know we do, and that's part of why I love seeing it so much with those Brits. We're going to win this thing, you know."

"We always do," she said.

"Penny didn't."

Anya groaned, and I wished a thousand times in a single instant that I could've taken back the comment.

The deck chief trotted up. "All personnel and equipment aboard with no injuries, sir. But, sir . . ."

"What is it?"

He glanced across his shoulder and screwed up his face. "Sir, one of the SBS swimmers caught a fish with his mouth, and he's eating it raw."

In unison, Anya and I said, "Dingo."

I pulled my radio from my belt. "Bridge, Sierra One."

"Go for bridge."

"All aboard and secure. No injuries."

"Roger. Stop throwing people off my ship, would you?"

I said, "Aye, sir."

We watched Dingo finish his meal, and I said to Anya, "Have our team run some drills with the Brits, and then set up a boarding drill. I want to watch the SBS guys try to take us."

She put on the American smile she'd worked so hard to learn. "Aye, sir."

"It freaks me out when you do that."

"I know. This is why I do it. We should make telephone call to our daughter later, yes?"

"Definitely."

I found Captain Millgood and said, "Good show, mate."

"I wasn't expecting to go into the water. Nice finish."

"When you train your men, how often do they expect what you throw at them?"

He gave me a slap on the back. "For a man who's just lost his wife, you're doing okay, I'd say. Do you always push this hard?"

"Don't you?"

Instead of answering, he asked, "Got anyone to talk to?"

"I talked to Jack Daniel for about a year after she was murdered."

"Understandable. Clear of that ghost, are you?"

"He still chases me around, but I don't let him in."

He shook the water from his hair. "Men like us, we don't exactly sit on sofas and tell other men 'bout our troubles, but them of us who've been there sit and listen pretty fair I reckon."

"Do you charge by the hour, Captain?"

He laughed. "Mates don't charge. Did a little diggin' on you, I did. That Board of Examiners in Georgia gave you a fancy plaque for your wall, and I see that you run a pretty fine shop for helpin' boys like mine get through fits of wanting to drive spikes through their own heads. By my estimation, that makes you the kind of man who cares a lot more about men like me and mine than about himself."

I said, "Maybe we've got that in common, Captain."

"How 'bout just Jimmy, eh, Doctor?"

"How 'bout just Chase, eh, Jimmy?"

* * *

Sick bay and its single patient looked a little different than the last time I visited. Dianne was sitting in a chair with a steaming cup of what I assumed was tea in one hand and a Russian copy of *War and Peace* in the other.

"You look like you feel better," I said in the language she'd been reading.

She looked up and smiled. "*Da.*"

We switched to English. "How was the recompression chamber?"

She grimaced. "May I be blunt? It sucked."

"It does," I said. "I've spent far too many hours in that thing. It's like being inside one of those pneumatic tubes at the bank drive-through."

"That's exactly what it's like," she said, "but you can't bring your book."

I said, "Nope. It might cause a spark, and a spark in a pure oxygen environment tends to make things exciting."

"That's what they tell me."

"How are you feeling?" I asked.

"Everything still hurts, but Dr. Shadrack says my kidneys are healing, my vision is improving, and I'm gaining weight. No woman wants to hear that, but in this case, I'll take it."

She held up the pulse oximeter on her finger, and I took a look.

"Eighty-four. That's a definite improvement."

"The doctor says I have to stay on the oxygen until I'm steadily in the nineties again."

Sometimes an abrupt change of subject spurs honesty better than anything else.

"You were poisoned by the Russians because they believe you killed your former husband, Ivan Sakharov, to inherit his fortune from Sibirskiy Geotekhnicheskiy Kholding."

"Of course that's what they think, just like they think the company belonged to the State. It did not, by the way. It was and is a privately held company."

"None of that is my business," I said. "I'm simply here because I don't believe the Cold War ever ended. I'm still fighting it every day."

"So, you're CIA."

"No, ma'am."

She looked around the ship's medical bay. "Naval Intelligence?"

I shook my head. "Also, no. I'm just someone who believes the Russians are still our enemy, and I absolutely must speak with your ex-husband, Scott Delauter."

"Tie those two things together for me, please."

I said, "The Russians want the money you inherited from your husband's 'privately held' company, just like you said. They were willing to murder you slowly and hand the antidote over your head to get that money. The problem is that you were smarter than them, and you had enough money to hide in an obscure little hospital in Greece where they'd never think to look."

"Keep going," she said. "You're doing fine so far."

"I found you because I have different resources and motives than the Russians. The money means nothing to me. All I want is a face-to-face meeting to ask some questions of Mr. Delauter."

She said, "Tell me the truth. Are you really a doctor?"

"I really am, duly licensed and board-certified by the states of Georgia, Florida, Virginia, and Alabama. I don't practice very much, though, and I had no authority of any kind to practice in Greece."

"What about the Russian woman?"

"Anya? Oh, she's definitely not a doctor or even a nurse. She's an assassin and an extremely good one. She was trained by the KGB and SVR, but she defected to the U.S. and now works for us. Her loyalty to the United States is beyond reproach. If it were not, I would kill her without another thought and never miss a moment's sleep. She detests Russia and the former Soviet Union and deeply loves freedom and the West."

She frowned. "Why haven't you asked me where my loyalties lie?"

"Because I don't care. I care for only one thing, and I've told you that repeatedly. I must speak directly with Scott Delauter, face-to-face. Once that's done, I'll walk away, and neither you nor he will ever see me again. It's that simple."

She closed the enormous book, placed it on the stainless-steel table beside her chair, and said, "Then bring me a telephone. We can make that happen in minutes."

I furrowed my brow. "You can produce Scott Delauter to stand in front of me in minutes with a simple telephone call?"

"No, of course not. Don't be ridiculous. But I can have him on the telephone to answer your questions."

"That's not what I said, Dianne. I said that I must speak with him face-to-face. A man can lie without repercussion on the telephone, but if he's looking into my eyes, I'll know in an instant if the words on his lips are the truth or deception."

"My God," she said. "You're going to torture him."

"I have no such plan. I only plan to ask him some questions. He'll either tell the truth or lie. If he tells the truth, I have a course of action that must be taken that does not involve him. If he lies, I have another. It's that simple. There is no torture involved. I don't care if he lies or tells the truth. I simply need to watch him do it in person. That's why I saved your life at great risk to my own and that of my team."

"You're a madman, Dr. Fulton."

"Yes, ma'am. Absolutely. And men like me are the only reason that you and the rest of the world get to pretend to live in sanity."

She seemed to consider my contention. "Make for Anguilla. You'll find him near there. Are you going to kill me when this is over, Dr. Fulton?"

"Only if you force me to, Widow Sakharova, but not if you cooperate and give me exactly what I want, Mrs. Delauter."

* * *

Inside the combat information center, I found Captain Sprayberry, WEPs, Ronda No-H, and a young officer I hadn't met. "Good afternoon, folks. Sorry I'm late. We've been playing Cowboys and Britains downstairs."

Captain Sprayberry grunted. "Oh, I know what you've been doing, and next time somebody gets thrown off my ship, it's going to be you."

"I should've expected that."

Barry motioned toward the young man. "Chase, meet NAVs. He's the newest officer aboard. As the name implies, he's now our navigational officer, fresh out of the United States Navy."

I shook the young man's hand. "Nice to meet you. I'm Chase Fulton."

"The pleasure's all mine, sir."

"Why did you leave the Navy?"

"I didn't leave the Navy, sir. They left me. I got shot, so they retired me."

"Retired you? How old are you?"

"Twenty-seven, sir."

"Oh, for God's sake," Barry groaned. "The kid's an Academy grad with two years of sea duty, two years of SEAL training, and he took nine bullets on his second deployment as a frogman. Is that a good enough résumé for you?"

I threw up my hands. "Sorry. Welcome aboard, NAVs. It's good to have another frogman. You and Shawn will have to swap stories."

"It ain't story time," Barry said. "We've got work to do. Tell Chase about the trench, kid."

NAVs pulled up a chart of the British Virgin Islands. "This is the BVIs, and this is Anguilla. Between them is a stretch of water known as Anegada Passage. It's the deepest stretch of water in that region of the Caribbean at around seventy-five hundred feet. On the banks of the trench are small, mostly uninhabited islands because there's no freshwater source. It's about eighty-five miles from Anguilla to Spanish Town in the BVIs."

"Don't get carried away," Barry said. "Move on to Oceana."

"Yes, sir. The island in question is right here." He moved the cursor to bring up a small island. "It's forty-five miles northwest of Anguilla, and, as you can see, it's completely barren. That's Oceana, sir."

I said, "Enough with the sir. I'm just Chase. What you do with the captain is his thing, but you're a freaking SEAL. I should be calling you sir. I'm just a one-legged civilian. Are you sure that's the island we're looking for?"

"Yes, sir. I mean, yes, Chase, I'm sure. Skipper delivered the coordinates, and that's it."

"How about satellite coverage?" I asked.

"We've got that, too." He pulled up a pair of monitors with high-def imagery, and the island was a desert.

"It's rocks and sand," I said.

NAVs grinned. "It would appear, sir, but . . . sorry."

"Just go on," I said. "What is it?"

He said, "Skipper is amazing. Take a look at this."

He zoomed in, and the imagery came alive as if the wind were blowing the sand around at ultra-high speed.

"What's happening?" I asked.

"Skipper ran a program to compile past satellite imagery, like time-lapse photography in reverse, and look. What do you see?"

I studied the pictures closely. "Tank tracks."

"Close," NAVs said. "Bulldozer tread tracks. They built something, but only at night, and they buried the equipment during the day. It took a really long time and a lot of patience, but they did it."

"What did they build?" I asked.

"We won't know until we can get a GPR drone over it."

I raised a finger. "Let's speak English that old guys can understand."

"Sorry. Ground penetrating radar."

I stared at the monitor. "How deep is the water around that island?"

NAVs said, "Immediately off the island, it's between two-sixty and three-forty, but just a half mile off the island, it's two thousand feet deep."

I raised my eyes to meet Barry's, and I didn't have to ask.

He said, "Two to two and a half days, but we can't run your boarding drill with the Brits if we're running on the foils."

"I don't care about the boarding drill. Get us to Oceana as fast as this thing will fly, and will one of you smart people get me a secure connection with Skipper?"

NAVs and the captain vanished, but WEPs and Ronda stayed behind.

Skipper's face appeared bright and clear in seconds. "Thank you, guys. I'll take it from here. So, I take it you met the new navigational officer. Cute, isn't he?"

I said, "Didn't notice, but you're married. Nice work on the time-lapse photo work on Oceana. Any theories on what they built?"

"I've got more than a theory," she said. "They built the underwater fortress. It requires an enormous above-water support system. It had to cost a fortune."

"How did they do it without anybody noticing?" I asked.

"I'm sure plenty of people noticed, but nobody cares. Rich people build all sorts of things on private islands all the time. Nobody pays any attention."

"I'll buy that," I said. "Your cute little navigational officer was a SEAL. Did you know that?"

"I did not, but I'm impressed."

"He wants to fly a GPR drone over the island and have a look at what's beneath the surface. Thoughts?"

"They'll shoot it down."

"You think?"

She said, "I know. There's no way they'll let us fly anything over that island. If they don't shoot it down, they'll jam it and/or make it crash."

"What do you recommend then?"

"I know you've had a tough year, but you've forgotten about the highest of high-tech gadgets Dr. Mankiller built for us."

I let my mind play through the enormous list. "I give up."

She said, "Remember DREAMUP, the deep-sea remote exploration autonomous manned utility platform?"

I palmed my forehead. "How could I have forgotten that thing? Please tell me it's somewhere we can retrieve it without adding a month to this mission."

"Take a little walk down five flights of stairs, through a pair of high-security doors, and you'll find her beneath a protective layer of space-age material I think they call canvas."

Chapter 36
Experience of a Lifetime

I sprinted from the CIC and grabbed Mongo from the live-fire training exercise on the weather deck. "Come with me. I need that enormous brain of yours."

Instead of protesting, he cleared his weapons, reported to his team leader, and followed me at a run. "Where are we going? Is everybody all right?"

"We're headed for the cargo hold just above the moonpool, and everybody's fine."

His gear rattled against his body as we traversed ladders and corridors as quickly as our boots would carry us. "Cinch that rig up. You sound like a can of marbles."

When we entered the code to access the secure doors into the cargo hold, one of the rarest events in all of clandestine operations occurred: Skipper was wrong.

The machine wasn't covered in canvas. She was hermetically sealed inside a thick membrane and mounted on a collection of pneumatic shocks apparently designed to absorb the ship's vibration and thunderous pounding at sea.

Mongo planted a massive palm against the bulkhead. "DREAMUP. Since we collected the vaquita with Dr. Taylor, this thing has been camped out in here with nothing to do."

"Do you remember how to operate it?"

He sighed. "Some. I mean, it can do so many things, and we can configure it to do almost anything. If it can be done from a mobile underwater platform, this thing can do it."

"That wasn't my question. I need to know if you can operate it."

He raised his shoulders. "Not without some practice. We need Dr. Mankiller. This is her baby."

"Let's make some calls."

Five decks closer to the sun, we brought the CIC to life, and Skipper had good news. "The boxes from your Dutch friend arrived."

"That's great," I said. "Please tell me we've got comms with Dr. Mankiller."

"Of course we do. The Bonaventure op center is temporarily wired through Michel's gear and encrypted. Even if the Russians are listening, they'll only know that we're talking. They won't understand what we're saying."

"You're really good at this spy thing, you know that?"

She said, "I'm really good at everything I do. Just ask Gator."

"Nope! Not going there, but I'd really like for you to be good at connecting me with Celeste and getting her on a plane to Sint Maarten."

"Maho Beach?" Skipper asked.

"Yes, ma'am."

"We're on our way, but only if we can ride the fence."

"We?"

"Sure. Why not? You said you wished I could be there to operate out of the CIC. If I'm sending Dr. Mankiller, why wouldn't I come too?"

I said, "Great, but I still need to talk to her."

"Stand by. She'll be on the line in thirty seconds."

True to her word, Skipper had Dr. Celeste Mankiller's face on monitor number three in less than half a minute. "Chase! How's it going?"

"I need you, Celeste. Feel like a trip down island?"

"You know it, baby. When and where?"

"Skipper will handle the details, but we'll put you on the ground at

Sint Maarten and chopper you aboard the *Lori Danielle* for a mission involving your DREAMUP."

"Seriously? We finally get to use her in a real mission for something other than catching vaquitas? Please tell me it's something cool."

"We're going to demolish about ten years' worth of construction, a billion dollars' worth of infrastructure, and I get to grill and eat the heart of the man who murdered Penny."

"I'll pack a bikini. Is Mongo with you?"

"He is."

"Good," she said. "He's the only one smart enough to bring DREAMUP back to life. She's been dormant a long time, and the process is long and slow. If you want to use her, I need Mongo twenty-four-seven until I get there."

"He's all yours."

"Ooh, I like the sound of that. A big strong man with a brain like his . . . ? Sorry, I've been locked up by myself in the lab for way too long. What's our time frame?"

"Two days."

I expected panic, but instead, she said, "No problem. Between the big guy and me, we could build a new one from scratch in two days. Put him on, and get out of our way. We've got a lot of work to do."

"Here he is, but I have to warn you, he looks a lot more like a soldier than a scientist right now."

She raised her eyebrows. "That makes him even hotter. Oh, and Chase . . ."

"Yeah?"

"It's good to see you back in the game. And Pogonya is the best. We missed you."

"Yeah, she's pretty amazing, isn't she?"

I left the big brains to work out the details of bringing the deep-sea remote exploration autonomous manned utility platform back to life while I worked on a plan to use the beast to its fullest capacity and bring the rest of the team up to speed on our latest intel.

Cramming our expanded team into the CIC made my decision to double the size of the space one of the better decisions of my command, especially since Dingo apparently didn't own a toothbrush.

I had WEPs bring up the same charts and satellite imagery I'd seen earlier, and I started the briefing. "What you see here is our target."

"Looks like somebody beat us to it," Singer said.

"That's the same thought I had the first time I saw it," I said, "but play back the time-lapse thing Skipper made."

While the video was cycling, I said, "For those of you who don't know, this is WEPs. He's our weapons systems officer and one of the best gunners at sea. If it floats, he can sink it. If it's submerged, he can sink it. If it's flying, he can sink it. Generally, he's pretty good at making things stop doing what they're doing, especially if they're a threat. I don't recommend starting a gunfight with him."

The video played, and the tracks appeared in the sand. The gathered crowd leaned in, and I said, "What you see is construction equipment tracks from coincidental satellite imagery collected randomly over several years. The imagery is random because there's no reason to constantly record data in the BVIs."

"Unless you're lookin' for topless babes, eh?"

I don't know who'd said it, but I had to concede his point. "Perhaps we should have NASA park one over Jost Van Dyke."

Another Brit said, "If you've got the bloody quid, why not?"

"Anyway, back to the briefing. What these tracks represent is a massive construction project over several years to turn this barren hunk of rock and sand into an underwater fortress called Oceana. I was wrong earlier when I briefed you about the island. We believed it to be a superstructure stronghold, but that's not what it is at all. Every inch of it is underwater, and that's what we're up against."

Captain Millgood said, "No worries. That's our world, mate."

I loved the SBS swimmers more with every second they were aboard. "I know, and that's why you're here. You may have noticed that we're doing a little flying. This ship is anything but conventional.

We're on foils and making . . ." I turned to WEPs, and he said, "Fifty-seven knots."

I did a little math. "I could convert that to kilometers."

"No need. Bloody fast is what it converts to, and we know 'bout knots. We been sailing longer than you Yanks been a country."

"Point taken," I said. "Show 'em DREAMUP."

WEPs brought up a 3-D rotating image of the machine, and I said, "This is the deep-sea remote exploration autonomous manned utility platform, or DREAMUP, for short. It's powered by a pair of hydrogen cells, and it strips hydrogen molecules from the seawater—by some sorcery that I don't understand—for propulsion. Apparently, there are a lot of benefits to that business, but I don't care. What I do care about is the fact that this beast can carry anything to any depth, fire any weapon, retrieve anything, and return it to the surface without humans being involved."

Captain Millgood asked, "What if we humans—excluding Dingo o' course—want to be involved?"

I grinned. "I thought you'd never ask. Remember that whole stripping-hydrogen thing I mentioned? I took just enough chemistry to know what ocean water is made of. It's hydrogen, oxygen, and salt. There are a few other little things in there, but we're interested in the oxygen. When DREAMUP strips hydrogen it needs, it spits out oxygen we need."

"I took chemistry, too," Gator said. "It also makes chlorine gas."

"Yes, it does, my young friend, and chlorine gas likes to react violently when you point it at things like alcohol, ammonia, and gasoline. They just might happen to have a few of these things in their little subaquatic lair, and we might get to have a little fun with them."

"All of this sounds cool, but what's the plan?" Gator asked.

"We're going to affix cameras and various other surveillance and observation gear to DREAMUP, launch her from a few miles away, and let her do some silent snooping. Did I mention that she's sonar- and radar-absorbing? She emits soundwaves that are precisely one hundred eighty degrees out of phase with every other sound she makes, and that makes her practically silent to all listening devices."

"Except seismographs," Kodiak said.

Before I could argue, Singer spoke up. "That place sits on the edge of the Anegada Passage. It's not exactly the Mariana Trench, but it creaks and cracks constantly. I did some sniper training out there, and I could watch the tremors in the crosshairs of my scope, so we don't have to worry too much about anything that could sound natural."

Captain Millgood said, "So, if we're going to hit this place with an ROV, why do you need us? You might as well drop a nuke on it and sail away."

"Sorry, Captain. I didn't mean to get sidetracked from your earlier question. First, DREAMUP isn't just an ROV. It's like nothing you've ever seen. Seconds, we're not hitting Oceana. We're doing recon and messing with it with the machine. When we hit it, we're doing so together—with your team and mine. When we get what we want and need out of there, we may let WEPs have a little fun with the place, but the hit comes from you and me."

I paused and pulled Millgood's knife from my belt. "Scott Delauter is inside Oceana, and I'm going in there to bring him out. He's going to stand under the sun just like I did when I watched my wife's soul leave her body, and he's going to watch me tear his wife's soul from hers, right before I teach him the same lesson Prince Yusupov taught Rasputin with your knife."

* * *

Two days later, we came off the foils, and the Azipods held us precisely in position as if the *Lori Danielle* were dead at anchor a mile off Maho Beach on Sint Maarten. Airplanes came and went across the tiny, world-famous stretch of beach where tourists hung onto the chain-link fence as the massive jet engines roared only feet away, giving them what they imagined to be the experience of a lifetime.

If they only knew the terror of shivering inside a hole barely deep enough to hide half of their head while snow and ice piled higher with every passing minute, and supersonic rounds hissed and cracked millimeters from their skulls as they fought not only for their own survival but for that of everything and everyone they loved ten thousand miles away. If they only knew the anguish of watching their brother fall beside them and feeling his blood and bone and flesh as the battle raged on. If they only knew the emotional cost of fighting a war they didn't understand, against an enemy they didn't hate, on behalf of a society that would never thank them, at the behest of politicians who'd never know or care to hear their names. If they could only feel the rage and hellish void of holding the woman they love more than life itself in their arms, while the light in her perfect eyes melts away because of a traitor bent on amassing wealth beyond imagination. If they only knew the true experience of a lifetime by knowing the warrior's life of endless death.

Chapter 37

The Big Teddy Bears

My crew of professionals were among some of the best in the world at their skill sets.

Barbie nestled the Vertol onto the helipad in the twenty-knot wind as if it were no more challenging than tying her boots. And her touch on the controls made it seem as if she were part of the machine—that her thoughts alone directed the intricate movements of the massive and complex flying machine.

That same degree of technical prowess flowed throughout the team, from the captain on the navigation bridge to the machinist's mate, who was deep in the bowels of the *Lori Danielle*, honing a blank, shapeless piece of steel into a priceless, precision-machined piece, without which the billion-dollar vessel would lie dead in the water, vulnerable and silent.

When the rotors spun down and the hatch slid open, out stepped two more of the most brilliant and unstoppable forces of my team: the venerable Elizabeth "Skipper" Woodly, perhaps the finest intelligence analyst in existence, and Dr. Celeste Mankiller, the mad scientist I unleashed from the collar that bound her to the subterranean federal government laboratories of Northern Virginia. We gave her a lab and a budget to run wild, and she gave us tools that would've made James Bond envious.

Both women dragged wheeled carts that were quickly taken by deckhands, but that was far from the limits of their burden. More deckhands joined, and more baggage was stacked. Unlike many women who join a ship for an unknown duration, the luggage didn't contain limitless shoes, ball gowns, and cute outfits for lounging by the pool. Most of the cases contained computers, files, classified documents, tools, equipment, and gadgets I'd never be smart enough to understand. However, since I'd promised a post-mission vacation in the BVIs, I had little doubt there were a couple bathing suits and sundresses stuffed somewhere among the tech.

"Welcome aboard, ladies."

Skipper said, "We rode the fence at the airport, and it was stupid. We got sand in our hair and eyes, and we're never doing it again. Let's get to work."

I glanced at Celeste, and she said, "Ditto. Where's Mongo?"

"He's in the cargo hold with DREAMUP."

"Good," she said. "Tell him I'll get changed and be down in fifteen minutes. I assume we're headed for Oceana now."

"That depends on what Skipper has to say when she gets settled into the CIC."

The analyst turned to the deckhands and pointed to containers. "Those six go to the combat information center, and the other four come with me. I'll grab a quick shower and head up to the CIC." She looked back up at me. "You're the boss, but I recommend getting us off this beach. We're getting a lot of attention."

My radio crackled. "Sierra One, Security One."

I said, "Go for Sierra One."

"Report to sick bay immediately, sir. Code Alpha."

"On my way!"

"What was that about?" Skipper asked.

"No idea," I said as I sprinted toward Dr. Shadrack's domain.

The security chief met me just outside the main hatch to the space with a pair of nurses beside him.

"What's going on, Chief?"

He said, "Dianne Sakharova offered these two a thousand bucks for a satellite phone."

I turned to the first nurse. "You didn't give her one."

He said, "What, and lose my security clearance over a grand? No way."

The second nurse said, "Same. Then she offered five grand, and that's when we reported it."

"Where is she now?" I asked.

The security chief said, "She's got Dr. Shadrack inside one of the recompression chambers, and she's pumping him down."

I grabbed the man by his shirt and gave him a shake. "Why haven't you shot her in the face thirty-five times yet?"

He pulled away and shot his eyes through one of the small glass windows into the space. I couldn't have been prepared for what I saw.

"Who left her alone with him?" I demanded.

"Nobody," the nurses said in unison.

The second nurse said, "Will Morgan was on shift, and Dianne sedated him with Propofol. It's an extremely fast-acting sedative. We found the syringe, and we think she might've been using that hollowed-out book she has with her to hide drugs and stuff."

I glanced at the first nurse's name tag. "Mark, can you tell how deep she's got Dr. Shadrack?"

He said, "She took my glasses, so I can't see anything."

The second nurse, Mary, said, "It looks like three hundred twenty feet. The limit of that chamber is three thirty."

"Where's Will, the nurse she sedated?"

Mary shook her head. "We're not sure. He was in the observation room outside Dianne's room, but we can't see either of those spots from here."

"Is there any reason to believe he won't wake up from the drug? What did you call it?"

"Propofol. It's fast-acting but also short-lasting. He should wake up in less than ten minutes . . . unless she overdosed him. In that case, there's no way to know."

I said, "Chief, here's what I want. Get me the person on this boat who knows more about that chamber and hyperbaric medicine than anybody else. Get me Singer and Gator. And I want to know how to get through this door as efficiently as possible without blowing it up." It hit me in that instant. "The breacher! Get me the SBS breacher with the sledgehammer!"

"The what?"

"Never mind. Just get me Singer, Gator, and whoever knows about that chamber, now."

I stared through the window at the macabre scene. Dianne stood over the clear glass tube with Dr. Shadrack lying on his back inside. He was clearly unconscious, and a nest of something grey lay between his knees. A Velcro band wound around Dianne's waist led to a collection of valves I didn't understand.

As I studied the situation, I said, "Step away from the hatches. I have no idea what she's planning to do, but that chamber is a bomb right now. That's enough pressure to do a lot of damage, so I don't want any of us close enough to eat that blast if she finds a way to set it off. I want you two as far away as possible. We're going to resolve this."

Mary took a step closer to me. "Dr. Fulton, in addition to being an RN, I'm the senior chamber operations technician, the person your security chief is looking for. I'm not going anywhere. I can explain everything that's happening in there, and you're exactly right—that thing is a bomb right now."

I stepped back and pulled my radio. "Security One, Sierra One. Disregard the hyperbaric med tech. I've got her. Just bring me Singer and Gator."

"Aye, sir."

My next call was to the bridge. "Captain, lay us five miles upwind of Oceana as fast as possible, and I don't care who sees us doing it."

"I'll have you there in less than an hour."

"What a minute. An hour?"

"That's right. It's forty miles away."

"That changes things," I said. "Put us there in ninety minutes.

That buys me some time and cools things down a little. Oh, and there's a bomb on your ship."

"What?"

I briefed the captain on the situation, and he said, "That's not great, but it's not as bad as you think. I'll have the engineers calculate the potential explosive force, and we'll secure the blast doors. The hull will be fine. The Russians don't have anything that can penetrate from the outside, so we're not going to hurt her from the inside. You're not going to sink my boat, soldier boy, so calm down. Just get that chick under control, and let's go catch ourselves a traitor."

"I thought it was *my* boat."

Barry said, "She's *yours* when she's not in peril. When she's a damsel in distress, she needs her daddy, and *I'm* her daddy. Bridge out."

I slipped my radio back onto my belt, but it came back to life.

"One more thing," Barry said. "If you let her kill my doctor, may God have mercy on your soul."

Gator and Singer sprinted into the opening just short of sick bay, where I stood with Mary, the hyperbaric nurse.

I said, "Take a look in there, snipers. Mary's going to tell you what you're looking at."

The nurse said, "Dianne knocked out Will—the watch nurse—and somehow subdued Dr. Shadrack. She put him in the hyperbaric chamber and compressed him down to three hundred twenty feet. That chamber's limit is three thirty. She seems to have some understanding of safety margins or the chamber isn't operating to its full capacity. It doesn't matter which. It's highly pressurized."

Singer turned to me. "That's deep, but it's not TNT. Do the math, dive instructor. What is that, like a hundred forty PSI? I don't want to be in the room when it blows, but we've been through a lot worse."

"The eternal optimist," I said.

"Eternal, indeed."

I said, "I'm sorry, Mary. Keep talking. These guys like to interrupt."

"Anyway, inside the chamber is a hundred percent oxygen, so that's an oxidizer. That means it makes everything around it that's flammable burn easier, hotter, and faster. That's more dangerous than the explosive force of the one hundred forty PSI you were worried about."

"I understand," I said. "Tell me about the stuff Dianne's holding and wearing. And what is that grey nest of stuff between Dr. Shadrack's legs?"

"The grey stuff is a huge problem. It's steel wool. The blue thing she's holding is a medical laser. The brown square draped over the top of the chamber beneath the laser is blocking the laser from striking the steel wool. If the blanket falls or is moved, the laser ignites the steel wool, and the oxygen inside the chamber turns everything flammable into ashes . . . including Dr. Shadrack. It also releases a lot of energy in the form of heat and probably blows the chamber apart. The resulting explosion and fire would be devastating to the sick bay and would kill Dianne."

"What about the belt?" I asked.

"That's worse than all the rest," Mary said. "She's rigged a rapid release valve. Think of it like a burst disc on your scuba tank. If you overfill your tank, the disc flexes and allows the compressed air to escape to keep the tank from rupturing. That's a good thing with a scuba tank, but not with a patient under pressure inside a chamber. Imagine being instantly blown from three hundred feet underwater to the surface. The nitrogen in your blood would come out of the solution immediately, and you'd get the worst case of the bends anybody's ever had . . . if you survived."

I raised my hand. "Been there, done that."

"From three twenty?" she asked.

"No, more like two hundred, but it still sucked."

"I'll bet it did. You're lucky to be alive."

I pointed through the glass. "Without that man in that chamber, I wouldn't be. So, let's get him out of there."

Mary said, "The belt she's wearing that's rigged to the valve is short enough to open that valve if you take her down. She's thought of everything."

"Not everything," I said. "She's never met my friends who always win the big teddy bears at the county fair."

"What does that mean?" Mary asked.

"Never mind. I'll just show you."

Singer asked, "What does she want?"

"She wants a cell phone," Mary said.

"Can she hear us through these doors?" I asked.

"Only if we yell really loud."

So, I did. "Dianne, listen to me! Tell me what you want!"

She scowled from inside. "What?"

I yelled louder. "Tell me what you want! What are your demands?"

She yelled something back, but I couldn't make it out.

"Somebody get me a piece of paper and a pen. And Gator, go get me that SBS breacher with the hammer. No explosives. I'm going through this door."

Mary handed me a notepad and pen.

I said, "No. Bigger. Like a sheet of printer paper."

She vanished and returned with a stack of paper.

I wrote:

I'm coming in, and we're going to talk. I will not hurt you. I only want to talk. I'm not armed.

She screamed, "If you come in, he dies!"

I wrote again:

If he dies, you die, and so does Scott. If you and I talk, that doesn't have to happen.

Gator returned with hammer boy, and I said, "I've got one more errand for you. Find a spot where you and Singer can see that laser and the static line running from her belt to that valve. Get yourselves a pair of rifles that can kill both of those things with a single shot, and be back here in two minutes. Oh, and bring me a chair with wheels."

Gator was back in ninety seconds, and I said, "Get into position, boys. We're going to win some teddy bears. I don't want her to see either of you when I roll inside, and I need you to tell me exactly where to land."

Singer had spent the last several years turning Gator into a world-class sniper, so he said, "Call it, shooter."

Gator didn't hesitate. "I want you behind that corner and on the belt. That's the more difficult shot, and out here at sea, you're the better choice to take it. I'll take the overhead behind and above. From there, I can clear the laser without risking the chamber glass. That gives Chase a wider fan, left and right. I can shoot over his head as long as he stays seated."

Singer said, "Nice. What's the call?"

"The call is Chase's," Gator said. "It'll be a single tap of his right hand against the bottom of his chair."

Mary asked, "What if she goes for the valve manually after you sever the cord?"

"She won't," I said. "I'll be within inches of her with the cell phone extended when they take the shots. As soon as they fire, I'll have her under physical control. If it goes south, the breacher will be on her in an instant, and if he can't manage, we've always got you, Mary. I'm sure you've got a dose or two of that Propofol handy."

I pulled off all my clothes except for my boxers, and Mary pretended not to watch. Well-positioned on my rolling chair, I motioned for Mary to clear out of the way, and I nodded at the breacher.

He whispered, "Nice go, mate. You can't hide no weapon if you ain't got no hidin' place, eh?"

"Hit it."

I held the phone in front of my bare chest. The breacher swung just hard enough to make the spring-loaded pins of the sick bay hatches surrender, and I rolled inside.

"Easy, Dianne. Take it easy. I told you I was coming in. You wanted a phone. My staff isn't allowed to give you one, but I'm in charge, so I can do whatever I want. Who do you want to call?"

"Stay back, or I swear to God—"

"Dianne, you're not dealing with a fool. You're not going to kill Dr. Shadrack because you know you can't survive it. You have far too much to live for. Do you want to call Scott Delauter to tell him to run? Is that it? Or do you want to call your broker and move the money? Think of it like being arrested, Dianne. You only get one call. So, who will it be? Which love of your life will you call? The man or the money?"

I dug my heels into the clinical tile of the deck and pulled myself ever closer to my target.

In an apparent attempt at redirection, she said, "You have a prosthetic. I didn't realize—"

"There are a great many things about me that you don't realize, Dianne. The most important of which is the fact that I've never lied to you. I'm going to give you this phone, and you're perfectly free to make one call. I'll even give it to you before you release my doctor—the doctor who saved your life, by the way. A little gratitude goes a long way, you know."

I studied the angles as I rolled closer with every passing second. Singer needed another inch from the left, so I pulled a little harder with my right heel as I extended the phone another half inch.

Dianne seemed mesmerized by my mechanical shin, calf, ankle, and foot, and I liked the advantage it gave me. Moving another six inches, I was within reach, and by my estimation, the angles were clear.

I leaned forward, clearing headroom for Gator's shot, and I rolled my left shoulder forward with the cell phone extended, offering Singer another half inch of free air.

Without conscious thought, my right middle finger tapped the bottom edge of my chair once, and the supersonic crack of two full-metal-jacketed rounds pierced the air within inches of my ears at the same instant Dianne's fingers wrapped around the phone.

The laser's blue plastic casing exploded into flying shards of splinters, bursting in every direction like grenade shrapnel. Black snowflakes of nylon filled the air behind the woman as the cord tethering her to the blow-off valve turned to dust. She lunged for the valve, but I captured her withered wrist in an instant. With her heel, she kicked open

Leo Tolstoy's masterpiece lying at her feet and reached for a syringe, but I pinned her hand against the great deception of one of the most celebrated works of literature of all time.

"This was peace, Dianne, but you turned it into war."

Chapter 38
Poised to Strike

Captain Sprayberry lay us five nautical miles upwind of the barren piece of sand and rock we'd come to know as Oceana. Doubt still lingered in my mind that anything other than more sand, shell, and stone existed beneath the surface, but if I was wrong, it was a masterpiece of cover, concealment, and camouflage. I'd never been a fan of being wrong, but that day, I was praying to be totally and completely wrong.

The combat information center buzzed with activity from people with brains bigger than my prosthetic leg.

Dr. Mankiller leaned across the console as if staring into the soul of the universe. "The camera array is online and functioning perfectly. Sonar, nav, infrared, and defensive systems are operational. All self-tests complete. DREAMUP is ready to fly."

She turned to me as if asking permission, and I said, "Show me the world, Doctor."

She gave the order. "Release primary and secondary tethers. Prepare to orbit the *Lori Daniel* on a diagnostic run."

"Aye, ma'am. Primary and secondary tethers released. Decks are awash. Positional systems nominal. Buoyancy control stable, propulsion stable. She's ready to swim, Doctor."

The pair of technicians at the console could've easily been mistaken for space shuttle pilots had they worn the uniform of NASA astronauts instead of jeans and T-shirts, but they were no less qualified to fly their craft than anyone Cape Canaveral produced.

Dr. Mankiller said, "Verify emergency recovery systems capability."

The reply came in seconds. "All ERS systems are go, ma'am."

"Outstanding," Celeste said. "Let's hope we don't need them. We don't want to chase a ten-million-dollar robot to the bottom of a two-thousand-foot trench. Cut the tertiary tether and let her fly, ladies."

The final cable securing one of the most highly advanced undersea multi-use autonomous platforms in existence surrendered its grasp and returned to its coil aboard the winch on the *Lori Danielle*'s midship crane.

The monitors filled with high-definition video of our ship's hull, detailing every barnacle, paint chip, and weld line. Ours was a remarkable vessel, unlike anything else at sea, but she suffered the same punishment as every other steel hull on the ocean. The unrelenting punishment of the saltwater environment left her in need of nearly constant maintenance, repair, and repainting. Unlike most other vessels, however, ours could do a little self-love with a high-pressure, freshwater rinse system that kept the hull far cleaner than nearly every other ship at sea, giving her faster speed, greater time between haul-outs, and overall better hygiene.

The room was silent as the deep-sea remote exploration autonomous manned utility platform flew a perfect inspection pattern around our ship.

When the circuit was complete, Celeste stood erect and said, "With your permission, Chase, I'd like to take you on a tour of the next thing you're going to destroy."

"Let the tour begin."

The cameras went dark, and I gasped. The operation had barely begun, and already, the single piece of equipment I needed more than any other had failed. Reconning Oceana, even with the team of Special Boat Service swimmers, would be a three-day ordeal if the threatening tropical storm didn't blow us to the North Pole. Failure of DREAMUP was the last thing I needed and just the latest in the string of events that had turned the previous eighteen months of my life into a near eternity of unimaginable torture.

"Take it easy, Chase," Celeste said. "Everything's fine. We're just running deep and dark. There's nothing to see down there, and there's no reason to run the lights and cameras. Black and blank makes us hard to see, and we like that."

In days passed, I would've poured a bourbon to calm my nerves, but on that day, I simply settled into my seat and said, "How about letting me know before you do that next time?"

My favorite mad scientist crinkled her nose. "Nah, I probably won't. It's too much fun watching you freak out. I'll let you know if we run into a great white, though."

"You do that. How long will it take to get to the island?"

"Just enough time for you to fill this room with sweaty, stinky boys —and Anya—who want to see everything we're about to see."

I made the call, and the CIC soon smelled a lot like a post-game locker room . . . except for Dingo. His beard was gone, his hair was closely cropped, his nails were clean and neatly trimmed, his uniform was pressed and clean, and it appeared as if he may have even brushed his tooth.

I glanced between him and Captain Millgood, and the captain rolled his eyes. "Don't pay 'im no mind. It's showtime. He always gets 'imself gussied up for a fight, he does."

Anya tucked her hand inside Dingo's elbow. "I think he looks rather dashing. All girls like a British man in uniform."

We don't choose jealousy, especially when it's insanely irrational, but I suddenly wanted a haircut and a pair of those British pants.

"Look what I found," Dr. Mankiller announced.

Every eye sprang from Dingo to the monitors at the front of the room. A massive column encased in barnacles, electrical cables, plumbing, and mechanical fixtures of every description filled the screens.

She said, "This display is grainy because it's in IR, just like your night vision. I don't want to turn on the floods and conventional cameras until I know no one is looking. They can't see or hear us with sonar or the naked eye yet, so we've still got the element of surprise for now. The closer we get to the surface, the more we'll lose that advantage. We're at two hundred sixty feet right now and descending."

Every eye was glued to the screen and Celeste's every word.

"There's our compound. Looks like a spaceship, doesn't it? That shape helps with the pressure. At this depth, it gets a little squeezy out there."

The techs flew DREAMUP around the facility, recording every detail, inch by meticulous inch.

Celeste said, "If you'd like, I can cut a hole in it the size of a sewing needle eye and watch them panic."

I shook her off. "As much fun as that'd be to watch, let's surprise them with something a little more dramatic."

She chuckled. "Oh, you don't think a pinhole at two hundred eighty feet would be dramatic?"

I said, "Let me restate, your honor. Let's surprise them with a dozen commandos with rifles and particularly nasty attitudes and make them *wish* for pinholes."

She pulled the microphone to her lips. "Fly the angles, and generate a three-D model from the seabed to the surface. Report natural light."

"Yes, ma'am."

She turned back to face the team of warriors who'd soon be inside the facility. "Any bets on how they get in there?"

"I've got one," Mongo said.

Celeste motioned for him to sit. "Get back in your chair. You don't get to play this game. You're too smart. Anybody else?"

"I'm going with an airlock of some kind," I said.

Celeste did a little dance. "Well, la-di-da. Aren't we the brilliant one? Who would've ever guessed an airlock to get inside an underwater facility? You're now the anti-Mongo. Sit down."

"But I wasn't finished," I argued.

"Sit down."

"Yes, ma'am."

Shawn, our first, but no longer our only SEAL, said, "It's pretty obvious. They bring the boats into a protected area up top with some kind of seawall they can raise and lower. Then, they probably pump it out like a dry dock and just walk inside."

In Vanna White fashion, Celeste extended her hands towards Shawn. "See? That's what I'm talking about. He's probably wrong, but that's a great guess."

Shawn yanked his wallet from his pocket and fished around inside until he came out with a bill. He waded through the chairs, shoving them aside until he reached the console and slammed the bill on it. "A hundred bucks says I'm darned close, Doctor Lady who's never been to medical school."

Celeste giggled. "You're on, but you'll have to trust me for the C-note. I'm good for it, SEAL who's never been to SEAL school. Oh, no, I guess that's not true at all, but I am good for the hundred."

Shawn winked. "Technically, you're right. It's called BUD/S, not SEAL school, but if you stiff me on the hundred, I'll make you wish I was a cute little SeaWorld mammal."

She cocked her head. "You kind of are."

"Natural light!" called one of the techs.

Celeste was all business again. "We're too close to the surface to be invisible any longer, so the cameras are coming alive. If they're looking, they can see us, and there's nothing we can do about it except run."

"Let 'em run," I said. "We've thrown the lariat, and the bull's horns are in the lasso. As soon as we take a wrap and lean back, we'll roll him over and turn him into a steer with Captain Millgood's knife."

DREAMUP continued rising, and the pictures grew clearer by the second. Near the surface, a curved wall appeared, running the perimeter of the vertical shaft, but it was at least a hundred feet in diameter larger than the column.

"Looks a lot like a dry dock to me," Shawn said.

Celeste studied the scene. "But it's covered by the island. You couldn't get a boat into it."

Shawn grimaced. "You're right. Show me the video of the whole column again. You can do it quickly. I just want to look for a hatch."

Celeste played back the video, and Shawn threw a chair across the room. "Dang it! I lost my hundred. It's not a dry dock. It's for a sub. They dock their ship on Anguilla and take a sub out here."

Celeste snatched Shawn's hundred-dollar bill from the console and pressed a finger to the screen. "You're right. That's an emergency escape airlock and hatch for a submarine connection. Somewhere in that sea-wall above, there's an entry point for a sub and another hatch with an airlock. Now we know how they're getting in and out, and it's genius."

I said, "It's genius, all right, but it makes things tough on us. We've got to blast our way through that seawall, blow the hatch without flooding the facility, get to the bottom, collect Delauter, and get him out without drowning everybody in the process."

Mongo said, "Take our baby back to the bottom, and get me some more precise measurements on that escape hatch. By the time you get DREAMUP back aboard the ship, I'll have an airlock and hatch built that will mate up with that thing as if they were cast in the same mold. We'll walk through the door like invited guests without getting so much as a drop of salt water on our boots."

"You're the genius," Celeste said.

"Yeah, I know. Where's Shawn's hundred?"

She eyed the giant as if he were speaking Swahili. "What are you talking about? He was wrong. I won the bet."

Mongo said, "That *is* a dry dock and an airlock up top. Otherwise, they wouldn't need the seawall. They'd just mate up with a hatch, just like the one at the bottom. You owe the SEAL his hundred, plus one of your own, Doctor Lady. You *didn't* go to medical school, did you?"

She handed over the cash. "No, I went to MIT."

Mongo turned to Millgood. "Do you guys know what a SEAL Delivery Vehicle is?"

"Sure we do."

"Can you run one?"

"Sure we can, but it's been ages."

Mongo eyed me, and I said, "It's your plan. Do what you want."

The big man said, "Good. You and your SBS swimmers are taking the topside with our SDV while our team hits the base with DREAMUP. You'll get wet. I hope you're okay with that."

Dingo's mouth flew open. "But what about my new haircut?"

"We'll see if we can find you a blow-dryer," Mongo said.

* * *

Just as promised, as soon as the techs had DREAMUP back on-board the *Lori Danielle*, Mongo and the machinists had a hatch designed and built for the personnel pod. Half an hour later, it was welded in place, pressure tested, and back in the water.

Shawn took the Brits through a refresher course on the operation of the SEAL Delivery Vehicle, and in short order, they were well-qualified operators and ready to strike hard, fast, and with overwhelming violence.

Captain Sprayberry moved the RV *Lori Danielle* into position two thousand yards from Oceana, and the teams lowered DREAMUP and the SDV—loaded with hardened commandos armed to the teeth—through the moonpool and into the water only minutes away from our unsuspecting target.

Chapter 39

Put Him in a Steel Box

"Sierra One, CIC."

The communications system built into DREAMUP was as precise as every other element of her design. Skipper's voice rang true, as if she were sitting beside me.

"Go for Sierra One."

She said, "Mary just reported from sick bay that she surfaced Dr. Shadrack from his dive in the recompression chamber. He's in perfect health, aside from a little hangover from the sedation meds."

"That's great news. Thanks. Is Dianne in position?"

Skipper said, "She's restrained in place a few feet behind me, under the watchful eye of two of the ship's finest security personnel."

I couldn't avoid the grin. "This should be quite the show for her. I know you've got your hands full, but if you get a free second, it might be fun to bring up her banking records on a side screen so she can keep an eye on the cash while she thinks it's still hers."

Skipper said, "As our beloved Clark would say, 'Two birds of a feather like to throw one stone at each other.' It's already done, and she can't take her eyes off of it."

"I assume she can also see the mission cams from my helmet."

"Affirmative. She's got a front-row seat to the show."

I said, "I've got a buggy full of itchy trigger-fingers down here, so let's get that show on the road."

"We've got a couple of housekeeping matters first, but it won't be long," she said. "Let's start with comms checks. Them One, CIC."

Captain Millgood came back through his garbled full-face-mask comms inside the SEAL Delivery Vehicle "Them One, crisp and volume clear. Over."

"CIC has you loud and clear as well. Say system status of SDV."

Millgood said, "Them One, status good. Mission ready."

Skipper said, "And now for inter-team comms."

I said, "Them One, Sierra One. Commo check."

"Them One has Sierra One loud and clear. Is that how you Yanks do it?"

"That's it, my friend. Sierra One has you the same. Remember, we'll be deep, but we'll have good comms thanks to Dr. Mankiller's tech."

"Got it, mate. For the record, say ROI one final time for all hands."

I said, "The rules of engagement are simple on this one. Preserve all life unless yours is threatened. They're going to be scared, but they're mostly service civilians—waiters, butlers, and such. If somebody points a gun at you, shoot him in the eye. If somebody points a knife at you, punch him in the throat. Scott Delauter is *mine*, and there are absolutely no exceptions to that. If you find him, pin him, but do not evac him. He is mine."

"Them Team copies all."

I said, "We'll leave as many behind as possible, as long as they're not in peril. If the facility is flooding, we'll pull them out, but we want Delauter and his security team. The service staff are meaningless to us. Let them get away. We're bringing Delauter back to the ship, and I'll deal with him here. Got it?"

Millgood said, "Understood. Them Team stands ready."

I said, "CIC, Sierra One. Comms check is complete. Tell the captain we're going hunting."

"Roger, Sierra One and Them One. Happy hunting. Bring us back a traitor. It's been a long time since we've had a good old-fashioned firing squad."

"Abort! Abort! Stand Down!"

I didn't immediately recognize the voice, but it didn't matter. Anybody with access to our secure communication system had the authority to halt an op for any reason at any time. We established that policy years before, and it had saved more lives than mine on more occasions than we could count.

Dr. Mankiller's tone softened. "Sorry. I got a little excited. It's okay, but I just got access to the internal security camera systems and some of the mechanical systems. They're flooding Shawn's dry dock topside."

I said, "That means this thing just got a thousand times easier. We simply intercept the sub, grab Delauter, and run for American waters."

I wasn't certain it was Dingo's voice, but it was definitely one of the Brits. "Blast it all! That mean we don't get to punch nobody in the froat?"

"We'll still find somebody for you to *froat* punch," I said.

Dr. Mankiller continued. "Sorry to disappoint you, but Delauter's not on the sub. Only three crewmen went aboard."

"Any ideas?" I asked. The radio was silent until I said, "Put a headset on the scarier of the two security guys holding Dianne, and tell him his call sign is Thunder One."

A few seconds later, the man said, "Go for Thunder One."

I said, "Take the gag out of your prisoner's mouth, and make her tell you why that sub would be leaving Oceana with only three crewmen aboard. Start easy, get loud, and then get rough if you have to."

"Aye, sir. Thunder One copies."

"Leave his mic hot," I said. "I want to hear everything."

Thunder One said, "Ma'am, I need to know why that submarine would leave the base with only three crew aboard and no passengers."

Silence.

"Ma'am, I don't think you understand. It's essential that you tell me now."

Silence.

The next sound was Velcro restraints being drawn tighter than they were designed to be worn. "You will answer my question, you will answer honestly, and you will do it now."

Silence.

Thunder One said, "Ms. Elizabeth, you'll want to call a medical team up here. This is about to get extremely bloody. Is there a particular part of this room you'd like me to take the prisoner to for this?"

Dianne called out, "Supply run or pickup! They're either picking up supplies or guests. That's all it could be."

I said, "Nice work, Thunder. You just earned yourself a new nickname. Were you really going to hurt her?"

"I was going to follow your orders, sir, but I hoped it wouldn't come to that."

Millgood said, "We've gotta go, mate. We have to get froo that gate when they open it for the sub."

I said, "Are we clear to go, CIC?"

"Execute!" came Skipper's answer, and the SDV peeled away with DREAMUP only inches behind.

My team and I dived for the bottom while Millgood and his team of SBS swimmers motored toward the seawall sub gate in the SEAL Delivery Vehicle. DREAMUP could make five times the speed of the SDV, and we took full advantage of that as we ran for the lower hatch.

I asked, "CIC, you said you had *some* control of the mechanicals inside Oceana. Is there any chance you can operate the seawall gate and dry dock pumps?"

Celeste said, "Maybe. I'm testing it while they're running the systems. If I can interrupt them, I can probably control them. It's a little too obvious if I just take over all of a sudden."

"Subtlety is one of the things I love most about you."

She laughed. "That's what they call me, Ol' Subtle Celeste."

We reached the emergency escape hatch at the base of Oceana and brought the infrared light system online. Mongo took the controls and guided us to the hatch. The coupling rig he designed and built aboard the ship locked into position perfectly on the first try, and the big man breathed a sigh of relief.

I asked, "You weren't concerned, were you?"

He said, "You know, there could've been barnacles or growth that could've interfered with the mating. Things can always go wrong."

"None of us had any doubt. How do you feel about the pressures and security locks?"

He said, "No problems. The pressures are simple, and the security locks always work from the outside. If there's a rescue going on, it happens from out here, so they don't mate up and knock for permission to come in. They lock on, open the hatch, and run inside. That's how it works. We're going to do the same thing as soon as our British mates up top are ready to kick down their door."

I made the call. "CIC, Sierra One. We are in position and ready to make entry."

"Roger. Them Team is inside the dry dock and will be ready in less than sixty seconds. By the way, Subtle Celeste has the keys to the castle."

A few seconds later, Millgood's voice came through the comms, crystal clear. "Sierra One, Them One is standing by to breach on your mark."

"Are you in the dry?" I asked.

"Affirmative. Your tech-services goddess let us in, pumped it dry, and we're in boots and breeches with rifles without rubbers. Let's kick their teeth in, Sierra One."

I checked Mongo. "Ready?"

Dr. Mankiller had designed and built a pair of safety glasses for each member of my team to wear beneath our helmets. They had tiny monitors in the lower-right corner that gave us the play-by-play footage of Millgood's team's body cams, so I pulled mine into position and waited for Mongo's response.

He nodded, and I said, "Execute, execute, execute!"

Simultaneously, Mongo broke the seal on Oceana's bottom-side emergency escape hatch, and Millgood's breacher not so politely knocked on the topside entry with his favorite hammer.

Millgood said, "Them Team is in. Minimal resistance."

The tiny screen inside my glasses gave me an interesting definition of Captain Millgood's understanding of "minimal resistance." Five security officers were on their backs, but none had been shot. All were clearly unconscious . . . at least. Three more had engaged in very brief hand-to-hand battles with SBS swimmers—battles that didn't end well for the guards.

Our typical entry stack put our smallest guys through the door first so Mongo didn't block everybody's view, but we inverted our stack for that particular entry since no one on board knew more about the connection between DREAMUP and the hatch than the man who designed and built it.

Our giant threw open the hatch and dived into the opening like a man half his size and age. The rest of my team crossed him like a doormat with our rifles at the ready and our eyes scanning every sector of the oddly shaped space. Screams from a few people inside were not only expected but also completely understandable. We subdued and flex-cuffed everyone who wasn't a threat and began clearing the space as if it were any other structure.

I had no idea what a high-velocity rifle round would do to the hull of Oceania, but the regulator, mask, tank of trimix gas, and DREAMUP gave me the assurance that I could survive even the greatest of calamities in nearly three hundred feet beneath the surface.

Chaos reigned among the staff inside the facility that we'd yet to get under control, and chaos is a double-edged sword in my business. Confusion that we cause can be managed at times, but a stampeding herd is dangerous in almost every situation.

"CIC, Sierra One. You said you had interior cameras, right? How about a little help with finding Delauter?"

"We're looking, but we only have security cameras and service cameras. There's nothing in private spaces."

"Roger," I said. "This place is pretty empty except for scared worker bees."

We continued subduing innocents and clearing rooms from the bottom up while Millgood and his team worked from the top down. With the lowest two decks clear, we arrived at a stairwell leading to a secured, heavy door, and suddenly, everything was right with the world.

I slid a hand across the door's surface. "I think we found what we've been looking for."

Mongo said, "I think you're right."

He gave the door a push, but it didn't budge. A mechanical cipher lock rested beneath an electronic version of the same type of lock, and our resident locksmith put on her devious smile.

Anya said, "I can take care of this. No problem. But also should be done from other door at same time."

I said, "Them One, Sierra One. Say status."

"All clear above and moving to depth. I assume things are rosy down below."

"I think we found our boy," I said. "We're three decks above the base at a secure door with heavy cipher locks. I'd like you and your breacher to move into position on the opposite side of the same compartment. I suspect there's a matching door on the other side."

Millgood said, "We're moving into position now and standing watches behind. Expect two minutes or less with no resistance."

He made the two-minute mark and said, "We're in position. Can you see the hatch with my body cam?"

"I can, and it matches mine."

"Stand by, and I'll radar it." A few seconds later, he said, "She's a sturdy door, she is. We can blow it, but that's a beauty of a shockwave down here."

"Can your radar see beyond the door? Is there a second inner door?"

He said, "There's something, but it doesn't look hardened. My guess would be an elegant door if this here be the master."

I pondered our situation and called the ship. "CIC, do you have any control over interior locks?"

"Negative, Sierra One. Sorry."

"How about the elevators?"

Celeste said, "Oh, yeah. I've got both of those locked down. There's a utility and a main. Both are frozen."

I asked, "Does either or both come to this compartment?"

"The main does."

"Unlock the main elevator, and let Delauter call it to this compartment. When he gets inside, lock it down. That'll put him in a big steel box where he can't get hurt in case I have to blast my way through this door."

Celeste said, "You're a diabolical one, Chase Fulton. I like working for you."

"You don't work *for* me, Celeste, you work *with* me. And I'm not the diabolical one."

The next sound that resonated through Oceana was the elevator car descending toward the compartment in front of us, and I called Millgood.

"Them One, don't blast it. Just hold position for now. We're going to work on picking it. We have a secret weapon straight from Moscow who's pretty good with her hands."

"I'll bet she is," he said. "Them Team is standing by."

Anya took a knee and pulled a kit from her pocket. She worked with the locks for several minutes, wiping sweat from her forehead. "These are Swiss and very good. I cannot open them."

Kodiak said, "I can."

"But can you do it without blowing us to Bermuda?" I asked.

"Sure. It's a shaped charge. It'll either work, or we'll all be too dead to know the difference."

"Them One, Sierra One. We're blowing the door. Can you blow yours with a shaped charge and contain the blast without opening the hull of Oceana?"

"Give me a minute to talk it over with me breacher." He came back a minute later. "We don't know for sure."

"In that case," I said, "save it for now. If ours fails, I want you to go back to the ship for a torch."

"Got it," he said. "But, Yank. How 'bout not failing, eh?"

"We'll do our best."

Mongo said, "I want to go back to DREAMUP and close the hatch. Right now, the pressure is equalized between Oceana and DREAMUP. The blast might blow her off the rig. If that happens, we flood, and this whole thing comes crashing down around us."

"I've got a better idea," I said. "Everybody get back aboard DREAMUP, close the hatch, and motor away. I'll blow the door. If I survive, I'll take Delauter up the elevator and back to the ship with Millgood's team. That way, we save DREAMUP and each of you if this thing falls apart."

Shawn laughed. "Yeah, that's what we do. We walk away from you when things get weird. Go shut the hatch, Mongo. We'll be here with the boss when you get back."

"It wasn't a suggestion," I said. "It was an order."

That brought even more laughter, and Shawn said, "New plan. Mongo, you hold Chase down while he's giving orders, and I'll go seal the hatch."

I surrendered, Mongo closed the hatch, Kodiak rigged the charge, and we moved as far away as the det cord would reach.

Kodiak held up the plunger. "Fire in the hole!"

An instant later, the heavy steel door folded like an envelope, and my team exploded through the smoke and debris with rifles shouldered and boots thundering.

I made my second attempt at giving orders, and that time, it worked. "Let the Brits in."

Anya released the bolts on the second set of doors, and the SBS swimmers poured in just as they'd done in the shoot house training scenario aboard the ship.

"Open the elevator, Celeste."

The ornately carved wooden doors parted, and the man inside fell to his knees with his hands high above his head and tears streaming from his face. "Please don't kill me. I'll give you everything. I'll make you rich. I'll give you anything you want. Just name it!"

I dropped my rifle, allowing its sling to catch it tightly against my body, and then I pulled my helmet from my head. With two trembling fingers, I plucked Penny's picture from beneath the lining of the rig and tossed it onto the floor of the elevator at Scott Delauter's knees. "Give me back my wife, you traitorous son of a bitch."

Chapter 40

Say Her Name!

I slid a thumb beneath the sling of my rifle and lifted it over my head. Singer took it from my hand, clearly understanding that I didn't want the burden of the weapon so close at hand as I approached the man I so desperately wanted dead. The sniper deftly thumbed the retention release and lifted the Glock from my holster for the same reason.

Taking a knee in front of Scott Delauter, I motioned down at the picture of my wife. "Come on, let's have her. You promised me anything I want, and she's what I want."

He whimpered like a terrified child as a puddle formed beneath him. "I don't have her. I don't even know who she is."

"So, you're in the business of promising things you can't deliver? Is that it?"

He leaned back against the wall of the elevator and continued whimpering. "No. I'll find her for you. I have the means. I can find her, and I can get her back for you."

I lifted the picture off the floor before the vile coward's fluid defiled it, and I held it inches in front of his face. "Her name was Nicole Bethany Thomas Fulton. She was my wife, and everyone who loved her called her Penny. You ordered her to be murdered on June third of last year, and I want her back. What time can I expect her home, Scott?"

His breathing turned from shallow jerks to trembling hisses of unimaginable horror.

"You promised, Scotty. You said I could have anything I want, so tell me . . . what time will she be here?"

"You don't understand . . ."

I drove the crown of my helmet into his nose so violently that a spiderweb of blood spattered onto the previously gleaming elevator walls. He started to wilt, but I dropped my helmet and grabbed his face. "Oh, no. Don't you dare pass out. Stay with me. We're *just* getting started." I reached behind me. "Somebody, hand me some water."

A bottle landed in my palm, and I squeezed the contents into Delauter's face, reviving his brain from the undeniable desire to fall unconscious.

I leaned close. "That's the nicest thing I'm ever going to do for you, traitor, so treasure it. Drink it in. Cling to that memory because it'll be the last pleasant one you'll ever know." I stood. "Get on your feet, and if you stagger, I'll break at least half a dozen bones in your foot. Stand up like a man, you worthless, spineless child."

He hesitated, and I raised a boot above his left foot.

"Okay, okay! I'm standing!" He pawed against the wall and forced himself to his feet.

"Good. Now, can you give me back my wife?"

His tears returned, and I drove a fist into his side, feeling two ribs break beneath my blow. "Hurts, don't it?"

He fell back to a knee, and I kept my promise of the half dozen broken bones."

Singer stepped into the elevator door. "Chase."

I turned and locked eyes with the godliest man I'd ever know. "Not now. If you can't watch, walk away."

When I turned back to Delauter, he was melting to his other knee, but I wouldn't have it. A handful of hair and a solid pull brought him back to his feet. Every breath had to feel like a torch in his gut, with the broken, razor-like ends of his ribs tearing at his insides with every inhalation.

"If you think that hurts, just wait until you take a step on that broken foot. Now, walk me to the safe, and do it like a man. Do you *know* what a man is, Scott? A man is someone who doesn't betray his country. A man is someone who doesn't hide in elevators and piss his pants when somebody like me—a *man*—walks in."

He took a step and cried out in agony, but his wails were music to my ears.

"Make another sound, and I'll break the other foot. Walk me to the safe."

Our men parted as Delauter shuffled toward a pair of mirrored doors. "It's in there."

"Then open it."

He pulled the doors, revealing perfectly spaced hangers filled with designer wear worth more than every stitch of clothing I would ever own.

"Doesn't look like a safe to me, Delauter. I guess it's time to break something else. How do you feel about a cheekbone this time?"

He breathed, "It's behind the clothes."

"Stop wasting time, and open the safe."

"If I do, will you let me live?"

I placed a palm between his shoulder blades and pushed, bloodying and ruining several thousand dollars' worth of clothes with his face. "Do you think we're still negotiating here, Scott? We're not. That game ended when you offered to give me anything I wanted and you couldn't deliver. This is a new game called do exactly as you're told or learn precisely how much pain you can survive."

I raked the bloody clothes aside, uncovering a custom-built vault with an extremely impressive system of controls. "Oh, this is going to be fun. If you'd like, I can explain what happens inside the human brain when it's under stress—how it forgets complex sequences of letters and numbers. Are you feeling stressed, Scotty-boy? You do remember, don't you? All those years you served on the Board, directing our work all over the world and using my brain and brutality to get the job done, no matter what it took? You remember, right? Yeah, I thought so."

Reaching around my prisoner, I dragged my index finger through the stream of blood still flowing from his demolished nose and drew the number one on the vault door. "This is attempt number one, and you've got fifteen seconds. Go!"

His vibrating hand oscillated above the keypad, and I counted down. "Twelve . . . nine . . . six . . . three . . ."

I paused. "When I get to zero, Scotty, I'm going to hand you your left ear. I thought you should know. Which hand would you like me to place it in?"

He didn't answer, and I didn't expect him to. I was merely doing to him what he had directed me to do to so many others for countless years.

"Oh, my. I've forgotten where we were. Let's start over for the sake of fairness. Fifteen . . . twelve . . ."

The countdown continued until I pressed my blade against the top of his left ear. "Four . . . three . . . two . . . one . . . "

"It's open! There! It's open!"

I spun him around and stared through his soulless eyes. "Do you believe I would've done it?"

In the mortified voice of a cornered vermin, he whispered, "I still believe you will."

My boot landed in the center of his chest, and lights from half a dozen weapons turned the interior of the safe into a Broadway stage.

One of the Brits said, "Bloody 'ell. Is all them stacks o' cash?"

"Bag it all up," I said. "There's likely more than just cash in there. Bag everything, and get it aboard DREAMUP."

I backed away, grabbed Delauter by the ankle, and dragged him to the center of the room. "Where's yours?"

"My what?"

"I've decided that it's going to be a vertebra," I said. "And it's either going to paralyze you and make the rest of the night pain-free, or it's going to send a thunderstorm through your nervous system. I'm willing to take the gamble. Answer the question."

He shoved a finger through the air to the right. "There."

I demolished a second closet with a sidekick so filled with rage that it would've killed any man who caught it. The clothes were equally elegant and, likewise, perfectly spaced. They landed in every corner of the room, and from the back of the space, a second vault shone like a beacon in the night.

With a yank from beneath his chin, Delauter was back on his feet. I pressed his blood-covered face against the vault door, then dragged it down the smooth surface, leaving a long, wide mark before pulling him away. "This time, I thought we'd number the attempts with your face instead of my finger. And it occurred to me that I was selfish before and didn't include you in the decision. So, which ear will it be, Scott? Right or left? You pick."

There was absolutely no hesitation, and the vault was wide open in seconds. Although the haul from his closet wasn't as impressive, it took four of our men with bags slung over their shoulders to make the trek to our getaway car.

I tossed Delauter onto his back in the center of the floor. "Do you still have your gallbladder?"

He shook his head violently.

"How about your appendix?"

His eyes turned to baseballs, and I said, "I'll take that as a yes. Would you like to see your appendix? I have no idea where it is, but I'm confident we can find it together."

He'd apparently exhausted his supply of tears, but his dry heaves were still plentiful, so I gave him a few openhanded slaps to get his attention. "My men are going to tear this place apart, down to the steel walls. Are they going to find another vault or safe?"

He shook his head, and I said, "If they do, parts of you are going inside whatever they find. Those parts will be very small, and they will come from very deep inside you. Are we clear?"

"Yes. There are no more safes or vaults. I swear."

"Your credibility is running thin, Scott. First, you betray your country. That's called treason, by the way, and it's punishable by firing squad. I just happen to have one of those. And second, you promised me anything I wanted. Remember that?"

"I swear, there are no more vaults."

"Good. How's the foot?"

"It hurts."

"And the nose?"

He didn't answer.

"How about the ribs?"

"They hurt . . . a lot."

"I'll bet they do. I know all about that. I've had all those injuries and a thousand more. You sent me out to get them from your nice, cushy chair on the Board."

I let that sink in for a moment before saying, "I've been thinking about something I said earlier, and I was being unnecessarily hasty. I told you I wasn't going to do anything else nice for you, but I'm not an animal, Scott. I'm not a treasonous liar like you, Scott. I'm a human." I reached a hand toward Singer. "Give me the morphine."

He pressed a syringe into my palm, and I stuck it into Scott De-lauter's thigh. "It'll take a few minutes, but this'll help. If you want, I can stick some in a vein. I'm not going to kill you yet. You've got a lot of questions to answer, and I'd like you to be relatively pain-free when we start that process. Tell me what you want."

He extended an arm, and I motioned to Singer. The sniper, medic, and brilliant man of God knelt beside the traitor and gently inserted a syringe into a vein near the man's elbow. "That's a small dose to give the intramuscular dose time to kick in. You'll feel it in a couple of minutes."

Delauter closed his eyes. "Thank you."

Singer patted him on the chest. "I need to know if you know the Lord. It's going to become very important in the few hours that you have left in your life."

"What are you talking about?"

Singer squeezed his arm. "We'll talk about it on the ship when the meds wear off."

While Singer was working on Delauter's soul, I was working on the Brits. "Get back up top and move back to the ship. We'll meet you there. If anybody needs medical care on your way up, see to them. We'll send the authorities back here once we're in international waters."

Millgood said, "You blokes don't exist, do you?"

I said, "No, sir, we do not."

Mongo shouldered Delauter, and I reclaimed my weapons.

As we descended the stairs back toward the hatch, I called the ship. "CIC, send me a shot of Dianne as proof of life."

We climbed inside DREAMUP, sealed the hatch, and motored away. The small portside monitor came alive with video of Dianne sitting on a chair and holding an image of Scott Delauter with his badly broken nose and blood-covered face.

I killed the monitor. "Before the drugs send you into the spirit world, I thought you should know that she loves you and she's alive. The Russians poisoned her, but we pulled her out of a hospital in Greece and saved her life. I'm taking you to her now. Sleep well, and think about what the guy who gave you the morphine said . . . because he's right. If you think the last half hour of your life in my little dose of Hell felt like a long time, just wait until you experience real eternity."

Skipper came through. "Sierra One, CIC. There's been an explosion at Pogonya's school in Bern. That's all the details I have, but I'm working on it."

Chapter 41
Lucky Guy

The ride from nearly three hundred feet beneath the surface back to the *Lori Danielle* was excruciating, and no matter how hard I slapped him or how many gallons of water I poured in his face, I couldn't abate the effects of the morphine from overtaking Scott Delauter's body and mind.

While we were still riding the crane through the doors of the moon-pool, I opened the hatch and ordered Mongo to get Delauter to sick bay and wake him up.

Anya and I sprinted through the door of the CIC to find Skipper on her feet and running to meet us. "She's okay! The Delta operator got her out just before the explosion."

Anya collapsed into my arms. "Oh, thank God."

I caught her and steadied her shoulders. "Is anyone else hurt?"

Skipper looked away, and I asked, "How many?"

She said, "We don't know yet, but it's bad."

"Where's Dianne?"

"She's locked up in the brig."

I paused just long enough to get the whole picture in perspective. "Have her moved to sick bay and strapped down. I want her and De-lauter to have time to talk, and of course, let's listen in."

"Consider it done. Is everyone okay from the mission?"

"We're all good. They're still coming aboard in the moonpool."

Skipper pointed toward a pair of headsets in the corner of the room. "I thought you might want to say *privet.*"

Anya ran to the console and threw on the headset. "Pogonya? Is Mama. You are there, yes?"

I was only a second behind her.

"Hello, Mama. Yes, I'm fine, but it's terrible. You cannot imagine. Is Father—?"

"I'm here."

"Oh, Father, how I wish you were here."

"I'm sending a plane for you, baby. You'll be here with us in a few hours. Are you sure you're okay?"

"Yes, thanks to Douglas. He's amazing and the bravest man I've ever seen—except for you, of course."

I covered my mic and looked up at Skipper. "Is Douglas the Delta operator?" She nodded, and I pulled my hand from the mic. "We'll see that he's well compensated. Is he there with you now? I'd like to thank him."

"No, he's still pulling people from the building. I told you he's the bravest person. You can't imagine. He doesn't care that the officials keep yelling for him to stay away. He simply won't listen. He's carrying two and sometimes three at a time."

Anya said, "I miss you, my *dorogoy rebenok*."

"Mama, English, please. And I miss you, too."

"And you are certain that you are not hurt?" Anya said.

"Yes, Mama. I am certain. I'm only frightened but not hurt. How will I graduate now?"

Laughter wasn't the appropriate response, but that's all that would come, and I chose not to stop it. "We've got a few PhDs hanging around here. If all else fails, I think we can put our heads together and write you a high school diploma."

"Oh, Father."

I took a long breath. "Hey, Pogo . . . We got him."

"The man who killed Penny?"

"Yeah."

"Did you kill him?"

"Not yet."

I left Anya on the phone with our daughter in the CIC while I made my way to sick bay, where Dr. Shadrack was administering a drug through an IV in Delauter's arm.

The doctor looked up as I came in. "So, this is your guy, huh?"

"That's him. Is that the drug to counteract the morphine?" He nodded, and I asked, "What is it?"

"Caffeine."

"You're giving him a cup of coffee?"

Dr. Shadrack said, "About a thousand cups, but basically, yes. What's the story on bringing her back in here?" He motioned toward Dianne as a pair of techs rolled her in, strapped to a gurney.

I said, "I thought these two might want to chat before I have a little heartwarming talk with them. You know how I am—all warm and fuzzy."

"I'll go along with the fuzzy part," he said. "Do you want me to do anything about his face?"

I leaned close to his mangled nose. "I don't know what you're talking about. He looks fine to me."

The doctor said, "Let me know when I get warm. Head-butt, face-plant, helmet blow, rifle butt strike, fell in the shower . . ."

"That one," I said. "That has to be it."

Shadrack said, "He's lucky. It's almost like he knew exactly how to fall without sending the cartilage of his nose right up into his brain. Lucky guy, this one."

"Hmm, yeah, I'd have to agree. He's one of the luckiest guys I've ever met."

* * *

I called the whole expanded team together in the CIC, including a pair of welders from engineering.

"Nice work today, folks. That was one of the cleanest missions we've ever run. We had no casualties, no equipment losses, and no damage. I love it when we can bring everyone and everything home in one piece. Well done. We recovered the target and additional assets without unnecessary injuries or collateral casualties. We're already almost fifty nautical miles from the scene in international waters, and the authorities have been notified to respond and pick up the civilians left behind. All in all, great job, everybody."

Cheers, applause, and whistles erupted from everyone except the pair of men in white coveralls standing in the back of the room.

I said, "I guess you guys are wondering what you're doing in a classified briefing, huh?"

"A little bit," one of the men said.

I said, "Congratulations are in order. You two are being promoted to captain and first officer. Who wants to be captain?"

Each man pointed at the other and laughed.

I joined them in the brief revelry. "Seriously, guys, I need a favor. I want you to cut the ship apart. Well, at least part of it. I want you to remove three sections of the starboard rail amidships. Can you do that?"

The two men looked at each other as if unsure whether I was serious. "Completely remove the rail, sir?"

"Yes, completely, but only temporarily. We're going to have a burial at sea, and I want three sections of the rail gone for the ceremony. Can you do that?"

"Yes, sir. Of course. When?"

"Right now."

The men disappeared, and the room fell silent until I briefed my plan.

When I finished, I said. "Okay, are there any questions?" No one spoke, and I said, "Dianne and Scott are down in sick bay having a little planning session of their own, and we've been recording every word, so that should make the show even more exciting. Let's have some fun with this. Everyone, grab some chow, and I'll see you on deck in an hour."

As they rose to leave, I grabbed Singer. "Would you like to have a chat?"

He gave me a grand smile. "Nah, I think you're doing fine, but I've got your pistol ready, just like you asked."

I took the Glock 19 and examined it closely. It was the exact weapon I wanted the sniper to build for me. Nothing less was appropriate for the task that lay before me. I would press the trigger on that weapon only once and never again. I would deliver the message that could only be delivered by firepower, iron will, and a truly broken heart. As much as Singer may have disagreed with my message, my method, and my madness, his willingness to stand beside me while I delivered the justice both Penny and I deserved made him more than just a brother. It made him part of me.

The CIC was empty except for Skipper and me, and I propped myself on the console beside her. "Do you have the numbers?"

"I do. When Dianne Sakharova inherited her dead husband's shares of Sibirskiy Geotekhnicheskiy Kholding, they were worth just short of three point four billion. That number has grown to just over three point nine since yours truly has been managing it for them, unbeknownst to them. Additionally, you recovered around four hundred million in cash from Oceana, various securities, precious metals, and jewels. On top of that, Dianne had been tucking a little away for a few years—we'll call it skimming—to the tune of about three hundred million. So, the sum total is just a skosh over four point six billion."

"Billion, with a B?"

"That's right, knuckle-dragger. With a big fat B."

"And what were our expenses?" I asked.

"You'd have to get with Ronda for an exact number, but it costs about a million bucks a day to run the ship, so I'd say at least ten million, plus salaries, the airplane you crashed into the ocean, and repaying the British Crown for their expenses. It's gotta be close to a hundred million. Oh, and I didn't factor in the vacation you're still giving all of us in the BVIs."

I said, "You may be the best analyst in the world, but you would've been a terrible accountant."

"And you would've been a terrible racehorse jockey."

"Get me the Russian ambassador in The Hague on the phone."

After a few snaps and clicks, I said, "*Privet*, Ambassador Shulgin. Chase Fulton. *Ty pomnish' menya?*"

"Of course I remember you, Dr. Fulton, and Sergei demands that you come back and make him stop clucking like a chicken."

I laughed. "Snap your fingers twice in front of his face and tell him he's released from the command."

"Will that work?" the ambassador asked.

"I have no idea, but you'll have fun giving it a try."

"You're still a madman, Chase."

"Yes, I am, Ambassador, but I have your money. I need the Kremlin's wiring instructions."

He was silent for a long moment. "You can't be serious."

"I'm happy to keep it if you prefer."

"No, no. Of course not. You have all of it?"

I said, "I do, but there were expenses, and I have to recoup those. I incurred just over one hundred million American dollars in expenses while recovering the three point four billion that Premier Putin believes he's owed. I'm sure you and he agree that's more than fair."

He cleared his throat. "We provided you with transportation, of course."

"I'll give you thirty bucks for that airplane and two thousand for the crew, Alexander. Do you want the three point three billion or not?"

"What of Dianne Sakharova?"

"What about her?" I asked. "You poisoned her and left her to die. What more is there to say about her? When you Russians poison someone, they turn into corpses."

He said, "Do you have any idea how to move that much money discreetly?"

"I guess you're right. I'll have it converted to rubles and airdrop it onto Red Square. Give me one account number or a thousand of them. I don't care. You'll have your money in a few hours. We had a deal. Funny thing about us Americans . . . We keep our deals."

I put him on the phone with Skipper, and they worked out a secure method to deliver a collection of account numbers before she handed the receiver back to me.

He said, "I have just one more question, Dr. Fulton. Did you get your man?"

"I always do, Mr. Ambassador. Thank you for keeping your end of the deal this time. The rest of your countrymen could learn a thing or two about diplomacy from you."

"As could yours from you, Chase."

Skipper disconnected the line and looked up at me. "We're really sending the money?"

"Three point three billion of it."

"What about the rest?"

"I'll let you know. For now, I've got some business to take care of on deck. Are you coming?"

She said, "I wouldn't miss it for the world."

* * *

When Skipper and I arrived amidships on the starboard side, the British Special Boat Service swimmers were gone. All that remained were my team and Dianne Belford Delauter Sakharova standing beside Scott Delauter, both shackled and chained, their backs to the sea as we made five or six knots across the docile waters of the Atlantic.

I stepped in front of Scott and whispered, "Did Singer talk with you about God and what happens when you draw your final breath?"

He swallowed hard and nodded, so I didn't take the line of questioning any further.

Determined to keep the emotion from my voice and the tears from my eyes, I spoke in measured, deliberate tones. "We figured it out. It was an incredibly complex scheme the two of you concocted, but my team is brilliant, and we have means of investigations that are more powerful than even the two of you could understand."

I paused long enough to shake the image of Penny's lifeless body from my mind and swallow the lump in my throat.

"While you, Scott, were a rising star within the United States intelligence service, the two of you divorced—at least officially as far as the state of Virginia was concerned—and you, Dianne, moved to Russia as part of a covert operation and married Ivan Sakharov. This was a brilliant piece of black ops on the part of the U.S. State Department to gather intelligence on one of the wealthiest capitalist-minded families in the former Soviet Union. Brilliant indeed, but even more brilliant still was the plan the two of you concocted to infiltrate deeply inside that family and even murder the man you were supposed to be surveilling to inherit his fortune so the two of you could live happily ever after in the secret undersea compound you built with Sakharov's money."

They stood in silence as I laid out their scheme in flawless detail.

"Then you, Scott, rose to heights previously unimaginable to serve on a mysterious board that directed teams like mine, that obviously don't exist to do things that the world never knew were done, and that kind of power would make any man drunk. It certainly intoxicated you right into treason. And as I already reminded you, treason, my friend, is punishable by firing squad after conviction. Oh, my goodness. We don't have a judge or jury way out here in the middle of the ocean. All we have is a firing squad. I'll give that some thought and see if we can come up with a solution."

The emotion was coming, and I was fighting it. I turned and paced a few strides to gather myself before continuing.

"Let's talk about the power on which you were so intoxicated that you, Scott David Delauter, ordered the murder of my wife. I've decided that we don't need a jury for that one. I'll be the judge and make a summary judgment. How does that sound? I carried her body from the airplane you had shot down. I watched the woman I love die, and nothing in life could be more painful than that. Nothing."

I gave the briefest of glances at Mongo, and he stepped beside Delauter, grabbed him by the shoulders, and spun him toward Dianne. He slammed his enormous hands across the traitor's face and forced his eyes open until it was impossible for him to blink or look away.

I took one step to my left, drew the highly customized Glock from my holster, raised it level with Dianne Belford Delauter Sakharova's chest, and pressed the trigger. Blood filled the air, splattering over Delauter, Mongo, and me, and the woman's body disappeared across the toe rail of the ship before the report of the pistol stopped echoing. Mongo gripped Delauter even harder, freezing him in place and forcing him to stare into the empty air where his wife's living body and soul had stood only an instant before. The man shuddered and screamed like a tortured animal, but the more violently he reacted, the harder Mongo squeezed.

The big man spun Delauter back toward the centerline of the ship, holding him in place and denying him the honor of seeing his wife's body one final time as it floated across the azure waters of the Atlantic, awaiting consumption by the ravenous creatures that devour their own.

I holstered the pistol and stood with my boots between Scott Delauter's bare feet on the steel deck of the RV *Lori Danielle*. "*That's* how it feels. That's what I see every time I close my eyes. That's what every bite of food tastes like in my mouth. That's what makes up every dream I have. That's what you did to me, and it can never be undone."

I forced them back. I would not let the tears come, no matter the cost. I would stand stalwart in front of my wife's murderer and deliver justice.

Reaching behind my back, I slipped Captain James Millgood's knife from my belt and held it in the inch of space that separated Delauter's face from mine. "Do you remember when I told you what it took to be a man when you were whimpering like a child and wetting the floor this morning, Scott?"

He nodded in minuscule, jerking motions.

I lowered the blade between Delauter's thighs, just as Prince Yusupov was rumored to have done to the mad monk Rasputin, and kept my word to Captain Millgood.

With the bloodied knife clear of the wound, an elbow shot to the center of his chest sent Penny's murderer overboard and me to my knees on the cold, steel deck of the ship that would forever be the shrine where I paid homage to the love Penny and I shared and the vengeance I claimed against the traitors who stole her from the man who could have never deserved her or the love she poured out for him with every breath.

Chapter 42
The Men We Used to Be

I sat on the edge of the deck, dangled my legs over the side where the rail should've been, and patted a spot beside me for Disco to join. He eased himself to the deck and slowly slid to the edge as if his instability might send him to the same fate as my victims. We sat in silence and watched the British Special Boat Service swimmers motor away in our rigid-hull inflatable boat with Scott and Dianne Delauter securely on board.

The rubberized projectile from Singer's specialized Glock was enough to knock the wind from her chest and send her overboard, even with several layers of Kevlar woven into the jumpsuit our security team had issued her. The cinematic, blood-filled capsule our sniper plugged the barrel with made the wound look horrific enough to fool even me for an instant.

Scott Delauter's injuries were not cinematic. Captain Millgood's knife was quite real, and the traitor felt the same agony Prince Yusupov delivered to Rasputin on the 30th of December, 1916, on the Moika River. Millgood's medics would control the bleeding but do little to ease the pain until they delivered him aboard the American submarine two nautical miles in our wake. The surgeon aboard the sub would plug Delauter's holes, and the skipper of the submarine would deliver both traitors to Guantanamo Bay, where they would be held until they could stand trial for treason against the United States of America. I would never be judge, jury, nor executioner, but should the day come when my country asked the latter of me in Delauter's case, hesitation on my part would not occur.

"It's not easy, is it?" Disco said.

"What's that?"

"Watching the men that we were drift away."

I twisted to face my friend and former chief pilot. "What do you mean?"

He pushed himself away from the edge of the deck. "With what happened to me, I don't feel so good sitting that close to the edge."

"Let's grab a couple of chairs," I suggested.

I helped him to his feet, and we settled onto a pair of nicely padded seats out of the wind as the RV *Lori Danielle* picked up speed and the welders returned to reinstall the railing.

He motioned toward our RHIB full of British SBS swimmers. "For almost a year and a half now, you've defined yourself as the man determined to find and destroy Penny's killers. You're not that man anymore. It feels strange, doesn't it?"

I stared at my boots and then into my soul, but somewhere between those two places, I came to understand that Disco wasn't looking for an answer. He was asking for an invitation. So, that's what I gave him.

"Talk to me, brother."

He turned his eyes skyward and watched the white clouds drift overhead as the ocean breeze blew through his greying hair and a tear fell from the corner of his eye. "The first thing I remember as a boy is the desire to fly. I remember looking up and seeing airplanes in the sky, and even as a little kid, I knew there were pilots in the front of those magical flying machines, making them fly. And that's all I ever wanted to do."

He paused and turned back to the heavens long enough to remember being that little boy again. "The day I turned sixteen, I took my first airplane ride, and it was a flight lesson. I'd never even been inside an airplane before, and I already knew I was going to learn to fly. I mowed grass, milked cows, shucked corn, and did everything you can imagine, saving up enough money to take lessons. When the wheels of that plane left the ground, it was my first time falling in love, and it never stopped happening. It was always magic. And each time was like my first kiss all over again."

He paused and just sat still, listening to the wind and reminiscing.

"I soloed at eight hours, got my private license at forty-four hours, earned my instrument, multi-engine, and commercial tickets before I graduated high school. I washed, fueled, and fixed more airplanes than I can count, and I kept milking cows, too. I paid for every single hour of flight training by working my butt off until this little nerdy dude in a blue uniform showed up at my high school and told me the Air Force would've paid for all of it."

The welders finished the rail and tossed us a couple of bottles of water before Disco continued.

"I became that nerdy guy in the blue outfit, Chase. Well, mine was a green flight suit, but I was still a nerd. I flew a lot of cool stuff, and it defined me. It became who and what I was. People would ask, 'What do you do for a living?' Instead of saying 'I fly airplanes,' I'd say 'I'm a pilot.' I am. That's an identity. You're a psychologist. You know all about that. But I'm *not* a pilot anymore. I *was* a pilot."

The second tear fell, and he didn't wipe it away. He motioned toward the RHIB approaching the surfaced submarine. "When that SOB blew me up at the airport, he tore my brain apart. The neurologists explained it to me, but I don't understand it. None of it makes sense or matters, except the part that means I can't fly anymore. The part that means I can't be the man I've always been."

One tear became many, but he still made no effort to wipe them away. "'We can treat it,' they say. 'We can medicate it and give you a relatively normal life,' they say. Yeah, sure they can. I walk like a crippled ape. I can't remember what I had for breakfast or if I had breakfast. I don't look up at airplanes anymore because it breaks my heart. Everybody looks at me like a crazy old man because I can't find my glasses that are on my head. I have to take a bucketful of pills twice a day or my head tries to explode. Some relatively normal life that is, huh?"

A few minutes later, he caught his breath. "That's the man I am, Chase. The man I was is dead and gone. Thank you for listening and not telling me how it's going to be all right. Thanks for not telling me how it could be worse. Thanks for just sitting there and caring enough to let me pour it out without being afraid I'd get it on your boots."

There was nothing I *could* say. Of the hundreds of thousands of dollars I'd spent learning to talk patients through their neurosis, none of that would've helped my friend. He needed an ear, not a mouth, so that's exactly what I gave him: someone to simply shut up, listen, and care.

* * *

When Disco stood and walked away, his stride was stronger, straighter, and somehow more confident. Apparently, it was our SEAL's turn in the chair, and I secretly hoped somebody hadn't put up a sign saying "The Doctor Is In."

"Is Disco all right? I didn't want to interrupt."

"He will be. I was just doing some listening. How are things with you?"

Shawn said, "Not bad. I like what you did back there with Dianne and Delauter. Personally, I think you should've killed them, but hey, different strokes, right?"

"No, you don't."

He shrugged. "I figured it out."

"What's that?"

"The SEALs on Captain Cassidy's sub. Remember him?"

"Of course I do. He's the submarine commander with the kids from the school shooting back in St. Marys."

"That's him. I made some calls to a few buddies of mine who were still on the Teams during that mission. The woman and boy they picked up. It was Dianne Delauter and the kid of an American State Department operative who got killed over there. The kid was perfectly innocent in the whole thing, but Dianne gave away the ID of the sub, the commander, some of the SEALs and crew, and the timing. She was a real piece of work. After her trial, regardless of the outcome, if they need a few extra trigger-fingers on that firing squad, I know a bunch of boys who'd love to volunteer."

"I'm glad we got her," I said.

"You should've let me shoot her for real."

* * *

Never vacation with British special forces troops. They're insane, they live without rules, but they're fun. The BVIs were a blast for everyone, and we needed a break from the reality we'd endured for far too long. Between Penny's murder, my terrible reaction to it, and the agonizing mission, a little time in the sun, sand, and surf was just what the doctor ordered.

Even Captain Millgood had fun, still dressed in his funny outfits, even on vacation. "Thanks for letting us join you, Chase."

"I'm glad you could come, James. It's nice to get away and relax sometimes."

He pulled off his hat and fanned his face. "This is nice, but I was talking about the mission. Thanks for asking my boys to come. It was good of you."

"Thank you for coming. We would've done it without you, but we would've lost a good man or two. It means a lot to all of us that you'd do it."

He slipped me a card. "That's a private number. Call anytime. Some of us are closer to being out of uniform than in."

I pocketed the card. "I just might do that."

He shook my hand and stood. "Holiday is over for us. Queen and country calls . . . Oh, and that knock on your door? It still may come some late night."

I stood. "If it does, I've got a posse that'll ride with you anytime."

* * *

Gordo, Tubbs, and Slider made their entrance in island style, and Tubbs looked more like Sonny Crockett than his namesake.

I said, "Looking good, guys. How was the flight?"

"We didn't land in the water this time," Gordo said, "and they can probably use the airplane again without rebuilding it, if that's what you're asking."

"That's an improvement."

They had a few cocktails while I drank fruit juice and tea, and we turned a few hundred dollars' worth of Cuban tobacco into aromatic white smoke.

"Speaking of using airplanes again, how's the refit coming along?"

Gordo said, "You know how these things go. It takes forever, especially when nobody's sure who's going to write the check."

"I'll write the check," I said. "And I'll see what I can do to light a fire under a few butts to get things moving. I've been on the phone with your former employer, and they seem to consider you guys free agents at the moment. Are you interested in an offer?"

"An offer?" Gordo said, eyeing his team. "I have a confession."

"Let's hear it."

He said, "I had a phone call with a cat named Disco. As it turns out, we've got a few friends in common. A-Ten driver, so you can't really trust those guys, but he seemed like a decent enough fellow. He tells me that working for you is the worst job a guy could ever love and that we should jump at the chance before we ever see the number."

"You'll like the number," I said. "There's just one really nasty part of the gig."

"What's that?"

"I've been on the ground for eighteen months, so I need a biennial flight review and refresher training to get back in the air in everything with wings, including our Mustang."

"Mustang?" he asked. "As in P-Fifty-One Mustang?"

"Exactly like that. A D-model, in fact, and one of the fifty-cals in the left wing still shoots."

He waggled his cigar in the air between us. "As long as these smokes are part of the deal, who cares what the number is? We're in."

* * *

British Airways delivered Pogonya to Anguilla. Before she stepped from the plane, a bearded, long-haired man—who looked far more like someone who belonged on my payroll than in the first row of first class on a British Airways jet—studied every inch of every face within a thousand yards before allowing my daughter to take another step. He turned out to be the former Delta Force operator who sometimes answered to the name Douglas—but not always. Although his picture never appeared in any Swiss newspaper or on a television screen, he saved the lives of more students on the day of the explosion than every other first responder combined.

Douglas no longer made mortgage payments, car payments, college tuition payments, or had any need to save for retirement. The Bonaventure Foundation made certain of that, and he became the chief of security for the Swiss school that was rebuilt in his honor with funds provided by a mysterious and unnamed benefactor.

Anya and I hugged Pogonya as if we'd not seen her in ages, and enough strings were pulled by people with letters after their names to grant her a high school diploma at the age of fifteen. She would start classes as a freshman at the University of Georgia in January of 2018 without a declared major, but she was leaning toward double majors in psychology and linguistics.

My perfect daughter, who looked so much like a gorgeous combination of her mother and mine, took me for a long walk on an even longer beach beneath one of the most unforgettable sunsets I've ever seen. "Are you going to marry Mama?"

"I love your mother, Pogo. I always have. I'm scared to death of her, but I love her."

"She loves you, Father. You're the only man she's ever loved. She says you're the only man who's ever been kind to her."

"That can't be true," I said.

"It is, I swear it. If it weren't, she wouldn't have waited all this time for you."

"I can't . . . not right now. I'm not ready."

"But we can stay, right?"

"What do you mean?" I asked.

"At Bonaventure. We don't have to leave, do we?"

"Of course not, Pogo. Bonaventure is your home forever if you want, and Anya is always welcome there. Without her, it probably wouldn't exist anyway. She and I aren't going to . . ."

She squeezed my hand. "I know. I'm not asking about that. You're an honorable man, and you and she can be my parents without sleeping together, but maybe the day will come when you will be ready to marry again."

"If that day ever comes, Pogo, it'll be to your mother."

* * *

With the vacation over and the team back at Bonaventure, I delivered a stack of gorgeous black-and-white Montblanc pens to Dr. Mankiller. "Dig into these, will you? They're supposed to be encrypted satellite phones and completely untraceable. A few of them came from British intelligence, and mine came from a Russian ambassador."

"Which one is yours?"

I placed it in her palm, and she immediately dropped it into a lead-shielded container inside a pair of pouches that apparently had been blessed by a wizard from a planet I'd never heard of.

She said, "I'll get right on it. Oh, and your daughter is waiting for you on the back gallery. She's got a present for you."

"Oh, that's right. I almost forgot. She told me she had a 'geeft' for me, as her mother would say."

Celeste said, "That girl is the greatest geeft her mother could ever give you."

"Trust me. I know."

I jogged from the hangar containing our mad scientist's lab and back to Bonaventure, where I found Pogonya rocking in one of the chairs that was at least a hundred years older than she was.

"Sorry, I was working on a project with Celeste."

"No worries. She's really cool. Maybe I want to be like her when I grow up."

"Please don't ever grow up."

"Oh, Father. Let's go. You must see your present."

I laughed. "Come on . . . Say it like your mother—just once, for me."

She did the teenager eyeroll. "I have for you geeft, Chasechka."

She led me across the lawn and to the barn that Pecan the horse and I destroyed before it was rebuilt better than new.

"Nothing about this looks good," I said.

"You're going to love it. I promise."

We walked into the tack room, and from the rack she pulled a gorgeous saddle like nothing I'd ever seen.

I said, "It's beautiful, but it doesn't have a horn or stirrups. How am I supposed to get on it or stay on it?"

She continued her mother's accent. "Stirrups will come, and this I will teach to you. Is only one part of geeft. You must come now with me."

She led me from the tack room and through the stable to the end stall, where the top half of the stall door stood open while the lower half was securely closed. Pogonya approached the half door, rubbed her hand across the top of the lower portion, and made a kissing sound. The glistening black head of the most majestic animal I'd ever seen appeared through the opening and took in every detail of his surroundings. His obsidian eyes met mine and appeared to immediately know every thought that had ever entered my mind. Something about him made me believe he was wise yet tolerant of my ignorance, and perhaps even my fear of him.

Pogo rubbed a gentle hand across his skin, and the animal seemed to adore her touch almost as much as I adored her. "Come, Father. Meet Richter. He is a four-year-old Arabian Warhorse gelding, and he is just like you. He is as gentle as a lamb when he wants to be, but stronger than any beast when necessary. He is my gift to you. You will love him, Father, even though you can't believe it yet, just as I never knew how much I could love a man I couldn't believe was real."

Author's Note

As with the previous book in this series, and for obvious reasons, I must ask that you please not post SPOILERS concerning Pogonya. A few of you emailed and guessed that Chase and Anya may have a secret child hidden somewhere on Earth, but I would love to keep that a surprise for as many readers as possible until they discover her in this novel. So, if you would play along, I would greatly appreciate you becoming my co-conspirator on this one.

As I've mentioned a few times, I rarely write about places I've never been. I broke that rule in this story. I've never been to The Hague; in fact, I knew very little about it until writing this novel. I didn't even know what the name meant or why it always includes the word *The* in the name. I did a lot of research and learned a bunch. I hope you learned a few things as well. I enjoyed tying the hedges of The Hague and the hedges of Sanford Stadium at UGA together for Chase. It's a fascinating city with a beautiful and storied history. I've added it to my list of places I want to see before I leave this world. Maybe I'll even try a Googen-floppin-duple-haapen while I'm there. I'd love to share that story with you, but it's an inside joke between a few close friends and me that happened aboard a Holland America cruise ship some time ago, and you just had to be there.

The ditching of the C-130 Hercules in the Atlantic, believe it or not, is possible, and it has been done. It's not been done in that particular spot, but a handful of skilled crews have pulled off the maneuver and survived. Much of the stunt I described is fictionalized, but my dear friend and technical advisor, Colonel Bray (retired Herk driver), helped me get the details correct. For the record, Col. Bray claims to have never successfully put a 130 on the water. I'm not fully convinced, but I didn't push him on the issue. Concerning the fuel sample that Slider took inside the airplane prior to evacuation into the life rafts, that was entirely fictional and probably impossible. I wanted to use it as a dramatization of Slider's conscientiousness and calm nature under extreme pressure. I think it worked. It also allowed me to play chemist a little later in the story and explain how food-grade gelatin could've caused the problem. Although I am a lifelong pilot, I am not a chemist, aircraft mechanic, or saboteur, so I don't know for sure if gelatin would cause what I described. It was fictional, but the math worked when it came to the weights of materials. On a personal note, I like Slider, so I hope I get to use him and his brain on a few more schemes in upcoming stories.

While we're talking about airplanes and trying to crash them, let's discuss the term "stall." When people hear the word stall, they often think about what happened while they were learning to drive a car with a clutch. They stalled the engine by letting out the clutch too quickly. That is *not* what happens when an airplane stalls. We could spend several pages and draw a lot of graphs explaining what happens during an aerodynamic stall, but that would get boring, and I would get a thousand emails from flight instructors and aeronautical engineers telling me how I got it wrong. At the time of this writing, I've been flying for over four decades, and I've stalled a lot of airplanes more times than I can count, *but* . . . I've never done it accidentally. I've only done it intentionally while training or practicing recovering from stalls. An airplane *generally* stalls when the wing exceeds its critical angle of attack. That's a complicated way of saying the nose of the airplane is too high and/or the air speed is too low. (Calm down, flight instructors and engineers. I know that's not technically correct.) It's far more complicated than that, but if a pilot pulls up too hard and slows down too much, a bunch of complex aeronautical stuff happens that makes the wings stop flying, and the airplane falls out of the sky. That's a stall, and that's what Gordo and Tubbs were trying to avoid by going too slow with the nose too high when ditching the Herk. They weren't afraid of stalling the engines. They were afraid of stalling the wings. The engines were already dead. For the record, there's a banking component to the whole complicated thing that makes the math even weirder, and that played a role in the cockpit conversation. If you really want to understand it, take a drive down to your local airport and hire a flight instructor to take you for a discovery flight. He'll be more than happy to demonstrate the whole ordeal for you. I recommend not having a big meal beforehand.

Just so there's no confusion, I know who William of Orange was, but I grew up in Knoxville, near the University of Tennessee. I may have even taken a class or two within those hallowed halls, and to this day, my sister, who I adore, and you know as the character Teresa Lynn, is a die-hard Big Orange fan. I couldn't resist throwing in a little SEC revelry—or rivalry. (Note: SEC is the Southeastern Conference, for those of you folks in the rest of the country who aren't fortunate enough to have professional-level collegiate athletic teams.)

Ambassador Alexander Shulgin is quite real and did serve, for a time, as a diplomat from the Russian Federation to the Netherlands. He is used fictionally, and I know absolutely nothing about him. I do, however, believe he would've loved having an FSB officer in the embassy who clucked like a chicken every time someone said "Good morning."

I lived an extremely strange childhood. I believed my father to be insane for much of my youth. He was not, by the way. I least I don't think he was. He spoke in riddles that made no sense back then, but now, as I age, they have begun to turn into words of enormous wisdom that add great value to my life. Occasionally, though, some of those riddles simply remain riddles. One of the things he would often say when we returned home from a trip of any length was, "Home again, home again, jiggety jog." I liked it, but I never understood it. I used that line in this story, and I thought it deserved an explanation. Even when I wrote it in this manuscript, I didn't know what it meant until I did the research. So, here's what I learned. It is part of an old nursery rhyme, and it goes like this:

To market, to market, to buy a fat pig;
Home again, home again, jiggety jig.
To market, to market, to buy a fat hog;
Home again, home again, jiggety jog.
To market, to market, to buy a plum bun;
Home again, home again, market is done.

I make up a lot of stuff in these stories, but not everything. *Ippokrateio* General Hospital in Thessaloniki is one of the things that qualifies as non-fiction. I've been hurt all over the world and seen the inside of a lot of hospitals, but never that one. For this story, I used it fictionally. I weakened its security and made its staff look a little less competent than they really are, but the hospital exists, and so does the city. In fact, the city appears in the Bible. The Apostle Paul wrote two letters to the church there. They are First and Second Thessalonians. I'd rather you read those two books than anything I ever write, and I'm sure Singer would agree.

There's a lot of talk about pronouns these days, but when I gave the British Special Boat Service team their callsign of "Them," I wasn't assigning a pronoun of any kind. Military call signs, especially special operations call signs, are classified and change very often, sometimes more than once daily. In doing my research, I learned that the Brits are big fans of just being called "Them." It brings a certain anonymity that they seem to enjoy, and I thought it was perfectly appropriate. I believe we've not seen the last of Captain Millgood, and especially the dashing Dingo. For the record, I know absolutely nothing about the British SBS and SAS, so I researched the heck out of them and did my best. I'm sure I'll get plenty of mail about what I got wrong, and I'll do better next time.

Oceana is entirely fictional. It might be possible to build such a structure, but it would be enormously expensive and impractical. It was fun to assault, though.

Falke Clothing Store in The Hague does exist, but to my knowledge, it is not a front for British intelligence and provides no service for intelligence operatives of any agency. But wouldn't it be cool if it did?

I know it isn't polite to beg for applause, but I have to do it, and I think I deserve it. I derived cyanide from sugar beets. How many other novelists do you know who could've pulled that off? Eat your heart out, David Baldacci. (Just don't eat one of my sugar beets.)

And now, the story of "The Loving and Just King." I can't claim credit for that one. I heard it told in a much shorter version some time ago, and I loved it. It's a beautiful story, and like any good novelist, I made it longer. I hope you enjoyed it as well.

Finally, why is this story so darned long? I had a lot to say. And the next one may be even longer. I don't know yet. Thank you from the depths of my heart for inviting my crazy world into yours. I sincerely treasure the privilege of being your personal storyteller, and I hope I never do anything to lose that beloved spot.

Cheers,
Cap

About the Author

Cap Daniels

Cap Daniels is a former sailing charter captain, scuba and sailing instructor, pilot, Air Force combat veteran, and civil servant of the U.S. Department of Defense. Raised far from the ocean in rural East Tennessee, his early infatuation with salt water was sparked by the fascinating, and sometimes true, sea stories told by his father, a retired Navy Chief Petty Officer. Those stories of adventure on the high seas sent Cap in search of adventure of his own, which eventually landed him on Florida's Gulf Coast, where he spends as much time as possible on, in, and under the waters of the Emerald Coast.

With a headful of larger-than-life characters and their thrilling exploits, Cap pours his love of adventure and passion for the ocean onto the pages of the Chase Fulton Novels and the Avenging Angel - Seven Deadly Sins series.

Visit www.CapDaniels.com to join the mailing list to receive newsletter and release updates.

Connect with Cap Daniels:

Facebook: www.Facebook.com/WriterCapDaniels
Instagram: https://www.instagram.com/authorcapdaniels/
BookBub: https://www.bookbub.com/profile/cap-daniels

Also by Cap Daniels

The Chase Fulton Novels Series

Book One: *The Opening Chase*
Book Two: *The Broken Chase*
Book Three: *The Stronger Chase*
Book Four: *The Unending Chase*
Book Five: *The Distant Chase*
Book Six: *The Entangled Chase*
Book Seven: *The Devil's Chase*
Book Eight: *The Angel's Chase*
Book Nine: *The Forgotten Chase*
Book Ten: *The Emerald Chase*
Book Eleven: *The Polar Chase*
Book Twelve: *The Burning Chase*
Book Thirteen: *The Poison Chase*
Book Fourteen: *The Bitter Chase*
Book Fifteen: *The Blind Chase*
Book Sixteen: *The Smuggler's Chase*
Book Seventeen: *The Hollow Chase*
Book Eighteen: *The Sunken Chase*
Book Nineteen: *The Darker Chase*
Book Twenty: *The Abandoned Chase*
Book Twenty-One: *The Gambler's Chase*
Book Twenty-Two: *The Arctic Chase*
Book Twenty-Three: *The Diamond Chase*
Book Twenty-Four: *The Phantom Chase*
Book Twenty-Five: *The Crimson Chase*
Book Twenty-Six: *The Silent Chase*
Book Twenty-Seven: *The Shepherd's Chase*
Book Twenty-Eight: *The Scorpion's Chase*
Book Twenty-Nine: *The Creole Chase*
Book Thirty: *The Calling Chase*
Book Thirty-One: *The Capitol Chase*
Book Thirty-Two: *The Stolen Chase*
Book Thirty-Three: *The Widow's Chase*
Book Thirty-Four: *The Sacred Chase*

The Avenging Angel – Seven Deadly Sins Series
Book One: *The Russian's Pride*
Book Two: *The Russian's Greed*
Book Three: *The Russian's Gluttony*
Book Four: *The Russian's Lust*
Book Five: *The Russian's Sloth*
Book Six: *The Russian's Envy*
Book Seven: *The Russian's Wrath*

Stand-Alone Novels
We Were Brave
Singer – Memoir of a Christian Sniper

Novellas
The Chase is On
I Am Gypsy

Made in the USA
Middletown, DE
22 December 2025

25299562R00210